Also by Sandrone Dazieri

Kill the Father

Kill the Angel

KILL THE KING

A NOVEL

SANDRONE DAZIERI

translated by **ANTONY SHUGAAR**

SCRIBNER
NEW YORK   LONDON   TORONTO   SYDNEY   NEW DELHI

Scribner

An Imprint of Simon & Schuster, Inc.
1230 Avenue of the Americas
New York, NY 10020

First Scribner hardcover edition May 2020

SCRIBNER and design are registered trademarks of The Gale Group, Inc.,
used under license by Simon & Schuster, Inc., the publisher of this work.

For information about special discounts for bulk purchases,
please contact Simon & Schuster Special Sales at 1-866-506-1949
or business@simonandschuster.com.

The Simon & Schuster Speakers Bureau can bring authors to your live event.
For more information or to book an event, contact the Simon & Schuster Speakers
Bureau at 1-866-248-3049 or visit our website at www.simonspeakers.com.

Manufactured in the United States of America

1   3   5   7   9   10   8   6   4   2

Library of Congress Control Number: 2019033157

ISBN 978-1-5011-7472-8
ISBN 978-1-5011-7474-2 (ebook)

Don't you never try to look behind my eyes
You don't wanna know what they have seen.

—Frank Zappa,
"A Token of My Extreme"

Colomba bent over Giltine and determined that she was dead, while Dante furiously wheeled around on Leo. "There was no need for that. There was no fucking need!"

Leo put a new clip in his gun, then went over to Colomba. "Is she dead?"

"Yes." *God, she's tiny*, thought Colomba. She couldn't weigh a pound over ninety. "What was that explosion, Dante?"

"One of Giltine's old friends tried to arrange an escape route for her."

"And he came mighty close to succeeding," said Leo, grabbing the knife that Giltine had dropped.

"Leo, you know that you're contaminating a crime scene, don't you?" asked Colomba.

"How careless of me."

Something about the way he said it sent a shiver down Dante's spine. "Don't touch her!" he shouted. But it was too late, because Leo had plunged the knife into Colomba's belly and then twisted it, ripping the wound wider.

Colomba felt her stomach turn to ice and she fell to her knees, dropping her pistol, watching as her blood filled her hands. She watched as Leo punched Dante and knocked him to the ground and then bent over Belyy. The old man stared at Leo in horror, incapable of moving because of the terrible pain in his pelvis. "If you spare my life, I'll make you a rich man," the old man said.

"*Dasvidaniya*," said Leo, and cut the man's throat with as much indifference as you'd use to cut a slice of cake.

Dante crawled toward Colomba, who was curled up in a fetal position, already in a lake of blood. "CC," he said, with tears in his eyes. "Don't move. Now I'm going to compress the wound. I'll compress your—"

Leo grabbed Dante and yanked him to his feet. "It's time to go," he said.

Dante felt his internal thermostat shooting past level ten, level one hundred, level one thousand, and Leo's face became a dark dot at the edge of a megascreen in Berlin, and then the passerby who, months before that, had triggered the psychotic episode that had sent him to the Swiss clinic. "So it's you," he murmured.

"Be good, little brother," said Leo, then he wrapped his hands around Dante's throat and squeezed until he lost consciousness. Then he slung Dante's inert body over his shoulder.

The last thing Colomba saw was Dante's hand trying to reach out to her over Leo's shoulder. She wanted to tell him that she'd save him, that she'd win out over everything, that they'd never be apart again, but she uttered the words only in her dream.

When the EMTs showed up to save her from death's door, Leo and Dante had already disappeared, and no one had seen them go.

It took a week of searching to determine beyond the shadow of a doubt that Leo Bonaccorso had never existed.

PART ONE

NIGHTMARES

CHAPTER 1

*D*arkness.

    Dante is suffocating. The darkness crushes him like cement, grinding him, shattering his bones. It enters his mouth, seeps into his lungs. He can't scream. He can't seem to move, much less vomit. He faints again, and his exhausted slumber is a black screen upon which his memories burn. He sees a woman in green who smiles at him, dripping with blood. The sound of an explosion. The screams.

    The screams awaken him.

    Darkness. Darkness. Darkness. Darkness. Darkness. Darkness. Darkness. Dar—

    Light.

    It's only for an instant, a fraction of a second too brief to measure. But Dante latches onto it. His eyes drink in the light, and he starts to think again. A little bit. He can smell wood and dust. He thinks back to the explosion he heard and felt . . . did something fall on his head? Is he in a hospital?

    The strain is too much for him. He recedes back to the black screen. He goes back to his memories. To the woman covered with blood with the strange name in that strange place that resembles a discotheque. To the five bullets hurtling toward her. Dante manages to see them moving through the air like snails and slamming into her back. The woman's flesh turns to gelatin, her face becomes liquid, her smile shatters into a thousand pieces. On her left collarbone and on her belly, two small volcanoes of flesh erupt. The volcanoes rip open and the two bullets that have made the complete passage through her body burst out into the open air, spraying blood and bone fragments in all directions. The woman starts to fall forward. Behind her . . .

Darkness.

Dante is awake but he doesn't make the mistake of opening his eyes right away. First he tries to feel his own body, to reconstruct it in spite of the waves of pain that wash over him whenever he moves. He realizes that he's lying on his back and that something is constraining his wrists and ankles. He has leather in his mouth; something soft is wrapped around his hips. Otherwise, he's naked. Has he been intubated? Is he in serious condition? He remembers the sound of a diesel engine that was vibrating in his skull. It was a boat engine. Maybe that's how they transported him to the hospital.

He tries to move his hands and the pain in his wrists only worsens. They're fastened with something sharp, something that sinks into his flesh with every movement.

Plastic zip ties.

Zip ties are the cheapest form of handcuffs available on the market, but they're not standard issue in hospitals. He isn't in a hospital. He's somewhere else.

He's being held prisoner.

The wave of horror takes him back to the screening room of his memory. The movie resumes and the woman in green continues falling, allowing Dante to look behind her. There are glass cubicles, little rooms shattering now, garishly colored plastic furniture, dust, and rubble. And bodies on the ground. Men in tuxedoes, women in evening gowns. All drenched in blood. Even in his hallucinatory state, Dante realizes that he saw that explosion with his own eyes. He was there. He doesn't know how long ago it happened. But he knows it was in Venice.

He opens his eyelids, back in the present once again, and he focuses on the tiny dot of light above him, looking at it out of the corner of his eye, more sensitive to light now. As he turns his head, he sees it shift, disappear, and reappear. He's not looking directly at the ceiling of a darkened room; there's something between him and that dot of light. Something, he realizes only in that moment, that's very close. A wooden grate.

Those are airholes.

He's closed in a wooden crate.

The blood started flowing again after the blizzard that hit the Marche region. Many small towns and villages between the Monti Sibillini and the steep slopes of Monte Conero remained cut off, and the department of disaster management, Italy's Protezione Civile, was forced to distribute food with helicopters. In those days of brutal snowfall, hundreds of heads of livestock froze to death after their stables collapsed—in one case, dying along with their owner. Though it was far from the epicenter of the blizzard, the long dirt road that connected the tiny village of Mezzanotte to the paved provincial road was buried in snow, and that meant the tanker truck that normally delivered liquid propane gas to the houses scattered over the hillsides was now stranded down in the valley. One of these houses—right at the far end of the dirt road, perched high atop a sheer cliff that tumbled dozens of yards straight down behind it—was a poorly maintained gray-stone farmhouse. It had been built by peasants at the end of the nineteenth century, and subsequently expanded and modified, generation after generation, often without taking into account the slightest concept of uniformity or consistency. There were windows of every size, shape, and color, five front doors, and patches of different materials in the walls; the most recent wing of the house had been built out of cement, following the curve of the soil instead of excavating a foundation, and so the farmhouse wound up with one section that was two stories tall and another section that had only one floor, like a gray wedge plowed into the earth. Withered bushes and hedges protruded out of the blanket of snow that covered the garden, along with weeds and vines that blocked it from view.

The boiler was in the cellar, its surface scratched by the countless wrenches that had been used on numerous occasions to unhook its pipes and scrape out the calcium buildup that constantly threatened to block them. The boiler sucked natural gas from a long conduit that ran under the garden, all the way out to the buried tank just beyond the fencing, one of the many fuel tanks that the truck had been scheduled to refill.

At two in the morning, the boiler sucked down the last drops of liquid propane gas, coughed like a decrepit old lunger, and stopped working.

A woman with iridescent green eyes, broad shoulders, and high prominent cheekbones lay on her back in bed, listening to the creaking of the radiators as they cooled now. Her name was Colomba Caselli, she was thirty-five years old, and she was an adjutant deputy captain of the state police, on leave since a phantom had stabbed her in the belly and kidnapped Dante Torre, the Man from the Silo.

Fifteen months had passed since then.

No one had heard a thing about either of them in all that time.

Colomba got up, switched on the electric kettle to brew a cup of tea from a used teabag, donned an old parka over her indoor tracksuit, and stepped out the front door into the harsh wind. Outdoors, everything was white and icy, the dirt driveway a brilliant white serpent that wended away into the milky nothingness. The only sounds that could be heard were the gusting of the wind and the cawing of the ravens.

Colomba pulled the hood down over her forehead to protect her face from the blasts of pulverized ice and trudged all the way around to the gray lean-to made of corrugated metal roofing that stood next to the gate. She had a box of kitchen matches that she'd stuck in her pocket, its rattling emphasizing every step she took. She'd never lit a fire in the fireplace, but she knew there was a stack of firewood under that lean-to, buried under years of clutter and plastic.

Instead, though, she froze in place before she got there, standing knee-high in the fallen snow.

From behind the woodpile ran a line of human footprints. Someone had climbed over the fence and lowered themselves to the ground on the other side, only to vanish behind the house.

Colomba couldn't move, she couldn't turn her head, she couldn't stop staring at the footprints that designed a half arc in the dazzling white snow, passing just inches from the outside wall.

Her hand darted down in search of her pistol, and only when she found the pocket empty did she remember that she'd left it in the drawer of her nightstand. The first few months after being released from the hospital she used to take her gun to bed with her, and she'd regularly wake up with the taste of mineral oil in her mouth. Why the fuck had she given up that habit?

Was it because you were starting to feel safe? a voice asked her, a familiar voice inside her head, a voice so clear that she could have sworn it had come from right behind her back.

Her lungs shut down, and she lost her balance. She fell on her back, right onto the skeletal branches of a rosebush that had run wild. Staring up into the white sky, she could only think that the end had finally arrived.

She braced for the swooping knife blade. She braced for the gunshot. She braced for the stab of pain.

But nothing happened.

Little by little, Colomba regained the use of her rational mind. Her trembling came back under control.

She slid down off the rosebush and got to her feet. Leo Bonaccorso—the phantom from her previous life—would never have left his footprints out in plain sight where she could have seen them. She would simply have found herself face-to-face with him one day when she opened her eyes first thing in the morning—as he silently finished murdering her in her sleep.

Unless he has something else in mind. Maybe he means to lure me somewhere else to . . .

"Cut it out," she muttered, furious at herself. "You nut job, you asshole."

She took another look at the footprints—she certainly hadn't imagined them—and ran into the house to get her Beretta. Holding it at arm's length, gripping it with both hands, she followed the intruder's footprints around to the tool shed at the rear of the house, which served as a store-room for old junk. The bolt was undone, the door was ajar, and something was rustling inside in the darkness. Colomba raised the handgun to eye level. "I see you! Put your hands behind your head and come out."

There was no answer. The rustling sounds fell silent.

"I'm going to count to three: don't make me lose my temper. One, two . . ."

Before reaching three, Colomba strode the couple of yards that separated her from the shed and shoved the door open with the tip of her boot. Daylight revealed the massive silhouette of a man standing amid the old sticks of furniture shrouded in cobwebs. He was half-hidden behind the side of a clothes closet, and Colomba could only glimpse his back.

"I told you to come out of there!"

She took a step forward: the intruder hunched even further behind the tall cabinet, but now at least Colomba could see him. He was strapping big, all muscle and fat, and his hair was yellow as straw. He was wearing nothing but an old tracksuit and a pair of felt slippers. Trembling with fear, he stood with his face to the corner.

"Who are you? Turn around, and let me take a look at you."

He didn't move, and it was Colomba who finally stepped closer to him, discovering a face that was pink and hairless. He couldn't have been any older than eighteen, and he was staring into the empty air, expressionless. Colomba wondered whether he was like that all the time, or if he was in a state of shock. All the same, she lowered her handgun. "What are you doing here? Are you lost?" she asked. The boy didn't answer. Without warning, he bolted toward the door, with stiff, uncoordinated movements, his slippers spraying dirty water as he ran. Colomba grabbed him. The boy bit her hand, and so she tripped him, sending him sprawling headlong, facedown in the snow. "Come on, stop acting like an ass," she said. "I don't want to hurt you. I just want to know who . . ." The words died in her throat.

The snow around the boy had turned red.

Colomba knelt down next to the boy, conquering her plunge into panic. Had he hit something? A rock? Any of the pieces of junk scattered across the ground?

"Where are you hurt? Let me see."

The boy turned over and lay there staring at her, his eyes wide open and full of confusion.

He's in a state of shock; before long he'll pass out from loss of blood. Colomba unzipped his tracksuit.

Underneath was a T-shirt drenched in blood—blood that was starting to clot.

Ignoring the boy's inarticulate laments, she lifted the T-shirt, revealing the bare flesh beneath. There was no wound. She felt around to make sure and the boy tried to pull back, then she decisively rolled him over onto his belly and examined his back: nothing there, either, and nothing on his legs.

Colomba tucked his clothing back in place: the blood wasn't his. Good.

Are you sure that's a good thing?

She helped him to his feet and the boy stood wobbling in front of her. "If you try to run away again, I won't be so nice, okay?" she told him. "Come inside before you freeze to death."

The boy didn't move.

"Into the house." Colomba pointed him in the right direction. "That way."

The boy didn't follow the hand that she pointed. Colomba took him by the arm, ignoring his efforts to wriggle free, and dragged him after her into the kitchen, which also served as a dining room, occupying half of the ground floor. That space had once been a stable, built directly beneath the master bedroom to heat it with the warmth from the clustered livestock. The walls were covered with stains, and the furniture, dating back to the pre-IKEA era, was covered with dust. Perched atop a three-legged kitchen stool was a portable television set, turned on, though with the sound off, and tuned to an all-news station. Colomba never turned it off.

She wrapped the boy in a blanket, then took the cordless phone from atop the credenza to call the nearest police station, only to discover without anything like surprise that the phone line was down. The cables ran high over the fields for miles, winding through the tree branches to a switchboard that dated back to before World War II. All it took was a gob of spit to short-circuit the whole network, much less a massive blizzard. Anyone who lived around there made sure to equip themselves with cell phones and short-wave radios, but Colomba had neither device.

She looked at the boy with distaste.

Once again, she tried to ask his name, but he wouldn't even look at her. Was he deaf? She dropped a spoon, and saw him start at the sound. No, he wasn't deaf. He just wasn't listening.

"If you don't talk to me, I'm going to have to try to see if you have any ID. All right?" she asked him. "Okay, silence is a form of consent."

The boy put up no resistance to her search, recoiling only when Colomba touched his bare flesh, after which he'd scrub away at it with his fingers as if he somehow felt filthy. In his pockets she found neither wallet nor identification, but on his wrist, under the sleeve of his sweatshirt, Colomba found a green plastic bracelet.

Hello, my name is Tommy and I'm autistic. I don't like to talk or be touched. If you find me unaccompanied, please call this number.

Colomba cursed herself for the idiot she was. "Ciao, Tommy. Pleased to meet you . . . Sorry I didn't understand before this." She turned the bracelet over and found the same message in Greek. Lots of foreigners had purchased little villas on the hills of the Marche, so much more affordable than the houses in the neighboring region of Tuscany. No doubt Tommy's parents were among their number. There was also a useless—for now—telephone number and a home address, a street in Montenigro about an hour's walk away, under normal conditions. In slippers? In the snow? Hard to say how long it would take.

"How did you get all the way over here? Were you with someone who hurt themselves?" Colomba asked, and as before received no answer. She sat down on the other end of the sofa, feeling exhausted as if the hour she'd just spent had lasted an entire day. She felt an overwhelming desire to get back in bed.

But she had Tommy to deal with. And his bracelet.

"I should have just let you run away," she told him. "Now you'd be somebody else's problem."

She put her parka back on and went out to start the old Fiat Panda 4x4. She hadn't used it since she'd last gone out for groceries three weeks earlier, but as soon as she hooked the emergency charger up to the car battery, the starter turned over and the engine roared to life.

As she waited for it to warm up, Colomba applied the snow chains she'd extracted from the car's trunk, freezing her fingers to the bone and cursing under her breath as she did so. Every so often she'd walk over to take a look at Tommy, who still sat hunched over on the sofa. He'd taken off his blanket and seemed indifferent to the icy temperature. Colomba vaguely recalled that indifference to the cold was one of the symptoms of autism. Dante had told her so.

Once she'd gotten the snow chains onto the tires, Colomba dragged Tommy into the car, tethering him in place with two seat belts in the back seat, and then crept up the driveway, with the engine grinding along in first gear.

Her hands were sweating. She passed the house of her first neighbor, so to speak, a good mile and a half away, a peaceful man who lived alone—a beekeeper—and then she reached the intersection with the provincial road. There were no other cars out, and she felt lost on an alien planet made of ice. Her breathing faltered, growing labored, and a cramp in her stomach made a sheet of icy sweat break out all over her body.

She pulled the hand brake and got out. Standing in the snow, she forced herself to breathe calmly, staring at a bright blue break in the cloud cover.

It's just a few miles. Nothing will happen, she told herself. But something, she knew, already had.

Tommy tapped on the glass of the car window, and Colomba snapped back to full consciousness.

"Okay, okay, I get it," she said. Tommy wouldn't stop and was going to keep tapping the rest of the way. Colomba took another couple of deep ice-cold breaths, then got back behind the wheel. The provincial road had only a thin layer of snow on it, and her snow chains on the asphalt sounded like machine guns. At the turnoff for Montenigro, she found herself looking at a Carabinieri checkpoint, two squad cars on either side of the road and uniformed soldiers with submachine guns and their faces bright red with the cold.

She slammed the brakes on. From the back seat, Tommy let out a shrill shriek and lay down, out of sight.

Colomba turned to look at him. "There's no need to be afraid, Tommy. There must have been a car crash," she told him, knowing how unlikely that actually was. "Now, you wait here for me, all right?" She shut the door, leaving the boy in the car, and walked over to the small cluster of Carabinieri. One of them was a young woman with a head of red curls, who was directing the nonexistent traffic with a paddle.

"Signora, you're going to have to turn around. The road is closed."

Colomba read her insignia. "Good morning, Corporal. What seems to be going on?"

"Routine police work, ma'am," said the redhead, in the tone of voice that amounted to *None of your fucking business*. "You'd better go the long way round."

"Maybe you can help me. I found a boy who's lost. His name is Tommy Melas. He's autistic and needs to get back to his parents as soon as possible."

"Wait here." The corporal hurried away and a few minutes later she was back, with a tall bald man in his early fifties, his chin trimmed with a small neat gray goatee. He was dressed in a well-worn hunter's suit, but there was no mistaking the fact that he, too, was in the military. The man hesitated a tenth of a second before extending his hand, and Colomba realized that he'd recognized her. "I'm Sergeant Major Lupo, commander of the Portico station."

"I'm Colomba Caselli, but you already knew that."

"Where is your security detail, Deputy Chief?"

"I don't have one," she said in a hurry. "Listen, the boy walked all the way to my house, he's just lucky he didn't freeze to death, but he ought to be seen by a doctor."

"Your house in . . ."

"In Mezzanotte. I shut him up in the car because I'm afraid he's going to hurt himself, but also because his clothing is covered in blood. Drenched in it."

Colomba pointed to him. Inside the car, Tommy continued to tap on the window at the same rhythm, indifferent to everything else.

Lupo ran his hand over his whiskers unhappily. "Listen, Deputy Captain, I'll get straight to the point. Tommy's parents were murdered last night."

"Oh, Christ . . ." said Colomba.

"We received the call two hours ago, and we've just put out the alert for the boy. Thanks for having spared us a lot of grueling work."

"It was pure coincidence."

"Do you mind waiting for me at the café while I get the boy situated?" he asked, pointing her to the establishment just before the curve in the road. It was an old tobacconist that also served as a milk bar, as was often the case in small towns. "Have an espresso and put it on my tab."

"I'm going to guess that I don't really have an alternative."

"I think you know so, even better than I do."

Colomba knew it perfectly well and she did as she'd been told, though she ordered a cup of tea with lemon instead of an espresso. She sat down at the only table, next to the little plate-glass window. In the café there were three old men, discussing what was going on, while the Asian barista was texting on her cell phone.

She saw Tommy appear at the far end of the road, surrounded by Carabinieri who were gently herding him along. The boy managed to bolt from the little group by knocking the redheaded corporal to the pavement, but instead of running away, he simply galloped straight for the ambulance and lunged inside. From where she sat, Colomba couldn't see anything more until Lupo came out with a large bag containing the boy's clothing. She looked back down into her teacup.

Lupo arrived ten minutes later and sat down beside her. "The boy seems in reasonable shape," he told her.

"Does he have any relatives around here?"

"Not that we know of. Right now we're taking him to a farmstay in Cartoceto until we can find a better place to put him up." He ordered an espresso, and the barista prepared it for him without once taking her eyes off the screen of her cell phone. "He's legally an adult, but he certainly can't be left all alone."

Colomba thought back to the boy's frightened eyes and tried to picture him in one of the old converted farmhouses that dotted the countryside, full of vacationers during the summer months but by now surely empty and alone. She felt sorry for him, a feeling that lately she'd largely reserved for herself. "He was home when the murders took place, I'd have to imagine."

"I imagine the same thing. And he ran away in his slippers. Did he tell you anything when you found him?"

"No, not even his name. I'm not even sure he knows how to talk."

"Had you ever met before? Did you know his parents?"

"No."

"Neither did I, we didn't see them out and about much." Lupo put on a pair of half-rim reading glasses and undid his jacket. Underneath it he wore a sweater decorated with embroidered sombreros and burros; he pulled a sheet of paper out of an inside pocket. "The mother's name was Teresa, she came from Turin. The stepfather's name was Aristides, and he was Greek," he said, skimming his notes. "Tommy is actually the mother's son from her first marriage. His last name is Carabba. His real father died when he was five or six years old. Now he's nineteen."

Colomba raised her right hand. "Thanks for all that. But it's none of my concern."

"Maybe, a little bit, it actually is." Lupo fooled around with an early-model iPhone before handing it to her. "This is Tommy's bedroom, the way we found it today."

All she could see of the bedroom was the headboard of the bed and a wall covered with photographs. Colomba pinched the picture to enlarge it and discovered that the pictures on the wall were all of the same person.

Her.

Colomba handed back the cell phone without a word. *Even here*, she thought. She chewed on the lemon that had been rinsed in the tea, with an even grimmer look on her face. She'd been hoping that she'd left her compulsive admirers behind her. Lupo studied her expression. "You don't seem very surprised, Deputy Captain."

"After the bloodbath in Venice, my face has become public property. And then there are all those fans of Dante's who think that I was the one who made him disappear."

"Yeah, I think I've read something about that. The world is full of idiots."

"According to Dante, seventy percent of the population. And a hundred percent of the men and women in uniform," she added with a sad smile.

Lupo grimaced sympathetically. "He must have been a lot of fun to be around, this Torre."

"He still is," Colomba snapped. Then, more calmly: "I don't know where he is, but he's alive."

"Certainly, sorry about that." Lupo smiled consolingly at her. "According to the neighbors, Tommy almost never talks, but when he wants to, he's capable of expressing himself more or less like a child."

"You need a specialist. I knew a few people in Rome, but here I wouldn't know who to point you to."

Lupo smiled apologetically. "While we're trying to figure that out, what do you say to giving it a try yourself?"

"My job was to bring him to someone who could take care of him, and that's what I've done. And that's where my duty ends."

"The boy admires you. Maybe he'd be willing to talk to you, and any additional information we can get would be a big help."

Colomba clenched the cup a little tighter. "Even if Tommy told me something, it wouldn't have any legal value. If he's as seriously autistic as he seems, he has no juridical capacity."

"But he could help us identify whoever was responsible for the murders. And now that you're no longer on the force, you don't need authorization to talk to Tommy, the way I would."

Colomba thought back to the pictures covering the wall. She sighed. "Have the SIS already examined the crime scene?" The SIS was the standard abbreviation for Scientific Investigation Squad, the unit in charge of crime-scene forensics.

"No. And I don't know when they'll get here, in this weather."

"Then I'd like to take a look at the house before talking to the boy," she said, hoping that Lupo would refuse so that she could take that thought off her mind.

Unfortunately, that's not the way things went.

Colomba followed Lupo, entering the center of Montenigro for the first time since she'd been a child. Now many of the houses in the little village that dated back to Romanesque times stood abandoned and in ruins. For the most part, it was inhabited only by old people who rounded out their pensions by hunting for truffles, and now the old folks were all out in the street, eagerly watching in spite of the risk of freezing to death. There were even a few new houses, the kind you'd find on the outskirts of Milan. The Melas home was one of these: ochre yellow with a large veranda propped up by garish fake-marble columns.

A small knot of soldiers were stamping their feet to keep warm behind the two-toned tape that was blocking access. An elderly brigadier let them through, and Colomba instinctively reached into her pocket to flash her police badge. Of course, it was no longer there. On her last day in Rome she'd hurled it against the wall of the squad room, coming dangerously close to hitting the chief of the Mobile Squad in the head. Maybe they'd melted it down, or crushed it in a hydraulic press. She had no idea what they did with the badges of officers out on extended leave.

They put on latex gloves and shoe covers, taking them out of a cardboard box on the front steps. "Any signs of breaking and entering?" she asked.

Lupo shook his head. "I haven't seen any."

The snow had started falling again, thick and fast; the rain gutters were gurgling and the windows were so many blind, luminous eyes. They passed a front hall filled with shoes and umbrellas and entered the villa's kitchen. Colomba saw a bottle of mineral water overturned in the sink, with an almost complete print of a bloody hand. There were more handprints on the refrigerator, and on the floor was an array of bare, bloodstained footprints. Colomba felt sure they belonged to the boy.

"What a mess," she muttered.

"Yes, Tommy made quite a mess. The fingerprints are his, we checked it out on the fly while we were changing him."

Colomba followed the crimson fingerprints down a hallway whose walls were covered with photographs of birds of prey, and then into the living room. On the main wall hung the wedding pictures of Signor and Signora Melas. Signora Melas was projecting a virtual fountain of uncontainable joy in her white wedding gown, too tight around her stout hips, while Signor Melas stood, lithe and athletic in his black suit, smiling into the lens.

Lupo removed a sheet of paper from the breast pocket of his shirt and put his glasses back on. "They got married a year and a half ago, according to their residence permits. But we just took a quick look at the system, there was no time to do any more searching than that." He used his elbow to shove open the door into the master bedroom.

"They were killed in here, and it's not a pretty sight," he said. "You can spare yourself the experience, if you prefer."

"I'm sure I've seen worse," said Colomba.

She was right, but the scene was still quite repugnant. The bodies of the Melases, man and wife, looked as if they'd wound up under a truck, if the driver had then put the truck in reverse and run over them again a couple more times for good measure. They lay in their blood-drenched bed, he on his side, his legs tangled in the covers, a hand half-detached from the wrist, and she on her back. The woman's right leg had slid to the floor, as if it had been nailed down while she was trying to escape, the bone of the tibia protruding from the flesh. The blows had been so violent that his red-striped pajamas and her lace-trimmed nightgown were in shreds. Colomba decided that the mortal blows must have been to the head. The back of the man's skull had been flattened, his scalp shoved forward until it sloughed over onto his forehead; the woman's head, in contrast, ended above the eyebrows, where there was nothing but a slosh of gray matter and hair. Colomba felt the taste of the lemon rising up from her stomach. "Did you find the weapon?"

"Not yet. What do you think it could have been?"

"From the indentations, probably a hammer, and a heavy carpenter's hammer, for that matter, with a square face. A big one, too."

"And how many assailants do you think there might have been?"

"I'm not a 'white jumpsuit,'" Colomba replied in a flat tone, using the jocular nickname for members of the forensics squad.

"But you were on the homicide squad, you must have seen more things than I have."

"I can make some educated guesses, such as that the blows were delivered with a single weapon, used in alternation between the two victims." Colomba pointed at the ceiling. There were arcs of blood that intersected like the beams in a barrel-vault ceiling. ". . . The vertical swipes were produced by the murderer when he raised the weapon after inflicting the blow. While the horizontal swipes were—"

"—when he changed targets. Back and forth," Lupo said, proving that he knew more than he was saying. "So there might have been just one attacker."

"There could have been ten, if they'd just handed the weapon from one to the other and were careful to maintain the same angle of attack."

"But you have to admit that that's unlikely."

Colomba hesitated, undecided about what answer to give. She didn't like Lupo's persistent stance. "Let's get out of here."

They went back to the living room, under the eyes of the photos of the murdered couple. Colomba could imagine the pictures on their headstones, not too far in the future.

"Do you think it was a robbery?" asked Lupo.

"Well, what do *you* think?"

"I'm usually called upon to investigate calf rustlers and quarreling neighbors," said Lupo, with a shrug. "My opinion isn't worth a plugged nickel."

"I've seen experienced officers lose their lunch at the sight of corpses in these conditions. You seem quite at your ease."

"Sometimes cattle thefts can go horribly wrong."

Colomba shook her head: if Lupo wanted to go on playing the ignorant rube, that wasn't her problem.

"A robber will kill out of fear, to keep from being identified, or as a punishment for victims who've refused to go along. The Melases, in contrast, were murdered in their sleep, or just about."

"And considering that a hammer isn't the kind of murder weapon we'd expect from a hardened criminal, what are we supposed to think? That this was a crime of opportunity? A crime of passion?"

Colomba finally saw red. "Just stop beating around the bush. You think it was the boy who did it. You're just hoping he'll sob on my shoulder and confess."

Lupo smiled. "What can I say, Deputy Captain? I'm open to all possibilities."

"What motive would Tommy have had?"

"The boy is sick, he doesn't need a motive."

"Autism is a syndrome, not a disease," said Colomba. "People with severe cases, like Tommy, do sometimes hurt other people because they don't know how to control their own strength or because they have violent outbursts of anger. Slaughtering your own parents in their sleep is quite another matter."

"Jeffrey Dahmer was autistic."

"Maybe he had Asperger syndrome," Colomba replied. "That's very different from Tommy, who isn't capable of taking care of himself. He could have caught his parents off guard, but his movements aren't coordinated enough to be able to kill them both before they had time to react. You saw the way he moves."

"He might have been lucky."

"Let's take a look at his room."

At first, Colomba thought she'd walked into a broom closet. The one window had been covered with a large piece of cardboard and there was only a single bed, a footlocker, and a small cabinet without doors, containing Tommy's clothing. The sheets were decorated with Disney characters, and there was an old PC on a small table, next to an equally old ink-jet printer that was, however, perfectly maintained. But what caught Colomba's eye were the photographs of her. There were at least a hundred of them, either printed on copy paper or cut out of newspapers. Tommy had hung them up so that they practically covered the walls and part of the ceiling.

"Quite a spectacle, isn't it?" said Lupo. "Do you think that they forced him to stay in here?"

Colomba studied the room. "No. There's no bolt on the door, there aren't any ropes. Maybe he was just more comfortable having it like this."

"Maybe he thought he was a vampire."

Colomba pretended not to hear him and instead inspected the bed and floor. Sheets rumpled, no blood: Tommy hadn't gone back to his room after finding his parents dead. Or after killing them. He'd run away without putting on anything heavy to keep him warm. Nothing but the clothes he'd been sleeping in. "Sergeant Major, could you leave me alone in here for a few minutes?"

"Is there some problem?"

"No, I just want to have a moment or two to think things over and get a general idea."

"Don't take too long, if you don't mind. If someone happens to see you here, I'll have a lot of explaining to do."

"Don't worry about it."

Lupo left the room. Colomba waited until the rustling sound of the shoe covers had faded away, then turned on Tommy's computer, hoping it wasn't password-protected. It wasn't. She quickly found the folder containing the pictures of her and deleted it, then emptied the trash and started the disk-scrubber program. A good technician could no doubt recover those pictures, but not the first reporter to pay a bribe to gain access to the interior of the house. She turned the computer back off and tore the pictures off the walls, starting with the one of her in her uniform, with the gold braid of a full detective. Some of the pictures were printed on the letterhead stationery of a certain Dr. Pala, *Psychiatrist and Developmental Therapist for the Young*; the address was in a neighboring town. She crumpled those sheets over the big ball of papers she'd already crushed together and stuck the whole agglomeration under her jacket. With the walls bare now, the room seemed even darker and more unsettling. Dante, she decided, would have died if he'd been confined to a place like that. Maybe it was the other way around for Tommy, though.

He walked two miles, don't forget that.

She turned off the light and left the room, discovering immediately that she'd really had no time to waste, because a van with the logo of the SIS was parked just outside the front gate. The "white jumpsuits" were almost fully dressed and were briefly lingering in conversation with Lupo. She pretended not to have seen them and quickly but nonchalantly darted around the corner of the house, where she set fire to the crumpled ball of paper with the matches she still had in her pocket. By the time Lupo caught up with her, there was nothing left but a will-o'-the-wisp clump of ashes and a vague outline of scorched cinders.

Lupo shook his head. "Well done. Very nice work! Thanks for having treated me like a complete idiot!"

"They would have been on the front pages of the newspapers even before the pictures of the victims," Colomba replied, in all sincerity. "I used to have people sneak into my apartment in Rome to tell me about their theories. I don't want them to know where I live now."

"The only reason I'm not going to file a criminal complaint against you is that I respect what you've been through. But don't push your luck, 'heroine of Venice.'"

"Don't call me that," Colomba snarled.

"I didn't make up the phrase. So now do you intend to do what you promised?"

"You mean, am I going to help you frame Tommy?"

"I don't want to frame anybody. I just want to avoid wasting a lot of time spinning my wheels."

"No doubt they'll send someone down to help you with the investigation."

"This is my district, Deputy Captain. Are you coming or not?"

"Whatever the boy might tell me, I'm not going to testify. He'll have to tell someone else the same thing, of his own free will."

"Any other conditions or stipulations? Do you want a stretch limousine?"

Colomba shook her head. "I just want you to forget that you know where I live. Do you think you can do that?"

Lupo nodded. "Let me show you the way."

The farmstay where Tommy was being held until a relative or social services could take custody of him was called Il Nido—the Nest—and it was a fancier version of the farmhouse where Colomba lived: three times the size, with a swimming pool, stables, and riding grounds, surrounded by a vast meadow where two piebald ponies were stamping the snow in unmistakable disgust.

Tommy was being guarded by the redheaded lady carabiniere and an older colleague of hers in a single room with the shutters closed and the one table lamp switched on. Tommy looked even more enormous in here, sitting on the bed in tracksuit pants and a yellow T-shirt that was too small to cover his belly. He had to weigh almost 350 pounds.

"Open the shutters, Concio, this place looks like a cellar storeroom," said Lupo.

"That's the way he likes it, Sergeant Major, sir," the redhead replied. "He doesn't like being outside. He whined and moaned the whole way."

"He walked two miles," said Lupo. "He's had plenty of fresh air to breathe, and then some."

"He was in a state of shock. You saw the room he was living in, didn't you?" said Colomba.

"Sure, I saw, okay. You two stand guard in the hallway," said Lupo. "I'll let you know when you can come back in."

The two officers chorused "At your orders" and stepped out into the hall.

"You need to leave, too, Sergeant Major," Colomba said.

"I won't say a word."

"If Tommy wanted to talk to you, he'd have done it by now. Get out."

"I'll be right outside the door."

Colomba shut the door in his face, then grabbed a chair and dragged it toward the bed. Tommy was playing solitaire with a deck of cards, bouncing slightly on his haunches. He moved the cards around according to no apparent logic, but with meticulous precision in his fingertips.

Once again, Colomba felt pity for him, and once again, it was as painful as using a muscle that had long ago fallen asleep. Big though he was, he still looked as defenseless as a bear in a cartoon. "Ciao, Tommy," she said to him with a fake smile. "How do you feel? Did they treat you all right?"

Tommy went on playing, but more slowly now, spying on her out of the corner of his eye.

"I'm sorry about what happened to your parents. I came here because maybe you'd like to talk about it with me."

Tommy sat there with a card hovering in midair. Then he slowly set it down, muttering something, and for the first time Colomba heard his baritone voice.

"Did you want me to protect you? Or did you want to tell me something?" she asked.

Tommy sang a jingle from a television commercial.

The music and tone were identical, but the words were pure nonsense. Colomba could feel her level of irritation rise, but she clamped down on it immediately. "Let's try again, Tommy. And let me tell you something. Being here makes me uncomfortable. I really wish I didn't have to deal with something as ugly as your parents' death. If I'm doing it at all, it's because I think I can help you."

The boy said nothing, but Colomba had the impression that he'd understood. "Did you do something you shouldn't have, Tommy?"

Tommy shook his head, with an exaggerated movement, like a little kid.

"Did you hurt your parents, because you lost your temper?"

No.

"Are you telling me the truth?"

Tommy nodded.

Colomba wanted to believe him. "Did you see who it was? Did you know them?"

Tommy took a very long time to set down the card, but he still didn't answer.

"I'd be afraid if I were in your shoes, believe me," Colomba said. "But you're safe here. No one's going to hurt you."

Tommy sat motionless, with doubt stamped on his face, Then, with shaking fingers, he gathered up the cards and laid them out again in rows on the bedcovers, divided by suit and in rising rank; once he'd finished organizing them, he raised his forefinger.

"Should I take one?"

Tommy nodded.

Colomba smiled. "There are people who talk and talk and you can't figure out what the fuck they're trying to say . . . You don't belong in that category." She reached out a hand toward a card at random, but Tommy tapped the blanket again. Colomba froze: Tommy didn't want her to choose, he wanted her to pick a specific card that he had in mind. "Okay. Not this one. Farther up, farther down?"

Moving her hands in concentric circles, she reviewed all the cards . . . until Tommy started tapping frantically. Colomba stopped her hand again: her fingers were dangling over the king of diamonds. As she picked up the card, the boy's eyes grew as large as saucers, as if he was afraid of it. The king was a young man, depicted in profile, with long hair, royal mantle, and crown. He was wearing a heavy necklace with a large pendant and in one hand he gripped an ax. The little sun that shone down on him was a gold coin, and at the center of it was a laughing red face. Colomba had never paid much attention to that card, and now it struck her as frightening more than amusing. The ax could certainly represent the murder weapon, but why a king?

She turned the card to face Tommy, but he didn't look at it. "Was it someone with long hair who came into your house? Or someone with a strange hat?"

Tommy shook his head. No.

"A burglar who took money?"

Another no.

Colomba was still struggling to come up with another question when Lupo came in. In his defense, it should be said that he knocked first, but then he hadn't waited for an answer, either. "The medical examiner wants to take a look at the boy. Do you think I could . . ."

Tommy reacted as if he'd just been jabbed with a live high-tension wire. He leaped off the bed, knocking over the nightstand and sending cards and blankets in all directions. He stopped, standing with his face to the wall, fingers laced behind his back, eyes shut tight. He was trembling violently and gasping for breath.

Lupo snapped his fingers in front of the redhead who stood as if in a trance in the doorway. "Wake up. Call the doctor, the boy's having an anxiety attack."

Colomba felt as if *she* were having the anxiety attack. She was trembling as badly as the boy.

This can't be, she thought.

But hadn't she seen him do the exact same thing in the tool shed? She hadn't deciphered his actions back then, because she hadn't seen his face, but this time . . .

Tommy moaned, gluing his body to the wall as if he were trying to pass through it. A stream of saliva dangled from his slack-jawed mouth. Struggling to move, Colomba hugged him from behind and, for a few seconds, clung to him, breathing in time with him.

"Everything's okay, Tommaso. You're safe now. You're a good son," she whispered in his ear.

She'd used the word "son" intentionally, even though it scorched her mouth. Tommy relaxed all at once and practically tumbled over onto her. Then he wriggled free and started gathering up the scattered cards, collecting them in order of suit and rank.

In the meantime, the redhead had come back with a gray-bearded man wearing a three-piece suit. If he hadn't been in his early seventies, he might have seemed like a hipster, but he was the medical examiner. "Everyone out, please," he said imperiously. "And next time, ask a *doctor* whether it's safe to get close to him. Ask *me*."

Colomba had left the room at the word *everyone*, and now Lupo chased after her down the hallway.

"I didn't think I was going to scare him like that. Before this, he never even looked me in the face."

"It must have been because he was surprised. Who knows why. Ask the doctor," Colomba said flatly. She sped up her pace.

"If he says the boy's all right, you could try again. Again, on an informal basis."

"No."

"Why not?"

"Because I can't help you more than I already have, Sergeant Major. If you wanted a confession, he's not going to give me one. Not only because he seems incapable of verbalizing, but because I don't believe he was the one who did it."

She tried to walk around Lupo, but he planted himself right in her path. "You saw the house yourself, Deputy Captain. The clothing, the handprints . . ."

"Get out of my way."

"I can understand why he would have gotten scared, but you?"

"I'm not scared. I'm just irritated about all the time you're making me waste."

"You're a bad liar, Deputy Captain. What did the boy tell you?" Colomba darted around him and got into her car, half expecting to see Lupo jump onto the hood to stop her, but that didn't happen. On the township road to Mezzanotte, she kept the accelerator floored, with the snow chains machine-gunning along on the asphalt. She swerved a few times and came frighteningly close to a head-on crash with a truck, but steering into and out of her slaloming skids, she always managed to regain control of the vehicle. She didn't even know that she was driving; hers were automatic movements guided by nothing more than a speck of consciousness. The rest of her mind had gone three years back in time.

On that day of a bygone year, a younger Colomba was standing in front of ten rusty shipping containers in the countryside not far from Rome; the ten containers were arranged among the stumps and scrub brush in the yard of an old working farm. The special forces had cordoned off the area and the bomb disposal team had deactivated the triggers of the plastic explosives that sealed the hatches. When they opened the containers, the bright sunlight had blinded the people being held captive in them. The oldest prisoner was twenty, the youngest six, and they were almost all in terrible conditions of health. Some of them had taken to their heels, running uncertainly on legs that could barely carry them, but most of them had remained motionless in their cells. They had been bent to the will of a man who believed himself to be God, and who had done as he'd pleased for thirty long years, kidnapping and murdering children, raising them like battery hens, inculcating in their minds the supreme directive, the order that demanded obedience, on pain of death.

Never look outside.

When the hatch opened, they had been taught to turn and face the closest wall, their hands behind their backs.

Just as Tommy had done.

Colomba didn't know how or when, but Tommy, like Dante, had been the Father's prisoner.

CHAPTER II

The Father is there, in the crate, with Dante. Dante can hear him breathing by his side. He hears his faint voice deriding him, the touch of his hands. Dante doesn't know how to escape, he can't even shift his position. The lid of the crate is just a couple of inches out of reach of his forehead. Otherwise, he'd eagerly slam his head into it until it killed him. He'd beg, if his mouth weren't gagged; he'd rip the veins out of his limbs with his teeth.

Why can't he just die? He prays to a God he doesn't even believe in to strike him down on the spot with a lightning bolt, to kill him now. The screams in his head become deafening; he trembles and drools.

He doesn't know how much time has passed when he regains consciousness, so exhausted that he's practically calm. The Father is no longer there with him. Colomba has killed the Father to save Dante's life.

Dante thinks as little as possible about the silo in the countryside outside of Cremona where the Father held him captive for thirteen years. But now he'd gladly trade this place for that. At least there he had a bucket for his physical needs and not the adult diaper that, he now realizes from tentatively touching himself, girds his hips.

His relative state of calm is vanishing, and now Dante can feel his inner drooling idiot begin to rear his head. He concentrates on the rudimentary form of self-taught meditation that he's developed, a discipline that before now he's used only as a way of fighting the symptoms of withdrawal from various pharmaceuticals. He visualizes the image that he's associated with calm and well-being: Gudetama. Gudetama is a character from Japanese anime cartoons, an egg yolk with arms and legs who spends his time napping and complaining. Maybe not what a Zen master would have recommended, but then Dante believes in freedom of choice.

Gudetama brings about the desired effects, and Dante's respiration starts to return to normal, he can feel himself calming down. Dante imagines Gudetama slithering lazily and oozily through the air holes in the crate and sprawling on the cover, inhaling fresh, open air. And he can surely do it, too; if he only gets busy, freedom is only inches away.

Dante has spent his life studying ways of picking locks and getting out of chains, in the constant fear that the Father might return to get him. He can open a padlock with a bobby pin held between his teeth, he can get out of a straitjacket by dislocating his shoulders, he knows the exact right spot to hit a metal handcuff to break it open. Even easier with a plastic handcuff. His left hand, the bad hand, is a single twisted mass of scar tissue. His metacarpal bones never did solidify entirely and that makes his hand even more flexible and compressible. Dante manages to jerk it repeatedly so that it slithers through the plastic noose, though the edge lacerates his flesh as he does so. Gudetama whines and thrashes unhappily. Dante lays Gudetama down again. With his bad hand, he now frees his other hand, and using both hands together, he unfetters his ankles. Finally, he removes the mouth bit. It was fastened with a buckle on the back of his neck, and now that he sees it he realizes that it's a bit of masochistic gear, the rubber ball that sex slaves put in their mouths to muffle their screams. He wonders how Colomba would have reacted if she'd seen him tricked out like that. Colomba, with that . . . straitlaced mind-set of hers. He misses Colomba, but he's afraid to think of her, because it summons her up the way he saw her last, clutching at her belly as blood spilled out of it, her eyes wide open in shock and pain. He doesn't know how much time has gone by (hours? days?), but he still hasn't quite digested the fact that Colomba failed to protect him from his abductor, that she had been unable to vanquish the bad guys, the way Wonder Woman might have. With all the time that he's spent with her as a . . . "consultant," Dante has learned to trust Colomba, to rely on her implicitly. He always felt safe when she was around, he felt protected.

Attracted.

But remembering the past will do nothing to save him. Dante stretches his limbs as much as he can in that limited space, only a smidgen bigger than his body itself, with a foot or so of empty air above him, between his face and the air holes. He tries to push it, but the lid won't budge; in fact, it doesn't even creak.

Like a stone tomb covering.

That's the wrong image and, sure enough, Gudetama promptly vanishes. Dante pounds with his hands and his forehead against the wood until he can no longer see a thing due to the blood dripping into his eyes. He loses consciousness and when he regains it, he can taste the vomit in his mouth. He has to get out of there before he goes stark raving mad.

Dante massages his good hand to restore feeling, then runs it around the corners of the lid above his head. There are no hinges or movable parts that he can detect. The lid is screwed down from outside. Dante makes a deal with himself: if he can't find a way of opening the crate, and soon, he'll slit his wrists. The buckle to the mouth bit has a pointy tongue about an inch long, he'll be able to use that. Strangely, the idea of killing himself cheers him up in his partial delirium: he won't have to die like a rat in a trap, it will be quick and painless. But in the meantime he has other tasks to tend to. Dante feels around on the bottom of the crate, and suddenly he touches something strange. Circular cuts in the wood, about the diameter of an eraser on the end of a pencil. He presses down on one with his fingernail and pops out a tiny wooden lid. And underneath it . . .

It can't be, he must be dreaming again. And yet, his fingers, trained by his thousands of solitary experiments, can't be mistaken.

Inside the hole there's a trick screw, the kind that magicians use for nut-and-bolt puzzles, or to close false bottoms. It seems perfectly ordinary, fastened with a normal nut on the outside, but there's a hidden detail: the threaded shaft isn't part of the head, it's only screwed in. So the head can be unscrewed without touching the nut. Dante tries it and can feel it turning under his fingernails, he can hear the wood creak, and the gap between the bottom and walls of the crate grows wider. Dante undoes the screw entirely and then does the same thing with the three other screws concealed at each of the crate's four corners. And now the bottom sags loose.

Dante pulls his legs up against his skeletal chest and pushes with both feet. The heavy crate rises above him. A gust of fresh air reaches his nostrils, scented with dust and grass. He slides out, reduced now to a quivering heap of aching muscles and tendons and nerves, and the sides and top of the crate fall back to the ground with a thump that echoes through the empty stillness. He loses control of himself for a few seconds, shouting and ripping the oversize diaper off his body. Rolling on the chilly cement floor. But it all passes quickly. He struggles back onto his feet, feeble but angry, ready to duke it out with anyone who might think of trying to lock him up again. Though he hates violence, he's willing to use teeth and nails if necessary. Eager to do it, in fact, yearning to inflict violence. He sees the face of the man who called himself Leo Bonaccorso before his eyes again, dreams of beating that smile off his face. He dreams of locking him in a dark hole in the ground and giving him a taste of his own medicine. But only after asking him, once and for all, what the fuck he was thinking when he used an illusionist's trick trunk to imprison Dante. Was that all he had at hand? Or was it some kind of a sadistic game?

He reaches down and picks a length of electric cable off the floor, as thick as a banana and twice as long. He's ready to hit his captor in the teeth with it, and he hopes it'll hurt. But there's no one there. He's inside a rectangular warehouse, three hundred or so feet long on the longer side, with a roof held up by cement pillars. The light he had glimpsed is the light of the moon, which is refracted through the filthy glass of the skylight. The moon has almost set, while the sky is growing brighter. Everything around him is ramshackle and decrepit; a tree branch has shattered one of the windows and is now growing into the building; there are climbing vines and rotting dead leaves. He hears the cry of a bird of prey and the wind. Nothing else. No cars, no people, no electric generators, none of the sounds that we associate with civilization. And the smell, the smell isn't the right one. Venice reeked of saltwater and fried foods, cigarettes and seaweed. This place smells of wild plants and animals and plastic, it smells of an old fire. And there's no scent of human beings, except for his own odor.

Dante thinks of The Day of the Triffids. Of Z Nation. Maybe the apocalypse has taken place while he was in the crate. Now that he's able to think with something approaching his entire brain, he knows that it's not solely to his own credit that he's been able to keep from going completely gibbering insane. For his entire adult life he's managed his moods and symptoms through drugs, and he can sense traces of something distinctly chemical circulating in his veins. An antipsychotic of some kind, most likely, a tranquilizer or something. He finds the spot where the moonlight is strongest and examines himself. His arms have swollen veins, and there are broken capillaries as well as bruises. Injections, IVs. They put him to sleep.

For how long?

He feels his beard, which is growing out, soft and patchy. That's only a couple of days' growth. But he can't know whether or not someone shaved him while he was sleeping. Panic pulsates inside him. Dante forgets just how strange the situation is and runs desperately toward the flaking metal door of the warehouse. In the second that it takes before he touches it with his good hand, he envisions himself pushing on it in vain, and then slowly starving to death.

Instead, the door swings open easily, pulling with it the branches of the climbing vines, and now Dante is standing at the center of a large cement courtyard. He's in a military complex, reduced to ruins. Some of the buildings remind him of the high Soviet style of the Cold War. At the far end of the courtyard looms a building that he's never seen in his life, but which he recognizes immediately. It's practically identical to how he's always imagined it, or dreamed it. That place has been called by many different names, but to its prisoners it's only ever had one name.

The Box.

The dumb luck that had been watching over Colomba's driving finally ran out at the last curve on the dirt road before her house, and the Fiat Panda rammed nose down into a ditch full of icy water. She slammed her face against the steering wheel and split her lip, which finally brought her back in touch with reality. She didn't remember much of the crazy drive from the farmstay, but she could still feel the tingle of fear up and down her spinal cord.

But fear of what?

The Father was dead. Only eleven of his prisoners had survived, Dante among them, and Tommy wasn't one of them.

Are you absolutely sure of that?

They still didn't know all there was to know about the Father. They were very far from knowing everything. The Father had died without giving any testimony or leaving any documentation of all he had done, and his only known accomplice, the German, was serving three consecutive life sentences without once having opened his mouth to speak. What proof did they have that there were no other prisons they just hadn't found yet, no other prisoners?

Colomba dabbed at her lip with the rag she used to clean the windows and abandoned the car to its fate. She trudged back into the house, battling the icy wind, treated her bruises and cuts, and drank a cup of tea that stung her lip.

Tommy with his demented gaze continued to hover in her mind, until she finally forced herself to concentrate on more practical matters. Like the frost that was starting to build up on the windowpanes and the dank chill that was rising out of the sofa.

Make a choice, either go get firewood or else you freeze to death.

Despite the fact that the second option tempted her mightily, she finally opted for the first. She went out with a shovel to clean the snow off the woodpile, causing little avalanches directly onto her head, then she walked into the tool shed and pulled out an old ax held together with nails. She could see Tommy in her mind's eye again, shivering in the shadows of the tool shed, his oversize silhouette pressed against the wall. She shut the door behind her, hoping that that ghost would stay outside, and started chopping. It was a slow and laborious operation, not only because of the dull blade, but also because after every other blow of the ax, Colomba stopped to listen. She felt anxious when she couldn't hear any background noises, even though she also felt practically certain that she wasn't going to see any new intruders, real or imaginary, at least for the rest of that day.

Reasonably certain.

The Father was dead and Colomba didn't believe in zombies. Even if Tommy had been one of the old lunatic's prisoners, that didn't mean he hadn't actually slaughtered his parents. In fact, that would have been a justification, considering what he'd been through. If that was what had really happened.

Tommy might have seen that position depicted in some documentary, or he could have listened to the account of one of the survivors from the silos. At least a couple of them had been capable of speaking coherently and had been interviewed hundreds of times. Or else it was just a coincidence.

And what are the odds that one of the Father's victims, someone nobody's ever heard of, would be living two miles away from your house? Far more likely that you'd be struck by lightning while winning a turn of the wheel at roulette.

Tommy's room really did seem like one of the Father's cells, though. And then there were all those pictures of her.

She filled the wheelbarrow with logs and emptied it in the kitchen, but lighting the fire in the fireplace proved even more demanding than chopping the wood. The flue drew little if at all, and the balled-up newspaper she used as kindling kept going out; in the end, Colomba ran out of patience and just poured a bottle of stain remover over the wood. The stench of petroleum filled the room, but the fire blazed up with a roar, and Colomba narrowly avoided losing both eyebrows. She took the card that she had stolen from Tommy out of her pocket and wedged it into the mirror of the medicine chest in the bathroom. A king, a rich man, a chief . . . She'd need to talk to Tommy again, try to figure it out.

In her pocket, she even had the scrap of paper with the address of his psychiatrist. He didn't live far away, in fact.

Cursing herself and her stubborn mind, unwilling to relax and forget about things, Colomba picked up the phone and, discovering that the line had been restored, called for a taxi.

D r. Pala had his office high in the hilly part of San Lorenzo, just a short stroll from the seventh-century Benedictine abbey. A black woman came to answer the door. She had an Afro and wore a cocktail dress. The dimly lit lobby had frescoed ceilings and was scented with patchouli. The woman smiled at Colomba, who stood in the doorway in her parka that reeked of wet dog. "*Buongiorno*, please come in. If you'll remind me of your name, I'll check your appointment for today."

"I don't have an appointment. I just need to speak with the doctor. Ten minutes, at the most. My name is Caselli."

"I'm afraid he's expecting a patient . . ."

"This is about Tommaso Carabba. Tommy. Or maybe he's registered under Melas, I'm not certain what surname you have him under."

The secretary sized Colomba up, eyeing her for a moment. "Melas . . . Can you tell me anything else?"

"No."

The secretary ushered her into the waiting room, a small parlor, dimly lit, with a small leather sofa and two etchings by De Chirico. After a couple of minutes, a hulking man in his early sixties emerged from his office; he had long white hair and two pairs of eyeglasses dangling around his neck. His sweater and trousers were both black, as were the flip-flops on his feet. His toenails were beautifully manicured. "Please come in, Signora Caselli," he said.

His office had colorful furniture made of plastic and rubber, nature posters, a wooden Pinocchio that stood a yard tall, and a blackboard with the conjugation of the verb "to be." Colomba sat down in an armchair that seemed to be made of Lego blocks.

"Is Tommy well?" Pala asked as he sat across from her in an orange armchair.

"Yes, but I'm afraid I have to give you some bad news. His parents were murdered last night."

Pala was stunned. "Oh Lord. Who did it?"

"The Carabinieri think it was Tommy. I've met him and I have my doubts."

"Are you a relative?"

"I'm an ex-cop. Colomba Caselli, you can look me up on Google."

Pala slumped against the backrest of his chair. "There's no need. Certainly, I wouldn't have recognized you with your short hair, and above all, I didn't expect to see you here today . . . but Tommy is an admirer of yours, Commissario Caselli."

"Deputy captain, actually. Ex."

"So you have no professional interest in Tommy."

"No. Strictly personal."

Pala shook his head. "Just give me five minutes. Let me make a couple of phone calls, you can stay here if you like." He asked Caterina, the young woman at the reception desk, to cancel the next appointment, then he pulled a pack of vanilla-flavored cigarillos from the desk. "Care for one?"

"No, thanks."

Pala opened the window and lit one. Outside was the building's inner courtyard, similar to a convent's cloister, and a chilly wind was blowing, but it didn't seem to bother the doctor a bit.

"How were they killed?" he asked, after a moment's hesitation.

"Hammered to death in their sleep."

Pala smoked in silence for a handful of seconds. "I know that this is a stupid question but . . . was it painful?"

"They probably lost consciousness immediately, if they even ever woke up."

"If they were in their bedroom, then they obviously weren't invading Tommy's personal space . . ."

"Exactly."

"Then I really don't believe that it could have been him. He's autistic, his bouts of rage don't take place without a trigger. Certainly, it's always possible they might have done something that Tommy could have interpreted as a threat, but I'd rule that out: his mother knew how to handle him. So it must have been someone else."

Lupo and his convictions about the murders wouldn't hold up for long with a diagnosis of that sort, Colomba thought, but deep down, she, too, would have preferred to get the thought out of her mind. "Any idea of who else it might have been?" she asked.

"Explain the reason for your personal interest, first."

"This morning Tommy ran all the way to my house. He was still covered with his parents' blood."

Pala seemed perplexed. "So you live in Montenigro?"

"No, in Mezzanotte, in the Valfornai."

"Tommy never goes out alone. Often his mother was unable to bring him here, and I'd have to go there. He suffers greatly from exposure to open spaces. He must have been terribly frightened to have covered all that distance."

"He was."

"I need to see him . . . Do you think they'd let me have a meeting with him?"

"That depends on the magistrate and the expert appointed by the court. They'll be expected to certify that Tommy is incapable of understanding and formulating intent."

"Tommy is perfectly capable of understanding and formulating intent. He just needs to be cared for." He heaved a sigh of annoyance. "I shouldn't be talking about a patient of mine with you."

"Clearly, I can't force you to confide in me, Doctor. But I should warn you that soon, my place will be taken by a sergeant major who can't wait to wrap up this investigation."

"You don't seem to place a lot of trust in your colleagues."

"Ex-colleagues. If you want to protect Tommy, don't answer their questions, and consult a lawyer. It will take a while before they're able to issue any court orders, and new facts may emerge in the meantime."

"What sort of new facts?"

Colomba shook her head. "I have no idea. Why don't you just start by helping me."

Pala stubbed out his cigarillo on the windowsill and sat back down. "One question each."

Colomba thought she'd misheard him. "Excuse me?"

"I don't know you and I don't know whether I can trust you. You could get me in trouble with the association, or you could start trouble for Tommy. So, what I'm offering is one question each, take it or leave it. Or else threaten me with the handgun you have in your belt."

Colomba realized that the bottom of her sweatshirt had hiked up, uncovering the grip of her sidearm. She tugged it down. "I'm authorized to carry it."

"I certainly hope so. You start. What do you want to know?"

"How long have you been seeing Tommy?"

"Seven months."

"And before that?"

Pala smiled. "My turn now. Do you think that Tommy's innocent only because he was scared when you saw him, or do you have another reason?"

"I don't think it. Now it's my turn."

"Hold on there. You didn't answer my question."

Colomba glared at him. "You're making up rules to suit your purposes . . . Let's just say that I have some doubts. And let's say that I'd like to resolve it. Now answer the previous question."

"The Melases didn't live here. They moved here eight months ago from Greece. The mother didn't have the resources to afford a specialist there, and so she entrusted him to the Greek public institutions. My turn now. What keeps you from turning away, from simply ignoring him? Your sense of duty?"

"My sense of guilt. I'm not looking to collect any more than I already have," said Colomba, falling silent a second after saying it. It wasn't like her to confide in a stranger. "Would you have noticed if Tommy had been subjected to serious abuse, considering his condition?"

"Do you mean sexual abuse?" Pala seemed alarmed. "Do you have any reason to think that's happened?"

"You didn't answer my question."

"Because it's a particularly thorny matter," Pala said, after pausing to reflect briefly. "An autistic child's reaction to abuse is frequently to accentuate their self-harming behaviors, such as banging their head against the wall or chewing on their fingers. But if the abuse had taken place before I first saw him, then I wouldn't have noticed any changes. And speaking of abuse and trauma, who's helping you to overcome yours?"

"No one. I don't have any traumas," Colomba said hastily. "Did Tommy have any marks or scars?"

"I've never seen him without a T-shirt. None on his arms. Now it's my turn again. You deny that you've ever suffered a trauma. And yet, you show yours to the world."

"Is that a question?"

"No, this is the question. How many days have you been wearing that Charlie Brown sweatshirt?"

"What the fuck is that supposed to mean?"

"Answer or stop playing."

"I don't remember. That's the truth, I swear it."

Pala put on a pair of glasses and paused to study her. "From the ring around the collar, I'd say it's been a week. You're not taking care of yourself, you're not getting enough sleep, and you're not washing up enough. I doubt that was your personal style, really, prior to the Venice terror attack."

Colomba planted both elbows solidly on Pala's desk, her green eyes seething like twin emerald tornadoes. "Listen. Last night I ran out of propane, and I don't usually see a lot of people. So, yeah, I'm a little dirty and down at the heels. But I'm trying to help Tommy, and if you don't want to lend a hand, then frankly you can go fuck yourself."

Pala recoiled against the back of his chair. "And I doubt you were this touchy before."

"You're wrong there, I've always hated having other people pick through my brains. Well?"

"Ask whatever you want to know." Pala sighed. "I'll keep quiet about the rest."

"What sort of people were Tommy's parents? And don't answer in monosyllables."

"I didn't see enough of the stepfather to be able to offer any kind of judgment. It was the mother who brought Tommy to see me or else received me when I made a house call. She seemed reasonably happy."

"Wow, some endorsement."

"I don't know how much she really loved her husband and to what extent she was just bound to him by a sense of gratitude for having changed her quality of life. It was hard for her, living alone with her son."

"Why did they come here, of all places? Didn't she want to get back to her home?"

"I have no idea. She said that her husband was in love with this part of the world. In fact he was constantly out and about in the woods taking pictures of birds and plants."

"He didn't have to make a living?"

"No. He had an independent income. I thought it must have been an inheritance, but we never delved much deeper into the subject."

"If he was rich, he might have made some enemies. Or maybe his wife was having an affair."

"I didn't see them socially, we never talked about anything of the sort."

"What kind of relationship did Melas himself have with Tommy?"

Pala took a few more seconds to answer. "I don't think he'd quite gotten used to him."

"Did he yell at the boy or anything like that?"

"No, no. Absolutely not. But I never saw them interact in any affectionate manner, unlike with the mother."

Colomba stood up. "Thanks. If you could avoid telling the sergeant major that I came by to talk to you, I'd be grateful."

"Don't worry, I'm keen to keep my license. But, Colomba . . . call me. If you need to talk to someone, I'm here. The important thing is that the next time you come, please leave your gun with my secretary. Weapons make me nervous."

"Why are you so eager to become my psychiatrist?"

"Partly out of selfishness. One way or another, Tommy obliged me to take a look at you, and I've seen the array of horrors you've been exposed to. You've looked Evil in the face, close up and personal, Colomba. And that's something that someone in my line of business is constantly striving to understand."

"All you want is to take a ride through the circus in my head."

"No. Aside from the fact that I want to understand, I'm really interested in helping you. Because you need a helping hand, Colomba. I know how much you've suffered in order to do your duty. You deserve a little peace."

Colomba was tempted to retort that he could take all his psycho-bullshit and stick it up his ass, but a knot in her throat kept her from speaking. Her chin was quivering, her lips were twitching downward. To her horror, she realized that she was about to burst into tears. *No, not in front of him!*

"The worst thing you can do when you're in pain is pretend that it doesn't exist. It won't go away, even if we pretend not to notice that it's there," Pala went on. "In fact, it never gets better."

Colomba raised her hand to her face. It, too, was trembling. "I'm not going to let you pull the wool over my eyes," she panted. But then, why wasn't she leaving?

"Talk to Caterina and have her make an appointment for a day and time for us to meet again. It's not your fault that you survived."

Colomba hurried away, struggling to keep from losing control.

Colomba returned home in another taxi that she caught after nearly an hour's wait at the street corner. The cold calmed her down and little by little dried up the pool of tears waiting to burst from her eyes. That was a good thing, because when she got back to the farmhouse, she found her mother out front, stacking up grocery bags and cartons in front of the door. Colomba's mother had only recently entered her early sixties, her hair was gray and her body was petite. "You never go anywhere, but the one time I come to see you, you're not here," she grumbled.

"Next time, call ahead," said Colomba, more harshly than she'd meant to.

"Do I need to make an appointment? Come on, give me a hand." Her mother saw Colomba's swollen lip. "What have you done to yourself?"

"I slammed my head against the steering wheel." Colomba pointed to the shape of the Panda stuck in the ditch.

"I thought that looked like our car," said her mother. "You need to call a tow truck."

"Thanks, I'll do that."

Colomba grabbed a crate of apples and carried it into the kitchen, while her mother followed behind with the grocery bags. "It's freezing in here."

"The boiler isn't working."

Her mother opened the refrigerator and started pulling out the food that had gone bad, tossing it into one of the half-full black bags on the side of the sink. "Look at all this stuff . . ."

"If you turn around and leave right away, you can avoid the bad weather," said Colomba, who already couldn't stand having her around. "They say it's going to start snowing again."

"I thought you might want to come home with me."

"I'm home already."

"You never wanted to come up here when your papà was still alive, and now I can't pry you loose from the place."

"And I didn't used to like eating spinach but now I eat it all the time." Colomba flexed her right arm. "Just look at these muscles."

"Would you cut it out?"

"Do you need to use the bathroom before you leave? Do you want a glass of water? A benediction?"

Her mother shut the refrigerator door. "All right," she said with a tremulous voice. "I do my best to be a good mother, but what can I do if you don't want me to help?"

"Nothing. I'm a grown-up woman, I have a credit card and a handgun. I can take care of myself."

Her mother took a piece of toilet paper and dried her eyes. "And are you going to stay here until Dante turns up?"

"So what if I am?" Colomba snapped.

"You've been here for a year! Doing nothing!"

"What of it?"

"What of it? He's *dead*! Everyone knows that he's dead!"

"That's enough!" Colomba shouted. "Get out of here!"

Her mother sat rigidly at the table and Colomba felt embarrassed at having lost her temper with the last person left on earth who truly cared about her.

She put the rest of the groceries into the refrigerator, ignoring her mother's litany of complaints, which went on for another half hour until she finally headed back to Rome. Finally alone, Colomba started the fire back up by spraying a bottle of acetone nail polish remover onto the firewood. A sickly green flame burst like a shattered Molotov cocktail, but this time she jumped back in time and avoided the scorching blast of heat.

You've been here for a year, doing nothing.

She waited until the fan blades started kicking out jets of warm air, then she washed up in a basin in the ground-floor bathroom with water from the teakettle. The bathroom looked like it came straight out of some depressing sixties-era motel, and a large rococo-style mirror boasted pride of place. Colomba was forced to look at her reflection in it. She'd gained a few pounds since she'd been in the hospital, but she still looked drastically underweight. The scars from her operation stood out in an angry pink above her sunken belly, and her breasts had lost a cup size. She brushed them with her hand, and then hastily yanked her arm away, because the sensation reminded her of the last person to have squeezed them with his hands. But by now, the memory had been triggered, and Colomba imagined Leo behind her, his face exactly as she had seen it in the mirror on the train heading to Venice, when they'd locked themselves in the bathroom before indulging in what might easily have been the last reckless act of idiocy in their lives.

She still felt dirty.

A year doing nothing.

Colomba begged to differ. She'd actually done a lot of things: she'd whined and complained and self-pitied the whole year long, like a genuine professional. And she'd built herself a gray world where nothing ever happened, where she never had to talk to anyone or go anywhere. A muffled world that made everything more tolerable.

Or at least it had before that morning. Before the arrival of Tommy with his tragedy, and with all this strangeness. Tommy, who with all the places there were in the world had chosen to burst into her comfortable gray cocoon, and seemed determined not to leave.

Wrapped in a quilt, she chomped down a couple of slices of stale zwieback toast, gazing sightlessly at the jumbled mess that filled the room. There was junk everywhere, dirty and clean clothing, books and boxes of food. The stairs leading up to the second floor were covered with spiderwebs and littered with dead insects. She hadn't made her bed in what felt like centuries. She didn't even always make it to bed before falling asleep, and sometimes she spent the night there on the sofa. One night she'd even slept on the bathroom floor, and she honestly couldn't say why. Now, though, she understood that sleep wouldn't come for hours yet. She rummaged through the kitchen drawers until she found an old lined elementary school notebook with a flowered pattern on the cover. She recognized her father's handwriting, and inside were lists of seeds to buy at the town market for the vegetable garden. Who knows if he'd ever managed to plant them, or whether that was the spring that the heart attack had felled him.

Colomba turned to a blank page and started writing her first police report in a long, long time.

5

While Colomba was transcribing her conversation with Pala, working from memory, two hundred miles away, the chief of the Rome Mobile Squad, Marco Santini, was holding his nose to avoid the stench that filled the long hallway on the sixth floor of police headquarters on Via San Vitale. The foul odor was the result of the stopped-up toilets, and the reason the toilets were stopped up was that the hallway had become a dumping ground for all the immigrants arrested by the counterterrorism squad. Nearly all of them were Arabs, with a few Africans. There were those who shouted in their native languages, others who wept as they were being hauled away. It was a scene that played out identically every time a new operation was undertaken. As he limped along on his aching leg, Santini tried to remember the name of their last operation. *Petal by Petal?* No, some other fucked-up name: *Flower by Flower*. To give the idea of precision and painstaking care, but only concealing that they were really just dragging a trawl-net through the city's immigrant population. At the door to his office, Santini found Corporal Massimo Alberti. He was a broad-shouldered young man in his late twenties with fair hair and a sprinkling of freckles scattered over a face that just now was grimmer than usual. Once again, Santini missed the cheerful young recruit Alberti had been until recently. But it'll age you quickly when you see too many of your fellow officers slaughtered like farm animals.

"So what's going on?" he asked. "More roundups? *Flower by Flower II: Revenge of the Horticulturalists?*"

Alberti shook his head.

"If it's bad news, save it. I've just spent three hours of my life with the unions, what I need is a reward."

Santini was in the corner office that had been occupied by all the chiefs of the Mobile Squad who had gone before him. The last in that line of chiefs had left him a legacy, his collection of Paulo Coelho novels, crammed in among the law books and file binders. Santini pushed the novels aside, pulled out the bottle of vodka hidden behind them, and poured himself a shot, then carried the glass back to his desk, where he took a seat, lifting his wounded leg onto the stool that he'd brought in from home. "Well? Give me the grim news."

Alberti made a sad face. "Dante Torre," he said.

"Have they found him?"

"No, but they found the boat that Bonaccorso used to take him away from Venice, the *Chourmo*. It's lying at the bottom of the sea, under six hundred and fifty feet of water."

6

Right after the terror attack at the Palasport della Misericordia, an electrical blackout had knocked out the security cameras at a yacht club in the city, and before power could be restored a sixty-five-foot sailboat had headed out to sea. The *Chourmo* was her name. According to their reconstruction of events, Leo Bonaccorso had moved away from the scene of the explosion with Dante slung over his shoulder, mixing in with the hundreds of people fleeing the blast in a state of panic. The *Chourmo* had immediately deactivated her transponder, and considering the fuel in her tanks and the power of her engines, she could easily have docked almost anywhere in the Middle East. Bonaccorso must have been long gone by the time Santini had arrived at the scene. Santini had reached Venice at two the following morning, and he'd lingered on the bridge, the Ponte della Misericordia, watching as the dead were tended to.

There had been forty-nine corpses, covered by the sheets and contained in the body bags of, respectively, the Protezione Civile and the city morgue. Many of those corpses lacked a limb, or had badly ravaged facial features, or else clothing that was ripped to shreds. Half of them were Carabinieri and policemen, the rest were guests and executives of the philanthropic association Care of the World, which was throwing a benefit party at the Palasport della Misericordia, a small sports arena. The large external metal staircase leading up to the second floor had partly broken loose from its moorings in the outside brick wall, and it was creaking and swaying dangerously as the army helicopters set down.

At ten o'clock the night before, Santini had still been sprawled on the sofa at his home, drunk out of his skull. He'd just returned from a government plane trip with all the high muckety-mucks of the Ministry of the Interior as well as the chief of police and his entourage, all of them pretending not to even notice his existence, the one and only advantage of being in a state of utter disgrace. Once he reached the scene of the slaughter, and after donning the requisite crime-scene shoe covers, he'd stepped into the area lit up by the floodlights, an expanse scattered with jackets, coats, shoes, purses, necklaces, and bracelets that had either been abandoned during the stampede or torn off their owners by the blast. The crater from the explosion was ten feet across and was a smoky black. That was where one of the terrorists had blown himself up, while the others were shooting and stabbing people left and right. Two of the other terrorists had been killed by gunfire, and a third had broken his back by falling on a boat moored at the side of the canal. Then Santini had entered the Palasport itself. The SIS were inside, surveying the crime scene, stepping carefully around overturned furniture and crushed finger food. There was a stench of wine and fruit that was reminiscent of vomit, and the main source of light was the sickly greenish glow of the emergency lights that had turned on in the aftermath of the explosion.

One of the SIS agents had accompanied him through the room, using an LED flashlight to illuminate the darker corners during their tour. Two private security guards were sprawled on the steps of the central monumental staircase: one had a crushed Adam's apple, the other had a broken neck. The SIS agents pointed out that both men had been killed by someone using their bare hands, someone who really knew what they were doing. Santini hadn't paid much attention to them, or maybe he had. His brain, to be honest, was little more than a bowl of mush, right then and there.

The upper floor was basically a narrow colonnade that ran along the main wall, furnished more or less like the VIP area of a discotheque. The furniture was all made of garishly colored plastic, the rooms divided by glass partitions that had been shattered into smithereens. Everything was covered with rubble and dust.

In one of those rooms, a young man sprawled with his neck resting on the jagged edge of a jutting piece of glass from one of the shattered partitions, nicely dressed and practically decapitated by the razor-sharp shard. In front of him, two other security guards spread-eagled in the sloppy positions of death. The white jumpsuit had pointed to a patch of blood on the ground. "Your colleague was right here," he'd told Santini. And for an instant Santini had secretly hoped that Colomba had been killed instantly, sparing him the headaches that were in the offing.

Alberti knocked on the doorjamb, bringing him back to the present day. "Your ride is here, boss," he said.

"Any updates?"

Alberti shook his head. "Just the confirmation."

The espresso from the little Moka pot still scorched Santini's stomach lining, while a civilian automobile with a blinking emergency light on the roof conveyed him to the military airport. Two NOA agents, members of the counterterrorism operational units, with ski masks and submachine guns, escorted him to the landing strip where an Italian Navy NH90 NFH helicopter stood, engines silent. It was a behemoth almost sixty-five feet long with a crew of three, and it could carry as many as twenty passengers. Standing next to the helicopter's open side hatch was Colonel Di Marco, and Santini had a moment of disheartenment. He'd been hoping against hope that he wouldn't have to deal with the man, but he should have known the whole time that Di Marco wouldn't miss out on the final act. Di Marco was a few years older than Santini, and he was straight as a walking stick and every bit as malleable. He wore a loden overcoat that was too light for the season, and he left it unbuttoned, revealing a dark blue three-piece suit with a regimental necktie. He extended his hand.

"Colonel Santini. How's it going with your leg?"

"Painfully. Are we traveling in this beast?"

"Yes, we are, unless you have a problem with airsickness," Di Marco replied, turning his back on him and climbing aboard. The pilot saluted him. "We're going to swing by to pick up Caselli," he said. "Fasten your seat belt."

7

At two in the morning, the NH90 landed on the roof of the Portico hospital, after awakening half the population of the little town. Many of the townsfolk assumed that war had broken out and they jammed the local emergency response phone lines. In the meantime, Colomba was summoned from a military jeep and escorted to the service elevator. Up on the roof, the helicopter's whirling rotors filled the air with ice dust. The beast was enormous, a roaring prehistoric monster flashing dazzlingly in the night. A soldier from the crew that had escorted her helped Colomba into the helicopter and made sure she fastened her seat belt.

Santini was sitting at the far end of the row of empty seats. Di Marco, in the cabin with the pilots, turned to look at her, and Colomba stifled her urge to wipe that smug little smile off his face with a windmill of punches. They took off fast, far faster than any civilian aircraft, and Colomba felt as if her stomach had been left on the ground. Portico dwindled until it became a patch of yellow lights in the mist. The helicopter's windows iced over, the sky became a slab of gray slate, the moon turned small and pale. As soon as they were out of the zone of turbulence and bad weather, Colomba undid her seat belt and moved over next to Santini. He'd lost weight since they'd last met, his face was lined with new wrinkles, and his mustache was felted and gray. She lifted his earmuffs and shouted into his ear. "So did your boyfriend tell you anything about the corpse?"

"No, and he's not a friend of mine," Santini replied in the same fashion and tone of voice. He noticed the cut on her lip, and her extreme weight loss. "How are you?"

"Living healthy. How about you, with all your new gold braid?"

"Tired."

"Then why don't you quit, too? You could use a little rest. So, where did they find the boat?"

"Have you ever heard of Keith Reef?"

"It's the part of the Skerki Banks that's closest to the surface," Colomba replied. She'd been an avid scuba fisher for many years.

"The reef rises to just a foot under the water's surface. The *Chourmo* didn't have its sonar running, or else maybe Bonaccorso fell asleep at the helm. Whatever the explanation, he ran into the reef and sank."

"Like a fool."

"*Quandoque bonus dormitat Homerus*," Santini said, spouting an old Latin adage. "Even good old Homer—"

"—nods off from time to time. Maybe Homer, but not Leo. Who found the boat?"

"The Libyan Navy. They identified the wreck and were kind enough to inform us. What with all the boats we've given them lately, they've started to become more collegial." He put a cigarette in his mouth, but he didn't try to light it. "The boat has been there since right after Venice."

The blood drained out of Colomba's face. "Are you sure of that?"

"That's what I've been told."

"By your boyfriend."

"He's not my friend, I already told you that. But it's credible, don't you think? We thought that Bonaccorso had superpowers, but instead he just chose the wrong course setting."

Colomba went back to her seat and pretended to sleep.

They landed at the military presidio near the port of Pantelleria and were transferred to an Italian Navy tugboat. They saw nothing of the island itself, except for the coastline receding into the distance. Still, Colomba remembered spending a very nice vacation there when she'd still been in the police academy. She was reminded of the lights of Cape Bon in Tunisia glittering on nighttime water, the pools of the natural hot springs, the African vegetation. The tugboat jolted them over the waves until the sun rose, and before their eyes emerged Keith Reef and the ships patrolling it. Colomba had been pressed against the side of the ship the whole time, doing her best not to vomit. It was almost hot by now, and the top half of a dead dolphin was pounding against the rocks, emitting the stench of rot.

They boarded the Comsubin support ship—Comsubin being the Italian Navy's elite frogman special forces unit. Sticking out over the water was the mechanical arm from which the Rover, a small remotely operated submarine, dangled on a bundle of cables. The Rover was used to explore shipwrecks and clear underwater minefields.

On the main deck, they passed by four scuba divers, who were being helped by a small knot of technicians into high-pressure diving suits. Hanging from the winches on the decks, they looked like so many gigantic black toy robots, with globular joints and heads. Colomba barely even noticed them. Her anxiety was devouring all her energy, and she could barely stand upright. She would rather have been back in Tommy's bedroom, she'd have preferred to bury her own parents' dead bodies with her bare hands, a thousand times—anything would have been better than this. But what she'd experienced the day before was already starting to fade, erased by a past that never seemed to be over.

Aside from the Comsubin escort, they also saw a small cluster of officers in battle dress on the bridge, including the vessel's commander and the medical officer. From the way they approached Di Marco, there was no doubt that he had the higher rank. A monitor displayed imagery of the hull of the *Chourmo*, illuminated by the Rover's floodlights.

"Where's the body?" Colomba asked even before they were done shaking hands.

"On the far side of the wreck," the commander replied.

"Have you identified it?"

"The condition of the body makes that impossible, at least remotely, Deputy Captain," said the medical officer.

"I want to see it."

"In a few hours, we'll start recovery."

"I want to see it *now*, not in a few hours."

Di Marco resolved the impasse by ordering the commander to stop making problems. Santini, who hadn't given him so much as a glance throughout the entire journey, shot the other man a look of frank appreciation that Di Marco pretended not to see. The sailor at the console twisted the joystick and the image shifted accordingly, sliding along the side of the hull. It appeared to be intact, in spite of the blanket of deep-sea tangle, kelp, and sargassum that covered it. The real damage started at the screws in the stern: the starboard screw was completely gone, and where the propeller ought to have been was a gash in the keel, while the port screw was bent like a dried flower.

"This is the point of impact," said the commander. "The engine shaft hit the reef and the vessel immediately began to take on water. The scuba divers will enter through there, enlarging the hole in the sheet metal with hydraulic jacks. Still, from up here, we can at least zoom in."

The gash in the hull widened on the screens, becoming the access portal to a gravity-free world infested with seaweed and posidonia plants. Tables and electric appliances hung from the ceiling—actually the floor—while a mattress and a lounge chair floated amid the thickets of underwater vegetation and lengths of fabric that had once been sheets or curtains. There were schools of small fluorescent fish and mollusks slithering slowly along, trying to escape from the beam of light. Out of the silt and muck, glass bottles and unrecognizable metal instruments stuck up here and there.

Colomba held her breath. The picture stabilized on a heap of rotting material from which protruded a number of greenish bones. It was the torso of a skeleton filled with multicolored jellyfish. Frightened by the glare of the floodlights, they pumped hastily away in all directions, revealing the skull, sunken in the chest cavity. From the eye sockets hung filaments of seaweed tossing like eyelids in the underwater current. Some kind of eyeless eel was crawling over the cranium, emitting clouds of mucus.

Colomba's teeth bit into her lip, reopening the wound there. Was that Dante? Could those really be his late lamented remains? She turned to the medical officer who had been standing beside her in grim silence, with his uniform cap wedged under his arm. "Doctor, were you given Dante Torre's medical chart?"

"Yes, ma'am."

"So you really can't tell if . . ." For a moment her voice failed her. "If that's him?"

"It's very hard to do by video feed. But let me take a look." He zoomed in on the skeleton. "From the bone mass I'd have to say it's probably a man." He zoomed in further. "From the cranial sutures he could have been somewhere between forty and fifty years of age."

"So this could be Torre every bit as much as it could be Bonaccorso," said Santini, opening his mouth for the first time.

"Or any of millions of other people," said Colomba, who just couldn't take her eyes off the screen as she searched for even the slightest sign that could help her. Dante had a deformed hand, but the skeleton had lost both of its hands.

"Let's see if the sonar can give us any help," said the medical officer. Colomba and Santini both learned that the Rover was capable of performing 3-D scans with extreme precision, down to fractions of an inch, a technique that was usually used for underwater mines. The medical officer rotated the image on the screen. "This skeleton had neck problems. The third and fourth cervical vertebrae are collapsed."

"What symptoms would that entail?"

"Pain, and in serious cases, lesions on the bone marrow."

"That's not Dante," said Colomba with a sigh of relief. "He climbs trees and leaps in the air like a monkey."

"Could it be the other son of a bitch?" asked Santini.

"No. He was pretty agile, too." Colomba managed to get out those words in a neutral tone. She relived in a flash her first encounter with Leo, during a police search of a mosque in Rome. He'd been wearing a ski mask like all the other NOA agents, but what had captured her attention was his gaze, with a foundation of irony and common sense. What she ought to have done, though, was claw his eyes out, not smile at him.

Di Marco snapped her out of her reverie. "Then we've found another member of the terror cell," he said. "Good."

"So he, too, cheerfully immolated himself in the name of his god," Colomba said sarcastically.

"Don't be childish, Deputy Captain," said Di Marco. "Begin the recovery."

It took more than six hours for the divers to empty the vessel. Colomba spent that time between the bridge and the deck where the winch and mechanical arm was hauling up watertight coffin shapes made of black polycarbonate and as big as steamer trunks, evidence containers that had been sent down with the divers. They were opened by a crew of auxiliary technicians and the contents were then transferred to other, smaller containers, sterile and painstakingly cataloged. Even the water in the containers was collected and assigned the number from the original container.

The skeleton came up on the first trip, followed by wreckage, bric-a-brac, and navigation equipment. Then came a number of intact wooden crates. They contained flasks of colorful liquids that were treated as if they were radioactive, test tubes, and bottles: it looked as if they'd cleared out Dr. Frankenstein's laboratory. The last crate contained nothing other than the remains of a man's black suit, the one that Dante had been wearing the day he'd vanished. There was also a single black leather glove.

Colomba leaned against the walls of the ship and vomited.

8

As always, they'd scared her dogs silly when they'd come to get her. The Doberman pinscher had started running frantically through the courtyard, disturbing her neighbors just at the time of night they were watching TV, and Deputy Captain Bartone had once again cursed the arrogance of the military, which preferred to land without warning in her backyard, submachine guns leveled, or at her lab at LABANOF, Milan's Laboratory of Forensic Analysis, instead of simply making a phone call or sending a cab to pick her up. Since Venice, it had become a regular occurrence, at least a couple of times a month, the instant a fragment of uncataloged bone surfaced, or a stain on the clothing of this victim or that. She was proud to be the Ministry of Defense's trusted forensic archaeologist, but she would rather have spent her time working on the dozens of nameless corpses that filled the morgue's freezer compartments under her office. Restoring their identities, allowing their relatives and friends to get on with their lives—that was far more important to her than tending to Di Marco's whims and obsessions. She would gladly have told him no, if it hadn't been for Dante. Ever since the day that Bart had been summoned, during the investigation into the Father's victims, to analyze the contents of a number of drums filled with acid and human body fragments, Dante and Colomba had practically become family to her.

They transferred her to the Comsubin tugboat with a thermal blanket wrapped around her shoulders, and trembling with cold she'd found Santini waiting for her. Bart decided that he was aging in dog years, seven times as fast as other human beings. In just a couple of years, he'd gone from being a rough, tough no-nonsense cop with chest hair sprouting out of his shirt to a sort of elderly uncle, skinnier and clearly suffering from his wounded leg. With that inevitable Irish tweed flat cap pulled down over his nose. "*Buongiorno,* Doc," he said to her, extending his hand.

"Same to you, Santini. Do you happen to have an extra cigarette?"

The policeman handed her one and brought her up to date on the recovery process. The divers were still at work: they were inserting enormous airbags into the hull, and by inflating them they'd bring the ship to the surface.

"How is Colomba?" Bart asked.

Santini shook his head. "She doesn't believe it's Dante."

"She might be right," Bart said as she exhaled a cloud of smoke.

"I hope you find something among the remains that can convince her."

Bart shook her head, disheartened. She really didn't know what to hope for. Not finding anything would mean leaving Colomba's hopes in place, but she didn't think that was particularly good for her.

Colomba stepped out on the main deck, and Bart had to make an effort to smile at her. She hadn't seen her in six months, since she'd paid an ill-considered visit to her in "Culonia," the ass end of nowhere, as they all thought of it, and Colomba had uttered no more than ten words in the whole time she'd stayed. Even now, she was still pale and skinny, bundled up in a fake fur coat that would have looked right on a homeless person, her eyes glistening, dark circles beneath them. Santini slapped Colomba on the back and strode away without a word, and she rubbed the spot as if a seagull had just pooped on her. "Hey," Bart said to her and gave her a hug, pretending not to notice the stench of sweat. Colomba had boarded the helicopter without so much as a change of T-shirt. "God, you're so skinny, do you ever eat anything?"

"Dante isn't here, Bart," Colomba said, as if she hadn't even heard the question.

Bart sighed. "I'll do everything I can to figure out what's happened."

"You won't find a single piece of evidence that doesn't add up. Leo is too intelligent."

"Do you think he sank the boat on purpose?" Bart asked, already well aware of the way her friend saw it.

"Yes. I think that was his way of getting us to stop looking for him. So that he would be free to do as he pleased."

"Listen, Colomba . . . I don't want you to start getting your hopes up," Bart said reluctantly.

Colomba stiffened. "You don't believe me?"

"Sweetheart . . ." Bart replied affectionately. "You feel guilty about him. You feel sorry for him. You miss him. And you'd do whatever you could to bring him home. You'd even exaggerate a little bit when it comes to the things you see. You're a human being."

"What are the odds that Dante is still alive, in your mind? From one percent to a hundred percent? Be straight with me."

"Statistically speaking, if a person is kidnapped and they aren't heard from after twelve months—"

"Rule of thumb, a rough guess," Colomba said impatiently.

"One out of a hundred."

"If you'd been kidnapped and there was one chance out of a hundred of bringing you back home, you'd be praying someone would try for that chance. I know I would."

Bart took one of Colomba's hands in hers. "I have no intention of throwing in the towel. But you get some rest, you look like a wreck. Why don't you come stay at my house in Milan for a while?"

"Because I have some things to take care of in Portico." A sailor waved to her from the launch, and she replied with the universal gesture for "five minutes." "In your opinion, have we found all of the Father's victims?" Colomba asked.

That caught Bart off guard. "Oh Lord, I certainly hope so. Why?"

"There's a boy near my house who has some behaviors . . ." She broke off. "Forget about it, you already think I've lost my mind."

"I don't think you've lost your mind . . . I know what kind of a period you're going through. Tell me more about this boy."

Colomba leaned against the side of the ship. "He's autistic and he behaves exactly like the prisoners we liberated three years ago."

"So you're saying either that someone else besides us liberated him, or else that he managed to escape on his own. What do his parents say?"

"They were both murdered. And he's severely autistic, he doesn't speak. So nothing comes to mind?"

"No. Nothing that I saw in any of my examinations pointed to the possibility of other prisoners or other prisons. But I can't rule it out. By now, though, they would have starved to death long ago."

"No, not if someone was taking care of them."

The launch, tied up not far away, sounded its horn and made Bart jump. "Another Father?"

"An accomplice, a partner. More than one, possibly . . ."

"That sounds like the story that Dante was telling."

"Exactly, and I really ought to have listened to him. Because he has a bad habit of being right most of the time."

"Some of the time, that's for sure. But because you kept him balanced, you were the rational part of the couple. You can't take his place now."

"I was the obtuse part of the couple. Don't make the same mistake that I did." The sailor started waving to her from the launch again, calling her name aloud. "I have to get going. Let me know if anything occurs to you. If you find some detail in your papers, in the testimony, and so on. If I'm right about this boy, he's already suffered more than enough."

"When I get home . . ." said Bart, dubiously.

"And let me know if you find anything on the *Chourmo*," she whispered in Bart's ear.

Bart, uneasily, said that she would.

"Do it, for real. I might be out of my mind, but right now Dante can't count on anyone other than me." Colomba drilled into her with her eyes. "And be careful, don't trust anybody. You never know whose side they're on."

"Whose side *who's* on?" asked Bart.

"*Anybody.*"

Colomba climbed down the dangling ladder and into the launch, while Bart leaned over the rail, watching her and wondering whether at long last her friend had well and truly taken leave of her senses.

9

The trip back to Pantelleria was shorter than the outbound journey because the seas had subsided considerably. There was no one to give her a hard time, so Colomba was able to read the online newspapers undisturbed in her seat aboard the launch. There wasn't much news about the double homicide. Signor Melas's corpse had been identified by his sister, who was named Demetra and had arrived from Greece shortly after Colomba's departure. From a video shot in front of the Carabinieri station, she looked to be about fifty, with a facelift and a trout pout. She was accompanied by a gorilla-looking guy who was identified in the caption as the assistant district attorney of Pesaro, Carlo Vigevani, in charge of the investigation. He towered a good foot and a half over everyone else in the picture.

No newspaper made any mention of possible alternate leads, no evidence was mentioned that could point to anything other than a family tragedy. Nothing that pointed to an ogre risen from the grave to devour children.

Back on the island, she was ushered onto another helicopter, the same one that had brought Bart, and at her request she was dropped off at a military airport in Rome. From there she took a taxi to Piazza dell'Orologio, just a short walk from the Quirinal Palace. It was three in the morning, and her mother answered the door in her nightgown, her hair messy and tousled. "What happened?" she stammered.

"Nothing. I just came to get some things out of the garage. Sorry, I didn't have time to call ahead and let you know."

Colomba entered the apartment and took a key from a hook rack shaped like a buccaneer's flintlock pistol. Many other keys dangled from it, where they'd hung since time out of mind, without any locks anywhere left for them to open.

"I'll make you some breakfast," her mother said, still bewildered.

"My stomach hurts."

Colomba went downstairs to the garage in the inner courtyard. Among her old clothing and the various Formica cabinets, she found Dante's boxes and suitcases, which she'd picked up from his hotel. There was also the complete archive of the files from the investigation they'd conducted on the Father. Colomba filled an old backpack with documents and flash drives. She also grabbed an old laptop she'd used during her time at the Mobile Squad, and which she simply hadn't returned.

She came back upstairs and found her mother sitting in the kitchen, looking mild and subdued. The smell of caffe latte filled the room and made her mouth water. "Should I make you an espresso?" her mother asked her.

"I don't drink it anymore."

"Right, on account of your friend. I'd forgotten . . ."

Colomba said nothing; she didn't want to get into another quarrel. "I have to get going. They say it's going to start snowing again. If that happens, the trains will be running late, and then it's an unholy mess." She gave her mother a peck on the cheek, and the scent of rosewater filled her nostrils. She walked through the whitened metropolis to the Termini train station, with stalactites of ice hanging from the fountains, and the last drunken tourists. Everything seemed fake and distant. The first regional train for the Marche region wouldn't be leaving for an hour, and she sat waiting for it on the bench on the platform, freezing to the center of her bones. Once aboard, she wrapped herself in her parka and fell asleep, waking up by random chance at the right station. The sky was black and lowering with snow.

She made her way to the auto repair shop at the edge of Portico, and then rode for the last part of the trip in the cab of a tow truck, complete with a rosary hanging from the mirror and the picture of a man with a mustache who looked like an older version of the mechanic at the wheel, an athletic young man with nice hands and long wavy hair. He reeked of oil and sweat, but he had an agreeable smile. His name was Loris. "I've never seen you before. So you like to spend time alone?" he asked her.

"Who says that I'm alone?"

"I have a clinical eye." He laughed. "What kind of work do you do?"

Colomba turned her gaze out to the road. A television news van was taking a panoramic shot of the snow-covered fields. "I'm retired."

"Lucky you."

When they got to the last curve in the dirt road before her farmhouse, Loris braked to a halt and then hauled the Panda out of the ditch with the tow truck's electric winch. "What kind of chains do you use, anyway?" he asked, looking at the ruined tire. "Those must be a thousand years old."

"They probably are. Can you fix it in a hurry? This is the only car I have."

"You ought to get another one, maybe used."

"I don't need much of a car. How quick can you fix it for me?"

"Only because it's you, I'll jump you to the head of the line," Loris replied.

"But we don't even know each other . . ."

"You've ridden in my tow truck, you're practically family."

When Colomba entered the house, it was freezing. She tossed some logs in the fireplace and lit them by training her mother's hairspray on her lighter, which had the general effect of a flamethrower. She dragged the sofa over next to the fireplace and emptied the contents of her backpack onto the floor, distributing the documents all around her. With a screwdriver, she broke the video camera and microphone off of her laptop, hooked it up to the wall plug, and then used it to read the story of the man she had killed.

10

The Father had been active in two distinct periods. The first had started at the end of the sixties and had continued until 1989. The victims of the first period, or at least the eight that had been identified, seemed to have been picked off in some random fashion from all over the map of Italy. One child had been kidnapped during a school field trip near Rome, another by faking his drowning among the whirlpools in the River Po in Emilia. The only thing they all had in common—all but Dante, the sole survivor—was that they wound up buried together in plastic drums of acid on some undetermined day in 1989. The documentation of the second phase, which began in the early 2000s, was as substantial as that of the first, and it concerned her and Dante, too. They had met when she had asked him for help in the investigation into the disappearance of a young boy on the outskirts of Rome. One step at a time, they'd worked their way back to the shipping containers where the Father was holding prisoner ten of his victims. All of the prisoners had been identified, but not all of them had been returned to their respective families. Some of them had been missing for years, and they had been declared legally dead. Their parents had divorced or died in the meantime, or else they had no desire to assume responsibility for the care and feeding of already highly problematic children, who had only become even more problematic during their imprisonment.

One of them had committed suicide in the hospital, a tragedy that, Colomba remembered, had come as a terrible blow to Dante. *One of us*, he had said. The opinion that the investigators had formed was that the Father simply acted when conditions seemed favorable, probably after some chance encounter with the victim, and after staking out his habits and schedules. He especially loved families on the verge of a breakup, situations where the parents were likely to heap the blame on each other. Sometimes he'd also kill one of the parents, to make people think that the other parent had run away with the child. According to the findings of the commission of inquiry, the Father's crimes had been committed in order to satisfy the "uncontrollable impulses of a gravely disturbed and schizophrenic personality." An explanation that Colomba had chosen to settle for.

Not Dante, even if his hearing before the commission had proved utterly pointless. Colomba could still remember it in perfect detail. The hearing had been held at Palazzo San Macuto, in Rome's Pigna quarter, which by a twist of fate had been one of the headquarters of the Roman Inquisition in the seventeenth century. A long table and a number of white plastic chairs had been set out on the cobblestoned courtyard, while fifteen or so onlookers shivered with the cold as they stood around the walls. On one side stood a couple of parliamentary journalists and a small knot of functionaries from the intelligence agencies.

Dante sat at the center of the courtyard, huddled on one of the chairs, his painfully skinny body lost in the folds of a long black overcoat, while sitting across from him was an elderly senator, his face red with burst capillaries, nodding off under a fur busby cap. A blond woman in a loden overcoat and knee-high boots, a recently elected member of parliament, had set a tape recorder on the table and hit "record."

"Would you care to give us your name and your date of birth? For the record."

Dante was twisting the pack of cigarettes in his hands. He was nervous but lucid, without the deranged look on his face he normally had when he stuffed himself full of psychopharmaceuticals.

"I don't know my date of birth," he had replied in a voice that gradually became increasingly confident. "According to the forensic anthropologist who examined me, I look to be somewhere between forty and forty-five years of age. The name I go by is Dante Torre. I have no idea what name I was baptized with at birth. If I was baptized at all, that is. I might well have been born into a family of Rastafarians, or even Pastafarians, for all I know."

There had been laughter from the audience and the blond woman had given him a wan smile, doing her best to conceal her irritation. "Right.

Signor Torre, this hearing was authorized in order to delve deeper into several aspects of the inquiry concerning the kidnapper and murderer known as the Father, who was killed in an exchange of gunfire while law enforcement was attempting to arrest him. And in particular because you maintain that there are aspects concerning which the commission ought to be further informed."

"That's correct."

"Would you tell us, then, exactly how you were involved in this matter? Again, for the record."

"The Father kidnapped me when I was a child and he held me prisoner for thirteen years. In a silo in the countryside around Cremona, to be exact. When and how he might have kidnapped me, I don't remember and I have no idea. I was convinced I was the son of Annibale Valle and Franca Torre, but I only recently learned that that child was someone other than me. The real Dante was murdered when I escaped, back in 1989. They found his DNA in one of the drums of acid where the Father dissolved his victims. A fragment of pubic bone, in point of fact."

"And the Father made you forget your true identity."

"With a combination of isolation, narcotics, and persuasion. He was a psychiatrist and a neurologist, as well as a medical examiner. He knew what he was doing. And in my case, he succeeded completely."

"Why do you think that the investigation wasn't carried out in a satisfactory manner?"

"Because the Father wasn't just a psychopath. He enjoyed protection and cover at the highest levels, and none of that was ever discovered."

"And these people protected him so that he could go on kidnapping and torturing children? Doesn't that strike you as a little far-fetched?"

"All around the world, children are constantly being kidnapped and used as slaves, beggars, and sex objects, and mined for their bodily organs to be transplanted," Dante had replied tersely. "Let me give you some instances, from memory. In 2007 the Nigerian government demanded reparations to the tune of billions of dollars for illegal tests done on two hundred children from poor families with a new vaccination for meningitis. Forty-nine children died in 2008 in India during clinical trials at the Institute of Medical Sciences. All of them were poor, of course, and the tests were always performed by subcontractors, thus making it harder to trace back to the masterminds. Therefore I would be loath to rule out the possibility that some multinational corporation or other, no doubt with annual revenues greater than Italy's GDP, might have financed the Father to conduct in vivo experiments. He operated for forty years without being caught; do you think he was just some lucky asshole?"

Everyone had believed him, Colomba thought to herself, even her. Only now everything appeared to her in a new light.

She brewed another cup of tea and leafed through the dossiers on the Father's accomplices, at least those known to the police. There were quite a few of them, but nearly all of them were dead now, either of natural causes (a very few) or of violent ones (a great many), and all of them hardened criminals: murderers, rapists, and ex-military. Some had been working with the Father since the seventies; others had been hired to kill a witness or else just to feed the prisoners. The Father's main accomplice was known simply as the German, because no one knew his real identity. He was in his mid-sixties, but he was still strong as a bull, and he'd never once said a word about his old boss, since the day of his arrest. But there could be who knew how many others just like him.

Colomba read police reports and court verdicts until dawn the next day and dropped off dreaming that she had been locked up in a transparent silo in the middle of the hill country. Bart awakened her by phoning at noon. In the background she could hear the muffled roar of waves. "I wanted to know how you were . . . and I have something to tell you," she said.

Colomba transitioned from sleep to anxiety. "Dante?" she asked, dry-mouthed.

"No. I tried to reach you on Signal, but you didn't answer."

Signal was an app for cell phones that encrypted the calls, a widespread favorite for pushers and anyone with something to hide. Colomba had persuaded Bart to install it on her phone. "Because I don't have a cell phone anymore. I'll go buy one."

"How long will that take?"

"Half an hour if I can find a taxi."

There were six of them in the whole province, cooperating in a small cab drivers' cooperative, and with all this snow they were swamped with calls. The switchboard operator told her that she'd have better luck in the afternoon. Colomba didn't want to wait that long, so she set out, trudging through the icy chill.

11

At first, walking along under the now-clearing sky was almost enjoyable. The farmers had plowed the snow off the dirt road with their tractors, and the temperature was milder than it had been on the previous few days. Her shoulder muscles gradually relaxed and her legs loosened, the cramps subsiding. Colomba fell into an easy stride after the first three hundred yards of steep uphill climb, but that didn't last long and about halfway down the dirt road, she stopped and leaned against a signpost, taking her hood off so she could breathe more freely. Her heart was in her mouth, her belly was pounding: she cursed the past months spent lazing about doing nothing.

She resumed walking. She went past the hut where dogs were trained, the farmhouse occupied by the beekeeper, and the farmstay, which had gone out of business long ago—the building had stood empty since time out of mind, and it now looked like nothing so much as the Castle of the Snow Queen. She crossed paths with a shivering three-toned cat, and a very few automobiles moving along at walking speed, kicking up fantails of mud. At the end of her second hour of walking, from high atop the last hairpin curve, she saw the morning sun glitter on the white rooftops of the medieval center of Portico. The smoke from the chimneys made the town look like a postcard, with the Church of Saint Gerardo dei Tintori at the center, and the stone houses pressed one against the other, stacked up like a wedding cake. Colomba stopped to admire the town—she felt a little bit of its blood ran in her veins—and decided that it was breathtakingly beautiful, a piece of Italy known to far too few, which might perhaps be why it hadn't changed much over the decades. One of the changes had been the arrival of a cell phone and computer shop, opened by an overweight thirty-year-old who always wore a *Final Fantasy* sweatshirt.

Colomba bought a cheap cell phone from him, along with a reloadable prepaid phone card: it felt as if it were scorching the palm of her hand.

Next to the shop was the Bar del Corso, where her grandfather used to take her as a little girl to get sour cherry gelato; until the 1930s, the building that café occupied had been a garage for horse-drawn carriages. Colomba took a seat on one of the metal benches, downloaded Signal through the town's Wi-Fi network, and texted Bart. Hers was one of the very few phone numbers Colomba knew by heart.

The archaeologist and forensic chemist called her a minute later. "Why don't you have your cell phone anymore?"

"Because that's the best way to be spied upon, whatever you might happen to be doing. Is this about the Father?"

"What? No . . . I haven't looked into him yet. But I did see the report from the explosives experts. There are traces of explosives along the hole in the hull of the *Chourmo*. PBX, a kind of plastic explosive. I don't know much about it, that's not my specialty, and I certainly can't ask the military about it."

Colomba felt her heart swell with relief. "Leo faked the shipwreck, I told you so."

"That's not all. The passenger didn't drown. Someone cut his throat with a scuba diver's knife. He was dead when he went into the water, but I can't tell you how long he'd been dead, and it's unlikely that more extensive testing will be able to tell us."

Colomba felt a stab of pain in her wound. "What else do you know about him?"

"Let me look at the computer . . . I'm on the bridge and it's freaking cold . . . All right, now, the dead man stood somewhere between five foot seven and five foot nine, average weight. He had a titanium implant between the third and fourth cervical vertebrae. The medical officer hadn't seen it because it had broken loose: I found it in the sediment."

"Does it have a serial number?"

"Yes. And I'm connected to the hospital system database. His name was Giancarlo Romero, he was forty years old, a freelancer. He lived in Milan. Does that ring any bells?"

"No. Could it have been a fake name?"

"Not likely. He had the operation done in a public hospital, and he filled out all the appropriate tax documents." Bart read in silence for a few seconds. "And he used the same name for three other hospital stays over the course of ten years, and always for the same problem. Radiculopathy, a pinched nerve, resulting in chronic neck pain . . . lesions to his vertebrae . . . Probably an undiagnosed case of Klippel-Feil syndrome."

"Never heard of it."

"A hereditary syndrome; its disease gene is GDF6, in case you were wondering. I have his whole medical file in front of me, and it perfectly matches the bones that I have on the table. It's him."

"Was he reported as a missing person?"

"Never, as far as I can tell."

Colomba jotted down the details on a napkin that had an ad for sour cherry liqueur. "How long do you think you can keep this information hidden from the military?"

"Five or six hours," said Bart. "Don't do anything stupid."

Colomba ordered a beer, and then used the same app to call Alberti. He had Signal already installed and answered, in a calm voice, from Santini's desk: his boss was still out on the open sea with Bart and the others. "Deputy Captain, how are you?"

"Alberti, you're a cop now, and I'm not one anymore. So stop calling me deputy captain. Leave that for the rookies."

"Sorry. Force of habit." Since the official status of their relationship had changed, Alberti constantly tried to use impersonal pronouns and neutral conjugations of verbs to avoid having to use the Italian informal, much less her first name. It just didn't come naturally to him; he felt reverential awe when it came to his onetime superior officer. "How is the deep-water search going?"

"I'm not on the ship anymore. I need you to check out a name for me."

"At your orders, ma'am . . . I mean, *go ahead*."

"Giancarlo Romero, a resident in Milan, age forty," she said. "Can you confirm that there haven't been any missing reports on him?" She dictated his details.

"Just a second, Deput— whatever." Alberti typed his way into the CED, the interforces data-processing system, where the uniforms kept all the data concerning everyone else in the world. "Confirm that. He lives in Milan."

"Does he have any priors?"

"Just public indecency. He likes getting blow jobs from trannies in the park," he said, summarizing the man's file.

"And that's the only record he has. Are you sure of that?"

"Yes. He changed his registered address in October two years ago. I'll give you the new address."

"What date in October?"

"The thirtieth."

Two weeks after the massacre. If the *Chourmo* really had been sunk right away, then Romero would have been dead already. Four old men were playing cards at the table next to hers. Coincidence or fate, she saw the king of diamonds flash past. "There's something else I need. Do you still have friends in the 'cousins'?"

Alberti had been a carabiniere during his mandatory military service. "A few . . ."

"There was a double homicide around where I live now, three days ago. See if you can find out anything. The Melas family. And ask if anyone knows Sergeant Major Lupo, in charge of the barracks in Portico."

"Does he have anything to do with Romero?"

"No. I'll explain later."

Colomba rushed to the auto repair shop, coming close to being run over by a snowplow. Loris emerged from the mechanic's pit, from under a Toyota without wheels. "Listen, I haven't started on your car yet, angel."

"Listen: please never call me *angel*," Colomba said with a shiver. "Just lend me any car you have. Yours would be fine."

"You just drove your Fiat Panda into a ditch. Do you seriously think I'd give you my pride and joy?"

"If I break it, I'll buy you a new one. This is important."

He seemed to give it some thought. "Martina says that you're a cop, just like her. Is that true?"

"Ex-cop. Who's Martina?"

Loris described her: she was the lady carabiniere with red hair. "She also said that you were in Venice and that you got shot by ISIS," he said.

"At her age I wasn't such a chatterbox."

"Is it true?"

"More or less. But if you want to know the rest, you can read a newspaper."

Loris laughed, reached into the pocket of his overalls, and tossed her a set of keys. "Leave me your ID. And if you damage it, I'll sue you. I won three Grand Prix races in that car."

The car was a Peugeot 208 with rally bodywork, covered with logos. Colomba took off, tires screeching and leaving a cloud of rubber smoke behind her.

12

Romero's apartment was in a five-story building between Milan's eastern bypass ring road and Linate airport. The area was a distinctly Milanese mix of green areas, buildings dating from the sixties, and old brick hangars that had once been the production site of the glorious old Caproni aircraft plant, dismantled in the years after World War II. It took Colomba only a little over three hours to get there, the whole way bitterly missing her old flashing roof lights. She parked nearby and waited for another tenant to enter the building, slipping stealthily in after them. The building had no doorman, and Colomba cursed under her breath: with an adroitly offered bribe, you could usually get a doorman or a concierge to let you into the apartment or at least disgorge a little information. Luckily, the names on the mailboxes also indicated the floor, and Colomba climbed the stairs to the third floor. A young woman was watering a flowerpot of geraniums. She was about twenty-five, and she had ripe red cheeks as round as apples, and impressively large breasts. Colomba hesitated just a second too long.

"Who are you looking for?" asked the young woman as she dried her hands on her housecoat.

Colomba unfolded the story that she'd concocted during her drive. "Giancarlo Romero. He's been out of touch for a while and his folks . . ."

"He lives right there," the young woman interrupted her, pointing to a door at the far end of the landing. "When he gets back I'll tell him that you were looking for him."

The young woman's tone of voice made the hair stand up on the back of Colomba's neck. "But when did he leave?"

"Monday. Why? Did something happen?"

A drop of cold sweat ran down Colomba's back. Up until that instant, she'd assumed that Romero was one of Leo's accomplices. But now everything looked radically different. "His parents are looking for him," she said, forcefully recovering her lost breath. "But we might not be talking about the same person. Just to make sure, is he short, fat, and bald?" she asked, tossing out a description at random.

"No, he's tall, with dark hair and glasses." The young woman laughed. "And he's anything but fat. He's plenty athletic. Now, if you'll excuse me, I hear my baby crying."

"Thanks," Colomba managed to cough out. In the pocket of her parka, she was gripping the butt of her pistol so tightly it hurt her hand. She waited for the young woman to go back into her apartment, then she broke open Romero's door lock, taking a running start and giving it a solid flying kick. She'd seen it wasn't an armored door, and in fact it flew open easily, though with a resounding crack. Colomba shut it hastily behind her, pressing it closed with her back and then leaning against it and holding her pistol with both hands. She could hear someone's voice echoing up the stairwell, loudly complaining about the ruckus, but no one seemed sufficiently motivated to investigate.

She stepped forward, deeper into the apartment that lay shrouded in the dim light filtering through the roller shutters, and so badly reeking of bleach that it brought tears to her eyes. Three rooms, a few sticks of nondescript furniture. No clothing, books, or articles of any kind. No sheets on the bed, and the mattress had been drenched with bleach. The floors and the walls, too, had been scrubbed with bleach, dissolving and staining the paint. Even though she was no white jumpsuit, Colomba was pretty sure that all organic evidence had been eliminated. She wrapped her hands in the makeshift mittens of her parka sleeves and opened a window to clear the air.

You know who he is, right? You know that he lived here all of this time.

The cell phone vibrated, and the words *Unknown Caller* appeared on the display. Bart and Alberti would have used Signal and she hadn't given out her new number to either of them. She knew only one person capable of finding her that fast. The same person who over the past year had taken Romero's place and pretended to be him, living in his apartment.

Only *one person*.

She answered the call.

"Ciao, Colomba, I've missed you," said Leo's voice.

CHAPTER III

The temperature outside the warehouse is close to freezing, but Dante is hardly surprised at that. He knows exactly where Leo has taken him; he's recognized the building of his nightmares: the cement cube known informally to its prisoners as the Box. It's just that Dante thought the Box had been destroyed, because it stands just a few miles outside of Chernobyl. The dead city. Populated now by no one but old folks waiting to die of cancer or some other lingering aftereffect of the radiation. The same radiation that Dante now feels prickling on his flesh. Like so many tiny needles. How long will it be before he's covered with blisters? Minutes or hours? The city was considered to be at low risk for short stays, but who ever believed that? When there's money to grease the skids, there's always a way to paint a rosy picture.

He ought at least to return inside the warehouse's solid cement walls, but if he did that, he'd only be doing it so he could wait around till he died. Outside, at least, he can hope to find a way to escape.

He's already starting not to be able to feel his feet anymore. The courtyard, as big as three soccer fields, is surrounded by a two-story apartment building and, on the other side, by the gate leading to the Box. Dante runs across the ice-cold cement, broken here and there by stubborn weeds, until he reaches the apartment building. There, he peers in through the front door; someone else has beaten him to it, and has plundered what must have been a ground-floor office, now reduced to a shambles. The few desks remaining have been stacked up and burned, machinery and electric cables have vanished, everything that ever had even a smidgen of market value has been broken up and hauled away. All that remains is ashes and assorted human and animal excrement. Dante screws up his nerve and walks in, crunching underfoot—barefoot—the filth that covers the floor. He must be contracting millions of mutant diseases; he'll become a monster like Matango.

He climbs the stairs, taking care not to stop on fragments of broken glass and the cartridge shells ejected by the Kalashnikov that had peppered the picture of Andropov on the wall with bullet holes.

On the second floor he finds a corpse. He'd sort of been expecting it; that was all that was missing in this nightmarish spot. Still, he's disgusted at the sight. He's even more disgusted by the thought that now he's going to take off the corpse's radiation suit. Dante wants it for himself, and if he can, he'd like to put it on before he faints from the cold and the stale air.

He kneels by the body, careful to keep the window in front of his eyes. It's covered by a grate, and over the grate is hanging what seems like a liana vine out of Tarzan, but still there's a speck of moonlight shining through the leaves. God bless whoever invented the moon.

The jumpsuit that the dead man is wearing also seems to be a relic of the Soviet era, old and threadbare as it is. The rubber-and-transparent-plastic hood is equipped with a filter that Dante judges to be largely ineffective, and which is in any case held together with spit and duct tape. The rest of the jumpsuit is as porous as a sweater. But better than nothing. He knows that it will do little if anything to protect him from contamination, but at least it'll keep him warm. But first, there's the small matter of extracting its contents. A corpse, no big deal. Not really all that different from a living person, just a little more unresponsive.

He tugs on the hood, which makes a liquid noise as it pulls away from what's underneath. Dante was afraid of an explosion of fluids, but the old man's face that emerges seems like the relic of a Catholic saint. The microclimate inside the jumpsuit has transformed him into a leathery mummy. Dante has certainly seen worse, and he's certainly touched worse. He unzips the jumpsuit, which makes the bones creak, then he rips it off the corpse in a furious unequal wrestling match that transforms Dante into a fountain of sweat.

The old man is also wearing a sweater and underwear and undershirt and socks, but Dante decides that he won't be able to get those off. He'll make do with the jumpsuit, which, once in contact with his body heat—or what remains of it—starts to stink terribly. Dante staggers outside, his bare feet in the rubber boots that make ducklike quacking noises. He's probably going to have to get them cut off his feet once it's all over.

The cold has become tolerable. From the center of the courtyard, he stares at the Box again. It has no windows, a six-story building the size of a public housing block without a single fucking window on the upper floors. They built it that way intentionally, because what happened inside there wasn't meant to be known about in the outside world. And no one confined inside was supposed to ever leave the building alive.

He doesn't know how Leo has managed to get him over the Ukrainian border, much less why he would do it. He doesn't know why, before kidnapping him, he should have told him that he was the brother Dante had never known, or if that's even true. The only thing he's sure about is that he won't survive much longer there, jumpsuit or no jumpsuit. He'll eventually fall asleep somewhere and that will be the end of him. Already he's having a hard time staying on his feet, he has no idea of how to get home or find help, and he can't hear the noise of cars or overhead electric lines. He goes toward the Box, the only strategy available to him. A monument to the only god Dante fears, the god of confinement, made up of darkness and impenetrable walls.

The gate leads to a smaller-scale replica of the courtyard he's just left behind him. The enclosure wall around it stands more than fifteen feet tall, with the barbed wire, and it runs out of the lower section of the Box, a cement foundation wider than the rest of the building and one full story high. There, windows can be seen, because that was the section of the building used by the staff. The windowpanes are shattered, and here, too, everything has been plundered and burned. He can still smell the stench, though it's not too bad, truth be told. It actually smells like . . .

Coffee.

He knows that it's impossible, but still he follows the track of the smell in the air. He finds himself facing the door of what had once been the kitchen. Furnishings and utensils have been stolen or destroyed, except for an oversize refrigerator overturned onto its back. Sitting atop it is a gas camp stove with a Moka Express coffeepot bubbling away. Dante thinks in rapid succession that it must be a hallucination, or a booby trap, or even an antipersonnel mine, but then he looks up and *sees the man who's using his handkerchief to clean a couple of chipped demitasse cups.*

Leo.

He's wearing a pair of military overalls without insignia, open over the thermal jacket beneath. He has no face mask, no jumpsuit; he seems indifferent to the radiation. "You got here just in time," he tells him cheerfully. "The coffee's about to boil. Come on, we have so much to talk about."

Colomba couldn't get a word out. She kept her pistol aimed at the front door and her cell phone in her left hand, far from her ear as if it were scorching hot. She expected to see Leo plunge into the room.

"Who is this?" she gasped.

"You know who this is," said the voice, with the same unruffled tone as before. "Do I really need to tell you that you're wasting your time? I haven't left anything behind me."

"Let me speak to Dante," Colomba said in a faint voice.

"He's not here."

"Where is he?"

"That's a complicated story, little Colomba."

Colomba managed to recover her breath. "What the fuck have you done to him?" she shouted. "Tell me if he's alive! Tell me where he is!"

"I can't do that. I'm sorry."

"You filthy son of a bitch!" Colomba couldn't restrain herself; her hatred and rage exploded in her voice. "I'll kill you, I don't give a damn if they sentence me to life without parole!"

"If you keep shouting I'm going to hang up." His voice had lost all intonation and Colomba realized that she was doing the exact opposite of what you need to do when you're talking with a psychopath. She needed to be polite, conciliatory, and massage his ego. Every word that Leo let slip might prove to be an invaluable clue. She wrestled back control of herself, biting her lip as she did so.

"Can I please at least ask if he's all right?"

"Change the subject, little Colomba, *Colombina.*"

Don't overdo it. Go along with him. "Why did you kill Romero?"

"Because he was so easy to hook up with. And I'm good at hooking up with people."

Colomba trembled but said nothing.

He laughed courteously. "Sorry, little Colomba, that wasn't very diplomatic."

"What happened on the *Chourmo*? Why did the boat sink?"

"I didn't call you so I could answer your questions."

"Then why did you call?"

"To tell you to cut it out. You'll never find me and you'll never find Dante. And it could be dangerous for you to go on searching."

"I'm not afraid," Colomba lied.

"Well, you should be. You know what I'm capable of."

She struggled to pull air down her constricted throat, and Colomba folded over onto her knees. "Please . . ." she croaked. "Just tell me if he's alive . . ."

"Make your choice, little Colomba. A long and peaceful life in the hill country or a quick but painful death. Choose carefully," Leo said and hung up.

Colomba stopped breathing. Her ears were whistling, everything was turning black and sticky. With the last strength remaining inside her, she scraped at the tiles. The nail of her left forefinger lifted away, folding back close to the base. The pain was a lightning bolt that lit up her brain.

Fuck, she thought as she sucked on her injured finger. The half fingernail remained in her mouth and she spit it out onto the floor along with a jet of blood. She was making a mess of things, but she just couldn't get her thoughts to connect.

A long and peaceful life in the hill country.

He knew where she lived. He knew what she was doing. She'd eliminated every electronic gadget that she owned, she'd been sleeping with one eye open for a year, and he'd still been able to keep her under surveillance.

With a length of toilet paper and some bleach she removed every trace that she'd been there, and she collected the fragment of fingernail. She tossed it all into the toilet, and flushed repeatedly.

He knew where I lived, but also that I was here. He knew it immediately.

She stepped out of the apartment, leaving the broken door pushed to, and headed toward the stairs. Or rather, that's what she *thought* she was doing, but the next thing she knew she found herself standing with her knuckles pressed against the neighbor woman's doorbell. The young woman answered the door with a flowered apron wrapped around her waist.

"What the fuck—" she snapped.

Colomba pushed her back inside and shoved the door shut with her elbow to keep from leaving fingerprints. "You told him," she snarled.

"Get out or I'll scream!"

Colomba slammed her against the wall and clapped her hand over her mouth. "The person that you ratted me out to is a murderer. A psychopathic killer. And thanks to you, now he might get away. He might be killing someone else right this very second. Do you understand that? Tell me that you understand."

The young woman was terrified. She pointed at the bedroom door, which stood ajar, and through which Colomba could see the arm of a baby poking out through the bars of a crib. At the very most, the infant might have been a year old. Colomba took her hand off the young woman's mouth.

"Don't hurt my baby," she said, her voice screechy with fear. "I swear to you that I didn't tell anyone."

"Did he pay you? Did he threaten you to turn you into his spy?"

"No!"

Colomba didn't believe her, but that didn't make any difference. If the girl was still alive, that meant she knew nothing that could help lead Colomba to Leo. She'd made a mistake by going into this apartment. The young woman hadn't gotten a good look at her when they'd first spoken, but now she'd be sure to remember her perfectly.

Too bad. "Tell me something more about him."

"I don't know what . . ."

"Visitors. Strange behavior."

The young woman shook her head. "Nothing."

"Well, well, nothing at all. A psychopathic killer lives across the landing from you for a year and he never did anything odd," Colomba said sarcastically.

"He was never here for long. He didn't talk much." The young woman seemed to be making an effort, her eyes fixed on the baby in the bedroom. "I think maybe he liked the mountains . . ."

"Did he tell you that?"

"No, but the last time I saw him, he was wearing a backpack with those things you put on your shoes to walk on the ice. Maybe he went to the mountains . . ."

"Did you go to bed with him?" she asked.

The young woman shot her a terrified glare. "No. I swear I didn't."

"I hope so for your sake."

Colomba went running out of the apartment building, fear starting to overwhelm her fury. She kept her head bowed forward and her hat pulled down over the bridge of her nose, just as she had on the way in to foil any potential security cameras. These days, the cameras could be anywhere, including privately owned webcams focused on courtyards just for the fun of it. Handy when you're the one doing the investigating, a little less so when what you want most is to keep your former partners from coming after you, especially if you've just tried to intimidate a witness.

It's not them that you need to worry about, she thought.

Leo's voice had remained inside her like a poisonous thorn and was starting to infect her. Leo might be anywhere around her, ready to lunge at her.

Calm down!

She dropped the car keys twice, slammed her injured finger and shouted with the pain, and finally managed to get the door open and the car started. She took the provincial road to avoid the security cameras, and then stopped for gas at a filling station and café. She started her cell phone back up and sent a message via Signal that was sufficiently desperate and riddled with grammatical errors that Bart called her back instantly. A call that she made from the restroom of the marine laboratory.

"Tell them the name," Colomba whispered. "It won't do any good, but do it anyway."

Even with the miserable sound quality of the call, Bart understood that she was in a state of shock. "What's happened?"

A truck driver heading for the outside toilets smiled at her, and Colomba quickly turned away. "Leo has been using Romero's apartment for all this time," she said, lowering her voice even more.

"How do you know that?"

"He phoned me, for fuck's sake . . . I was in his apartment and he called me." She was stammering; her heartbeats were fists punching her right in the throat. "He has me under surveillance. He knows everything I'm doing."

"Colomba . . ." said Bart, making an effort to remain calm. "How can you be so sure it was him?"

"I'm sure! Do you think I could make a mistake about a thing like that?" Colomba dried her bloody hand on her shirt. The finger continued bleeding.

"Listen . . . go to my house. Ask the concierge to give you the keys. I'll get back there as quickly as I can." Bart lived in Milan with her two dogs, in a loft built in an old printing plant.

"No, no . . . I'm almost home," Colomba lied. "I'll call you back." She ended the call, deactivated the phone by inputting the wrong PIN six times in a row, then disassembled it over a trash can, snapped the SIM card in half, and threw it all away. It wasn't enough to change the phone number; the device itself could be traced. Each phone had an IMEI code that transmitted every time it connected to a cell tower, and if you had the right technology, you could identify it. And no doubt about it, Leo had the right technology. She ought to have turned her phone off before going to Romero's apartment, but she'd become so accustomed to not having one that it just hadn't occurred to her.

Idiot.

She didn't feel up to driving all the way home in the dark, so she got a room in a motel, bribing the attendant to let her check in without registering her ID. She waited until daybreak, watching the lights of the passing cars on the provincial road. She was thinking about Leo, and nothing else, the whole time: she just couldn't stop. His voice was a toxin that infected her; she felt as if she were balancing on a tightrope suspended over a tank full of sharks.

Why had he reached out now, after a year and a half? Why had he chosen to confirm that he was still alive, instead of letting her suffer in uncertainty? In Colomba's experience, killers never called the police to challenge them, never sent signals in code, never subconsciously tried to get the cops to stop them. They ran for their lives, they killed, and they took to hiding, knowing full well that every contact added an element of risk. Old Mafiosi, with all the money they had, rarely even saw the light of day. They lived like moles in underground chambers, sending notes around, the classic Mafia *pizzini*, messages that couldn't be traced on the internet.

Leo might be crazy as a waltzing mouse, but he knew that contacting her was dangerous. If he'd done it, he must have a good reason, one that at least made sense to him.

A long and peaceful life in the hill country.

Crampons for the ice.

Leo had stayed in Italy instead of running away, he knew where she lived, he was out there wandering through the snow. The invisible tight-rope beneath Colomba's feet lurched and wobbled, coming dangerously close to making her tumble into the void. In her vertigo, she relived the brief vacation that she had taken at the Bagni Vecchi spa in Bormio with Dante, in the aftermath of the Father's death. While she was swimming in the heated pool, Dante had answered his cell phone. A stranger on the other end of the line had congratulated him for having survived, and before hanging up, had informed him that he was his brother. No names, the self-proclaimed brother had never called back, but that phone call had changed everything. Dante didn't remember anything about his own early past, and everything he had thought he knew turned out to have been false memories implanted in his mind by the Father during the long years of childhood isolation. It's easy to influence a child cut out of the world at large, and no doubt about it, the Father knew what he was doing. And for Dante, knowing that he had a brother out there somewhere, the search for his own past had become a genuine obsession. There was someone who had the key to open the door inside his head, there was a person out there who could tell him who he really was, or who he'd really been, anyway.

And that person was Leo. Leo had admitted it while he was kidnapping Dante and she was slipping into a coma. If it was true, then what had his relationship been with the Father? Was he the accomplice who'd murdered Tommy's parents?

Leo had been capable of pretending to be a fellow cop for weeks, just so he could arrive in Venice in the middle of the bloodbath. He planned things out, he followed a painstakingly drafted script. Someone like him could certainly arrange to have one of the Father's prisoners transferred to a spot two miles from where she was living, but to what end? Was he just interested in tormenting her?

With her finger, Colomba wrote *Leo* in the condensation on the windowpane. The headlights of a truck lit it up. The Melases had been murdered the day that the *Chourmo* was found. Maybe Leo was burning his bridges. Or maybe he had a deeper, darker reason. And unless she managed to stop him, more blood would flow.

The Portico Carabinieri station was a small three-story building no differ-ent from any of the others that lined the road leading to the museum, that is, aside from the barbed wire and the yellow sign warning that this was a military complex, and that there was absolutely no admittance. The door for the general public was on the ground floor, and admittance required passing through a metal detector. The second floor, on the other hand, was strictly for Carabinieri, including a small interview room, which was also used for conversations between suspects and their lawyers. Lupo lived on the third floor. In the smaller Carabinieri stations, it was quite normal for the commander to live on-site. There wasn't enough staff for the night shifts, so he simply answered emergency calls in the off hours.

Inside as well as out, the station looked more like a private residence than it did a military barracks. The standard furnishings provided by the procurement branch of the Ministry of the Interior were spruced up here and there by a couple of counterfeit Magritte paintings, done by a local forger whom Lupo and his squad had arrested a couple of years ago. They were on display in the lobby, next to the photograph of Italy's prime minister, because Chiara liked them. Chiara had been the only civilian employee in the station, and a sort of commander in chief, particularly irascible when it came to logistics. When Chiara had finally retired, her position had been taken by a part-time switchboard operator hired with funding from the law on the handicapped: his name was Donato, and he was deaf in one ear and a double amputee.

Right after Chiara's office (that's what they still called it, as if her spirit continued to hover over the place) was the door to the galley kitchen, where the Carabinieri made espresso or heated up something to eat in the microwave oven purchased the previous Christmas with a collection taken up among the barracks staff. There was also a small fridge packed with food brought from home, in airtight containers. There were no names written on the containers, as everyone was perfectly capable of recognizing their own. At eight in the morning, two Carabinieri on duty were there, having their second breakfast: Master Sergeant Nerone and Brigadier Bruno, both sipping espressos from the Neapolitan espresso pot that Bruno alone—born and raised in Mergellina, outside Naples— was authorized to operate. Nerone had the physique of an ex-rugby player, with a belly and a beard; Bruno, almost eligible for his pension, was tall and skinny. Martina came in with a thermos full of Herbalife smoothie that she hoped might take a couple of inches off her hips, and the attention of her two partners immediately focused on her. Martina was no top model, but she was still the only woman to be found in that latter-day variant on the all-male monastery.

"*Buongiorno*, Master Sergeant Nerone, ciao, Bruno. Is there any left for me?"

Bruno lifted the lid on the Neapolitan flip coffee pot. "Not much. You want me to make some more?"

"No, it'll do, thanks." Martina poured the coffee into a little paper cup. "I've already had two."

"Did you bring the Melas boy here?" Nerone asked.

"Yes, Master Sergeant."

Upstairs, in fact, a meeting was under way with the magistrate and the court's child welfare expert to discuss Tommy's situation and legal standing.

"Too bad you can't take your children back to the store if they turn out to be defective," said Nerone. "Just think how convenient it would be. Is your son an idiot? Send him back."

Bruno laughed. "When my son was a teenager, I would have done it without a second thought."

"Tommy isn't stupid," Martina ventured cautiously. She was the latest arrival at that police station and she didn't want to openly contradict her superior officers. "He has different kinds of problems."

"His parents found out about the problems he has," said Nerone. Bruno laughed again, and Martina forced a smile.

"But there's no question that it's their fault if he turned out like that," Nerone went on, luxuriating in the attention of the others, without the slightest suspicion that most of that attention was due to his rank alone. "They must have done something wrong."

"You're born autistic . . ." Martina said, in an even more subdued tone of voice.

"One in ten is on account of the vaccines," Nerone pontificated. "Maybe more than that, because the multinational pharmaceutical companies do all they can to conceal the damage."

Bruno seemed to understand Martina's embarrassment and weighed in, changing the topic. "So what did they do to Vigevani? Have you seen how tall he is?" The Pesaro assistant district attorney was a giant. Tousled hair, horse-faced, he stood six foot eight and weighed 270 pounds. His tie was so wide it could be used as a beach wrap, and his shoes looked like Goofy's, from the Disney cartoons.

"He looks like a caveman," laughed Nerone, swallowing the bait.

Martina decided not to point out that cavemen were shorter than modern human beings, and drank down her supplement-filled smoothie, thinking about Tommy, about the way that he sobbed in terror every time she had to move him from one place to another. His eyes reminded her of the dog she'd had as a girl, who had died in her arms, teaching her at a single blow the harshest and most frightening lesson life has to offer: that it ends.

Someone came galloping down the stairs. Martina pictured Tommy running out the door and rushed into the lobby to block his way. She'd seen how her partners treated him when no one was looking—like an ox to be shoved roughly through the slaughterhouse door, a beast to be made fun of—and she didn't want to see that happen.

But it was just Lupo, red in the face with irritation, who looked right through her as if she were invisible and went out the door without a word.

"I'd have to guess that the meeting didn't go particularly well," said Nerone. He tossed the crumpled-up plastic cup, missing the trash can and spattering Martina's boots with coffee.

"I'm afraid that's not it, Vice," said Bruno. Master Sergeant Nerone was second in command, and he loved that nickname, though in a barracks with total staff of six it was rather ridiculous. "That's the look the chief gets on his face whenever he has to go ask someone for a favor . . ."

When Colomba returned to the farmhouse, she found it steaming hot and full of gnats. In her absence and as a result of the tons of salt scattered on the roads, the fuel truck had been able to wend its way up to Mezzanotte and refill the boiler's tank. Colomba walked in, pistol drawn, and checked the rooms, double-checking to make sure that all the shutters were fastened tight, putting the padlocks back on the ones she'd unlocked in order to let in fresh air. It was only after she'd secured them all that she sprayed insecticide on the leftover food and took a shower to rid herself of the persistent phantom stench of bleach. The stench of Leo. The king of diamonds stared out at her from the mirror.

With a bit of imagination the card's glance could be said to resemble Leo's, at least as well as she could remember it. Was that what Tommy had been trying to tell her? Had he picked the card that most closely resembled Leo?

She looked away from the mirror, cursing herself for an idiot. If things continued like that, before long she'd be glimpsing his face in the stains on the wall.

In the motel, she'd bandaged her finger with toilet paper, and now she disinfected it and applied a Band-Aid. The fingertip was twice its normal size, and the empty fingernail bed hurt just to look at it. As she chewed on an aspirin, she heard the sound of a car horn. "Deputy Captain, congratulations on the new car!" Lupo's voice shouted from the road.

She wrapped herself in her bathrobe and leaned out the window. The sergeant major was propped against the front gate like a prisoner peering through prison bars. "The mechanic let me borrow it," she shouted back. "Loris. Do you know him?"

Lupo nodded and Colomba understood that he had no love lost for Loris. "But I'm not here about him. Can I come in?"

"Why?"

"Do I have to tell you from here?"

Colomba took the keys to the gate out of her parka pocket and threw them to him, then went downstairs to open the front door.

"Everything all right? You look a little tired," Lupo asked as he came in and took off his heavy jacket.

"I didn't sleep well. That must be because of the heating, not something I'm used to anymore."

Lupo took a sheet of paper out of his jeans pocket. "I've brought something to use for lighting your fire. You can hold on to it until the next time."

Colomba unfolded the piece of paper: it was a photograph of her, printed from the computer. "Was this Tommy's, too?"

"You overlooked one under the bed, a classic oversight. This way we're done with them."

"Thanks." Colomba used it to light the burner under her teapot. She was sick and tired of those pictures. "So what brings you here, aside from this little gift?"

"You want it straight? The prosecutor doesn't want to charge Tommy," Lupo said as he sat down at the table. "Vigevani is afraid of looking like a fool."

"Because Tommy's autistic?"

"That's right, and also because he's afraid that a few years from now, some homeless bum will show up and confess to the murder. Or that Melas's sister will sue him."

"To get the money she needs for plastic surgery?"

"Probably. She doesn't give a damn about her nephew or her brother, but she'd squeeze blood from a stone. If only she'd get out of here, but she's determined to stay until the magistrate unfreezes her brother's assets. And that's not going to happen until the investigation is concluded. A cat that bites its own tail, or actually, I should say, *my* tail."

"Then you'd better start looking for that homeless bum," Colomba said.

"Too bad that we don't have any homeless people around here. I don't know which way to turn at this point. We went house to house and no one had anything useful to tell us." He threw both arms wide. "The Melases' social life? Zero. Relatives? Zero. Enemies? Zero. Friends? Zero."

"Have you talked to Tommy's therapist?" Colomba asked in a casual tone.

"Pala? Yes. And he had nothing to offer, either. I tried to convince him that the boy's going to be better off when the investigation is finished, but he doesn't care. All psychiatrists care about is money."

Colomba didn't tell him that Pala had made a very different impression on her, but she was glad to see that the therapist hadn't mentioned her. "And you continue not to want to ask the regional Carabinieri headquarters for a little extra support?"

"No, ma'am. When I was in Florence, I had to check with a thousand different offices before I could take even the simplest steps. Here I have my own little patch of heaven, and I'd prefer to hold on to it."

"So is that why you're looking to send Tommy off to the slaughterhouse?"

"The boy is going to be given medical treatment, nobody wants to give him the electric chair."

"There's no cure for autism, and Tommy isn't guilty."

Lupo rolled his eyes in exasperation. "I swear to God, I just don't understand why you and Vigevani keep on being so stubborn about this."

Colomba poured the boiling water into the cups and carried them to the table, along with the box of tea bags. "If you're looking for a shoulder to cry on, you're going to have to go somewhere else."

Lupo chose a tea bag that didn't look moldy. "I came because I think that finding the murder weapon might get Vigevani to budge."

"Haven't you found it yet?"

"We've used metal detectors and I made sure the guys from Protezione Civile checked every pothole on the road from Montenigro to here. Nothing."

"So?"

"Well, your property is all that's left, and I was planning to come search it this afternoon. With the whole squad, we'd take an hour at most. Then we'll clean the place up till it shines. We'll even wax the floors."

"Why would you want to search my house?"

"He stayed here, didn't he?"

"Tommy didn't have anything on his person."

"Maybe you didn't see him hiding it. You know that I wouldn't even need your permission, I'm just asking out of courtesy."

"You don't need my permission, but you do need the magistrate's authorization. And if you came here to ask me, it means that he wouldn't give it to you."

Lupo's fingers tightened around the mug until his knuckles whitened. "Deputy Captain, I'm trying to behave with a minimum of civility with you . . . Why don't you return the courtesy? We're both on the same side, aren't we?"

"The last person to say something like that to me perforated my intestine with a knife blade."

Lupo's jaw clenched. "Thanks for the comparison."

"When I met him, Leo Bonaccorso seemed like more of a cop than you do. Especially today, when you come to me in search of an easy solution that'll allow you to go back to scratching your belly."

Lupo leaped to his feet and put his cap on his head. "I have to go now. And your tea is awful, if you want to know the truth."

"Don't worry, that's the last cup of tea you'll ever get from me!" Colomba yelled after him.

Lupo vanished around the hill, turning on his siren just to annoy her. Colomba immediately put on her combat boots and hurried to check the tool shed, just to make sure. She even moved a few layers of boxes, finding nothing but spiderwebs and dust. To finish up, she searched along the fence line.

No hammer.

The theory that it had been Leo was once again her first choice. A theory based upon nothing but her personal impressions. She finished getting dressed and dipped into the files for a composite sketch of Leo. There were no pictures of him, but the 3-D identikit resembled him closely. Short hair; strong features; frank, open smile. The picture had been circulated extensively for months, but without any results, and Colomba herself had had no opportunity to show it to anyone since. Until right now. She got into the Peugeot 208 and drove down to Portico, where she bought a new cell phone at the usual shop and signed up for another rechargeable SIM card, hoping that it would be the last. She parked the car in the little plaza in front of town hall, turned on the heat, and placed her bare feet next to the heater vents, then Colomba called all the local hotels she could find on TripAdvisor, working her way through them, starting with the closest one and then expanding outward. She found Melas's sister at the ninth place she called.

5

Demetra was eating lunch in the dining room of the farmstay called Baita in Collesecco, with no company other than the mounted heads of stags and mountain goats. She was shorter and younger than Colomba would have thought from the video, and she was wearing a black dress and purple makeup over her facelift.

"Signora Melas? *Buongiorno* . . . I know that you speak Italian," said Colomba. "My condolences."

Demetra ignored the extended hand. "I already told your colleagues that I don't give interviews free of charge." Her Italian was perfect, aside from the thick accent.

"I'm not a journalist. My name is Caselli and I'm a police officer on extended leave. I have a few questions to ask you."

Demetra waved her hand dismissively; she had a French manicure. "Stop bothering me."

Colomba sat down across from her. "I'll say it again: I'm very sorry for your loss," she said in a low voice. "But if you don't answer my questions, I'll call counterterrorism and inform them that you're a member of some Greek anarchist group or other. Sooner or later, they'll figure out that it isn't true, but you'd be spending a very unpleasant week, even if you voted for Golden Dawn."

Demetra finished the last spoonful of soup. "You're not a policewoman anymore, you just told me."

"But I still have plenty of friends. Do you want to find out if I'll really do it?"

"What does my brother matter to you?"

"Not a thing." Colomba showed her the identikit of Leo. "Do you know this man?" she asked, unable to conceal the stress in her voice.

Demetra shot a quick glance at the sketch. "No."

"Take a careful look. He might have a beard or glasses now. Or he might have dyed his hair."

"No. Who is it?"

The man who might have killed your brother, you hag. "Have you ever seen him with your brother?"

Demetra pushed away her bowl, decorated with hunting scenes. "For the third time, no. You still haven't told me who he is."

Colomba put the picture away. "If you don't know him, then it doesn't matter," she said. "Did your brother have any enemies?"

"I have no idea. I didn't know him all that well."

"You didn't know your own brother? Forgive me if I have my doubts."

"*I thought* I knew him, but I was wrong about that."

"Explain it to me."

Demetra took a deep breath, expanding her lungs so that her silicone breasts pushed against her blouse. "My grandfather was a sailor," she said. "After the war, he stopped sailing and opened a workshop to repair boats in Markopoulo Mesogaias, on the east coast. When he died, my father inherited the business, growing it into a corporation with a hundred employees. When my father died, Aristides sold it to a Turkish company."

"When was that?"

"Two years ago."

"What month?"

The woman thought it over. "December. Is that important?"

Colomba gestured vaguely, and she really didn't know the answer.

"What kind of boats and ships did you build?"

"You name it, up to three hundred tons. But we didn't build them, we just repaired them. Yachts, for the most part, they came to us from all over Europe."

"Do you remember a boat called *Chourmo*?"

"I wasn't dealing with the boats directly, only the financial operations. You could ask the new owner."

"Okay. Why didn't you oppose the sale?"

"No one cared what I thought. My father didn't like that I had a life of my own, instead of staying home and washing his underwear. So he put it all in Aristides's name before he died."

"Didn't you even try to get your brother to change his mind?"

"We quarreled and he stopped talking to me."

"What role did his wife play in all this?"

Demetra grimaced in disgust. "How am I supposed to know? I saw her the first time here, in a photograph."

"Weren't you invited to the wedding?"

"I didn't even know he was married. He liked women, but I'd never seen him involved in a serious relationship."

"Sometimes people grow up."

Demetra took her cell phone out of her purse and showed Colomba a picture of Melas with a statuesque young woman in her early twenties, looking quite Eastern European. "One of his many girlfriends. She was an underwear model. Do you think *she* looks anything like the woman he married?" She shook her head. "Men may change, but not that much."

6

Alberti called Colomba as he was walking back to Rome police headquarters with a protein smoothie that he'd just picked up at the corner
café. There was less noise than usual in the hallway, maybe because half
of the NOA counterterrorism agents had been sent to Milan and there
were no illegal immigrants to process. "Deputy Captain, good evening."
He sat down at Santini's desk, as he often did when his superior officer
wasn't there. He even put his feet up on the desk. "And don't tell me to
call you by your first name, because I'm no longer on a first-name basis
with anyone who's come this close to getting me sent to Guantánamo Bay."

"What are you talking about?" Colomba asked. She was driving just
then, and she slowed down and put in her earpiece.

"I'm talking about the operation under way at the address I gave you
yesterday. An address that I imagine you visited before everyone else."

"Maybe I did. So what's the word?"

"The word is that a dead man linked to the terror attack in Venice
went on using his ATM card and paying his rent. I'm guessing that the
dead man in question was Romero."

"Don't worry, I'll leave you out of it if they catch me. What did you
find out about the double homicide?" she said dismissively.

Alberti read the notes on his cell phone. "The Melases are clean.
There was an investigation into the death of her first husband, but it
was ruled an accident. He was going mushroom hunting near Turin, and
he slipped and fell into a crevasse. That happened thirteen years ago."

Colomba did some quick arithmetic in her head: Tommy would have
been six years old, during the Father's most recent period of activity.
"Was the woman present?"

"They say she wasn't. Are you thinking she killed her husband?"

"I'm thinking anything I can."

"As for Sergeant Major Lupo . . . do you want the short story or the long one?"

"The short one."

"Suspected of taking bribes when he was still in Florence, but couldn't be tried because the statute of limitations had expired. Still, they transferred him to the provinces, where he couldn't do any harm."

Colomba was so focused on what Alberti had been telling her that she blew past a red light. It was one of those battery-operated lights they use in construction zones, synchronized with another traffic light like it a mile and a half downhill to alternate columns of one-way traffic. Colomba found herself heading straight for a snowplow and just managed to avoid a head-on collision by running over a line of rubber traffic cones. She managed to brake to a halt a hundred yards later, her heart racing. She got out of the car to fill her lungs with fresh air, and only then did she remember that she'd left Alberti on the other end of the line. She picked the phone up from the floor of the car: the call had been ended, but instead of calling back, she reached into her pocket for the scrap of paper with Pala's phone number on it.

"It's a pleasure to hear from you," he said when his secretary put her through.

"I wanted to thank you for not telling Lupo anything," Colomba said.

"I promised I wouldn't."

"Yes, that's true . . ." Colomba didn't know exactly what to say next. She felt as embarrassed as a young boy who wants to buy a porn magazine at a newsstand. So she said nothing.

Pala seemed to understand. "Did you want to make an appointment?"

"How about right now?" she said in a rush.

"That's not the way it works, Colomba . . ."

"Five minutes and I'll be right there."

It took her ten, and she parked the car with the front wheels buried in a snowdrift.

Caterina accompanied her in chilly silence until they reached her desk. "Are you armed?" she asked.

"Mm-hmm . . ."

Caterina held out her hand.

"Is it enough if I give you the clip?" Colomba asked.

"Just for today. Next time I'll turn you away. And I want the bullet in the chamber, too."

Colomba racked the slide of her gun, and Caterina caught the bullet in midair.

"Nice reflexes."

"Three brothers. All hunters. I grew up around rifles and bullets."

"So do you hunt, too?"

Caterina smiled, pushing the pink tip of her tongue through her teeth. "Not with a rifle."

That evening, Pala looked like a villain in a James Bond movie, all in white, even his glasses and sandals. "How is Tommy doing?" she asked.

"Pretty well. He's been transferred to a group home. If the trial went against him, what would happen?"

"People like Tommy can be tried in a court of law, and you know that yourself," said Colomba. "The magistrates will examine the experts' documentation, they'll declare him mentally incapacitated, and they'll confine him to a home for minors to serve out the term."

"For how long?"

"Hard to say. But it won't happen anytime soon. The magistrate is very cautious, he wants a smoking gun. And I'm pretty sure that it doesn't exist." *Unless Leo plants one*, she thought.

Pala laced both hands together on his belly as he tipped his chair back. "Why did you decide to come back to see me?"

Colomba didn't know how to answer that question, and she didn't have a very clear idea of what she wanted, either. "There's a guy in Rome that I see . . . that I *used* to see, near police headquarters. He shouted all day to anyone who would listen that the pope was talking to him personally through the television set."

"I think there must be one in every city."

"I've always wondered what made him so sure that the pope was trying to speak to *him* in particular. What made him think he was so important?"

"Have you been hearing from the pope yourself?"

"No, but I don't know how much I trust myself. I'm afraid that my wishes are winning out over reality. That I'm fixating on what are mere coincidences."

"Do you want to tell me about it?"

"No."

"I understand . . . Do these wishes involve your boyfriend's return home?"

Colomba was caught off guard. "Are you talking about Dante?"

"Yes. What's the problem?"

"We've never been boyfriend and girlfriend, or lovers. Just good friends. He helped me out with some investigations and bought me dinner a few times at his hotel, but we've never gone to bed together."

"And yet I have the distinct impression that you have an intimate relationship."

Colomba kept picking at her injured finger. "We've shared some important experiences, but he's not my type. We're too different. He's the smartest person I've ever met, but he's also deeply paranoid, and utterly contemptuous of common sense and the law . . ." She shrugged. "He believes in nothing and no one."

"Not even in you?"

"Yes, he believed in me. And that was his mistake."

"Because you weren't able to save him."

Colomba felt the bitter taste of her tears in her throat. "Fuck you. Give me a tissue."

Pala tossed her a box of Kleenex without a word. Colomba blew her nose and stood up. "We'll meet some other time."

"We still have some time."

"I don't."

"Five minutes, let's give it a try," Pala said kindly, helping her to sit back down. "You have your limits, Colomba, like all human beings, and you suffer from the terrible experiences you've been through, but I doubt you hear voices through the television. You're not here to figure out if you're still a rational person, but whether you can trust yourself and your judgment."

"So what's the answer?"

"I'm afraid that the answer can only come from you. That's just one more reason that life is hard. I don't know what problem has been tormenting you, Colomba, but I'm certain that you'll find the right path."

"Unless even that's only in my head."

"Take it anyway and see where it leads you. There's always an answer, at the end of the road."

The operation was almost over. The NOA counterterrorism officers, with the assistance of officers from various other law enforcement agencies, had secured Romero's neighborhood and interviewed all the residents. In order to help man the operation, which involved nearly five hundred officers, personnel had been streaming in from all over Northern Italy, and the local police headquarters had sent men out onto the street who normally had their asses screwed tight to their office chair. One of them looked like a gorilla with a shaved head. That was Inspector Claudio Esposito, who had successfully requested a transfer north and out of the Mobile Squad. Now he was working in HR: regular office hours, colleagues who treated him with kid gloves in order to obtain time off and personal favors, while his sidearm gathered dust in an office safe.

Esposito had been sent out to direct detoured traffic, but after greeting the chief of police, he headed toward the only bar and tobacco shop inside the perimeter. It was jam-packed with uniforms making an infernal racket, and Santini had taken a seat at the only outside table, damp from the rain, with his overcoat buttoned up to his chin and his Irish tweed cap pulled down over his aquiline nose.

"Have you seen what a circus this is?" he said.

"That's the way it always is lately." Santini stuck a cigarette in his mouth and Esposito lit it with a Zippo lighter emblazoned with a picture of Mussolini before taking a seat. "People are saying that we're looking for Bonaccorso. Wasn't he in Syria?"

"Apparently not." Santini gave him a quick summary of the discovery of the sunken yacht. It was supposed to be classified information, but Esposito had proven he knew how to keep his lips sealed. "There's such a thing as lifeboats and that piece of shit certainly had one," he concluded.

"So what did he come here for? To organize a terror attack at Linate airport?"

"Watch out when you spout bullshit, or you might wind up believing it yourself," said Santini.

Esposito snickered. "I think what you tell me to think, sir." Among Esposito's better qualities was his utter loyalty. "What about Torre?"

"Even if we think that Bonaccorso is still alive, and I'm not saying that he actually is, he certainly wouldn't be dragging Torre around with him. May he rest in peace." He glanced at Esposito sidelong from under the visor of his tweed cap. "Wipe that sad expression off your face, you couldn't stand the guy."

Esposito shrugged his shoulders. "So how did the deputy captain take it?"

"Why don't you go pay her a visit and you can ask her yourself. She's gone back to where she's been living."

Esposito ordered a grappa. "I'd rather not. She makes me feel like a piece of shit because I'm not devoting every minute of my life to finding Torre."

"That's the same effect she has on everybody," said Santini.

A group of officers in civilian clothing walked out the front door of Romero's apartment building, and among them was Di Marco, the only one not wearing a bulletproof vest.

"I guess the colonel thinks he's invulnerable," said Esposito.

"A genuine tough guy: he shaves by blasting the whiskers off his face with live ammunition."

Just then, Santini's cell phone rang: he recognized the number of his personal extension. "Why are you at my desk, using my phone?" he asked.

Alberti had forgotten, he'd been too busy struggling with his sense of loyalty. "My phone is being fixed, sir," he said in a rush. "I was just putting some documents to be signed on your desk."

"Okay, so why are you calling?"

"I think I might have fucked up . . . I helped Deputy Captain Caselli get a name. I thought it was just a routine inquiry . . ."

Di Marco was heading straight toward him, and Santini shut his eyes and imagined he was piloting a jet fighter straight back to his office in

Rome, where he could machine-gun Alberti through the window. "A name in Milan, I'm going to have to imagine."

"Yes. But she never told me that—"

"You know that there's only one thing that she cares about, don't take me for a fool," Santini interrupted him.

There was a moment's silence. "Also, she asked me about a double homicide near her house. Do you think that's connected to all this, too?"

Santini bit his cigarette filter so hard that it snapped in half. "Write up a report and put it on my desk, that way at least I know what hellish fate awaits me. And keep your mouth shut. If this gets out, you're finally done for."

Santini hung up. The colonel had stopped next to the table.

"Let the colonel have your seat, Esposito."

"There's no need, let's take a little stroll," said Di Marco. Santini went strolling slowly with him toward the back of the building, where the office coordinating operations had been set up, and where the armored vehicles were all parked. That was also where all the foreigners who had been found with their visas and residence permits not perfectly in compliance with regulations were being held, thirty or so of them, from the Middle East or North Africa, both men and women. All of them were complaining loudly, and the police were yelling back at them, while the children wailed.

"Have you found anything in the apartment?" Santini asked, looking away. He was sick of those scenes.

"Not even a molecule, for now. But the neighbor woman gave us a perfect description of Bonaccorso. He was there for more than a year, even if he tended to stay out of sight. Then he took off when the *Chourmo* was identified."

"Someone alerted him. The Libyans?"

"That doesn't much matter for the time being." Di Marco looked up toward Romero's window. "The neighbor woman described another person, too, who assaulted her last night, threatening to kill her and her son. An attractive woman, with short hair and green eyes . . ." Di Marco stopped to look at him, and Santini showed no reaction whatsoever. "Well?"

Santini picked at his mustache. "Well what? I didn't know that Caselli had come here, but I'm not all that surprised, either."

"Caselli is your problem, and it's your job to keep her in check."

Santini lit another cigarette, and as he did so he realized that he'd stolen Esposito's lighter. He concealed Thunderjaws, as Mussolini was jocularly known, in the palm of his hand. "She's no longer on the force and she doesn't even live in Rome anymore. And you're the one who decided to bring her along to the grand underwater maneuvers."

"I was hoping that she'd identify a corpse and stop busting our chops. What are the odds that Caselli could have found something useful and taken it away?"

Santini opened his mouth to say that he had no idea, but he never got the words out. A red-hot blast wave shoved him from behind with the force of an onrushing semitrailer and slammed him into Di Marco, and then the two of them into the air, swept away by a roar that erased everything, even their screams. Santini hit his chin against the curb. Di Marco let himself fly loose-limbed the way he'd been taught in boot camp, but he landed on a manhole cover and broke both his wrists.

Neither Di Marco nor Santini lost consciousness. So they were able to see Romero's neighbor throwing herself in flames out of the third-floor window with what looked like a baby boy in her arms.

CHAPTER IV

*D*ante looks at what was once the kitchen of the Box, though now little or nothing remains of it. The big window is broken, the wall is riddled with holes.

Leo is sitting on an overturned crate. Next to him is the refrigerator, lying flat on the floor, and on it he has placed his camp stove. Leo gestures to Dante to come closer. And Dante obeys. What else can he do? Run away? He's exhausted and cold, his internal thermometer has exploded.

"You stabbed Colomba," he says with all the horror he is capable of mustering in his condition. "You killed her . . ." He feels himself being dragged down into the maelstrom; he's forced to let himself sink into the mud of that infamous place.

"She's fine," Leo says.

"I saw the blood, I saw—"

Leo tosses him a pack of Marlboros and a lighter. "I didn't say I didn't hurt her. Have a smoke and relax."

Dante puts a cigarette into his mouth with his gloved hands. The taste of tobacco is wonderful, and he imagines the nicotine kick. Instead he spits it out after taking half a drag and tosses the pack back to its rightful owner. A weak throw that doesn't even reach the refrigerator upon which his captor is pouring coffee into two little plastic cups. "I don't want anything from you," says Dante. "And you can stick that coffee up your ass."

"Quit getting yourself all worked up. If I'd wanted to kill Colomba I would have twisted the knife in the opposite direction. Zip, and there goes her artery." He sips the coffee.

Leo is such an accomplished liar that Dante can't manage to detect the signs of it. And what if he's telling the truth? "Do you care about her?"

"We don't have time for idle chitchat." With a sweep of his arm, Leo knocks the camp stove aside, and the coffeepot overturns, spraying black liquid in all directions and rolling toward him. Dante decides that he can use it as a weapon, but when he reaches down to grab it, he finds that it's vanished under four inches of water.

"What the fuck is happening?" he asks, moving his feet. It seems that the water is filtering up out of the kitchen floor. Radioactive water.

"Nothing."

The water has already risen to his ankles. It's falling from the ceiling, too, now, and running down the walls. It stinks of ozone and diesel fuel. Dante tries to make it to the door, but he slips and falls backward. He lies there, bobbing on his back, in the dead man's float. "Help, the radiation!"

"That's the last thing you need to be afraid of, little brother," says Leo as he bends over him.

Dante flails around, unsuccessfully trying to get back up on his feet. His jumpsuit keeps him afloat like a life preserver, but it also keeps him from standing up. "So what should I be afraid of?"

"Not what. Who."

Leo says something else, but the sound of rushing water swallows his voice. Dante is swept away like a bobbing cork.

Now Leo is a dot amid the ruins. His voice is an electric buzz. He waves goodbye, then disappears among the waves.

And the water closes over Dante's head and devours everything.

As the day drew to an end, Colomba returned the Peugeot 208 to the Portico repair shop. Loris was just about to close up for the night, but he let out a shout of joy when he saw her. "I thought you'd absconded with my pride and joy. Did you treat it well?"

"With kid gloves. What about my junker?"

"Finished it half an hour ago. I didn't know how to let you know."

"So much the better." She tossed him the keys.

Loris painstakingly checked over his "pride and joy," then led her to the Fiat Panda. The old jalopy had been washed inside and out; the hubcaps gleamed. It seemed, well, maybe not brand-new, but at least not stolen from a junkyard. Compared to the Peugeot 208, though, the engine sounded like a fart.

"I even changed the air filter and the clutch," said Loris. "And you had a wasp's nest under the back seat, luckily empty. I can get you one in better shape for not much money."

"It's a memento, it has sentimental value."

"Why?"

"It was my dad's. He only used it to drive down into town and then back up to Mezzanotte, the way I'm doing. For long trips, he had a Škoda." She could still remember the smell of the perforated leather steering wheel cover.

"So you really are from around here."

"Only on my father's side of the family. My grandfather worked in Sant'Anna Solfara, and when they shut down the plant, he moved to Rome. Do I have to sell a kidney to pay for the work?"

"That's not the body part I'm most interested in." He smiled.

"Funny guy."

Inside the office, a twenty-inch television set was reflected on the sliding window used to pass documents from room to room. Her eye caught a flash, and so Colomba raised her head to see the words ƧWƎN ƆNIʞAƎᴙᗺ overlaid on the spray of water from a fire truck that was trying to put out a seething blaze spewing out black smoke. The footage changed into an overhead view from a helicopter flying at low altitude over a carpet of emergency vehicles and police cars and, last of all, the apartment building that Colomba had visited not even twenty-four hours previously: it had collapsed inward like a cement soufflé, leaving nothing standing but the outside walls.

Loris said something, but Colomba ignored him and grabbed her cell phone, blessing almighty providence that she hadn't thrown it away yet. Alberti answered her as he stepped out of the squad room where everyone was watching the same scenes on the television set there. He informed her that Santini and Di Marco were in the emergency room, but that they weren't in particularly serious condition. Still, there were twenty officers and soldiers not accounted for, as well as seven residents of the building. There was talk of a gas leak, but nobody believed it had been an accident and everyone assumed only one person could be responsible for this, though their lips remained zipped.

Leo.

Colomba paid for the repairs with the gestures of a zombie, and at the same lugubrious pace she headed off toward Mezzanotte behind the wheel of the Panda, which smelled of soap and Scots pine. Loris had even changed the snow chains, putting on new ones that machine-gunned less thunderously. Colomba wouldn't have heard them anyway. She thought about Leo with his finger on the button of the bomb as he asked her to choose between life in the hill country or a quick death. What if she had given the wrong answer? Would she have had time to realize it, or would it all be over in a flash?

Colomba had already been involved in three bombings, and she'd survived them by the narrowest of margins. A little bit like the Japanese man who had been in Hiroshima when the atomic bomb was dropped, and had survived, and had then gone to Nagasaki just in time to be there for the second one, too. If there had been a third atom bomb, maybe he wouldn't have survived. And neither would she.

Colomba went back into the farmhouse, and she'd just taken her boots off when she saw a column of flashing emergency lights sliding down the side of the hill toward her. Instead of simply breaking down the door as she had feared, the two Carabinieri squad cars and the two unmarked vans stopped outside the gate. The passengers got out and gathered in the little plaza: Colomba recognized Lupo and his squad. She put on her parka and stepped into the doorway, careful to keep her hands far from her body. "Am I under arrest?"

Lupo walked over to the chain-link fence with the look on his face of someone enjoying themselves. "No, Deputy Captain. But after what happened in Milan, the danger of bombings has been raised to Alpha One"—which meant terror attack now under way. "And we've received the order to take charge of sensitive locations. And clear them of explosives."

"What does that have to do with me?"

"You're on the list of people at risk, Deputy Captain."

"It's a minimal risk, we both know that."

"But we'd rather not run that risk. For your sake, and your neighbors' sake."

"I don't have any neighbors . . ."

"The bomb-disposal squad had to travel all the way from Perugia, they did me a favor and headed out here immediately," said Lupo, ignoring her observation. Colomba smacked the chain-link fence with her hand, and Lupo jumped backward.

"So is that how you want to play this game, Sergeant Major?"

"No. That's the way *you* chose to play it. I begged you on bended knee to be cooperative." He gestured to one of the bomb-disposal experts, who had already donned his jumpsuit.

The man came over. "Lieutenant Franchini," he said with a strong Neapolitan accent. "Is there anyone else in the house?"

"No."

"It'll take a couple of hours. If you like, you can take a walk or a drive."

"No, thanks. I'd rather stay and watch."

"From the safety area outside the perimeter, though. That's the regulation."

Colomba couldn't put up any opposition and didn't even try.

"You're wasting your time, Lieutenant."

"I always hope I am. Do you have any explosive material in your house?"

"Only a box of bullets in the kitchen drawer."

"Are the doors open?"

"Yes."

"Very good. Please step outside," he said, gesturing for her to go.

Colomba stalked out of the house fuming with rage and leaned on the hood of one of the squad cars. Franchini and a younger colleague of his finished donning the protective attire that made their bodies look enormous, their limbs short, and their heads—clad in black helmets and with massive goggles—tiny. Slowly they examined the ground up to the house with two portable detectors, then the lieutenant inserted fiber-optic cables through the keyhole and checked to make sure there was nothing dangerous on the other side.

"Don't you think you're overdoing it a little?" Colomba shouted.

"Don't worry, Signora, we know what we're doing," said Martina, who had stayed within a few steps of her to keep an eye on her.

"Of course you do. And you can call me *Deputy Captain*."

The lieutenant carefully extracted the fiber-optic cables. "There's too much junk in the way," he shouted to a third bomb-disposal technician, who had remained back next to the van, without protective armor. "Send the remote-controlled robot," he added.

"Are you kidding me?" Colomba snapped. No one answered her, and she had the impression that everyone was working off a preconcerted, especially annoying script to make sure they plucked her every last nerve.

The third bomb-disposal technician opened the rear hatch of the van and guided the robot with the hydraulic platform. It vaguely resembled Wall-E, with three wheels in a belted tread on either side and a series of unsettling pincers. The bomb-disposal technician set up a tripod and opened a control console atop it with a small LCD screen. He pushed a few levers and the robot's treads began to turn, carving a path through the snow. The robot was equipped with a portable X-ray machine, an endoscope, a surface particle sniffer, and a scrambler to block outside radio commands. It was possible to equip it with a small high-pressure water cannon, but luckily they'd spared her that.

The robot poked its video camera into the farmhouse through the open door. The officer at the monitor zoomed in on Colomba's dirty dishes. "Nothing visible," he said on the radio.

The bomb-disposal technicians entered cautiously. Inside and under the furniture, they found nothing but stale scraps of food and dust. When they were done with the ground floor, the robot climbed the interior staircase, spattering the walls with mud and moaning like Godzilla. Lupo walked in behind it, and Colomba abandoned her position to run after him. "You're not a bomb-disposal technician, Sergeant Major."

"I have to supervise. Lodge any complaints with headquarters, Deputy Captain."

"You're taking advantage of the situation."

Lupo leaned toward her. "Yes," he said in a low voice. "And you have no idea how I'm enjoying it. Bruno, could you please see the deputy captain out?"

The brigadier stepped forward to carry out the order, but one glance from Colomba froze him to the spot. He stepped back behind the screen, breathing on the neck of the third bomb-disposal technician, who pretended not to notice.

The examination of the upper floor came to an end and everyone went downstairs again, in the same tank-tread formation. As it went past, the robot slammed into the kitchen sink, knocking a dish off. As the plate shattered on the floor, Colomba turned to complain to the operator. "Sorry," he said with a blush.

The robot went back out into the yard, and Lupo sat down on the front step of the house. Colomba looked around for a stone to hurl at his bald pate, but she didn't do it because Martina came running up to her.

"The bomb-disposal technicians have found something. We need to get away from the house, Sergeant Major."

"No kidding?" Lupo asked, unruffled. "Where?"

"In the back. Next to the shed."

"Okay. Everyone out!"

On the screen, the two bomb-disposal technicians were bent down in the snow beside the tool shed.

"What is it?" Colomba asked.

The operator showed her the metal detector's scan. "It's a foot and a half deep," he said. "Metal, and it doesn't look like a pipe. Ring any bells?"

"No."

The two bomb-disposal technicians dug with their hands, moving the dirt a thimbleful at a time. Once they got closer to the object, one of the two technicians stuck his hand decisively into the hole and pulled it out. He unfolded the pillowcase it was wrapped in.

"All good," he said into the radio, waving the object. "It's just an old hammer."

Then he noticed that the other technician was staring at it in horror and he followed the other man's gaze.

On the hammer's claw, a human ear hung, pierced through by the metal prong.

Colomba lay sprawled on the sofa in the kitchen, looking around the room as she waited, surveying the marks of muddy tank treads and boots, watching TV. The number of missing tenants of the apartment building had dropped to five, and those declared dead had risen to seven. Lupo reappeared a few minutes before one in the morning. "Melas's corpse was missing a chunk of its ear. The medical examiner says that the piece matches and that, in the cold, it's been preserved very nicely. So we have the murder weapon."

Colomba said nothing.

"I'd have preferred to have you volunteer it, or at least allow me to search the house freely. Instead, this way, it's all going to be much more complicated."

"It's impossible that Tommy could have dug a hole without my noticing it. And if he had, I would have seen the marks in the snow."

"You know, Deputy Captain, that's what I think myself. I imagine that you found it and that you hid it yourself, in an attempt to protect the boy."

"With all the places in the world I could have disposed of it? Try not to make me laugh. The most likely explanation is that it was someone who's eager to wrap up the case and, just think of the coincidence, happened to show up at my house with a metal detector."

"Show some respect for the uniform I wear."

Colomba glared daggers at him. "What kind of respect were you showing for that uniform when you took those bribes?"

Lupo clenched his jaw. "We'll file a confiscation report tomorrow morning, along with everything else. I'll expect you at eight sharp in my office."

Colomba waited for the caravan to vanish into the distance, except for the squad car assigned to annoy her, which pulled out to a point on the dirt road a few yards from her front gate. It was too dark for her to identify the person at the wheel, but she knew that whoever it was, they would sit there all night, staking out her house to make sure she didn't go anywhere.

Fuck you, whoever you are.

She rummaged through her kitchen in search of something to drink. There was nothing in the fridge, but in the pantry, with an expiration date from last year, she found a six-pack of cans of premixed rum and Coke. It tasted horrible, especially at room temperature.

She put her parka back on and dragged a chair out to the little covered porch at the back door, concealed from any prying eyes. She kicked the snow into piles, stuck the cans into it, within easy reach, and started guzzling them. By the time she got to the third can, it was cold enough to suit her. An icy wind was blowing, and the temperature had dropped below freezing. Small icicles tinkled on the tree branches. Lupo had taken his revenge, and Di Marco would be the next to make his appearance, she felt sure of it. If it hadn't been for the explosion, maybe he'd have turned a blind eye to her interference in the investigation, but now . . . This might well be her last night of freedom.

She looked at her wristwatch, a men's model in stainless steel that had belonged to her father, with glow-in-the-dark numbers and hands.

It was two in the morning. If this was her last night, she might as well make the best of it.

At 2:10 a.m., Martina wiped the condensation off the inside of the windshield and tucked the blanket around her. Why anyone should have left the forgotten blanket in the squad car she couldn't say, but considering how cold it was out, she was happy to have it. She didn't want to keep the engine running: you could hear it miles away. She hadn't complained when Lupo had assigned her to the all-night stakeout, even though she'd long since done more than the maximum number of hours of overtime. Lupo didn't like people who questioned his orders in any way, shape, or form: he called them *labor agitators* and he had cleaned house, getting rid of everyone who failed to comply with what he thought of as the proper *family spirit*, which was another way of saying: doing what they were told. Martina had shrugged and gone along with it, but she couldn't wait to get out of there, to some big city or other, where the commander wasn't constantly breathing down your neck and the deputy commander wasn't such an idiot. Now that her objective was within view, she was beside herself with anticipation, in spite of the doubts and pangs of conscience that had tormented her.

She plugged the earbuds into her cell phone and started the app for Radio Ananas—Pineapple Radio—so she could hear the latest news about Milan. The number of victims had risen to ten, and she continued to stare at Colomba's silhouette. Her target had left the trees and gone back inside, moving around, backlit. Colomba had gotten on Martina's nerves from the first time she'd laid eyes on the woman, with that know-it-all way she had about her, and even more so now that she was making her spend a sleepless night in her squad car. If they let people like her into the Mobile Squad, then Martina had made the right decision to join the Carabinieri, after all. *Just think what it must be like to work with her*, she thought.

The snow started falling again, as fine as dust. The low wind made it whirl into shapes that glittered in the light of the full moon. They appeared and vanished, sliding into and out of the shadows under the trees . . .

The snow sketched out the silhouette of a man, standing right in front of the car.

Martina instinctively turned on the headlights, and the clumps of snowflakes turned into fiery phosphors that erased everything. She immediately turned the headlights back off, cursing herself for an idiot, and on her retina she could still see the ghost negative of a white road dotted with black and an evanescent silhouette. Martina blinked several times, and the silhouette faded. She checked to make sure that Colomba was still in the house, and saw her shadow moving around on the ground floor.

Maybe it was the guy from the dog training establishment, who had gone to feed the animals, she thought. Martina could hear them barking in the darkness, calling back and forth to other dogs scattered across the valley. Who knows what the hell those dogs had to say to each other all this time. Maybe it was a canine version of WhatsApp. *What did you eat today? The usual kibble? That's right, and after that I gave my asshole a nice long licking.*

Martina snickered to herself, and then she glimpsed the evanescent shadow of the man again. It seemed to be moving now, around behind the curve of the trail. In some manner, the silhouette looked familiar to her, though she still couldn't say why.

She unlocked the car door and opened it slightly. A gust of wind pushing a handful of needle-sharp chunks of ice hit the back of her neck, sending a shiver down her spine. Maybe it wasn't worth getting out into that shitty weather simply to identify someone who probably just lived around there. Almost certainly the owner of the dogs, who was out checking to make sure they were all right.

And yet . . .

And yet the dogs kept barking, and it wasn't the cheerful barking of dogs greeting their human friend. This was the baying of an animal catching the scent of a stranger, doing its job as a wary sentinel.

All right, then, Martina asked herself in that split second of uncertainty, *should I go see who it is, or should I pretend I didn't see it?*

While that second ticked past, Martina made the wrong decision.

5

At one minute to three, Colomba finished equipping herself and slung her backpack over her shoulders. It contained a flashlight screened by duct tape, a pair of kitchen gloves, and a stubby crowbar she'd found under the sink, as well as a pair of wooden snowshoes from the seventies. If Leo had a pair of these, too, Colomba thought, then he'd probably used them the night he'd murdered the Melases. And for some reason, spared Tommy's life. Just as, for some reason, he'd spared hers in Milan, instead of blowing her up with the rest of the apartment building.

She hated that thought.

Instead of her fur-lined parka, she put on a ski suit. She went out the back door, where whoever was staking out her house wouldn't be able to see her. She moved as quickly as she could in the darkness, until she reached the border to the garden, under the shelter of the skeletal hazelnut trees. In the distance, nothing but the undulating darkness of the fields, separated by a steep slope, a good thirty feet down. It was almost impossible to descend that slope, on account of the thorn bushes and the crumbling terrain, but Colomba knew the route by heart.

She got a firm grip on the lowest branches and used them to ease herself halfway down, then she let herself slide on the snow, taking care to avoid the projecting rocks. She hit bottom, knee-deep in the snow, and then fastened the snowshoes to her feet, struggling with the fasteners. She'd used snowshoes only once before, in officer training school, and those had been made of plastic: these seemed to come straight out of a World War II movie. She took a few steps, walking awkwardly like a duck, expecting to sink into the deep snow—but she didn't. Antique wartime surplus they might be, but for whatever mysterious reasons, they worked.

Remaining under the ridgeline so that she was invisible from the road, she headed toward the yellow lights on the hill straight across from her. It was an uphill climb the whole way, and once she'd burned through the remaining alcohol in her bloodstream, her calves and her spleen started to hurt, and then her back began to ache. She had to stop frequently to rest, and once she even had to wait until a family of wild boars stopped rutting and rummaging and moved on. She reached the outskirts of Montenigro at five in the morning, exhausted and frozen solid.

Sitting on a snow-free rock, she caught her breath and celebrated with the last can of drink mix, then studied the little village. It was deserted and dark, like a ghost town. The only gleam of light came from the Carabinieri squad car parked in front of the Melas home, at the end of the road. She'd hoped that Lupo might at least remove the police detail from there, but she hadn't been so lucky.

Sliding along down the slope, Colomba reached the far end of the town's main street, crossed it, and made her way across a little soccer field until she came to the back of the Melas home. She climbed over the gate.

From the far side of the house, she heard the dull chug of the Carabinieri squad car as it idled, and the notes of a sickly sweet piece of lounge music in the background. She couldn't hear the voices of the officers in the car. They were probably dozing off, half-asleep.

Holding the end of the flashlight with her mouth, she forced open the kitchen shutters. She used the blade of her pocketknife, producing faint cracking noises that sounded to her, in the utter silence, like so many explosions. The window behind the shutter was ajar. *Hallelujah.*

Colomba clambered in over the sill and landed on the floor next to the sink. The bloody objects had all vanished, and the footprints were outlined in SIS duct tape. In the bedroom, both corpses and the bed itself had been removed, but blood still splattered the walls and ceiling, dark and grainy as pitch.

The stench was minimal at this point, and Colomba thanked the brutal cold and the farsighted wisdom of whoever had turned off the heat. She put on her latex gloves and rubber shoe covers and started searching the house.

She found nothing hidden, no coded notebooks, no microfilm or cyanide capsule. Nothing but the physical signs of a life lived frugally, with little or no luxury. Furniture of a decent standard, with understated colors and standard decor. The occasional cheap Greek souvenir, a few articles of designer clothing, all of them belonging to the woman, while the man's clothing was of average quality, in gray or brown, bought at Italian department stores. The only fancy suit was the one he'd worn for his wedding, carefully wrapped in a plastic dry-cleaner's bag and, to all appearances, never again worn.

There were no mysteries left in Tommy's bedroom, but in the living room cabinets, Colomba found half a dozen cameras, and she remembered that Melas loved to take pictures in the forest. She turned on one of the cameras and started scrolling through the shots. Nothing but nature photography, done by someone who lacked even the most elementary artistic abilities. It was a rare picture that featured a whole bird, properly framed and in focus. For the most part, they were indistinguishable blurs of tree trunks and foliage. Often, judging by the time code, they'd been taken in rapid bursts over the course of a few minutes.

Melas didn't give a damn about these pictures.

Taking pictures was just an excuse to get out of the house every day and do whatever it was he'd come to this part of the world to do. Spy on her, kill someone, meet with Leo. His wife, on the other hand, stayed home with her son. She was happy to have found someone willing to take care of them both. At the back of the cabinet shelf, Colomba found a box that contained fifty or so memory cards. Clearly, Melas didn't want to be caught flat-footed if someone asked to see the fruit of his labors.

Colomba changed the memory card in the camera and started the slide show again. More trees, this time with autumn colors, more out-of-focus birds, more off-kilter framings. She realized, however, that the settings repeated themselves. Hadn't she seen that twisted tree before? She checked by putting the previous memory card into another camera and then setting the two screens side by side. Yes, sure enough, it was the same tree, taken in a different season. For that matter, the view of the mountains was very similar, too. If Melas always frequented and photographed the same places, she'd be able to determine where he went by his pictures . . . maybe. She scattered all the memory cards on Tommy's bed. Each card contained two hundred pictures, so there were at least ten thousand shots to look at and flag. Trying not to think of how long it was going to take, Colomba set to work.

At twenty to five, Lupo was fast asleep in his apartment on the top floor of the Carabinieri building, which was furnished in a mix of government-issue and Tex-Mex. The little living room, for example, combined a Formica-topped conference table with a large green plastic cactus, and one of those old posters featuring a sepia-toned photograph of Billy the Kid leaning on his rifle. You could be sure that the decent-quality stereo system would blare out American country western music even before you turned it on. In the bedroom, on the other hand, there was a poster-sized picture of Lupo on the Harley-Davidson he'd driven coast to coast in the United States, the finest vacation of his life.

The phone call from the Vice made him sit bolt upright in bed. "What is it?" he asked, mumbling into his cell phone.

"Martina is missing."

Lupo woke up all at once. "What do you mean, missing?"

"I couldn't sleep, so I called her to ask if she wanted me to spell her, or maybe keep her company. I know that you don't like it when we trade shifts, but still—"

"We can talk about that some other time," said Lupo, who knew that the Vice was still trying to get his direct report into bed, even though he'd been given clear orders to knock it off.

"I tried to call her over the radio, but there was no answer. Same with her cell phone. So I went out to see. The car is still sitting there, but there was no sign of her."

"What about Caselli, is she there?"

"The lights are on, but for now, I've stayed away from the house. If she left and Martina was following her, she would have called it in."

"Wait for me at the start of the dirt road."

Lupo put the espresso pot on the flame while he got dressed and drank the scalding-hot brew as he read the temperature on the window barometer: –1° C. It could be worse. He poured the rest of the coffee into an empty fruit juice bottle and put a plastic cap on top, then he went to meet Nerone in the green jeep they'd inherited from the Forest Rangers. The Vice signaled his position with his highway flashlight, set to red. The crimson glow made him and the vegetation look like something out of a nightmare.

"Here you go, it's still lukewarm," said Lupo, handing him the juice bottle through the car window.

"Thanks, Chief." The Vice unrolled ten feet of scarf and downed the coffee at a gulp. "I tried calling her again, but no response. Same thing at her home number."

"Could she have gone into Caselli's house? Maybe she needed to pee."

"She'd sooner have pissed her pants. Give the girl some credit, she's working her ass off."

Lupo pretended he hadn't heard. "Let's all communicate by phone, let's leave the operations switchboard out of it for now. And give me your flashlight, my battery's dead." He grabbed the flashlight out of his hand and headed down the dirt road in first gear, stopping a few yards short of the abandoned car, and then continuing on foot. The keys were still in the ignition, and on the passenger seat were Martina's cell phone and bag. No traces of blood, at least.

He changed the color of the flashlight and illuminated Martina's footprints, which could barely be seen. She had gotten out of the car when it had only just started snowing, and now all that remained of each print was an evanescent outline, covered with fresh snowflakes. Just as Colomba had done only a week earlier, Lupo started following the footprints with his pistol drawn.

Unlike Colomba, however, he was an expert in the field. When your last name is Lupo—Italian for "wolf"—you need to make your mind up early in your childhood to find a survival strategy. Back then he'd been skinny and scared at the idea of getting hurt, so he'd invented a Native American ancestry on the part of a nonexistent grandfather, who was named Lupo just like him, but with a different first name, Grigio. Gray

Wolf. They'd given him a Christian name just because he had to live in Italy, but where *he* came from, he was known as Little Brave. The story had only worked for a while—at age ten he'd been shown for a pathetic liar in front of all the other students, out on the blacktop—but he'd always had an abiding passion for the tribes of the Free Peoples. And he'd done his best to learn their skills and adopt their ways. He knew how to identify the tracks of hundreds of different animals, as well as their spoor, though he never talked about it much. And he could also see how fast an animal was moving. Whether it was grazing peacefully or running in panic from a predator.

Martina's footprints showed she was running.

Not from the start. When she'd stepped out of the squad car, she'd been moving at normal speed, and then, after a couple of yards, she'd accelerated in a straight line along the edge of the dirt road. Here the trunk of a tree that had been felled marked the beginning of a narrow path, almost invisible, that cut across the fields, in the opposite direction from Colomba's farmhouse. Immediately after the tree trunk, Martina's footprints seemed to be following another pair that were clearly preceding her. They were only the vaguest of ghost prints by now, and Lupo couldn't tell if they were a man's or a woman's shoes, much less their actual size. *Martina got out of the car and chased a person. And then what?*

The footprints vanished entirely under the fresh snow, but Lupo was still in time to identify the point where the first and second series of footprints had met. There were two crescents, the mark a foot leaves when you turn on your heels, dragging the tip of a boot across the ground.

The new arrival had stopped, and Martina had caught up with him. He had turned around.

And then?

Lupo could see a confused scene of bodies locked together in the darkness, and he imagined a shout of terror. But there were no signs of a struggle on the trail. No signs of fallen bodies, no blood, no broken branches. The footprints were invisible by now, but those other traces would have been visible. So did that mean they walked off together?

He continued along the trail as the sky cleared, until he reached the edge of the woods, two thousand square miles of trees spreading out over the hills. Countless trails intersecting beneath the branches of the firs and the larches. So Martina could be five feet away, or fifty miles.

On the way back, Lupo called Nerone, who had climbed back into the car. "Martina was chasing someone."

"Caselli?"

"Who knows. I'm going to go take a look at her house. But you wake everyone up and alert the Protezione Civile. Call the local priest, Don Vito, too, find out if he can send anyone to help us search. You organize the search teams, I want you all out looking before daybreak."

Lupo climbed over the gate and knocked at Colomba's front door. There was no answer. He walked around to the back of the farmhouse, where he immediately spied the footprints heading down into the fields, prints that were already disappearing under the fresh snowfall that was coming thicker and faster now. The policewoman had clearly done her best to avoid being spotted by Martina. Or had she just gone the long way around so she could take her from behind? Lupo realized that that wasn't a credible hypothesis, because the footprints were pointing toward the far side of the valley. Toward Montenigro.

Practically falling down in his haste, Lupo ran toward his car.

7

Colomba was awakened by the sound of the door lock turning and for two seconds there was nothing in her head but a pulsating void, like a television set tuned to static. Then she remembered that she'd fallen asleep like a rock on Tommy's bed after scrolling past the millionth blurry picture of birds and trees. She leaped to her feet and hid behind the bookcase, scattering memory cards all over the room. She even had one pasted to her forehead, and when she peeled it off it left an impression of the logo on her skin.

Her wristwatch with the old-fashioned glow-in-the-dark hands said it was ten after six. *I wasted an hour, and now I've been caught like a fool.*

The second lock turned and the door swung open, and Lupo entered the house. Colomba's hope that he might have just happened along for no reason to do with her shattered on contact with his words. "Deputy Captain. If you're in here, show yourself," he said. "And I know that you're in here."

"I'm not armed," she shouted, remaining hidden.

"Come out into the open."

Colomba peered out at him, from behind the doorjamb. Lupo was spattered with mud up to his ears, his sidearm was still in the holster, and he was scratching the back of his head, his thoughts clearly elsewhere. She walked toward him. "How did you find me?"

"Maybe I'm less of an idiot than you've taken me for. So, breaking and entering. For now, I'll just arrest you, and then Vigevani can make up his mind. Let's go."

Lupo grabbed her by the arm, and Colomba repressed her instinct to kick him. "Hold on a second, Lupo. Let me catch my breath. What's happened?"

Lupo huffed. "Martina walked away a couple of hours ago, and she's not answering over the radio."

"Walked away from where?"

"From staking out your house." He yanked on her arm again, this time just to make her look him in the face. "Did you see her? Do you know something you're not telling me?"

"If something's happened to Martina, then the one who did it is the same person who slaughtered the Melases and planted the hammer at my house. That's all I know for certain."

"You're still sticking to that bullshit theory . . ."

"It's not bullshit! And the Melases definitely had something to hide." Colomba pointed to a photo on the wall. "Just look."

"It's a woodpecker," said Lupo. *A pileated woodpecker*, to be exact, one that can't be found in Europe, but Lupo kept that detail to himself. Little Brave didn't want to come across as a hopeless nerd.

"Purchased at a bookstore. Because none of the pictures that Melas took in a year are worth blowing up. I've seen half of them, and I know just how bad they are. So why did he hike around in the woods all day snapping pictures?"

"All I care about is finding Martina again. Everything else comes after that."

"How can you be so sure that the two things aren't connected? That Martina didn't see something she wasn't supposed to see?" Lupo hesitated and Colomba noticed. "What are you thinking about?" she asked him.

"There were some footprints next to your house, footprints that were made a long time after we left it," Lupo said, reluctantly.

"Did you send anyone to see where they led?"

"They were already being erased by the snowfall, otherwise I would have followed them myself. Anyway, I put all available men out on the street."

"Then you can afford to waste a little bit of your precious time trying to figure out what Melas was actually doing in the woods. We could find out the identity of the man or the woman who left those footprints. And figure out whether they're involved in Martina's disappearance."

"You're diabolical, you know that, right? You're taking advantage of my concern for that young woman."

"Yes, I'm taking advantage of that fact to try to get you to listen to reason," Colomba admitted. "But the devil I'm really afraid of is out there, in the middle of the snow."

8

When she was a girl, Carabinieri Corporal Martina Concio had been a promising young figure skater, the next Denise Biellmann, according to her trainer, especially her spins. At age thirteen she was a national junior finalist, until she suffered a nasty fall that took several teeth out of her mouth and some of the grit out of her determination to excel. Like everyone who has pursued a goal and then given up on it, she'd been left with an open wound that she picked at relentlessly in her dreams, either by skating over the ice at supersonic speeds or else by crawling along on the same surface as slowly as a snail. Right now she must be dreaming, because in front of her was a tree trunk sheathed in ice and she couldn't move. She was cold and it was dark out. She turned back into a girl for a second, and she thought she could hear her trainer shouting to look out for her supporting leg. She opened her eyes again: the icy tree trunk was still in front of her. She was starting to be able to feel her body again, along with something creeping inside her, on the level of her belly. A serpent of flame and ice, the hand of the Hulk, her first Cuba Libre at age fourteen.

Pain.

When she'd been taken to the emergency room after her fall, the examining doctor had asked her name, and then had said: "My cousin is named Martina, don't you think that's a nice coincidence? Now tell me, from one to ten, how much does it hurt if I move your leg like this?"

Thirteen-year-old Martina had shouted, "Ten," but now she would have had to shout a hundred, or a thousand. She tried to, but when she opened her mouth all that came out was a sort of belch, and then a spray of blood and slobber. She couldn't say what position she was in. Was she flat in her bed, standing up, or seated? It was as if her body were floating on a cloud. She couldn't feel her arms, she couldn't unclench her fingers. She tried moving her feet and the pain stabbed her in the belly again, surging up her throat with a sickly sweet burst of taste. Her feet could touch nothing beneath her. Not the ground, not the sheets of a bed. Just thin air.

What's happened to me? What was there behind the tree? She tried to turn her head, but once again her belly screamed out. Something inside her was lacerating her flesh with every breath she took. She spat out more blood.

I shouldn't move, I'm injured. Probably she'd been in a crash of some kind, but she was still alive. And she was experiencing pain. That's a good sign. If you're gravely wounded, you feel nothing, right? *Right?*

She searched through the jumble of confusion in her head. The nighttime stakeout, Caselli.

The shadow in the snow.

Could it be that that was her last memory? The sound of the car door opening echoed again in her head.

The shadow on the road. Her getting out of the car . . .

And then what? Did he bring me here? But where is here?

This time she bent her head downward, a fraction of an inch at a time, maybe even less, her progress broken by fleeting intervals of unconsciousness. Beneath her, off to the right, she thought she could glimpse something glittering in the darkness. Ice, most likely, and yet it seemed to move, to ripple.

It was a river, a mountain stream, and the moonlight was being reflected in it. She had the impression that she was flying over it. Shifting her head another fraction of an inch, she saw the shadow of her legs, which seemed to dangle in the empty air. How could that be, what was holding her up in the air like that?

Clenching her teeth, she bent her head by a good half inch, and the image of the river disappeared. There was something blocking her line of sight. A zone of darkness that was darker than the rest. Another half inch, and now that zone of darkness completely obscured her line of sight. Something between her and the river, and when she vomited another gush of blood, and saw it fetch up against the dark zone, she realized that it was much closer than she had imagined. It wasn't anywhere in the indefinable zone between her feet and the stream, but actually attached to her body. It was holding her up.

Am I sitting on a branch of the tree? she asked herself. Had she fallen during her stakeout and grabbed the tree on her way down? She wanted to be able to move her hands to touch the tree and assure herself of its actual existence, but they were like lengths of yarn, completely indifferent to her mental commands. As were her legs.

She vomited more blood, and this time she saw it oozing, establishing the outline of the branch before dripping into the void, colorless like the rest of the universe around her, made up of shades of gray. And she finally understood what someone had done to her.

9

Colomba showed Lupo the pictures she'd selected of a trail that ran, out of focus, behind a line of spruce trees. "I think that Melas must have followed the same route every time. This trail always turns up in his photographs, for example."

"It's definitely looking south by southwest," he said, after taking a quick glance, checking the shadows against the time code on the picture. "In the distance, that's the Sibillini Mountains."

"Can you be any more specific?"

"No."

Colomba scrolled through other pictures on the camera. "Look at these. They were taken on different days and in different months, but it's always the same stuff. You see this tree, or whatever it is?"

"Yes," said Lupo, more interested now, staring at the twisted holm oak.

Colomba pointed at a badly weathered gray concrete pole. "Does that ring a bell?"

"I think those are the hills of the Val Cesana. It's one of the old pylons of the high-tension wires."

"So that's the line of hills beyond Mezzanotte, on the road from Montenigro."

"Keep showing me pictures, we need to narrow down the area a little more. It's still much too extensive."

Colomba handed him the camera that she was using as a viewer. "I put them in sequence," she said. Lupo ran through a sort of stop-action film clip of the trail with the twisted tree: it curved repeatedly and ended at a brick-and-cement wall. "So that's a windowless building. What, stables?"

"No, stables are built differently. This is a hayloft." He pulled out his cell phone and opened Google Maps.

                    o   o   o

Five minutes later they were climbing into Lupo's green jeep. It was only seven thirty in the morning, and outside the temperature was barely above freezing; the cloudless sky was starting to brighten.

Lupo put in a call to the Portico barracks, where no one was around but the civilian employee, because everyone else was out pounding the zone in a dragnet search. Volunteers from the Protezione Civile were arriving from all over the region, and so were K-9 dog teams. He ended the radio call and then, out of nowhere, said: "I never took a bribe."

"Good for you," Colomba replied, in a flat tone.

"The only mistake I made was that I didn't report my fellow cops who *were* taking them. I thought we were supposed to wash our dirty laundry strictly inside the family. Then I found out that the family I thought I belonged to had never existed. They turned their backs on me, everyone, even the guys I'd tried to protect."

"That's what happens."

"I imagine that you would have behaved differently."

Colomba shrugged her shoulders. "I can't lecture anybody else. I made too many mistakes of my own."

"Which is why you're off the force with time on your hands now," said Lupo.

"That's right."

The last section of the trail was too narrow to use the squad car. They got out and headed into the woods on foot. Colomba put her snowshoes back on, while Lupo relied on his knee-high Gore-Tex boots. "It ought to be a few hundred yards from here," said Colomba, checking the direction on her cell phone.

"But we're not the first ones to come through here." Lupo pointed to a series of parallel stripes along the trail, which seemed to have been drawn with an off-kilter rake. He leaned down and broke a bulge in the snow with his hand, revealing pine needles. "Someone erased their footprints with a tree branch," he said.

"Who could it have been?"

"Poachers, probably. Careful where you step, they might have set traps."

"*If* they're poachers. I'm just happy that you're armed, at least."

They started down a green corridor of interwoven branches that let the daylight filter through and dropped clumps of snow on their heads as they passed. The sky was blue for the first time in many days, and everything was dripping. "That looks to me like the tree we want," said Lupo after they'd taken about a hundred steps, and he pointed to a corkscrew-shaped holm oak that stood straight ahead of them.

Colomba, accustomed to the snowshoes by now, sped up to get to the tree, careful not to step close to the crumbling steep edge of the trail. A section of trail had recently collapsed and there was a comma-shaped stretch of mud that contrasted sharply with the white of the snow. Colomba leaned down to look and realized that one of the trees projecting from below glittered with a color that often meant only one thing.

The color red.

The purplish snow was scattered over the tree trunks and was sliding toward the ground, dense as tar. The tree was a thorny medlar, and the branches looked like a gigantic version of the stalks of a rosebush. One of those branches, thick as a man's arm and bent upward, ran right through the lifeless body of Martina Concio.

10

Martina's mouth and eyes were wide open, her hands were clenched, and she was covered with blood and vomit. Colomba shoved a fist into her mouth to keep from screaming.

"What did you see?" Lupo asked, still a few steps behind her.

Colomba looked in the opposite direction. There it was, in the distance: the hayloft. It was made of rocks and cement and part of the roof was missing, but even from the trail, Colomba could see the padlocked chain that fastened shut the solid wood door.

She duck-walked, or duck-ran, really, hoping that the snowshoes wouldn't fall apart on her now, of all times. She could hear Lupo shouting her name, and then his scream of horror when he reached the collapsed trail edge.

She didn't stop.

Before they had a chance to lock her up in a cell somewhere, she wanted to get a look at that goddamned hayloft.

Lupo called in emergency support by radio, then shouted Colomba's name in an angry voice. She ignored him. She placed both hands on the stump of an outside wall where the roof was missing to hoist herself up to get a look inside, but all she saw was snow, garbage, and rotted beams. There was, however, an intact room, the one into which the padlocked door led. Impossible to see into it. She picked up a large rock and started hammering away at the padlock with it.

Lupo, closer now, berated her: "You knew it the whole time! That's why you brought me here!"

Colomba pretended not to have heard him.

"Cut it out!" Lupo shouted as he slammed into her. Colomba whirled around and smashed the rock into his face. She'd aimed for his chin but she hit him on the nose, which broke and started gushing blood. Colomba hit him again, on the cheekbone this time. Lupo staggered, fell, and on all fours started crawling toward her, moving blindly, completely dazed by the impact. Colomba relieved him of his pistol and slipped it into the pocket of her ski suit; then she went back to pounding on the padlock.

"It was you," Lupo muttered. "You killed her."

"Don't be ridiculous. We came here because the pictures were of this place."

Lupo grabbed her ankle. "You're the one who put the pictures in order."

Colomba stamped on his hand, then smashed the padlock with the rock again. The hasp sprang open. She opened the door with a hard shove of the shoulder. If there had been nothing but a heap of rotten wood, she'd have let Lupo arrest her.

Instead the weak sunlight of the early winter morning illuminated a sort of rustic living room, with a wooden table and a plastic chair. On the other side of the room was a motocross motorcycle covered with a plastic tarp, a Honda CRF450. It had knobby tires that looked new. Next to the bike was a set of mechanic's tools and a pair of summer tires ready to be installed, as well as three different helmets of various colors, and three men's motorcycle jumpsuits, size medium. The keys were under the seat, along with another bunch of double-bit keys.

Lupo had gotten up onto his knees and now he was fooling around with one of his boots. Colomba kicked him in the belly and he dropped a .22 derringer that wouldn't have looked out of place in the hands of a poker player in the Wild West. It had four barrels arranged in a square and a scrollwork handle. Colomba put the pistol in her pocket, then handcuffed Lupo to a ring in the wall meant to tether animals. He swallowed a chunk of broken tooth. "You're insane."

Colomba relieved him of his cell phone and radio, turned them both off, and laid them down on the table. Then she called Alberti on her own phone, catching him in the cellar room where he composed music on his computer, music that he posted online under the pseudonym Rookie Blue. Right now, however, he'd only gone there to catch some sleep, after returning home from police headquarters at four in the morning.

He often did that when he got home late and didn't want to wake up his girlfriend. Little by little, she was moving in with him, even though they'd never really discussed it, and Alberti still couldn't say whether or not he was happy about it. "The chief is okay, he's back from Milan—"

"I don't give a damn. I need something and I need it fast. A license plate."

"Deputy Captain, this really isn't a very good time."

"It's the last thing I'm ever going to ask you. And it's really important."

"Does this have to do with Bonaccorso?"

"Yes! For fuck's sake."

"Okay. I'm listening."

Colomba dictated the license plate number. Alberti asked a trusted partner to run it through the system. The owner of the motorcycle turned out to be a London real estate agent, who had bought it at auction from a clinic in Rimini that had gone into bankruptcy along with its former owner. And he'd bought the clinic, too, while he was at it. In February of the year before.

February, exactly when she'd first moved to Mezzanotte. Colomba collapsed in the snow, her lungs struggling to take in air. Another coincidence?

Maybe Pala was wrong and she really was insane.

She walked back into the hayloft, where she found a red-faced Lupo feverishly trying to yank the ring out of the wall. "Set me free, you fucker! What do you think you're doing?"

Colomba climbed onto the motorcycle and started the engine. "I'm getting all the way to the end of the road," she replied.

11

One of Colomba's ex-boyfriends, a guy she'd broken up with and left on terms that were anything but friendly, never went anywhere except by motorcycle, and at the time, she had bought herself a motorcycle to go with him on their free weekends. She'd never had such a miserable time, but at least she'd learned how to ride one. She opened the hayloft door wide and braced it in place, then she put on one of the helmets. It was too big for her head, and she thought she could smell the breath of whoever had worn it before her. Leo or Melas, either a homicidal monster or a murder victim.

She started the engine, put the bike in gear, let out the clutch, and almost broke her neck.

In order to control a motorcycle on the snow, you need to go fast enough not to sink, but not so fast you lose control. Making things even more complicated for Colomba were the fact that she was out of practice and her unfamiliarity with that particular bike. She fell four times in the first two hundred yards, and the last time she wound up flat on her face in the snow, weeping tears of frustration. *Get up, you stupid asshole*, she told herself. *Do you want them to catch you here? At least try to make it hard for them.*

She got back up and fell again, but when she thought there couldn't be a square inch of her body left unbruised, she finally made it onto the blacktop of the provincial road. As the speed increased, however, so did the wind-chill factor.

She avoided the highway on account of the security cameras and instead rode along the dark sea and the deserted beach that in the summer months turned into a playland. The dank, chilly humidity got under her skin. When she reached Rimini, a pearlescent day was dawning, and she found her way thanks to a highway sign that still featured the name of Villa Quiete, even though the clinic had long since gone out of business. With Google Maps, she would have found it more quickly, but she'd removed the battery from her cell phone, in order to keep from being tracked down too soon.

The clinic was located in a residential neighborhood, just a short walk from the waterfront, a slab of a building sheathed in ceramic cladding the color of a highway rest stop. It stood three stories tall, and was surrounded by untended grounds littered with garbage. Colomba parked the motorcycle in a side alley and stood observing the clinic from a distance. It wouldn't be hard to get over the top of the gate, in spite of the sharp tips of the bars, and there were only two security cameras at the main entrance . . . or anyway, only two that were *visible*. Was this another one of Leo's hideouts, after the apartment in Milan? Did he and Melas use this place to meet? Was this where they had readied the explosives that Leo had detonated in Milan?

She clambered over the top of the gate and dropped over on the other side to the untended park, running bent over toward the building, careful not to let herself be seen from the street, even though there was practically no one out and about. The windows were shut tight by roller blinds and it was impossible to see into the interior. Colomba avoided the central doors and instead chose to try the personnel entrance on the side of the building, screened by a stand of trees. Like the other doors, this one was made of shatterproof glass and further protected by a metal accordion gate. The lock took a double-bit key, and she thought back to the bunch of keys she'd noticed under the motorcycle seat. She went back to the motorcycle, and the third time she climbed over the gate, she understood that she wouldn't be able to do it a fourth time: she was exhausted.

She tried the keys in both directions, each time praying to heaven and the Almighty to help her. The third key turned, so easily that at first Colomba was afraid that she'd broken the lock. Instead, the gate opened without difficulty, and the door behind it opened with a simple turn of the knob. She found herself in a short hallway where it was colder than it had been outside. There was dust and cobwebs everywhere, and the filthy floor was covered with footprints, coming and going.

Colomba hoped that they were recent, that Leo really was sleeping in one of the wards of the former hospital, blithely unaware of her arrival. She imagined herself waking him up to the taste of a pistol barrel in his mouth. *So you think I'm afraid of you?* she would bellow into his face.

A metal door swung open, leading into the clinic lobby, long since plundered of nearly all its furniture; the fluorescent overhead lights were shrouded in spiderwebs. A large mosaic depicted the Virgin Mary watching over a sleeping patient. Strips of light came in through the shutters, and Colomba was just able to read the numbered map on the wall. The clinic was subdivided into two long hallways on the second and third floors, while the offices were on the ground floor.

Colomba checked the offices first, creeping along silently with both of Lupo's sidearms gripped firmly in her fists, which were shaking from the rush of adrenaline. The offices were empty and smelled of dead rats.

She found the waiting room, and then the stairs leading up to the second floor. She cautiously, slowly climbed the stairs, keenly aware of the slightest noise. The only sounds came in from the street, except for an electric motor buzzing who knew where in the building.

The hallway was painted a pastel hue, lined with rooms without doors or beds. Empty.

Hanging on a bulletin board was an official directive whose yellowing sheets of paper instructed all hospital personnel to learn the correct operation of the new hospital beds, which looked like spaceship berths for patients incapable of autonomous movement, and that's when Colomba realized that it wasn't a normal clinic at all, but a chronic care unit for the comatose.

The buzzing of the electric motor was louder now, and Colomba noticed another crucial detail: it was coming from the top floor.

More stairs. The pistols were heavy, and Colomba stuck the .22 into her belt, keeping Lupo's regulation sidearm outstretched, gripped with both hands, aimed high, her body moving in time with the weapon. By now the buzzing had turned into the shrill noise of a dentist's drill, accompanied by the rhythmic creak of a mechanism. *Zzz. Click. ZZZ. Click.* A room on the third floor still had a door. From underneath it filtered a pale-blue light that juddered in time with the creaking noise.

Zzz. Click. ZZZ. Click.

What was Leo doing? Did he have a weapon in his hand, had he learned how to hurl lightning bolts? Colomba didn't understand a thing anymore; the noise was baffling her and fear was mixing with the adrenaline.

The door had a lock on it, electronic and massive, with a red light pulsing deep inside a hole that seemed to have been custom-fitted to the little cylinder hanging on the bunch of keys. She inserted it, quickly assuming firing position again the minute she heard the lock click and saw the light switch to green.

At ten a.m. on the dot, exactly sixteen hours after the detonation of the bomb in Milan, Colomba used her elbow to press down on the levered handle and then push the door open, stepping forward into a cloud of pale-blue light that blinded her for a second. Then her eyes grew accustomed to it. She saw a human-sized doll being shaken in the air by some invisible hand, brightly illuminated by an LED spotlight.

She saw that the doll was strapped to a million-dollar bed. The bed kept changing shape, rotating and stretching the doll, jerking it vertical, then horizontal, then bent in half, without any break in continuity.

She saw the electrodes that covered the doll, the empty IV bags dangling from its skeletal arms.

She saw the plastic intubation pumping air down its throat. Then she realized that it wasn't an oversize doll.

It was a man.

It was Dante.

PART TWO

AWAKENINGS

BEFORE

*T*he IT expert has been working without a break since the day of the Palasport massacre, a whole week in which he got an average of three hours' sleep a night; and he's still not done.

He hands the flash drive to Di Marco, gets out a star-bit screwdriver, and starts dismantling the computer to remove the hard drive. He's going to give it a ride in the microwave oven, the same way he's already deepbaked the three cell phones he found in the apartment. With a rain of sparks and smoke, their internal memory has been definitively damaged. Better than smashing them with a sledge hammer.

Di Marco sticks the flash drive in his pocket, leaves his squad to finish cleaning up the scene of the attack, and leaves for the Comsubin launch awaiting him, tied up at the side of the quay. As he climbs aboard, the soldiers salute him, all the while leveling their assault rifles toward the four cardinal points of the compass.

The launch slides swiftly over the water to the port of Mestre, where an armor-plated car is awaiting the colonel and his security detail, ready to take them to the Edmondo Matter barracks. Before passing through the gray gates of the special forces headquarters, Di Marco spots the slight figure of a man standing on the sidewalk, smoking a cigarette, wearing a threadbare trench coat and an Irish tweed cap. He taps on the shoulder of the driver, who complies by braking to a halt, whereupon Di Marco gets out and goes over to the man. He wasn't mistaken: it's Santini, former chief officer of SIC, the Central Investigative Service, now just killing time at the Mobile Squad in Rome until he can take his pension. "What do you want?" he asks, planting himself, feet wide, before him.

Santini flicks the cigarette away and sticks his hands in his pockets. "Did you know?" he asks in a flat, dead voice.

"I have no idea what you're talking about."

"I'm armed." Santini moves his hand, and under the fabric of the trench coat the lump of a pistol barrel appears.

"You're too smart to shoot me in front of witnesses."

Santini seems nervous, but he doesn't retreat. "If I were intelligent I wouldn't be here now. Did you or didn't you know what was going to happen at the Palasport della Misericordia?"

"No," Di Marco replies, without moving a single facial muscle.

"Caselli was there."

Di Marco takes a step back to examine Santini's face more closely. He thinks it over, and there is practically the sound of gears clicking and grinding in his head. "She's making it up," he says after a few seconds. His voice has lost a bit of its arrogance.

"She's in the hospital, but she's going to survive. Torre, on the other hand, is among the missing." Santini is shaking. "They can't have arrived in Venice by pure chance. They knew that something was about to happen at the Palasport. How could you not have known?"

Di Marco pauses to think, and his gears tick away some more. "Get in the car," he finally says.

Santini staggers, in a mixture of drunkenness and sheer surprise. "What for?"

"I'll tell you something you don't know yet." He points to the front gate of the barracks. "In there."

"My ass I'm going in with you."

"Your mistrust is ridiculous. I'm the chief of counterterrorism in a country that's just suffered the worst terror attack since the end of the war. I have nothing to fear from you, so you have nothing to fear from me."

It's a threat, but Santini is concentrating on another issue. "You're not the chief of counterterrorism."

Di Marco flashes him a smile that is nothing more than a stretching of lips. "Everything is changing, and in a hurry, Santini, after what just happened. There will be the drowned and the saved. Which group do you want to be in?"

CHAPTER I

Dante was unstrapped from the million-dollar bed and loaded onto an ambulance by a group of paramedics. First, though, the firemen blasted open the lock of the main gate of Villa Quiete, seeing that those keys weren't in the bunch in Colomba's possession.

Under the name of Signor Caselli, Dante was examined by the emergency room staff at the hospital of Rimini, who all wondered what the hell could have happened to that poor wretch, not so much because of his miserable state of general health as because of the surgical implants in his body. The patient had a PEG valve next to his belly button, for force-feeding, and it was covered with a filthy gauze bandage, while in his arms there were two venous catheters, and in his trachea the tube from a mechanical respirator, so someone had at least started to care for him. Not anytime recently, though: all of those surgical implants were dirty and infected, surrounded by swollen necrotized flesh; what's more, the patient was undernourished and dehydrated, shriveled up and seemingly crippled, filthy, reeking of excrement and rot.

One nurse suggested he might have escaped from some other hospital before hiding out at Villa Quiete. A friend of hers, a head ward nurse, had once had a patient vanish on her, and the old woman had only been found six months later in the boiler room in the basement, stiff as a mummy. But she had had Alzheimer's, while the brain of the patient from Villa Quiete looked perfectly healthy on the CAT scan, without any sign of trauma or disease. So why had he remained confined to bed for so long?

"I don't know," Colomba replied, in specific response to the specific question posed by the chief physician. Exactly as she had answered practically all the other questions.

"Do you know what they gave him to keep him sedated?"

"No."

"But what is his condition? What is he suffering from? Why is he intubated?"

Colomba shook her head once again, and the doctor wondered to himself whether the woman really was in any state to understand his questions. The green eyes that she kept fastened on the door to the wards were feverish and glistening. "We need to remove the infected implants and clean his wounds," he said. "We need the consent of a guardian or a next of kin. You're his sister, isn't that right?"

Colomba signed without even glancing at the papers.

"Will he get better?" she asked.

"He's very debilitated, Signora. And I'm not going to hide the fact that this operation involves a degree of risk, given the state of his metabolism." He hesitated. "Do you want to speak to the chaplain?"

Colomba shook her head. "He's not a believer."

Half an hour later Dante was being wheeled into the operating chamber. Colomba, standing in the hallway, saw him go by and walked with him as far as the elevator. When the metal elevator doors slid shut again, she saw Alberti and Santini reflected in them.

"Fucking hell," said her former boss, from behind her. "Jesus Christ, you actually managed to do it."

The power of the domino effect: the firefighters at Villa Quiete had alerted the police, the police had called the Carabinieri high command, the Carabinieri high command had alerted the chief of police of Rimini, the chief of police of Rimini had reached out to the chief of police of Rome, and the chief of police of Rome had phoned Santini, who at that moment was sprawled out on the sofa having basically overdosed on pain pills. The gist of the phone call was this: What the hell was "the heroine of Venice" doing in an abandoned clinic in Rimini with a dying man? Was she working undercover or had she finally and definitively gone insane? In either case, this was Santini's problem to handle.

Santini had called Alberti and they'd assembled a team, and the whole way Santini had been praying to just die. But after he'd actually laid eyes on Dante, alive, he'd thanked his lucky stars that he'd gotten there immediately. He walked Colomba to one of the armchairs in the waiting room, carefully relieving her of the .22 and the other sidearm tucked under her belt. It was a Glock 17, not her usual Beretta.

"Where did you get this?" he asked, slipping the handgun into his trench coat pocket.

"Lupo," Colomba murmured from somewhere very far away.

"Lupo?"

"He's the sergeant major of the Carabinieri in Portico," Alberti put in. Up till now he'd been standing, watching silently, overwhelmed by everything that was happening.

"I don't even want to know why you know that," Santini replied. "What's happened, Caselli? What the hell do the Carabinieri have to do with Torre?"

Colomba let out the story in dribs and drabs, helped along by a grappa that Alberti went down to the hospital bar to fetch her. When she got to the part about having handcuffed Lupo to the hayloft wall, Santini hurried to make a couple of phone calls.

Lupo, chilled to the bone and cursing furiously, was liberated by two of his own men. In spite of the fact that the left side of his face was twice the size of the right and his nose was broken, he refused medical treatment and stayed there to supervise the recovery of Martina's corpse by the alpine rescue team. To avoid compromising the autopsy findings, they simply sawed off the branch, leaving it in place in the wound, and lowered the corpse, stiffened by rigor mortis, dancing in the sling of a cable hanging from a winch. There was also a medical examiner, dressed in the style of an old-time barber surgeon, his beard encrusted with ice.

In accordance with his instructions, the corpse was unhooked from the winch and laid on the folding gurney. The branch that Martina still had in her viscera acted as a pump. There was a gushing sound, and from her belly there emerged two gigantic tremulous lips that spewed blood on the search and recovery team. This was her peritoneum, lacerated and pushed out by the internal air pressure. The medical examiner, Dr. Tira, wiped the round lenses of his eyeglasses with a silk handkerchief; the EMT attendants hurried to cover the corpse with a sheet.

"I want a warrant for the preventive custody of Colomba Caselli. And I beg you not to nitpick about it this time," Lupo said to Vigevani, walking with him behind the corpse. In private they were on an informal basis.

"Are you sure you can justify the charges, Wolf? If she testifies that you were the first to put your hands on her, that might put you in a bad situation," the magistrate replied.

"And am I supposed to have just handcuffed myself?"

"You ought to know that wouldn't actually be all that hard."

Lupo stopped walking, forcing Vigevani to turn around. "If you don't believe me, just go ahead and say so."

"No, no, of course I believe you . . . But come on, the idea that Caselli killed Concio?"

"Why not?"

"She's been a straight-arrow cop, Wolf."

"Exactly. *She's been*. She was almost killed in Venice, someone kidnapped her boyfriend—"

"I don't think that she and Torre were an item."

"And before that she worked on a serial killer case," Lupo went on without listening. "I've seen cops resign from the force after a single shootout, whereas she's had more gunplay than Buffalo Bill. She's pushed well past the breaking point; who knows what could be going through her head."

The ambulance with Martina's corpse took off, heading in the direction of the autopsy room at the hospital of Pesaro. The only cars left in the clearing belonged to Lupo and his boss, Vigevani. Vigevani's driver got out to open the door for him, but the magistrate waved for him to wait and walked Lupo to his jeep. "So how are you thinking events unfolded? Describe the mechanics of the thing to me, since a motive is unnecessary, if she's insane."

"She left her house and Martina followed her to see what she was getting up to. Caselli hit her over the head, loaded her into her car . . ."

Vigevani huffed in exasperation. "Then she brought her here, took her car back to Mezzanotte, and set out on foot toward the Melas home where you found her, because she was sure that you'd turn up there."

"Maybe she was looking for something and so she just made up the story, right then and there."

"So that she could convince you to come here and make sure you found the corpse, and then hit you in the head with a rock and make her getaway on a motorcycle that she'd taken care to hide here in advance?"

"When you're out of your mind, logic doesn't matter."

Vigevani shook his head. He added: "Let's do this, I'll take your theory to the preliminary investigating magistrate, but then you'll have to go in and convince him."

Lupo felt mortified, and his rage ballooned. "Fine, okay, I'll say that maybe, and I mean *maybe*, Caselli didn't kill Martina, all right. So she's not crazy, okay. Then she had a reason to kick my face in, and I want to know what it was. Assaulting a law enforcement officer, theft of military weapons, kidnapping, grand theft auto . . . She may have survived the attack in Venice, but sweet Jesus, you can't amnesty all of it."

A strange expression appeared on Vigevani's face—a sincere surge of concern, Lupo would have been willing to bet—but then he turned around anyway and headed for his car, walking as if on eggshells to keep from slipping and falling. "Hey, are you just leaving like that?" Lupo yelled after him.

Without turning around, Vigevani asked: "Do you know what joke is going around at the attorney general's office about Venice?"

"No," he replied.

"That if ISIS had a good lawyer, they wouldn't serve a day behind bars for the massacre at the Palasport della Misericordia."

"Is that supposed to make me laugh?"

"It's supposed to make you think. Be careful what moves you make, Wolf. As far as I'm concerned, this is probably the last time I'll set foot around here." And he drove off, leaving Lupo standing in the snow.

S antini let Colomba look at Dante for a few minutes through the plate-glass window of the intensive care unit—the operation had been successful, but it was too soon to tell whether the infection would react to the antibiotics—but then he accompanied her to the car that was awaiting them both at the hospital entrance. Waiting inside the car were two men who looked like brothers: musclebound, with crew cuts and padded leather jackets. Colomba was still pretty much out of it, but she understood that Santini had alerted the counterterrorism division.

"Was that absolutely unavoidable?" she asked him.

"And you even bother to ask?" he replied.

They took them both to the special forces headquarters in the Gamella barracks in Pisa. Santini accompanied her down the corridors and past armed guards, then left her standing in front of a closed door.

"If you want my advice," he said, "cooperate."

"Fuck yourself," Colomba replied, having recovered somewhat during the drive. She went in.

Di Marco was waiting for her in an office with just one desk and two chairs. Both his wrists were in casts, hanging from a sling around his neck, with his usual dark blue suit and his usual smug arrogant face. "Excellent work, Deputy Captain. Next time, give me a call before throwing half the country into a frenzy."

Colomba had one last surge of energy. "You goddamn son of a bitch!" she shouted, kicking the desk hard enough to make pens and pencils roll across the top. "Dante was in Rimini! Not at the bottom of the sea or in a cave in Afghanistan. In Rimini! Where the fuck were you even looking for him, all this time?"

"Deputy Captain, I'm as surprised as you are. It's an unexpected development."

"Oh, really? With all the men at your disposal, with the whole army at your fingertips, you couldn't find him, right under your own noses! Maybe you didn't *want* to find him."

"Stop being childish and sit down."

Rather than give him the satisfaction, Colomba would have popped her ligaments, but she finally ran out of strength and her legs gave way beneath her.

"I ought to have had you arrested when you went snooping around in Romero's apartment, Deputy Captain," said Di Marco. "Instead, thanks to Colonel Santini's good offices, I'm going to try to keep you out of prison for the second time. You ought to be grateful."

"Grateful? I can't wait till I have the chance to tell everyone how you left Dante to rot," she said.

"After which, you'll be arrested and tried for treason and violation of state secrets."

Colomba ground her teeth. Oh, how she was aching to wrap her hands around his throat. "Is that what you wanted to tell me? Okay, not a word to a soul. Now have me taken back."

"Matters have gone too far to wrap this up on an informal basis. The prime minister is going to take part in the next select executive council meeting of CASA, scheduled to begin in a couple of hours. And you, Caselli, are going to be the guest of honor."

CASA was the Committee for Antiterrorism and Strategic Analysis. Those allowed to attend were almost exclusively the highest executives in the intelligence agencies and the police forces.

"What would I be attending for? I'm a civilian now."

"You can tell the story of how you managed to find Torre and how, the whole time, you were operating on direct orders from my office. Santini will confirm your version of events."

"But I won't. I'm sick of lying for you."

"Would you rather wind up behind bars in a military prison without being able to sit by your friend's sickbed?"

Colomba slumped back in her chair. "No," she said in a low voice.

"Then cease once and for all this pointless hostility. For that matter, it's going to be an especially interesting meeting. The prime minister has been in office for six months and he's finally been given the all-clear by the security agencies. He's finally going to find out what actually happened in Venice."

5

Lupo went back to his apartment and called the young woman's family, awakening them with the worst news that a parent can receive. Speaking to them, he minimized the extent of her wounds, deciding to inform them that Martina had died instantly, and told them that they were doing everything possible to track down the perpetrators. After ending the call, he poured himself a glass of moonshine bourbon, distilled just like in the old days, during Prohibition, colorless and powerful. Lupo practically never drank, but right then he felt broken inside and out.

He'd just thrown back his second gulp when Bruno knocked at the door. The elderly brigadier's eyes were puffy and his hands were shaking. "I saw your light was still on."

"No problem." Lupo gestured for him to come in. "Care for a glass?"

Bruno nodded and sat down on the ottoman next to the large plastic cactus, barely wetting his lips after Lupo poured him a drink. "I'm going to apply for retirement," he said all at once. "I'm at ninety percent if I factor in my obligatory service, that should be enough."

Lupo felt a stab of regret. Bruno had been serving under him for six years; they'd arrived at Portico together. They'd never become friends, but after all that time, there were few secrets between them. And Lupo had been well aware that Bruno was reaching his limit, though he'd pretended not to notice. "I know that if you've made up your mind, there's no way I'll be able to change it, but I wish I could. Think it over for a few more months."

Bruno's expression didn't alter. "I've been thinking about it for a year now; my mind is made up. And it's not just because of Martina. It's because of all the shit I've been forced to swallow. I've seen what's happening right now far too many times before."

"Exactly what are you talking about?"

"I'm talking about *people* who cut and stitch the truth the way they see fit."

Lupo rolled his eyes: with the passing of the years, Bruno had become more and more of a conspiracy theorist. "The *people* who invented the vaccines to control us all?" he asked wearily.

"I'm not crazy. I have eyes to see. And I do see things. Caselli won't be indicted, how much are you willing to bet?"

Lupo was caught off guard. "Vigevani is strangely reluctant. He made it clear to me that it has to do with the massacre in Venice . . ."

"Because there's something rotten about Venice," Bruno said laconically. "I've talked with plenty of my colleagues who had some involvement in it. The intelligence agencies managed to make everything disappear. Evidence, eyewitness accounts . . . possibly corpses."

"They must be carrying out further confidential investigations."

"I know them, their confidential investigations. You weren't around in the seventies, but I was. And back then, it was impossible not to get sucked into one thing or another by the intelligence agencies. But this is different."

"Different how?"

"They're hiding something big. Trust me. And Caselli is up to her neck in it." Bruno wet his lips again. "She claims that she went to Venice for a two-day vacation with Torre and that she just happened to be passing by the Palasport della Misericordia during the attack. Then Bonaccorso stabbed her and kidnapped Torre, and nobody knows why. Right?"

"That sounds right to me . . ."

"In the days just previous, she had a shootout with an Islamic extremist, and then a cop on her squad murdered his wife and committed suicide. Guarneri was his name."

"I didn't know that," Lupo said, impressed. "But what does that have to do with anything?"

"Well, just look at the coincidence, he killed himself the day before Venice. Pure chance? I doubt it."

"But that's the most likely explanation."

"Would you have gone on vacation if your partner had just killed himself?"

"No."

"And there's another thing that very few know: Caselli knew Bonaccorso."

"What do you mean, she knew him?"

"*Apparently* they met by chance. But an eyewitness reported that he'd seen them together on the train to Venice, before the massacre. Her, him, and Torre."

"That's bullshit," said Lupo, unconvinced. It seemed like a crazy story, but then Colomba's had been even crazier.

"I'm just giving you the facts. But if Caselli was working for the intelligence agencies, then we'll never know the truth about what happened to Martina."

6

The military had emptied a corner of the central warehouse by moving hundreds of bags of cement, stacking them in a semicircle around a long metal table and a paper pad easel, like an oversize legal pad standing on four legs. Besides Colomba, Santini, and Di Marco, seated around the table under fluorescent lamps were the chief of the national police and the general and commander in chief of the Carabinieri. Everyone was asked to leave their electronic devices in a plastic bin that was then carried away by a soldier to a safe distance. Di Marco had been able to get himself seated without using his hands, glaring daggers at the man sitting next to him who'd made a move to help him.

He was a functionary, the man sitting next to Di Marco, whom Colomba had never seen before: in his early forties, bronzed, and with the lean body of a long-distance runner. She just had time to shake hands with him—"Pleasure to meet you, Walter D'Amore, AISI," he said, using the acronym for the Italian Internal Information and Security Agency—before the prime minister made his entrance in a mustard-colored camel hair coat.

It was strange to see him all alone: his security detail had been detained at the entrance to the warehouse, because they weren't even authorized to see who was attending the meeting. Without his usual entourage, the prime minister looked around like a tourist out visiting monuments. He was forty-five years old—a young leader, by the standards of the Bel Paese—and to Colomba he always seemed to be making an effort to appear relaxed. She'd only ever seen him on TV, and not very often at that, because politics wasn't an interest of hers. She thought that he looked like a pastry chef in a children's book, with a round head and a dazzling smile.

"Good evening, everyone, if I can use the phrase, considering what time it is," he said, "and forgive the delay, but today I had one meeting after the other." He raised his wrist and glanced at his watch. "It's already one thirty in the morning, so I have no more than fifty minutes. I need to catch a plane to Paris for a free-trade area conference."

"I doubt that fifty minutes is going to be enough time, Mr. Prime Minister," Di Marco said in an icy voice.

The other man threw both arms wide with a regretful smile. "I'd gladly do without it, given the emergency at hand, but it will be an opportunity to talk to my European counterparts about security, if nothing else." He turned to Colomba and extended his hand. "I'm very pleased to meet you, Deputy Captain Caselli. People like you are a credit to our nation."

"Thank you," said Colomba, embarrassed at the compliment. At least she'd had a chance to take a quick shower in the women's barracks: a camo uniform without insignia had replaced the filthy ski suit.

"I hope that there will be some other opportunity for us to meet and speak with more leisure. But I'm just too curious to know how you managed to find Signor Torre."

D'Amore laid both hands on the table; a small wooden Buddha dangled from his left wrist, Colomba noticed. "Before talking about that, we need to deal with a very sensitive subject, Mr. Prime Minister." After a brief pause, he added: "The massacre in Venice."

The prime minister looked at him as if he'd just insulted him somehow. "Are there any new developments, aside from Signor Torre's return home?"

"I wouldn't call them new developments exactly. More like a review of old ones," said D'Amore, unruffled.

The prime minister fell back on his pastry chef's smile. "I already know everything that there is to know about Venice. I recently read the unredacted document issued by the commission on massacres. And I had a frank and wide-ranging discussion about it with the director of the CIA when he came to meet with me in Rome."

He must have had a good laugh, Colomba thought.

"A very intelligent individual. I would imagine you must have met with him frequently, Colonel," the prime minister said.

"Mr. Prime Minister . . . I'm going to have to ask you to remain on topic," said Di Marco, as annoyed as an elderly schoolteacher. "Very few people know anything about what we're going to discuss now in this warehouse. Not a single word of this session is going to be transcribed, exactly as with the preceding sessions."

The prime minister looked around in search of support, without finding any sign of it. "Are you saying that there is other, *classified* information about Venice?"

"Yes, Mr. Prime Minister."

"It's against the law to classify information about massacres."

"Thanks very much for reminding us of the fact," said Di Marco. "But I assure you that once we have completed this investigation, it's going to be our solemn duty to inform the offices with proper jurisdiction of this classified information."

"But this is madness . . . You can't do this."

"In the opinion of the previous administration and a number of illustrious constitutional scholars, we most certainly can. If you please, then, D'Amore. This time we'll *do our best* to listen to what you have to say."

D'Amore cleared his throat. "As you know, Mr. Prime Minister, most of the victims in Venice belonged to a nonprofit organization called Care of the World, or COW to its friends."

"Spare me the ABC," the prime minister replied in an icy tone. "The killers were four Daesh militants, trained in Syria and under the command of the so-called Leonardo Bonaccorso."

D'Amore didn't bat an eye. "I'm afraid not. The information you're talking about was *fabricated*."

The prime minister's jaw dropped. "Wait. You're saying that the details are fake?"

"Yes."

"And just who fabricated the information?" He looked around again.

Who do you think? Santini thought as he picked at his mustache.

"The terror cell that carried out the attack did not form part of any known jihadi organizations," D'Amore continued. "The Caliphate claimed credit for it as it so often does, trying to attribute to itself attacks performed by others. And for once, we let the claim go uncontested."

"All the intelligence agencies confirmed the reliability of the claim of responsibility. The members of the terror cell were already wanted by half the countries on the planet . . ." said the prime minister.

The chief of police smacked his lips: he was starting to get sick of this. He was a powerfully built bald man in his early sixties, with fingers the size of sausages. There was no love lost between him and Santini, but they were forced to put up with each other. "I'm afraid not. They were respectively a child molester, a serial rapist who had partially cooked and eaten his roommate, an alcoholic ex-cop, and a guy who had drowned his wife in boiling water. And not one of them was a Muslim."

"What about Bonaccorso? Isn't he a foreign fighter?"

"For as little as we know about him, he might as well be the Blue Fairy from Pinocchio."

"A significant slice of foreign intelligence agencies took the information that we handed on to them as solid. Other agencies actually gave us a hand," said Di Marco. "And as for Bonaccorso, he did not take part in the actual attack. He showed up at the scene afterward, in the company of Deputy Captain Caselli, and killed all the members of the terror cell he came into contact with, as well as COW's founder, John Van Toder. It is our belief that he had nothing to do with them, and that he must have been working on behalf of some other organization, with objectives as yet to be determined. The investigation that we're now in the middle of, and which demands absolute and all-encompassing discretion, is focused primarily on him."

"But the one who kidnapped Torre really was Bonaccorso, right?" the prime minister, ashen-faced, asked Colomba. "Or is that a concoction as well?"

"Yes, it was him," Colomba put in, speaking for the first time. "But not on behalf of the Islamic State, Mr. Prime Minister."

"Then for whom?"

Colomba gritted her teeth. "I'd like to know that myself."

"Do the Americans know the truth?" whispered the prime minister. "Do the Americans know? Do the Russians?"

The general of the Carabinieri lit a Toscano cigar in spite of an angry glare from Di Marco. "Mr. Prime Minister, let me give you a piece of advice: don't talk about this with anyone. That's what I do and it's never a mistake."

The politician's face reddened. "Four perverts can't have orchestrated a bloodbath on this scale. Not alone, not without the support of some larger organization."

"You're right about that, they did have some support. In fact, more than just support. They were recruited and organized by someone." D'Amore reached into the file that lay on the table before him and pulled out a photograph of a corpse, which he slid over to the prime minister. It was a petite woman in an acid-green dress, covered with wounds and blood. Her face was frozen into a smile. "By her."

That woman's real identity was something that Santini had first learned the day he followed Di Marco into the Edmondo Matter barracks, immediately after the massacre. To his great astonishment, the colonel had led him through the kitchen, and then ushered him into a large walk-in freezer that was guarded by special forces officers. Surrounded by hanging sides of beef was a body bag, and in it was a woman in her early forties, with slightly Asian-looking eyes and a faint smile on her face.

"She called herself Giltine," Di Marco had told him. "As a girl she was a political prisoner in a Ukrainian prison better known as the Box. She was acting out of highly personal motives."

Santini had taken another look at the woman, shrunken and stiff in death. "So ISIS doesn't have a fucking thing to do with all this. Caselli was right."

"I'm afraid so."

"And when do you intend to make this information public?"

"Once it's ceased to prove useful."

"Useful for who?"

"For our country. Right now, it's a secret known only to a very select few."

"Which includes me."

Di Marco had stared him in the eyes and Santini had realized that his fate was being weighed at that very moment.

"There's a movie called *Fight Club*. Have you seen it?" Di Marco had asked him.

"A long time ago."

"And do you remember the first rule of Fight Club?"

"You do not talk about Fight Club. That's the second rule, too."

Di Marco had nodded. "Welcome to our Fight Club, then."

Santini lit a cigarette and refocused his attention on the conversation. The prime minister was speaking, and he looked like a punch-drunk boxer. "But why . . . what do we have to do with this Giltine?"

"Nothing. She wanted to get the founder of COW," said D'Amore, now showing a photograph of an old man with long white hair, his face frozen in a grimace of terror stamped by rigor mortis on his tanned face. "Whose name wasn't John Van Toder at all, and who wasn't South African, but Russian. His real name was Aleksander Belyy, and he was a criminal in the Cold War, let's say the Soviet equivalent of Josef Mengele. He was in charge of political prisoners for the KGB. He arranged for hundreds of them to vanish into an insane asylum in the Ukraine known as the Box. Whole families, including the children. One of those children was the woman who carried out the massacre."

"My God," said the prime minister. "And she killed forty-nine people just to get to him? People who had dedicated their lives to charity . . ."

Santini heard the chief of police choke back a laugh.

"Even COW wasn't what it claimed to be," said D'Amore, with something verging on regret. "It was merely a cover organization for a network of private military contractors established by Belyy in his second life. COW laundered cash and used humanitarian missions as a cover to transfer weapons and men into areas that were under embargo."

"But why didn't you say anything about this? You needed to report the acts of this criminal!"

Santini sighed, his head now throbbing with a brutal migraine. "Mr. Prime Minister, many of the military contractors under the umbrella of COW were working with allied nations," he said wearily. "None of us were interested in starting World War III. Caselli, could you tell us the rest, please?"

With some embarrassment, Colomba got to her feet and started talking, stripping her account of any mention of Tommy and leaving out the fact that Leo had declared that he was Dante's brother before kidnapping him. Exactly as she had previously told Di Marco, she explained that she had taken an interest in the Melases because Lupo had asked her opinion about the double homicide. But she did tell nearly all the facts about Bonaccorso.

"I met him after a shootout, and he pretended that he wanted to help me in my investigation, even though I had been suspended from active duty," she said. "Together we were able to reconstruct Giltine's progress through Italy, and together we went to Venice, though unfortunately we arrived too late to understand what was really happening. Also traveling with us was Dante Torre, who provided crucial assistance in our investigation, but I don't know why Leo kidnapped him. By the same token, I have no idea why he hid Dante Torre in Rimini. It was pure dumb luck that I found him, but I'm glad I did." Leo's phone call echoed in her thoughts. Then, in her mind's eye, she glimpsed his smile as he slashed her belly open, so similar to the smile she'd glimpsed in the mirror on the train. She felt a surge of nausea and sat down again.

The prime minister had listened to her only distractedly, his mind tormented by grim thoughts.

"So you were all in cahoots in concealing the truth," he said once Colomba had finished telling her story. "Police, Carabinieri, intelligence agencies. And even the previous administration. That's just . . . disgusting."

"Don't be naive, Mr. Prime Minister," said Di Marco. "Having friends in the UN or in the top European institutions is *much* more advantageous than creating a scandal would be."

"I wasn't elected to conceal the truth from the Italian people."

"What the Italian people want from us is to be protected, Mr. Prime Minister. And that's exactly what we're doing, in part thanks to the veil of confidentiality we've been able to preserve over this investigation."

"Confidentiality? Cover-up is more like it!"

"Mr. Prime Minister . . . you know better than I do that the truth is overvalued. And as often as not, people who insist on telling the truth are far less attractive to the larger public than a certified liar."

D'Amore gave him a smile that wouldn't have been out of place on a pitchman selling frying pans on TV. "We'll provide you with a list of foreign officials who'll be glad to lend you a hand the day you have to enter into some thorny negotiation. Our country paid an enormous price in Venice: Don't you think we ought at least to gain some advantages in exchange for it?"

9

D'Amore accompanied Colomba and Santini to their car, leaving Di Marco behind to lecture the prime minister about the urgent necessity of full and wholehearted cooperation. Santini made a pit stop in the men's bathroom and D'Amore took advantage of the opportunity to talk to Colomba confidentially.

"We don't know anything more about Bonaccorso than what we said during the meeting, but maybe we've figured out why he killed Romero: the port."

"The port?" Colomba asked in some surprise.

"The area around the yacht club where the *Chourmo* was tied up is notorious as a hotbed of male prostitution," D'Amore explained. "Romero was identified a couple of days before the Palasport attack in the intimate company of a rent boy. We think that, before leaving Venice again, he returned to the site, just as Bonaccorso was boarding the sailboat with Torre thrown over his shoulder. Maybe Romero offered to help."

Colomba imagined the scene. "Poor sucker . . . But didn't anybody think to look for him?"

"He'd already checked out from the hotel. Is there anything particular that you find surprising?"

Colomba shook her head. Leo had told her on the phone that Romero had been easy to hook up with, but he hadn't actually and explicitly said that he'd hooked up with him. "Well, if you include him, we have a nice round number," she said grimly. "Fifty. Without counting the collateral victims like the Melases."

"The investigation into their murder is going to be handed off to the attorney general, who'll operate in close coordination with you. But for the work that needs to be done on the ground around Portico, we'd like to have someone we know, someone who understands what's at stake."

"Ask Santini. You've already got him on retainer."

Just then Santini showed up, his mustache dripping wet. "I'm going to get some sleep," he said as he limped toward the car. "You two take all the time you want. Ciao, D'Amore, it's been indescribably delightful."

D'Amore watched him go. "He's already got his hands full. I was referring to you. You found Torre all by yourself, Colomba." He called her by her given name for the first time.

"Dumb luck."

"No, it was because you're one of the people who knows Bonaccorso best."

Colomba wanted to shout at him, but she lacked the strength. "I don't know him, all right? He made a fool of me, the same way he's making fools of you all."

"Don't let your dislike of Di Marco lead you astray. He's always put duty above all else."

"Unlike the rest of you." Colomba climbed into the car and put an end to the conversation by slamming the door behind her. Inside, the usual two nonbrothers awaited her, along with Santini, who was already snoring and wafting out clouds of alcoholic fumes. When they arrived in Rimini, the eastern sky was brightening with the onset of dawn. In the hospital, Colomba looked in on Dante behind the plate-glass window, and then stretched out on the single bed for guests, outside the sterile zone, and fell asleep without even taking off her combat boots.

Santini, on the other hand, continued to Rome, dreaming of shirtless barefoot fight scenes.

10

Colomba didn't leave the hospital again. Alberti, newly appointed head of security for the duration of the hospital stay of "Signor Caselli," brought her changes of clothing from her house, but she never strayed farther than a couple of yards from Dante's bedside.

They transferred him out of the intensive care unit and into a single room in the ward, and Colomba paced back and forth in his room like a zombie, while her awareness that he was actually lying there, before her—*alive*—little by little washed away the clotted mass of pain and sorrow, only to replace it with the fear that Dante might die before her eyes now, just when he seemed to have been rescued, or that he might be crippled for life or suffer permanent brain damage. She was also afraid that Leo might come back to tear him away from her yet again.

To be safe, Dante's rescue wasn't made public and Di Marco's men scoured the area between Portico and Rimini on the invented excuse of a new terrorism alert, which led to the expulsion from the country of a couple of Pakistani migrant laborers and a Moroccan dishwasher, if nothing else to justify the outlay on overtime. Lupo was persuaded by his commanding officers to stop busting Colomba's balls, which only reinforced Bruno's suspicions about the cover-up being orchestrated by the intelligence services. He was also relieved of his investigation into the Melas double homicide; it was handed over to the high command, which did no more than to demand custody of all the documentation and then studiously ignore his calls and emails. They told him nothing about Dante, of course. Just as Vigevani kept him in the dark, deciding to go on vacation and blocking Lupo's number on his cell phone.

Bart, on the other hand, was alerted to the news by D'Amore, at six in the morning on the third day after Dante's rescue. She woke up to the sound of the dogs howling in the courtyard below and the *flap flap flap* of helicopter blades overhead.

"Again? What a pain in the ass . . ." she muttered. She threw a down coat on over her pajamas and then ran outside to get the dogs, who were leaping in the air in their fright, scratching furiously on the neighbor's doors.

Her neighbor across the landing, a bearded photographer covered with tattoos, opened his door wearing nothing but a pair of boxer shorts. "Would you tell them from me to just go fuck themselves?" he snarled.

"Sorry, it's not my fault."

Bart went out the front gate and ran to the weed-ridden field behind the building, where the helicopter was just setting down. A soldier in full camo uniform and a handsome suntanned man in civilian attire both jumped out the hatch and to the ground.

"Are you seriously trying to get me declared persona non grata in my neighborhood?" she shouted. "What have you got against using the telephone?"

"Forgive the earliness of the hour, Deputy Captain!" shouted the good-looking man in civilian clothes, trying to make himself heard over the roar of the rotors, which were churning around at minimum RPMs. He extended his hand: "Pleased to meet you. D'Amore. AISI. Internal Information and Security."

"Roberta Bartone. What's happened? Another terror attack?"

D'Amore smiled. "For once, it's good news."

As soon as Bart found out what it was all about, she ran inside to get changed, called the dogsitter, and called her assistant to tell him to make other plans.

11

When Colomba awakened, Bart was sitting in the chair next to Dante's bed, holding his hand.

"Hey."

Bart turned around, her eyes glistening. "You're my favorite cop in the world, you know that, right?"

"Ex-cop." Colomba got up and hugged her. "It's a miracle."

"You performed the miracle, sweetheart."

Colomba looked anxiously into Dante's face. Did he look healthier? Was his complexion a little rosier? "How is he?" she asked her friend.

"I looked at his chart and talked to the chief physician. I'd say he's progressing nicely. The infection is subsiding and his blood pressure has been rising."

"Then why don't they bring him out of the coma?"

"Give him time, he's still very fragile. Take a shower, I'll go get something for breakfast."

Bart came back with a tray of assorted sandwiches, and found Colomba reading him a novel, dressed in a kimono-style bathrobe. "Where did you find that?"

Colomba dog-eared her page in the book and grabbed three small salami sandwiches. "Someone gave it to me when I was sixteen. It's been in storage in Mezzanotte all these years."

Bart smiled. "I'll bet you were a lot of fun when you were a girl. Hurry up and eat, because I want to hear your version of events."

Colomba took a swig directly from the water bottle on Dante's nightstand. "Alberti!" she shouted.

He hurried into the room. "Yes, Deputy Captain?"

"Stay here with Dante until I get back," said Colomba. "We're going to take a walk in the garden."

They went downstairs to the hospital grounds, a park filled with oaks and weeping willows, and strolled past patients in hospital gowns with jackets over their shoulders, pushing IV stands. "Do you really think that the Father has some connection with Tommy?" Bart asked after Colomba was done summarizing what had happened.

"The Father or someone in his place."

"Do you mean Leo?"

"Dante has always been positive that Leo and the Father knew each other. Leo started stalking Dante immediately after the Father's death. And if he knows who Dante really is, that might be true."

"Another psychopath."

"Dante was convinced that the Father was testing a cure for autism on children, on behalf of Big Pharma."

"A drug that could cure all the syndromes afflicting those who are on the spectrum would destroy the patient's personality."

"But it would be worth a lot of money, right?" Colomba asked.

"Heck, yes." They moved toward the perimeter wall, where Bart bummed a cigarette off a doctor. "Why didn't you tell the intelligence agencies about your suspicions? They could investigate in that direction."

"I don't trust Di Marco, I never know what his real agenda is. The only thing that I'm forced to recognize is that he's a patriot. If there were anything dirty about him, the people he's climbed over to become the chief of counterterrorism would certainly have ratted him out by now." Colomba threw a pebble, trying to hit the side of a metal trash can. She missed it. "And anyway, they've already dug into Tommy's past and they didn't find a thing. Has anything occurred to you?"

Bart shook her head. "No. I've gone over every square inch of the only two prisons we know anything about, the shipping containers and the camper parking area where you killed the Father. I didn't find anything that suggested other prisoners had been processed or that there were other torture sites. And by now, I have to say, they'd all be dead anyway."

"Unless Leo took care of them," said Colomba. She tried with another, slightly bigger rock, and this time she hit the rim of the trash can with a deeply satisfying *tonnng*. "I just hope that Dante wakes up soon. In this incredible mess, I really need his twisted brain."

12

Luckily, Dante's brain hadn't suffered any physical damage in spite of the long period under anesthesia. Once he got over the first onset of meningoencephalitis, a week after his arrival in the hospital, the doctors ordered the removal of the breathing tube that connected him to the ventilator and started reducing the level of sedatives being administered. Dante thus found himself swimming through an extremely boring version of heaven, without fluffy clouds or colors. It took forever before the unbroken fields of white started filling up with silhouettes that fluttered in silence. In time, the shapes started to acquire depth and sound. They turned into shadows that danced around him in an endless succession of grumblings and squeaks and buzzes. They were words, but Dante couldn't understand them: he'd lost all knowledge of language, along with all physical sensations. He didn't even know that his eyes were open.

That is why, on the tenth day, it was in fact his first physical sensation—thirst—that brought with it the first fully meaningful word.

Water.

The word pulsated, floating overhead. Dante felt icy drops falling on him, little tiny pinpricks.

Rain.

He could taste their flavor in his mouth, as metallic as

Blood.

It almost felt as if his head were filling up, swelling up like a bag of concepts and stimuli that once again made him feel like a

Human being.

Seen from outside, his eyelids were only quivering faintly, but inside, he was turning

Somersaults
of sheer
Joy.

And now the silhouettes were slowing down; he could make out details. A green flash that gave him something like an

Electric shock.

That silhouette in fact became his point of reference. It appeared on the far side of the unscalable mountain formed by the

Bedsheets.

The other silhouettes approached and churned away, but the one with the green flashes was always there. Time slowed down further, as if the words that filled his head were serving as a counterweight. The landscape became definable, the world took on warmth and color.

Odor.

The odor set his brain on fire. Every molecule brought with it sensations and memories of what had been. The silhouette became three-dimensional. It was a woman sitting in an old armchair with a book that was crumbling in her hands. She wore a sweater made of undyed wool and a pair of jeans; her bare feet were perched up on the bed.

When the woman looked up, training her green eyes upon him, Dante remembered her name.

13

A ir," Dante uttered soundlessly, forming the word with his lips.
Colomba leaped to her feet, rang the bell to summon the nurse, unlocked the wheels on his bed, and pushed him out of the room and quickly down the hall to the emergency exit. Dante's eyes were darting around furiously, his gaze filled with terror.

When Colomba pushed down on the panic bar, the door alarm went off instantly, summoning Alberti and two other officers, who came galloping down the hall, sidearms drawn. Colomba ignored them and went on running, pushing the bed out onto the balcony.

The fresh air seemed to have miraculous properties. Dante calmed down, trained his eyes on Colomba, and his lips formed a pair of syllables. When Colomba finally figured out that Dante was silently uttering "CC"—the nickname that she had learned to accept—tears came to her eyes and she leaned over to hug him, taking great care not to crush him. He was weirdly light, as if his bones were hollow.

After a couple more weeks of physical therapy and treatment, Dante was able to be moved, and the powers that be in the intelligence agencies' protective services started lobbying for him to be transferred to a military hospital. Colomba resolutely opposed that approach and instead convinced them to move Dante to the Portico hospital, where rumors about a certain Signor Caselli rescued from an abandoned clinic hadn't circulated as they had in Rimini. The hospital, small though it might be, was a perfectly adequate facility and it bordered a thoroughly untended garden, concealed from the public street by a high enclosure wall. In the overgrown, weed-filled garden, they set up a Red Cross field hospital, which became Dante's new residence; another adjoining tent served as the operations base for the security detail. It was unlikely that anyone could even see in, but just to prevent loose talk, they set up a series of other tents in the garden and put up a sign announcing the coming opening of a camping supplies outlet. This also theoretically served as an explanation for the security detail, who dressed in night watchman uniforms.

At Dante's request, Colomba opened her pocketknife and made a cut in the canvas and then pushed the head of his bed outside. It was still cold out, in spite of the electric radiators that an army engineer had set up, hooking them up to overhead high-tension wires, but Dante spent nearly all of his time with his face poking out of the tent. And with all the time that he spent looking up at the sky, little by little he managed to learn to focus and understand where he was. His mind was like a broken kaleidoscope. In the days that followed his transfer to the new hospital, it sometimes worked, but other times it just made the noise of shards grinding: in those cases, Dante blathered a mixture of tenses and languages. He recognized a few faces, he took fright if sounds were too loud, and he struggled to detect parts of his own body. He wept frequently, especially at night. More than once, Colomba got up to rock him to sleep, the way you do with little kids. "It's all right," she'd tell him. "You're safe now."

At the end of the third week since his awakening, Dante was capable of stringing together some simple phrases as well as swallowing semisolid food, with Colomba spoon-feeding him and taking care not to let him choke.

Every time he opened his eyes, he knew he'd find her beside him. Sitting outside if the weather was nice, or else inside, at the foot of his bed, with some old book or other in her hand. She was his guide in his return to the world, for the moments when he couldn't remember ordinary everyday acts. Dante often looked on in wonder or fear at objects in common use. He would drift into a state of rapt bewilderment at the sight of a button or a spoon. He'd have fits of rage, crying jags, and panic attacks, and when he overcame them, he was mortified and filled with shame. In much the same way, he was ashamed of his stilted command of the Italian language, of the way his body had turned weak and flaccid, of his momentary intervals of absentmindedness.

Colomba never ran out of patience, not even when he threw tantrums like a child. She'd read to him from an Italian edition of *A Farewell to Arms* so old that the price was in lire (350 lire, to be exact), or else she'd read reviews of the films he'd missed, or the latest news. At his request, she hung a sign on the tent that read *Crystal Lake* (which Colomba suspected was an obscure reference to some film or other), she told him about the Marche region and her family, and a little at a time—very cautiously—the things that had happened during his time away: Tommy, the Melas murder, Dr. Pala, Lupo, Romero, and all the rest of the chain of clues that had led her to him.

One night Dante screamed as if someone were trying to slit his throat. Colomba, who was sleeping in the other bed that had been set up in the tent, separated from Dante's by a small partition, ran around to see what was wrong, sidearm drawn and ready. "What's wrong?"

"Leo . . . I saw him," Dante said, his voice hoarse from the tracheotomy.

Colomba looked around, wildly swinging the pistol that had only recently been given back to her. "Where?"

Dante twisted his lips in the effort. "The Music Box." He coughed.

"I don't understand," Colomba said gently. "Try again."

"Opening. Cold. What a long trip!" Dante was on the verge of tears. "Shit. Fuck." He concentrated, trying to pin down the wriggling eel that his brain had become. "The Box."

"The Box? The prison that Giltine was in?"

"Wunderbar!" Dante said happily. "Wonderbra!"

Mixing languages and references that came from who knew where, Dante managed to tell Colomba the broad outlines of his awakening in Chernobyl and the meeting with Leo that had resurfaced in his mind. She told him that it had been nothing but a dream, and in order to convince him of the fact, she let him scroll through satellite pictures of the Ukraine and Chernobyl. "You see? There's nothing there. The Box was dismantled after the meltdown of the nuclear power plant. You told me so yourself."

At first, Dante didn't believe her. It all seemed too real to him, more real than the tent that had become his new home. But as his grip on reality grew stronger and more stable, he soon realized that Colomba had to be right: he'd dreamed it all, and the year and a half that he'd lost he'd spent fast asleep. No heroic escape, no radiation eating away at him, no act of courage, no confrontation with the man who claimed to be his brother. All the same, Dante was convinced that that dream must have a meaning. Or at least he hoped so, in order to find something positive in all that misfortune.

Looking up at the moon in the sky that was losing its wintry gray hue, with his body in the tent and his head out in the chilly garden air, Dante wondered if even this was a hallucination. Maybe he was still back in Venice, frozen in the moment when he'd recognized Leo for the man who'd been spying on him for years. Maybe they really had shut him up in a crate and he'd lost his mind, and Colomba was still looking for him, because there never had been any Tommy to show her the way. Or else there never had been any crate, any massacre, any Leo.

Maybe he was still locked up in the silo, still the Father's prisoner, imagining a life that he would never have.

CHAPTER II

Colomba, wearing a too-heavy woolen cap and a pair of sunglasses, climbed the front steps of the cathedral of Portico, now crowded like a soccer stadium on game day. There were officials and authorities from all over the province and police officers in dress uniform come to commemorate the death of the Melases, the only double homicide in the surrounding area since the Stone Age. The magistrate had authorized the funeral, seeing that all possible and imaginable tests had been performed on the bodies of the victims, including the DNA. Even though she'd been away from Portico for a month, and she'd never spent much time there in the first place, Colomba kept her eyes downcast to avoid meeting the gaze of anyone who might recognize her.

Right before the funeral began, it started to rain. Dozens of multicolored umbrellas opened on the piazza and Colomba found herself shoved into the human riptide, able to stop only when she came even with the coffins in the nave. The heaps of flowers piled atop them weren't enough to conceal their shoddy construction: Demetra must have chosen the cheapest ones available in the catalog.

In any case, there she was, in the front row, with ten strings of pearls around her neck and a face that looked more angry than it did sad. The investigation into the murder of her brother and sister-in-law was far from complete, and that meant she was obliged to remain in Italy. Her passport had been suspended and she had been questioned by magistrates and Carabinieri, forced to reveal every wrinkle and detail of her life.

Next to Demetra clustered the city authorities, including Lupo and four of his men in dress uniform, plus the legless guy on crutches who answered the phone at the police station.

Colomba slipped behind a column and continued studying all the attendees. In the crowd she recognized the medical examiner and the nerd from the cell phone shop who had for once renounced wearing his T-shirt with the slogan in Klingon, and even the Korean barista from Montenigro. Pala was there, too, dressed of course in black from head to foot, standing off to one side admiring a fresco while waiting for the service to begin, with Caterina at his side, speaking intensely with him in a low voice. Colomba continued observing those present, in search of someone who might seem out of place. She hoped that Leo might appear around there, wearing a fake mustache to laugh at his victims. She knew that her hope was practically impossible, but if she'd stayed home she'd have been tormented by doubts nonetheless.

The priest began the commemoration. Colomba crossed herself and recited the Our Father, and then turned in search of the exit. That's exactly when Tommy entered the church.

Accompanying him was a brusque gray-haired woman, perhaps a social worker from the group home where Tommy had been transferred. He seemed relaxed and even more mastodontic, bundled in a navy-blue wool turtleneck sweater and a pair of dark brown elephant cord trousers that seemed ready to burst around the thighs. He looked around, jerking his head from side to side like a small bird, dry-washing his hands and uttering at every step a repetitive series of noises that covered up the priest's voice. Every head in the church turned toward him as if in a wave at the soccer stadium, and the officiant stopped speaking. Feeling far too visible, Colomba quickened her pace toward the front doors, but with the crowd packing the house of worship, it wasn't easy. Tommy noticed her and emitted a piercing shout so high-pitched that it shook the stained-glass windows. He rushed toward her, knocking over his attendant, with an enormous smile that left his top teeth uncovered.

"Calm down, Tommy," Colomba said gently. "Don't knock me down."

Tommy took her by the hand, forcing her into a sort of unruly ballet among the crowd. In the distance, Colomba glimpsed Lupo and his men turning to look at her. When he recognized her, Lupo turned red as a beet.

"Tommy, I have to go," she said, delicately freeing herself from his grip. She wanted to keep Lupo from getting *his* hands on her.

Tommy frantically twisted his head around, right and left, in the throes of agitation. Colomba stroked his hair. "I'll come see you soon. That's a promise," she said, and left him in the care of his attendant, heading out into the driving rain. Behind her, the bass notes of the cathedral's pipe organ started up, and as if they'd summoned him, D'Amore appeared in the middle of the piazza, with a large rainbow umbrella.

"Of course, you're here, too," Colomba said.

He smiled. "Discreetly, as is our nature. Seeing that it's almost lunch-time, what you say we eat something together?"

"They're serving meat loaf at the cafeteria today. I can't miss that."

"Come on. I've left you alone in the past few days, but you can't expect me to forget about you. My treat." D'Amore raised his umbrella. "Come on under."

Colomba remained a step away from him. "I'd rather drown. Lead the way."

They lunched in a trattoria that everyone in Portico called Dal Fascista, because of the oversize mural of Mussolini painted during the Fascist regime and passed off as a historical piece of art. The elderly waitress served them two bowls of wild boar stew and a basket of grilled crescia flatbreads, and in the din of conversations at the adjoining tables, they felt perfectly safe carrying on their own discussion. "Demetra Melas has asked for legal custody of Tommy. We're doing our best to put obstacles in her way, but if no other relatives step forward, in the end she'll probably get what she wants."

Colomba looked up from her bowl in astonishment. "I didn't think you cared."

"She has her good reasons. Twenty-five million good reasons," said D'Amore.

"Excuse me?"

"Her brother was filthy rich. He even owned Villa Quiete. He became a majority partner in the company that owns it, through an equity fund. Before dying, Melas put everything in Tommy's name. He doesn't even have to inherit it. It's already his."

"He's still officially listed as a person of interest for the double homicide," said Colomba. "Why haven't you cleared him?"

"Because there's no proof that it was Bonaccorso who made him an orphan. The attorney general is very sympathetic to our investigation, but he's not willing to clear Tommy based strictly on an abstract line of thought. We haven't found any connection between Bonaccorso and the members of the Melas family, much less any traces of his passage through Italy."

"Aside from the bombing in Milan."

"The only person who's seen him is covered with burns on seventy percent of her body. Even if he'd left something useful in Romero's apartment building, it's gone up in smoke."

"I didn't imagine that the investigation was still so completely at sea," Colomba murmured. She took a piece of flatbread and devoured it.

"If you have any suggestions, you're more than welcome to volunteer them."

Colomba swallowed, helping the food down with a swig of wine. "If anything occurs to me, I'll be sure to let you know."

D'Amore smiled. "How long are you going to go on sulking? You have a score to settle with Bonaccorso and we need a hand. Even if only to figure out what the fuck he had in mind when he moved to this part of the world."

Colomba toyed with her sauce. "By now, he's probably on the far side of the world."

"That's what we thought at first, too, but we were wrong." D'Amore forked the last piece of wild boar into his mouth. "We're willing to support you, whatever aspect of the investigation you choose to undertake, and we'll give full and free rein, all the independence you need. You can even use the surviving members of your team. And we'll pay you, too."

"Very generous on your part."

D'Amore gave her a smile that dripped red with sauce. "You're right. I doubt you've ever gotten a better offer."

During the trip back to the "field hospital," Colomba seriously considered the offer. She knew that working all alone she'd never be able to lay her hands on Leo, and the thought of him had started to obsess her again, now that Dante no longer required continuous attendance. He was able to speak clearly now, and he could stand on his own two feet and even walk, though he needed a walker to do so, and he especially hated that because it looked just like the one used by the old child molester, Herbert the Pervert, on *Family Guy*. His voice was very hoarse, and now and then he'd still lose the thread in a conversation, but his medical progress was considered, if not miraculous, at the very least, exceptional. It was hard, though, for the doctors to have any terms of comparison, since there's not a lot of documentation on the prolonged sedation of healthy patients.

"After the third coma, it becomes easier," he'd told her one evening at dinner under the translucent cloth of the tent. Dante had eliminated all animal-based nutrients from his diet. In spite of the fact that the doctors turned up their noses at it, he supplemented his soups and purées with vegan smoothies befitting a body builder.

That evening, Colomba, by contrast, had ordered a depressing chicken breast with salad. She was putting on weight and building up her muscles, and that was all to the good, but she didn't want to get a potbelly. "Three? You're pulling my leg."

"Narcotics overdose. I called it simple experimentation, but the doctors begged to differ."

"It's bullshit, but I'm going to pretend to believe you because you're still half out of it." Colomba had handed him the wishbone, after gnawing all the meat off it. "Pull."

Dante had pulled and had gotten the long part. "I win."

"What did you wish for?" Colomba asked.

"To be able to get back what I've lost without having to exert any effort. But I don't think it worked."

After his thirteen years of complete isolation while being held prisoner by the Father, Dante had set out to collect hundreds of cartons filled to the brim with pop culture from the years that had been stolen from him. Clothing, videocassettes of television programs that not even the actors remembered anymore, deodorants no longer in production, vinyl albums still unplayed, surprise toys from Kinder eggs, soccer player trading cards, toys that had lasted only a single brief summer such as Clackers balls, as well as fashion catalogs and interior decorating magazines. And now he had another eighteen months to get back, in a world much more complex than the world of the eighties, made up of snatches of nothing that went viral on social media before being filed away and forgotten.

Every time he failed to grasp a wisecrack or an allusion tossed off by the nurses or the guards was a knife to his heart. It took him back to the awkward adolescent who had escaped from the silo, clueless about how to use a bathroom or knife and fork, shoes or a telephone. If he'd survived that dark period, he owed it to the only advantage that the silo had conferred upon him: his spirit of observation. In order to understand the aliens that surrounded him, he'd codified and memorized thousands of their gestures, sounds, smells, and facial expressions, as if he were studying a complex foreign language. Before age twenty, he'd become capable of reading human beings like so many open books. And he'd made the discovery that had changed his life: Everybody lies. Out of self-interest or fear, to cheer someone up or to win their charms or favors, out of stupidity or viciousness, they all lie and frequently believe their own lies.

This is something that Colomba knew, and she also knew that their relationship worked because she had always been brutally frank with him. At least, until he'd awakened from his coma, and she had decided to spare him the details of everything that had happened while he was away.

When she entered the tent and saw a brand-new television set at the foot of the bed, though, Colomba realized that the secret was no longer a secret.

Dante looked up from the television set, and Colomba couldn't meet his glance.

"Hey," she said, looking down at her feet. "When did that get here?"

Dante turned it off with the remote. "This morning, while you were out. Did you know that Netflix made a documentary about Venice?"

"Yes."

"What the fuck happened, CC? What the hell did they do?"

"They covered it all up. Or, actually, *we* did. I went along with it, and it's partly my fault."

"I don't believe that." Dante was so upset that he'd started cutting short his words like he'd done right after his awakening. "You'd never do anything of the sort."

"But that's what really happened. Do you want to know the whole story, or should I just go hang myself?"

Dante shut his eyes. "Oh, Jesus. Tell the story. From the beginning, please."

Colomba sat down by his bed and took off her combat boots. "After Leo stabbed me and kidnapped you from the Palasport della Misericordia, I passed out. I came to at the Venice hospital three days later. I'd lost plenty of blood and I was pretty much out of it." And every time the morphine started losing its effects, it felt like a hand grenade had blown up in her belly. "So out of it that I didn't notice that no one was coming to see me, except for Santini. He listened to my ravings, he told me what was going on outside without any of it sticking in my mind. Only after a week did I figure out that no one knew yet that I had even been there, in the Palasport della Misericordia. I had been registered under a false name, and they hadn't even informed my mother."

"They'd quarantined you," Dante murmured.

"It was Santini's job to coach me, before I came into contact with civilians or investigators. The cover version was that you and I had been on holiday in Venice, and that we'd fetched up by chance at the Palasport della Misericordia." Her former commanding officer's voice still echoed in her ears. *There were forty-nine deaths! Forty-nine. And you knew that it was going to happen.* "Santini told me that if I told the truth, I'd be charged with failure to prevent a massacre, obstruction of justice, and criminal conspiracy to commit mass murder."

"But you tried to warn them . . ." said Dante.

"They arranged to get rid of all the reports where I explained that I suspected Giltine's existence. Santini knew that he was an accomplice to a criminal act, but he also told me that he'd had no choice in the matter." That day he'd been wrecked and half in the bag. "Because if my version was accepted, he, his boss, and everyone who had refused to listen to me would wind up in deep shit, right alongside me."

"I'd have tried anyway," Dante said angrily. "God, I would have loved to see them *drown* in shit."

"I would gladly have run the risk of going to jail, but I wouldn't have risked your life. There would have been indictments, counterindictments, commissions of inquiry, and scandals, and any time a magistrate tried to open up the investigation again, he would have found himself facing the hostile ranks of everyone I'd gotten into trouble."

Dante lowered the head of the bed, and then raised it again, punching the button furiously. "In the documentary, they say that you were given a medal."

"I never went to pick it up." Colomba pulled the blanket over her feet; it was cold out. "When they transferred me to the hospital in Rome, the real circus began. The journalists snuck in everywhere to try to get a firsthand account. Then there were all of your fans who wanted me to confess that I'd murdered you. That was a rumor that started to circulate, too."

"I know. *The Truth about Dante Torre.* I'm almost proud of it."

"One guy disguised himself as a nurse to get into the hospital to force a confession out of me, but luckily they caught him at the entrance." The man had borrowed a smock from a friend of his who was a baker, covered with flour, to serve as his lab coat, and carried a knife. "The people I felt worst about, though, were my fellow cops."

"Why?"

"Because they just weren't finding you. I had become an oathbreaker, and no one knew where I was. I was rude to everyone. And even before I finished the initial period of convalescence, the psychophysical evaluation arrived saying that I was no longer fit for active duty. The best I could have hoped for would be to be put in charge of the passport office, or something like that. Anyway, I had no interest in staying on the force. Not after what I'd done. I turned in my resignation and left."

The first time, she'd managed to drive exactly three miles before fetching up against a Jersey barrier and totaling her car. The anti-anxiety drugs made her dopey, and her reaction times were flattened. The second time she'd taken the train and established residence in the old family house. And there she had remained.

"There was nothing I could do to find you. And there was nothing new about you. Ever," said Colomba. "There were plenty of times when I thought I should have just told the truth and hoped for someone better than Di Marco or the magistrates who'd taken over the investigation to come along. I continue to think it. Maybe someone else would have found you faster."

Dante rolled from one side to the other, like a caterpillar in agony. "No. Get that idea out of your head," he said. "You did what you could."

"No, I got it all wrong." Colomba sniffed. "I couldn't stop Giltine. I ran the risk of getting you killed. I told lie after lie. And all for nothing. They just let you rot." Colomba sniffed loudly again.

"But that wasn't your fault, CC. I'm furious at that crowd of spies and politicians who rewrite history as they please. And who blackmail decent people." He shook his head. "Nothing new about that, it's never been any different. Luckily, once I get out of here, I'll never have to deal with any of them again."

Colomba sighed. "Speaking of which . . . There's another thing you need to know."

5

Colomba told Dante about her meeting with D'Amore. "He asked me if I wanted to work with the counterterrorism division."

"And you told him to go to hell, I trust?" Dante scrutinized her face.

"No, I didn't."

He pulled a pack of cigarettes out from under the covers and lit one.

Colomba lunged at him. "Have you lost your mind?" she screamed. She tried to grab the cigarette out of his hand, but Dante made it disappear between his fingers like a magician practicing sleight of hand, only to pull it out of his ear a second later. He pretended it came as easily to him as it had in the old days, but to judge from the grimace on his face, the cigarette might as well have been made of lead.

"CC, I'm an adult, registered to vote and legally responsible," he said, taking a puff in the style of Humphrey Bogart.

"And you're convalescent." Colomba tossed cigarette and pack into the courtyard. "You can be as angry as you like, but it's not a good reason to commit suicide. In any case, if I did accept, I wouldn't really be working for them, I'd just pretend, and then we could use the things that they know. The information would travel in only one direction."

"Why would you want to do such a thing?"

"To find Leo. Don't you think that's a good enough reason?"

"Definitely not."

"There was a time when Leo was an obsession for you. You'd have given I don't know what to lay your hands on him," Colomba said in her astonishment.

"Then he laid *his* hands on *me* and I got over my obsession."

"I have a duty to find Leo, too."

"You're a victim just like I am, CC. And a victim's only duty is to try to feel better." A shadow passed over Colomba's face, and she looked away. But Dante noticed that, and in his head another piece of the puzzle fell back into place: him on the train to Venice, watching Leo and Colomba leave the compartment together, with the same glint in their eyes. "You fucked him."

Colomba chewed a fingernail. "I knew it was too much to hope you hadn't noticed. Anyway, it's none of your business who I go to bed with."

Dante raised his voice and coughed until he couldn't speak. "He kidnapped me! And he's my brother! If he'd gotten you pregnant, now I'd be your child's uncle!"

"Stop talking bullshit. And Leo's DNA shows no connection with yours."

"Where'd they get the sample, from the crotch of your panties?"

Colomba threw a combat boot at him, and missed him by a whisker. "Asshole! They did the test on a hair, but I'll say it again, it's none of your fucking business. I feel guilty toward myself for having fallen for it, not toward you."

The late-afternoon light hit the side of Colomba's face. Dante had a familiar stab in his stomach. *My God, she's pretty*, he thought. And he realized that he felt something deep inside he'd never experienced before: jealousy. It was a feeling he despised, and his tone of voice turned even harsher. "Okay," he said without looking at her. "Sorry. It's been a bad day. But you can go ahead and tell D'Amore that I won't work for him."

"It's me he wants," Colomba replied in an icy tone.

"Don't fool yourself. They're using you to try to get me to change my mind. That's the way Di Marco manipulates people."

"I'm not so easy to manipulate."

"Did you tell Leo that when you were locked in the bathroom on the train together?" Dante asked, and he regretted it as soon as he said it.

"Fuck yourself." Colomba hopped over to get the combat boot and left.

6

Colomba leaped into her car with a welter of rage, shame, and disappointment in her stomach. How the fuck could Dante be so ungrateful, such a complete oaf . . .

When she felt as bad as this, Colomba usually went for a run, but that morning she'd already taken one around the hospital and she wasn't sufficiently back in shape to go for another one. So she headed toward Conigliano, a small town not far away that had a shooting range in a large industrial shed in the countryside. She'd planned to go see the place one of these days. The owner sold her two boxes of fifty bullets each and took her out to the firing line. There were twenty ranges, most of them occupied by shooters of every sort, ranging from a bodybuilder covered with neo-Nazi tattoos to an old man who cleaned his glasses after every shot.

The proprietor gave her a pair of shooting earmuffs. "From the way you handle your weapon, I can see that you know what you're doing, but the law requires me to give you the basic safety instructions, since this is your first time here."

Colomba nodded her head. The man showed her how to load and unload her gun, and how to move on the range. He fired three shots in rapid succession at the silhouette of a man with hat and pistol, at twenty yards, and got a pretty good score in spite of the way he squinted behind the thick lenses of his eyeglasses. Then he handed her the weapon. "It's all yours."

Colomba reloaded. The instructor noticed how she moved her fingers. "Army?"

"Police. Retired."

"Many of your fellow cops don't even know which way to point the barrel."

"Many of my fellow cops never needed to know, which is just lucky for them."

Colomba emptied the first magazine with slow, careful shots. She was an average marksman, and her lack of exercise wasn't helping any. She hit the lower belly of the target instead of the chest, then she raised the gun slightly and hit heart, throat, and face. The instructor nodded. "I'd say you can take it from here. Enjoy yourself."

Colomba emptied eight magazines and reduced ten silhouettes to tatters, then she bought another hundred bullets and shot those off, too, this time in rapid fire. When she was done, her wrist and shoulders ached, but she felt much more relaxed. She cleaned her sidearm and then went to say goodbye to the proprietor.

"I noticed that you're not using a holster," he said. "If yours is worn out, I have a couple at an affordable price."

"I'm just used to doing it this way," said Colomba, slipping the pistol into her jacket pocket: the lining was full of holes and soaked in gun oil.

The proprietor raised his goggles. "Signorina, if I were twenty years younger, you'd be my dream woman."

"Thanks. That's the nicest thing anybody's said to me in quite a long time," she replied.

She walked out into the deserted parking lot, her ears still buzzing from the gunshots. In spite of an orange streetlamp, it was much darker than when she had parked, but Colomba was too relaxed and charged with endorphins to worry about that.

Then she felt a breath on the back of her neck.

7

Colomba tried to draw her sidearm, but she wasn't fast enough. She felt someone grab her by the hair and shove her violently against the window of the Panda. Her nose crunched, her lungs contracted. She screamed with her lips smeared against the glass, but no sound came out.

Leo.

Another shove, this time slamming her down on the car's hood. Sounds turned soft and echoey, her mouth filled up with the taste of blood. In that frozen moment she relived all the times that she'd imagined him in a flickering shadow, in a soft creak. The gloved hands clenched down hard around her neck and darkness grew denser and thicker.

All right, okay, she thought, and in some strange fashion she felt strangely lightened. *At least now it will be over.*

Then she caught a whiff of the stench of the man who was strangling her. It was an acid odor, reeking of filth and sweat. Colomba remembered Leo's odor, the taste of his mouth, the shape of his body.

This wasn't Leo.

This wasn't Leo.

Her rage pumped her up with strength. Colomba slammed her foot backward and behind her felt an ankle collapsing beneath the sole of her combat boot. The compression of the hands around her throat subsided, and her lungs opened to the outside air. She managed to get turned three-quarters of the way around. Her assailant was a skinny man with a ski mask and the jumpsuit of a blue-collar worker.

This isn't Leo, she told herself for the third time.

Colomba tried to yank her pistol out of her pocket: the man knocked her over with his full body weight and she slammed onto the pavement; her pistol slid far away.

She felt one of her incisors chip against the dirty cement, she tasted burnt oil and diesel fuel. She twisted her face and snapped her teeth shut, blindly, biting deep into the muscles of a thigh. The man howled in pain, and Colomba heard a familiar note in that voice, though she couldn't quite place it because the ski mask camouflaged the sound. She rolled away, without even trying to get to her feet, and slid under the Panda. She lay there, flat on her back, monitoring the moves of the man, pulling her switchblade knife out of her left boot. She opened it slowly, silently, hoping that her assailant would bend down so she could slide the blade into him. Instead she saw the tennis shoes running away, and an instant later she heard the sound of something metallic scraping across the cement of the parking lot.

My gun! Colomba thought as she dragged herself toward the front wheels. The man with the ski mask knelt down and fanned the gun as he fired, sending the bullets in a spreading array underneath the car. One bullet ricocheted off the chassis's underframe, hitting the cement on a trajectory perpendicular to her face. Colomba yanked herself out from under the car with all the strength in both hands and started running when she was still down on all fours. The man with the ski mask fired again, and the bullets went astray, spewing sparks in the darkness. The side window of one car shattered into smithereens, and the siren of the alarm went off.

Zigzagging at a dead run, Colomba crossed the parking lot back the way she'd come, taking shelter behind the corner of the industrial shed that housed the shooting range. She flattened herself against the wall, clutching the knife with both hands, spitting out blood and saliva. No sign of the man with the ski mask. Colomba cautiously looked behind her: the parking lot was deserted and darkness had enveloped the surrounding fields.

All of the customers who had been in the shooting range were now arrayed outside the front door, alerted by the shouting. Colomba announced that she'd been attacked, and that she would personally file a criminal complaint. "Do you have security tapes of the parking lot?"

"The only security cameras are inside and at the front door. I'm sorry," the proprietor replied.

Of course, thought Colomba. "In that case, a list of your members."

"Signorina . . . there are regulations concerning privacy . . ."

Colomba rubbed the blood from her nose and then wiped her hand off on the proprietor's shirt. "If you don't get moving, I'll take this place apart, piece by piece."

The proprietor got moving.

8

It was ten o'clock by the time Colomba arrived back at the hospital, covered with blood and oil. Alberti, who just then was chatting with a male nurse outside the front entrance, took off toward her at a run the minute he saw her. "Deputy Captain? What on earth happened to you?"

"Mind your own fucking business," she retorted. "And it'll be your ass if you buy cigarettes for Dante again."

The tent was glowing faintly in the darkness. Colomba went in through the ambulance entrance and shoved the mosquito netting aside. Dante was sitting on the bed, smoking a cigarette while he watched TV.

"They made a special just about me," he said, quickly tucking the new pack away under the bedsheets. Then he got a look at her. "Oh, fuck. Who was it?" he murmured.

"It's not as bad as it looks."

"I hope not, because it really looks awful," said Dante. "Let me call the doctor."

"No. I want to find the asshole who attacked me." She sat down stiffly on the edge of the bed. "Take a look and tell me if you see anything."

"Blood," Dante replied, on the verge of panic.

"Look again. You're my only alternative to the Forensic Squad, seeing that I can't alert the cops."

"And why can't you alert them?" Dante asked, moving away from her dirty jacket.

"Because it might have been one of Leo's accomplices."

"So you have to find him all by yourself, you against everyone." Dante shook his head. "It would certainly help if you could tell me what happened."

"A guy attacked me in the parking lot at the Conigliano shooting range." She told him all about it, while Dante delicately removed her jacket and examined her, mostly in an effort to keep her calm.

"This doesn't seem much like Leo's MO," said Dante cautiously.

"Do you seriously believe that you know how he thinks?"

"I definitely think that it's possible to find more efficient killers than whoever attacked you in such a clumsy way." Dante sighed. "Lift your sweater, please."

Colomba did as she was told. "You might be right. It could have been that asshole Lupo . . . He couldn't take the way I made him look like a fool."

Dante directed the swing-arm side table lamp to illuminate her neck. He saw blood, dirt, and bruises. "Um."

"Um what?"

"Um, I don't know. Was he wearing gloves?"

"Yes, work gloves, no fingerprints."

Careful not to touch her, Dante pushed his face close to Colomba's neck and sniffed. He could smell blood, sweat, automotive oil, dust, and soap. And lemon. A chemical lemon smell. A smell he was familiar with. A smell that summoned up grit on the tongue. "Have you washed any dishes or used any kind of detergent or cleaning fluid in the last few hours?"

"No."

"Okay, then you can tend to your injuries. I know who it was. But I'm not going to tell you unless you go have yourself looked at in the emergency room."

"You're not bullshitting me, though, right? You really do have a solid idea?"

"There's been plenty of bullshit between the two of us already. Go get yourself looked at."

"I'll tend to my own injuries, I don't have any time to waste." She washed her face in the hospital's ground floor restroom, filling the sink with blood. Her nose was twice its normal size, but her septum wasn't broken. Her lip was split open, though, in exactly the same spot it had been cut the last time. And it burned like acid. Colomba soaked a wad of toilet paper in water and wiped off the blood, and then she twisted more toilet paper into two wads and stuffed them up her nostrils, which in the meantime had started pissing blood again. Five minutes later she was back at Dante's bedside, where he'd been waiting for her, twisting his hands anxiously.

"God, what a shitty day," Colomba said as she sat down; only then did she notice that her T-shirt was torn over her belly. "Who is it?"

"I'll tell you, but only if I can come, too," Dante said with some reluctance. "That way I can get some fresh air."

"No. You can't even stand on your own two feet and it would be a disaster if anyone recognized you. But if you want, I'm happy to sit here chatting about it while the guy makes his getaway."

Dante snorted impatiently. "You're intolerable."

"No, *you* are. Was it Lupo or Leo?"

"Would a carabiniere have come without a weapon?"

"Their sidearms are registered."

"Are you trying to tell me that you wouldn't have been able to lay your hands on a clean firearm when you were still on the force?"

"All right, then, who was it? Make it short and sweet."

"Your attacker avoided the security cameras at the shooting range. And he can't have prepared in advance by studying the location, because not even you knew that you'd be going there. So he must know the place. Most likely, he followed you from the hospital but then he just improvised."

"I got them to give me the list of the members. Do you want to read it? I did, but I don't recognize any of the names."

"He's not a member for the same reason he's not a carabiniere. He would have had a weapon, something to hold on you at least until he could have taken yours. Did you have the safety on your gun?"

"Yes."

"Did he have any difficulty turning off the safety or racking the slide when he picked it up off the ground?"

Colomba thought back. "No."

"So your assailant knows how to shoot, but he doesn't own a firearm. He doesn't even have a hunting rifle, and around here they give you shotgun shells for change at the bar."

"He has a dirty criminal record."

"Exactly. You haven't had dealings with many people in Portico, and out of them, if you count out the cops and the women, how many are left who are male and of an age to be physically fit to attack you?"

"Quite a few. And that's not counting the dozens of journalists who've been this way."

"Journalists don't use hand-washing paste. I recognized the smell of lemon on your neck. Which is what you use to cut grease."

Colomba knew exactly what that was. It was another thing that her motorcycle-nut ex-boyfriend had taught her to use, when she got home covered with black grease.

Just like, say, a mechanic.

9

Colomba got in touch with Alberti and Alberti managed to get a squad car. Once they reached the little house where Loris lived, next to the repair shop, they all agreed that there was no time to waste by this point: the door gave way after a couple of hard shoulder blows.

Loris wasn't there. But there was the stink of food gone bad, as well as a general state of disorder, tangled filthy bedsheets, hundreds of cigarette butts scattered on the floor, and the bloodstained cotton that the man had used on his cuts. The stereo speakers had been kicked in, the TV set lay on its back on the floor. There was a plate with a Conad supermarket loyalty card, dusted with white powder. Colomba cursed herself for the fool she was: How had she failed to notice that Loris was an addict?

"He must have started pretty recently," said Alberti. "Shall we take a look in the repair shop?"

"Definitely."

The burglar alarm wasn't activated and from under the metal roller gate came the light of a fluorescent lamp. Colomba and Alberti each took one side of the gate and lifted it, keeping their bodies out of the line of fire, behind the wall. Loris was sitting at his workbench. In front of him stood a bottle of whiskey and a cup, and in one hand was an old cordless phone that was practically falling apart. Alberti aimed his pistol right at him. "Police! Down on the floor with both hands behind your head. Move it!"

Loris dropped the cordless. Under his half-open overalls could be seen a dirty sleeveless undershirt and the bruises that Colomba had given him. Loris had lost weight; his face was gaunt and his eyes looked as if he hadn't slept in a century. Instead of standing up, he grabbed the cup off his workbench and held it in his hands, staring at it with great interest.

"Are you deaf?" Alberti shouted again.

"I just want to drink a toast," said Loris in a toneless voice. "In memory of Martina."

"What do you have to do with her?" Colomba asked, sincerely baffled.

"She was my woman. She was expecting a baby. My son."

Colomba felt her rage melting away, replaced by pity. "Listen, I'm sorry to hear that, but I had nothing whatsoever to do with her death. Now put both hands behind your head."

"Bottoms up." Loris lifted the cup and threw it right at her.

Instinct made Colomba duck, and the cup shattered against the wall behind her. The liquid sprayed in all directions and a few drops landed on her heavy jacket, sending up small plumes of smoke.

Colomba lunged at Loris, slamming him against the workbench with a powerful shoulder blow. He grabbed the bottle, trying to break it over her head, but Colomba grabbed his wrist with both hands and twisted it.

"Put it down or I'll shoot," shouted Alberti, moving one step closer to get a clean shot.

Loris kicked Colomba in the belly, then he lifted the bottle to his lips and took a long swig. Alberti shouted in horror. Colomba, hunkered down and breathless, rolled away as Loris collapsed to the floor, coughing and in the throes of convulsions. The bottle slipped out of his hand and shattered on the floor, spraying most of the liquid onto Loris's legs, which, like Colomba's jacket before, started to fume.

Taking great care not to touch the wet parts, Colomba and Alberti dragged Loris away from the puddle, which reeked of rotten eggs. The lower portion of the mechanic's face was swollen and purple, and his mouth had been reduced to little more than a foaming hole full of teeth, which had then fallen out as the gums dissolved. With a gasp, Loris spat out his tongue: it was black and riddled with holes like Swiss cheese, and it continued to writhe and jerk on the cement floor.

Alberti fished his cell phone out of his pocket to call an ambulance, while Colomba ran over to the hose, turned on the faucet, and aimed the freezing spray of water at Loris. The mechanic practically wasn't moving anymore, both hands clutching at his throat, which was slowly splitting open, oozing black blood. Colomba went on rinsing him off, but Loris had stopped reacting. The spray of water stripped even more flesh off his ravaged hands, and one finger floated away with the stream and down the drain. By now, Loris's face was black.

"The ambulance is on its way," said Alberti, putting his cell phone away.

Colomba put a hand on Alberti's shoulder; the man was pale as a sheet and on the verge of vomiting. "Can you take care of this on your own?" she asked him. "You can just tell them that you heard him moaning as you went past and went in to see."

Alberti nodded.

"I'll try and reach out to counterterrorism and see if I can get your name taken off the reports. Whatever happens, you have nothing to worry about."

"But what did he drink?"

"From the smell, battery acid."

"Good God."

Colomba gave him a slap on the back, and then she searched the workbench, finding her own gun, empty of bullets, and a framed picture of Martina. She was in uniform, and it had been cut out of a newspaper. Colomba decided that Loris might like to have it while they were taking him to the hospital, but by the time she turned around to give it to him, he'd already stopped breathing.

10

When Colomba walked back into the hospital tent, Dante jumped out of bed in his anxiety.

"Are you all right? How's Alberti?"

"Everyone's fine. Except for Loris. He's a goner. And it was . . ." Colomba couldn't continue. "Jesus, why does everyone around me keep dying?"

"Come here and let me give you a hug."

"No. You wanted to get outside, let me take you."

Dante threw his coat over his flannel pajamas, scattering sparks of static in the darkness. Colomba helped him into the car and took the road leading out of Portico. Distractedly, focusing mostly on driving, she told Dante what had happened, and when he heard how the mechanic had died, he turned a little green.

"I understood that they knew each other, Loris and Martina, but not that they were a couple," Colomba finished up.

"Can you pull over? I think I'm going to throw up."

Colomba stopped at a pizzeria on the provincial road with a couple of outdoor tables for smokers. Putting her arm around his waist to support him, Colomba helped him to get seated, then turned to the waiter and ordered a couple of beers. It was still cold out, but the sky was clear and the stars were shining brightly for the first time in a good solid month. Dante let the sight fill his heart. "I wonder what acid tastes like," he said.

"I don't even know why certain things pop into your head. Anyway, Martina wasn't pregnant," Colomba said. "We would have known."

"Unless the medical examiner lied to defend her postmortem reputation, Loris must have misunderstood, or else someone else tricked him into believing it."

"Loris didn't need Leo to have it in for me."

"Are you sure of that? If you ask me, he needed Leo to connect you to the murder of the lady carabiniere. How could he have known that you were a suspect? He was a drug addict and he had a criminal record; can you seriously picture Lupo telling him all about it?"

"No." Colomba ordered another beer, promising herself she'd only drink half. "One thing's for sure, Leo knows how to pluck all the right strings. He even made me believe in a phone call that he'd fucked Romero."

"And did that bother you because you thought he liked Romero better?"

Colomba's beer went down the wrong pipe, and she spat it out, coughing and breaking out laughing. She'd been physically attacked and had then watched her assailant intentionally melt his face with acid, and yet, for the first time in a very long while, she really couldn't restrain herself. "Did I ever tell you what an asshole you are?"

"Asshole is my middle name."

"You don't have a middle name. Or a first name, for that matter."

"Ouch. Cruel!" Dante chuckled. The limited alcohol content had immediately gone to his head.

"I can't force you to lend a hand, because if you're not up for it, you're just not up for it, but I have to admit that you'd definitely be a help," said Colomba. "And then . . . there's Tommy."

"Who may have spent some time in the Father's diabolical clutches."

"This would finally be proof that the Father wasn't some solitary nut job, but that he had a whole organization behind him. You've tried to prove that for years; now you could actually do it. And you'd be helping a kid."

Dante stole her bottle. "One of *us*," he said, and took a gulp.

He handed the beer back to Colomba, who polished it off. "One of *us*," she repeated. Everyone who'd brushed up against the Father in any way had had their life changed, and Colomba was part of that group. "So, are you going to give me a hand or are you just planning your escape?" she asked.

Dante cocked an eyebrow. "I have three escape plans figured out and ready to go, and I've skimmed enough money off my adoptive father to live comfortably for a couple of years anywhere on earth I choose to take up residence. But I have no intention of abandoning you." He took a half-crushed cigarette out of his sock. "Unless I have a smoke, my mood is going to collapse. Do you want to pick this fight?"

"No. Enough's enough, I'm not your mother."

Dante lit up and emitted a moan of satisfaction as he breathed a plume of smoke skyward, in the general direction of Sirius. "Considering that we're doing something much more dangerous than ingesting tobacco, it wouldn't really make sense anyway. Alberti told me that protective services is ready to reveal that I'm still alive."

"As soon as you're released from the hospital."

"If you want me to go on being part of this operation, then you need to ask them to delay that announcement. No public statements about my liberation. No pictures with the Italian flag as a backdrop. However much I may love groupies, I'd prefer to have the rest of the world continue to believe that I'm dead, so I can be left to work in blessed peace."

CHAPTER III

Alberti helped Dante get into the gray Alfa Romeo outside the overgrown garden that had been his home. "Next stop, Mezzanotte," he said. Dante leaned his head against the half-open window, deathly tired. It had been four days since Loris killed himself, and he might have gotten ten hours of sleep in all that time, forcing himself to read through the whole stack of documents that Colomba had had sent to him, a roundup of the current state of the investigation. Especially what they had on Martina, whose death struck him as even weirder and more nonsensical than the mechanic's demented suicide.

At the time of her death, Martina Concio had been twenty-five years old, perfectly healthy, with good muscle tone, and presenting no sign of previous or current disease. She died of massive hemorrhage as a result of penetrating trauma to her abdominal cavity caused by the pointy tree branch; the angle of entry—forty-five degrees—was compatible with the theory that Martina had landed on that branch after roughly a six-foot fall. It was likewise compatible with the ragged outline of the wound, which fit the shape of the branch, and the bruising on her body as a result of the fall. There were no assault bruises.

Tests done on her bodily fluids had shown no presence of toxic substances: there was nothing in her stomach but coffee and sugar. She also had sugar in her mouth and esophagus, which, considering the rapidity with which the body tends to assimilate sugar, meant that it had been ingested only minutes before her death. She had in any case been awake at the time of the fall, because she had tried to grab a branch, but there were no defensive wounds, nor had any flesh been found under her fingernails.

Martina was dressed in her heavy winter jacket, her uniform, and her government-issue sidearm, safely fastened in its holster. In her pockets were a publicity brochure for a beautician, an apple, a handful of coins, and café sugar packets, empty and full, but without any branding or advertising. IDs, keys, and wallet had remained in the car, in her handbag.

An examination of the ground between the car and the place of her death had revealed nothing. Hours of snow, wind, and freezing rain had gone by, to say nothing about the tromping of the rescue teams, but the SIS still ruled out any signs of a body being dragged, nor had they found any blood either on the car or around the tree on whose branch she'd been impaled. If Leo really was the one who'd killed her, he'd done a good clean job of eliminating all traces of his work.

Between reading documents and his physical therapy sessions, Dante had also had to face a closed-door session of questioning from the magistrates of the counterterrorism pool. He'd told them that he remembered nothing of the massacre in Venice, nor of the weeks that had preceded it. *Really, I was in Venice? Oh my goodness.*

They'd actually believed him. Dante was as good at telling lies as he was at spotting them, and no one had any interest in digging too deep to find a different story than the one already told in the proceedings of the inquiry. In the meantime, Colomba had been almost uninterruptedly in the Pisa barracks talking with D'Amore and a CIA operative stationed in Italy who had updated her on the international manhunt for Bonaccorso and the specialties of Italian cuisine he was obsessed with, to a phenomenally mind-numbing extent.

They'd just taken the turnoff for Mezzanotte when Alberti was forced to slow to walking speed on account of a tractor with extremely high wheels that was taking up the whole roadway. Dante grumbled. "Delightful in this part of the country," he said. "Like bingo games at the hospice."

"Don't you love nature?" Alberti asked.

"Only in documentaries. In real life, it's a perfect setting for a horror flick. A couple of idiots, living completely isolated in the countryside, being hacked to death. I just hope that there's at least a fast internet connection. They've aired whole seasons while I was asleep, and I'm going to have to download hundreds of episodes." Dante lit a cigarette and looked at Alberti's arms. "What do you take to pump up your biceps like that?"

"Just nutritional supplements and some time in the gym."

"Were you trying to exorcise your sense of guilt about having lied to the world?"

Alberti's freckles glowed phosphorescent. "It's not like I knew *all* that many things, after all. And right after the massacre, Esposito and I had the 'cousins' on us like a pressure cooker. For two weeks we couldn't leave the house or make a phone call or even talk to each other. So I kept my mouth shut until the deputy captain felt better, and then she told me what to do."

They'd reached Mezzanotte and Alberti opened the new gate with a remote control. The farmhouse had undergone a few modifications in the previous days, with the utmost discretion. A series of video cameras—small ones, practically invisible, and all facing outward—now surrounded the building, while the ramshackle old gate, hanging off its hinges, had been replaced in record time with a brand-new electric one, complete with sharp spikes and barbed wire—and the barbed wire continued along the fence, surrounding the entire perimeter of the property.

On one of the house's outer walls, a small dish antenna had been installed to provide an internet connection via satellite, and both incoming and outgoing signals were fully encrypted, while the dog trainer's little hut had become an operative DCT (Department of Counterterrorism) station, which monitored every slightest movement on the road. The owner had agreed to cooperate, as long as he was allowed to come feed his dogs twice a day.

The scraps of wood and the broken furniture scattered across the backyard were clearly visible now that the untended grass had taken the place of the snow. The technicians who had installed the security systems had carted off their own garbage, but not the preexisting garbage.

"Does Colomba really live in all this mess?" Dante asked.

"It's a little better inside."

Alberti opened the door and led him in, passing through the kitchen and taking him to the room overlooking the backyard. It was still unfinished, with walls and floors in bare gray cement: Colomba had laid out a large white wool carpet, a king-sized tatami, a small table with a chair, and a chest of drawers purchased on sale from IKEA. What made it perfect for Dante, though, was the longest wall, overlooking the fields beyond the back garden, and entirely faced in plate-glass windows, which had recently been replaced with bulletproof and shatterproof panes. No curtains—Colomba knew that Dante didn't use them, even in his bathroom—but privacy was ensured by a thicket of prickly pears.

"It's not like your hotel suite in Rome, but there's a nice view," said Alberti, gesturing toward the line of the hills, where the brown was sprouting into green.

"Do you have any idea of where I've been lately?" Dante let himself flop down onto the tatami. "This is definitely an improvement."

Alberti pulled aside an accordion door at the other side of the room. "Here's the squat toilet."

"Seriously? Are there still houses with squat toilets?" Dante grumbled.

"If you need to go, I can give you a hand before I have to leave."

"No, thanks. I consider time in the bathroom to be a solitary pleasure." Dante rolled over on his back, lighting a cigarette as he did. He felt mighty proud of himself for having successfully performed that routine. "And you're not going anywhere."

"Protective services are sending me home today . . ."

"And counterterrorism will be sending you straight back, my friend. You might as well spare yourself the trip."

Alberti sank down dispiritedly on the only chair. "Signor Torre . . . I've been here for a month."

"It's called the Wheel of Karma," Dante said with a faint smile of false pity. "You do something disgusting, and in exchange you get the short end of the stick. In your case, they press-ganged you to hunt down Bonaccorso under Colomba's orders and protect me from stray bullets. But don't worry. You're not the only one who's going to be paying the price of poetic justice. Colomba just went to pick up your new partner in 'forced labor.'"

E sposito emerged from arrivals at Rimini airport with an enormous
suitcase and the look on his face of someone who's been catapulted
straight into hell without advance warning.

"Get moving, can't you see I'm double parked?" Colomba shouted at
him through the side window of a Jeep Grand Cherokee.

Esposito dragged the oversize suitcase as if it were the ball and chain
and he the prison-farm convict, and stowed it in the vehicle's trunk.
The back of the Grand Cherokee was so packed with crates of fruit and
vegetables that he had a hard time finding room for it.

"And this?" he asked, once he was situated in the passenger seat of
the Grand Cherokee.

"A thoughtful loan from the NOA," she replied, referring to Italy's
counterterrorism operative branch.

Colomba slid the vehicle into the stream of traffic, giving the paddle
shifter a series of rapid taps that made the engine groan. "Sorry I didn't
get a chance to let you know in person. But it's been kind of a shitty
period," she said.

Esposito hadn't seen Colomba since her time in the hospital in Rome,
and now she looked like her own self, though she did have a face full
of bruises that were only starting to heal. "Well, just think what a great
time I've been having," he replied. "I only found out yesterday that I'm
supposed to go get myself killed by Bonaccorso." The Rome chief of
police had given him just twelve hours' notice, with a phone call while
he was out for dinner at a pizzeria with his wife and kids.

"Don't be such a pessimist. It just means you're going to have to do
a little police work, if you even remember what that is."

"I've only been working in HR for a year; it's not like I've become a certified desk jockey, you know," Esposito retorted, his feelings hurt.

Colomba took the entrance onto the state highway. "You've always been a certified desk jockey, but if you want to get back home in a hurry, then you'd better get busy fast. And after all, I've arranged for you to have a nice soft reentry: for the next few days, all you have to do is take care of Dante and stand guard on the house."

"You don't have protective services?"

"Open the glove compartment."

Esposito did as he was told. Inside was a tangle of electric wires and pieces of plastic.

"Ambient microphones," Colomba went on. "Every time the house is empty, Di Marco's men plant them everywhere."

"I thought we were working *for* the spy shop . . ."

"We're *pretending* to work for them and they *pretend* to believe it." Colomba took advantage of a red traffic light to shoot him a razor-sharp icy glare. "But never forget that you work for me."

Esposito nodded. "Understood. So where do we start?"

"We start with the Father."

Esposito gave some serious thought to just throwing himself out the door of the moving vehicle. He hadn't taken part in the investigation into the serial killer known as the Father, but he knew as much as he needed to. "Wait, wasn't he dead?"

"Oh, he still is. But we may not know all there is to know about him. Tommy, the son of the Melases, is behaving just like the other kidnapped children." Esposito held up his pack of cigarettes and flashed it in Colomba's direction. She nodded and lowered her window: no point in objecting when you're used to working with a tobacco fiend like Dante.

"How old is the boy?"

"Nineteen. He might be part of the second wave of kidnappings. Finding out whether that's true might be the best way of getting to Leo."

"Have you tried questioning him?"

"Unfortunately, he isn't able to answer our questions. Luckily, I know someone who can help. We're going to stop by and see him before we head home."

S tefano Maugeri was a skinny man in his early forties, and in spite of the cold he wore a pair of knee-length denim cutoffs. He received his visitors in the setting of his apartment in Assisi, surrounded by coffered ceilings and antiqued furniture in the historic center of the small Umbrian town, midway between the piazza outside of city hall and the Basilica of Saint Francis. He'd bought the place with the proceeds from the sale of a shop he owned in Rome and legal reparations for false arrest and imprisonment and police brutality. He'd been charged with murdering his wife and son, but Colomba and Dante had proved that it was the Father who'd kidnapped the boy after murdering the woman.

"Deputy Captain Caselli, what a gift it is to see you again, and here in my home," he said as he danced around them. "And Esposito, it's good to see you, too. Please, come in, be my guests. Have you had an accident, Deputy Captain?" he asked, peering into her face.

"No," she replied in an icy voice. Maugeri hadn't murdered his wife, but he'd knocked her around more than once, and Colomba wasn't interested in celebrating old home week or trading confidences with him. "As I informed you over the phone, Signor Maugeri, we're here strictly to talk to your son."

"I thought that the investigation into the Father had been archived as a cold case."

"That's right, it has."

"So, then, what's up? Has something new happened?"

Colomba's eyes darkened. "You remember that I exonerated you, right?"

"Yes, of course, and I'll never get tired of thanking you for it," said Maugeri.

"There's no need. Just let us have twenty minutes with your son. Of course, if you insist, you can be present, but if you weren't, we'd prefer it."

Maugeri nodded discontentedly. "Why of course, certainly. Go right ahead."

Luca Maugeri was a lanky towheaded boy with a pair of round glasses and a striped T-shirt. He was sitting in his room at a child-sized desk, writing in a checkered graph notebook.

"I brought a couple of old friends to see you, Luca," said Maugeri, shutting the door behind him. "Do you remember them?"

"Yes, Papà, thank you," said Luca in a ringing voice, without turning around; he had already spied the new arrivals in the reflection on the windowpane. Colomba had only met the little boy twice, on the day of his liberation and in court, but Luca hadn't spoken to her either time. He was autistic, had higher-than-average intelligence, and was self-sufficient, but it had taken him years to get over the shock of the kidnapping and his mother's murder.

"All right, then, I'll let you talk. I'm in the next room, if you need anything," Maugeri said, shutting the door behind him.

"You look well, Luca. You've grown a lot, you know," said Colomba. "How old are you now?"

"Ten. Thanks for coming to see me, Signora Colomba," said the boy, in the same tone of voice as before, slightly mechanical and an octave too high. "You too, Inspector Esposito. I sent you a card last Christmas."

"That was really nice of you, Luca, thanks," said Esposito, with some embarrassment. He'd escorted the boy and his father back and forth to court.

"But you didn't write back."

"Because he's nothing but a bumpkin and an oaf, Luca," Colomba broke in. "But are we interrupting you? Were you doing your homework?"

Luca nodded. "Italian is hard, but I'll pass." He paused. "Has something bad happened?"

"No," said Esposito. "What would make you think such a—"

"Yes," said Colomba.

"Thanks for telling me the truth. Lots of people won't because they think I don't understand," said Luca. He pulled out a toy walkie-talkie from his desk drawer and called his father. "Papà, we'd like tea and cook-ies." He put the radio away and turned his face ever so slightly toward Colomba. "When you have guests, you ought to offer them something to drink."

"Yes, that's right, thanks," said Colomba.

"Go ahead and sit on the bed, I just vacuumed it."

Colomba took a seat, but only after glaring icy daggers at Esposito with a glance meant to keep him on his feet. "The bad thing that's happened, Luca," she began, trying to find the right words to keep from scaring him, "is that there's a boy a little older than you who's just lost his parents."

"Where did he lose them?"

"No, I meant that they're dead," Colomba corrected herself. "It's a metaphor. Do you know what that is?"

"Yes, Signora Colomba. Every time I hear one, I write it down so I'll remember it." And to show that he was telling the truth, he got out another notebook and copied down the phrase.

"Well, that boy needs our help, Luca. But if we're going to help him, we need to talk to you about some things that aren't very pleasant."

"The Father?"

"Yes."

The boy nodded, perfectly composed. "All right. After our tea."

The tea arrived along with a trayful of cookies. Esposito, who hadn't eaten since breakfast, scarfed down half the tray while Luca used a magnifying glass to study the picture of Tommy.

"I've never seen him," he finally said, then set the photograph down on the desk so Colomba could take it back. "I never saw any of the other prisoners until we were freed. But I never saw him at the hospital, either, afterward."

Luca had been kidnapped just like nine other individuals, and kept like them in a shipping container, but upon their liberation, he was the only one who'd been in any condition to be questioned. His imprison-ment had lasted only a few days, and that had ensured that he was able to describe his kidnapper, the Father's accomplice, a man who was known as the German; as a result, his father, Stefano Maugeri, had been absolved of suspicion once and for all.

"I don't think he was with you, Luca. I remember perfectly well what you told the judge, and you were fantastic when you testified. But I still need to ask you a few more questions. May I?"

"Certainly, Signora Colomba."

"When you met the others at the hospital, didn't any of them mention other prisoners to you? Did they talk about people they'd seen whom we never found?"

"No."

"Did the Father or the German ever mention other boys besides the ones we liberated? Did they ever talk about a boy named Tommy?"

"No. The German never talked to me. And the Father only said that stupid beasts would die." He paused. "It was a metaphor. It meant I should behave myself."

"Did he ever talk to you about prisons other than the one where he kept you?"

"No. Never."

A little at a time, Luca had turned to face them. He had light-blue eyes and fine features: he was going to grow up to be a handsome man. It warmed Colomba's heart to think that she'd rescued him, and she felt guilty for reawakening horrendous memories: "But I know that there were others like me."

"Why didn't you ever tell us about that?" Esposito asked. "That's a big piece of news."

"Because I promised I wouldn't, Inspector Esposito. And a promise is a debt of honor." Luca turned to look at Colomba. "But you saved me. If you want me to, I'll tell you all about it."

"I do want you to, Luca. And I assure you that I'll be very careful about how I use what you tell me. Where were these prisoners you speak of?"

"They were where *we* were. *Before* we were there. I think they're all dead now."

Stupid beasts die . . . Colomba bit her lower lip.

"Do you know what DNA is?"

"Deoxyribonucleic acid."

"And do you know that in the police department, we use DNA in our investigations?" Luca nodded. "Well, in your shipping container and everybody else's, the only DNA we found belonged to the ten of you. And also . . ." She stopped midsentence. The police had churned through the soil all around the site in search of buried bodies, but to no avail. "So, I'm wondering, how can you be so sure?"

"Because some of us saw them."

"You said that you didn't talk about them . . ."

"I said that we hadn't talked about them *in the hospital.*"

Colomba and Esposito exchanged a glance. "The shipping containers were separate, Luca. You couldn't talk to each other from one to the other," Colomba said. "We checked."

"That's right, Signora Colomba. But there were other systems. And that's what I'd promised never to tell a soul."

"You weren't supposed to talk about how you all communicated?"

"Yes. It was a secret." Luca rapped his knuckles on the desktop. "The Code."

After they had finished their tea, Luca had insisted on ordering cups of hot chocolate for them all, again over the walkie-talkie, in spite of his father's feeble attempt to protest that he'd already brought them tea and cookies. "It's an exceptional occasion," Luca had retorted, remaining stubbornly entrenched in his demands.

"So, you communicated by banging on the walls of the shipping containers?" Colomba asked as she blew on her cup of piping hot chocolate.

"That's right," Luca replied, stirring the sugar into his. He was careful not to touch the sides of the cup with his spoon.

"It was like Morse code. In a way. When I got home, I checked it against the official Morse code. It's different."

"Do you remember it?"

"Yes."

The boy got a sheet of paper and wrote:

A .
B ._
C ..
D ._ _
E ._.
F .._
G ...
H ._ _ _
I ._ _.
J ._._
K ._ ._

L .._ _
M ._ .
N . . . _
O . . . .
P ._ _ _ _
Q ._ _ _ .
R ._ _._
S ._ _ ..
T ._ . _ _
U ._ ._ .
V ._._
W ._ . . .
X .. _ _ _
Y .._ _ .
Z .._._

Colomba took a moment to check on her cell phone, and sure enough, it was the way Luca had said: Morse code was similar, but radically different. "Are you sure that you're remembering correctly?" she asked.

Luca nodded. "The dots were a tap, or a bang, and the dashes were a scratch." He offered a practical demonstration on the desk, using his fingernails. "It wasn't easy, but the boy on my right was really fast."

Colomba thought back to the location of the specific prisoners in the shipping containers: the one to Luca's right had slashed his wrists after being rescued; he'd been a prisoner for five years.

"How did you learn it?" Esposito asked.

"There were some words written on the ceiling of my shipping container. I could only see it when the sun shone through the air grate," said Luca. "It was written in poop. But it didn't smell bad anymore."

My God, Colomba thought. *How can you force a child to experience anything of the sort?* "What was written?" she made herself ask.

"It said to memorize it and then erase it. Which is what I did." A pause and then: "But I'm not sure exactly what the others were talking about. I just passed the messages on, and they were always too fast for me to be able to understand them."

"What do you mean by 'passing messages on'?" Esposito asked, his mouth dry.

Luca sketched figures out in the air. "There were ten of us. If you were at the beginning of the line and you wanted to talk to the last one in the line, then the people in the middle had to pass on the messages. Like in a game of telephone."

"How did you know who the messages were for?"

"We each had a code name," said Luca. "Mine was . . ." He tapped and scratched it out on the desktop. *Tap. Tap. Tap. Scratch. Pause. Tap. Scratch. Scratch.* Colomba tried to decipher it, but she couldn't.

"Translated, it says ND. I don't know what it means," Luca explained. "I wondered if it might not be an abbreviation for Nerd. I hope it was. Peter Parker is a nerd, too."

"And were you all in agreement not to tell anyone about the Code?"

"Yes."

"Why?"

"For the others." Luca paused and for the first time, his voice wavered uncertainly. "They would have had some . . . problems. With the Father."

"The Father isn't alive anymore, Luca," Colomba said gently. "He can't hurt anyone now."

"I don't know."

Colomba shivered. "You don't know if he's dead? I assure you, he is. It's not a very nice thing to say, but I was there when he died."

Luca sat in silence for a few seconds, then he started talking again in a lower voice: "Sometimes I go to see the boy who was in the second shipping container. They put him in a hospital. He says that his parents never go to see him. I think that's an awful thing."

"Yes, Luca, this is an awful thing," said Colomba, with a knot in her throat.

"I called him OG. With the Code. That's what I still call him. And that's how we still talk. He . . . prefers it that way. OG believes in magic, Signora Colomba. He believes that the Father can change bodies like the Shadow King. That's an enemy of the X-Men." Luca looked at her in the reflection in the mirror. "But I believe that he had a son and that he raised him to become just like him. Maybe more than one. But that doesn't matter. If they do exist, I know that you will kill them all."

5

Dante had put on an ankle-length gray overcoat over a gunmetal-gray three-piece suit with a red tie and a Borsalino hat, all of it with a vaguely retro flair to it. The only hints at modernity were the Alexander McQueen shoes with two-inch soles and the black glove sheathing the bad hand, camouflaging its deformity. Nothing that he wore was even remotely suitable for a walk along muddy trails, and in spite of his walker, he was constantly slipping and sliding.

Likewise covered with mud was the spot where Martina had been killed. Alberti helped Dante to sit down on a rock that still had a length of Carabinieri two-toned crime scene tape attached to it. The tree that had impaled the young officer had been uprooted, but Dante had no difficulty imagining her corpse dripping blood onto the snow.

"That's not the way the Father killed," Alberti said from behind him.

"You're right. He was more discreet. He let the German stab the victims, then he'd dissolve their bodies in acid," said Dante, continuing to watch the young woman's death agonies in his mind's eye. "Martina must have suffered terribly."

"I could have told you so, sir, without having to come all the way out here. What's more, the deputy captain wanted us to stay at home."

Dante peered at Alberti from over the top of his mirrored sunglasses.

"What do you think of my brother?"

"That he isn't your brother."

"I've decided that, until proven otherwise, as far as I'm concerned, he is." The dream of his meeting with Leo remained particularly vivid, more than all the rest.

"The DNA—"

"The DNA taken from a hair from his head left in the NOA dormitory.

Don't you think he might have planted that hair there intentionally?" Dante threw both arms wide. "And in any case, there are many different kinds of brothers. Adopted, members of a single religion, the Masons, the Knights Templar . . . even if I'm reasonably certain that the Knights Templar have nothing to do with this. Still, let me know if you spot anyone around who looks like they stepped out of *The Name of the Rose*."

"All right, Signor Torre . . ." said Alberti patiently.

"To get back to Leo, do you think he's the kind of person who'd do spectacular things just for the hell of it?"

Alberti thought it over. "He seemed very rational when I met him."

Dante nodded, crushing out his cigarette butt and putting it in his pocket. "At least a part of him operates with a certain lucidity, otherwise he would already have been long dead. So, what does that tell us?"

"That he must have had . . . a motive?" Alberti asked, hesitantly.

"You've improved while I was away. Bravo." He pulled himself up, gripping the hated walker with both hands. "Let's go to the hayloft."

The door had been repaired with a couple of boards, and a Carabinieri crime-scene seal announced that the structure was now under an order of judicial confiscation. Dante leaned against the cement wall and removed his dark glasses.

"Don't you want to take a look inside?" asked Alberti, peering through the boards.

"Whatever there was to find has already been found." Shielding his eyes with one hand, Dante gazed around. "Do you have a crowbar in the car?"

6

Colomba received the call via Signal while she was still a little over ten miles outside of Portico. She'd just ended a call with Bart, who was setting out for Rimini with her team. Bart had been drafted to redo a full examination of Villa Quiete, after the military experts had finished theirs without finding anything useful. She was certainly happy to lend a hand, but disgruntled about the lack of any advance warning and the dozens of backed-up cases she was abandoning on her desk in Milan.

"Where are you?" Colomba asked, hearing the wind behind Dante's voice.

"At the old mill."

"Didn't I tell you not to go out?"

"Do you remember that you're not my mother? In any case, I called you because we need to go to the lady carabiniere's house. If you'll tell me the address, I'll try to get in on my own. Alberti will act as my lookout."

Colomba swerved. "Just wait for me in Portico and don't do anything fucked up."

They all met in front of the museum, which housed the famous Roman-era Gilt Bronzes that the populace of Portico had actively defended against plans to move them to the National Museum in Rome. Colomba remembered it because her father had been one of the townsfolk of Portico who had chained themselves together as part of the protest. It had almost kept Colomba from being admitted to the officer training academy. The admissions panel took any hint of subversive family ties very seriously, even though Colomba's father was anything but a radical. In fact, if anything, she'd inherited from him the conservative blood that ran in the family.

The meeting between Esposito and Dante was almost a tear-jerker, because Dante actually allowed himself to be hugged. "Genius," Esposito declared, "I was sure I'd never see you again. I mean I was really, really one hundred percent sure, you get me?"

"I came back specifically to disappoint you. And you're a smoker, aren't you? I just finished my last cigarette."

"I should have known . . ." Esposito handed him half a pack, then went on to throw his arms around Alberti. "Damn, you got big, *amigo*. Give me a glass of whatever it is you've been drinking."

"My God, all of you are obsessed. I'm not taking anything. I just lift weights, *amigo*."

"Sure, sure, of course you do . . ."

Colomba sent the two of them to keep an eye on the house and update each other on the day, while she remained behind with Dante, who suddenly seemed anything but exhausted. His pupils were also enormous now. "What the fuck kind of pill did you take?" she asked him.

"Nothing."

"Do you remember the rule, 'No lies between us'?"

"On our way here, we ran into a crowd of amateur long-distance cyclists, all of them in their early sixties, who were pumping uphill like nobody's business. I just asked Alberti to check them out." Dante patted his chest under the jacket. "They'd dissolved some damn witch's brew in their water bottles, and now my heart is racing a mile a minute."

"You're determined to die, aren't you? I don't know why I even took so much trouble to find you."

Dante pirouetted around his walker. "Because without me your life is gray and uninteresting, CC. So, how was your meeting with Luca?"

Colomba told him about the Code and Dante lost all his giddy verve. "Hey . . . did that make you feel sad?" she asked him.

He shrugged. "I just started to feel jealous of a group of boys who were exchanging messages with shit."

"Jealous of what?"

"At least they had someone to talk to. For thirteen years, all I had was the Father with a mask over his face."

"Luca and the other boys seem certain that either the Father or his successor is still in circulation."

"Who could be better than Leo for that spot? The son who takes the Father's place. The best son." Dante lit a cigarette. "So, shall we go see the lady carabiniere's house?"

"I'm not sure about that, Dante. If Lupo finds out, he'll declare open war on us. And after all, if there was anything useful, they already would have found it."

"Let's trade. I'll explain Luca's Code and you can accept the risk."

"Did you know it?"

"No. But I've just figured it out." Dante tapped and scratched on the car hood. "I just tapped out *ciao*. All right then, do we have a deal?"

Colomba's curiosity got the better of her. "I'll make you pay for this. But yes."

Dante held up his good hand. "Look closely. I'll teach you a new way of counting. I learned it from an essay by Isaac Asimov."

"I read a book of his. It was about robots."

"That's like saying that Raphael drew pictures of Madonnas, but okay." He raised the thumb of his good hand. "One." He lowered the thumb and raised the index finger. "Two."

"That doesn't strike me as all that innovative."

"Hold on, now comes the good part." He raised thumb and index finger. "Three." He raised his middle finger and lowered the others. "Sorry, no offense meant. Four." Thumb and middle finger. "Five."

"Okay, I confess that I'm lost now."

"I'm counting in binary. It's a language created for computers—"

"That much even I get."

Dante went on delightedly. "And it only has two digits: zero and one. In effect, instead of being base ten, it's base two, and it's written from right to left and it's positional. Luca's Code transforms the zeros and ones into dots and dashes. After that, they just lined up the letters alphabetically and numbered them starting from one, without using the codes that are normally used in binary for letters, which are longer. Here, give me that sheet of paper . . ."

"There's no need, I'll take your word for it," said Colomba, who was starting to get a headache. "I'll call D'Amore and see if there's anyone who has a set of keys."

7

Martina's landlady was named Floriana. She was about thirty years old and she greeted Dante and Colomba outside the front door of a three-story apartment building that overlooked a small piazza.

"A pleasure to make your acquaintance, Signorina," said Dante, tipping his Borsalino hat and talking at machine-gun speed. "Chief Inspector Valle," he added, borrowing his adoptive father's surname. "This is my partner, Carelli. Deputy Captain, from the Eighty-Seventh Precinct."

"A pleasure to meet you," said Colomba, glaring at him. She'd read a couple of books from the series, and she'd even enjoyed them, even though she usually avoided detective books. If they were too realistic, it felt like work, and if they were too imaginative, they irritated her.

"The apartment is on the mezzanine, but I'm afraid we don't have an elevator," said Floriana.

Dante pointed to his walker. "Because of this? Don't worry, it's only temporary. And she's the only one who'll be going in. I'll examine the place from outside."

"But you're the one who wanted to come . . ." Colomba said in a faint voice.

"But that doesn't mean I wanted to *go in*. Go on, CC, you're better than me at rummaging through other people's possessions."

Colomba turned her back on him.

"Do you know, your partner reminds me of someone?" said Floriana, leading her up the stairs.

"Whoever that is, I'm sure they're a tremendous pain in the ass."

Martina's apartment was a one-bedroom with a galley kitchen. Cheap furniture, probably the castoffs of deceased old people, and in the bathroom a square mirror with fluorescent lights and two black-and-white medicine chests. It looked like one of the apartments that Colomba had rented, already furnished, when she was a rookie. It wasn't worth paying the money to get something decent if you were just going to spend most of your time out in the street. Her boss back then was called Rovere. The Father had sent the German to plant a bomb in Rovere's apartment.

"We weren't friends or anything, we just saw each other when she came to pay the rent. But I was really sorry to hear what happened." Floriana scratched at an encrustation on the jamb of the door to the living room. "I ought to rent it out again, but it seems wrong somehow. Even if there's nothing of hers left in here."

"Had she been living here for long?"

"A year and a half, more or less. But she was telling me they were going to transfer her soon."

"She was going to be transferred?"

"So she told me. It's not like we talked about it all that much, though. Here . . . it's not as if she had to give me official notice." Colomba's intense gaze made her hesitate. "We didn't really have a written rental agreement . . . I told the other officers about it. It's not a crime or any-thing, is it?"

"Actually, I think it *is* illegal, but I couldn't care less about that, right now." Colomba reached out her hand and Floriana dropped the keys in it, then turned and hurried back to her shop. Colomba waited for the sound of her footsteps to subside, then she opened the wooden roller blind. Dante was chasing pigeons, laughing like an idiot. She called him with a shrill whistle, fingers pressed between her lips. He came over to the window, his head reaching almost all the way to the sill, so they could talk in low voices. "They've already cleared the place out," she said. "Just like I expected."

"Did they even take away the leftover food?"

"Is that a serious question?"

"Yes. Usually they throw away any open containers, but I'm just hoping that Martina's parents were too upset to do a deep cleaning."

Colomba looked into the greasy cabinets and came back to the window.

"Do you want a complete list?"

"If you don't mind."

"Two boxes of salt, one coarse and one fine; a half-empty bottle of olive oil; a box of slimming herbal tea. A pack of chocolate wafers and a pound of pasta."

"Whole wheat?"

"No."

"Look under the burners on the stove. That's where the interesting stuff can usually be found."

"Why don't you come do it yourself?"

"Because I'm so disabled I'm practically a paraplegic."

Colomba did as she'd been told, and scraped up curls of filth and a piece of dried-out macaroni with the blade of her pocket knife. She shoved the garbage out the window and right onto Dante's head. He shouted in disgust.

Chuckling under her breath, she shut the window and went down to hand over the keys. When she stepped out onto the little piazza, Dante was examining the piece of macaroni, poised on the nib of the fountain pen that he never used. "Does that look like it's the right color?"

"What color is it supposed to be? It was stuck to the floor."

"Don't remind me." Dante blew on it, then stuck it in his mouth and chewed on it for a couple of seconds before spitting it out.

"Can you do that again? I want to take a picture," asked Colomba.

Dante wiped his mouth with his glove. "I'm sacrificing myself for the sake of the investigation. You ought to be thanking me."

"You never would have put that filthy thing in your mouth if you hadn't had some idea you haven't told me about yet. So hurry up and spill the beans, unless you want me to hit you over the head with that dingus that's keeping you from falling over."

"I just wanted to make sure that Martina didn't eat foods for diabetics. Or take medicines on a regular basis. All you found under the burners was a chunk of aspirin. No hypodermic plungers or bits of blister packs . . ."

"If Martina had been a diabetic, she'd have been kicked off the force. That's a disability-level disease."

Dante mopped his sweat-pearled brow: the cyclists' beverage had stopped working on him. "From the autopsy, it appears that her C-peptide was lower than normal. You know what that is, right?"

"Pass me the walker."

Dante raised both hands. "Okay, okay. It's more or less a precursor enzyme of insulin. If it's too low with respect to the insulin levels in the bloodstream, then it means that the insulin wasn't produced in the pancreas, but was injected externally. I learned that from the reports on suicides among paramedics in the United States, because injecting insulin is the method they most commonly use. To kill patients, too."

"And you think that Leo used it on Martina?"

Dante mimed an injection. "He caught her off guard and gave her an injection in the belly, where he knew that the wound would cover up the needle mark. A powerful dose on a nondiabetic with an empty stomach can be fatal. In just a few seconds, they practically can't stay on their feet anymore. Then he gave her some sugar to raise her blood sugar levels, and when he realized she was coming to, he impaled her."

"Fuck."

"And she experienced every instant of the agony, wide-awake, the poor thing," Dante said with an absent look in his eyes.

"If she'd moved away, maybe she'd still be alive," said Colomba. "She told her landlady that she was going to be transferred, even though there's no mention of the fact in the reports that I read."

Dante raised his right eyebrow until it arched over his glasses.

"*Interesting.* So who can tell us if there's anything that was left out of the reports?"

"No one but the Carabinieri."

"Then I have some bad news for you."

At the front desk, Brigadier Bruno looked at the electronic image of Colomba in the video intercom as if someone had just dumped a truckload of manure on the front steps. She didn't have her eyes turned toward the lens, and she seemed if anything more disgusted than he was. "What do you want?" he asked into the microphone, which turned his voice into a rasping electrical buzz.

"Lupo. Please tell him that I'll be in the café at the corner, and that I want to talk about Martina Concio."

"Don't you dare speak Martina's name, you understand?"

"I'd gladly have avoided it. Tell him to get out here or I'll just go home."

Bruno marched the length of the hallway. Lupo was in his office reading his men's reports about various routine activities. His bruises had healed, but he'd been in a terrible mood for the past few weeks; as a result, the messages he'd been leaving on Vigevani's voicemail had grown increasingly harsh. "For fuck's sake, they can't cut me out of this," he would shout. When Bruno gave him Colomba's message, he seethed with an icy rage.

"I'll tell her to go fuck herself," Bruno said.

Lupo clenched his jaw. "No. Let me do it."

"Don't get yourself into trouble," said Bruno. "Don't forget she has protection in high places."

Lupo didn't even bother to reply. He put on his jacket and charged out of his office, hand instinctively resting on the butt of the pistol on his hip. Just a few yards away from the café, he recognized Colomba's profile, but he also noticed that she was not alone. She was sitting at a table with someone who looked like a bearded version of David Bowie.

That was who turned around and watched Lupo approach, gazing out over his mirrored sunglasses with an ironic glint in his eyes. "Sergeant Major, *buonasera*. I'm so happy to make your acquaintance," he said.

"And who, sir, are you?"

"The world's most frequently kidnapped man: three times, twice by the same person, and the third, they tell me, by ISIS. Just imagine me without a beard and without a glove." Slipping off the leather glove, Dante showed him his bad hand.

Lupo felt his legs give out beneath him. "Jesus, Joseph, and Mary," he said. "I don't believe it."

Dante handed him the glass of vodka tonic he'd been drinking, and which had restored his good mood and sped up his heart rate. "You can check my fingerprints. I'm in the files. When Colomba beat you up in the forest, she was on her way to rescue me."

Colomba nodded. "I'm sorry about that, Lupo, but I didn't really have any choice in the matter."

"You could have told me so, instead of coming at me like that!"

"You never would have believed me, not with Martina's corpse front of mind."

Lupo felt his rage oozing out of his pores. "Afterward, though, I would have. I've spent the past month asking myself what the fuck's going on. Who killed her? Was it ISIS?"

"Sure, exactly, it was ISIS," said Dante sarcastically.

"In the person of Bonaccorso," Colomba intervened. "We think it was him."

"That piece of shit was buzzing around here?" Lupo asked in disbelief.

"You don't know anything about the investigation because the DCT doesn't trust you," Dante put in, referring to the Department of Counterterrorism. "But we're not from counterterrorism and we're here to offer you an olive branch. As well as something to drink."

Lupo sat down and ordered a glass of bourbon, even though he never drank in the daytime. The situation struck him as surreal. Here he was, having a relaxed conversation with a man whom everyone else thought was dead, sitting at a table in a café with the woman who had broken his nose. "Why would you do that?"

"We need information. Let's just say that we're in a race with the DCT to find Bonaccorso first," said Dante.

"Obviously if you went around talking about it, we could all be charged with leaking state secrets," Colomba said. "So keep your mouth shut."

"Do you really think that all Carabinieri are idiots?" asked Lupo.

"No, that's what *I* think, *sheriff*," said Dante caustically.

"Don't call me sheriff. So do the Melases have anything to do with this story?"

Colomba paused and, looking the sergeant major in the eyes, said: "They were the boy's jailers. Bonaccorso killed them before leaving town."

Lupo shook his head. "This is just a shower of bullshit."

Dante loosened his tie and unbuttoned his shirt. "You see this scar? That's where Bonaccorso stuck a tube in me to get me to breathe. He held me hostage for a year and a half. Call it whatever you like, but it's not bullshit."

Lupo looked away. "What do you want to know?"

"Did Martina have a boyfriend?" Dante asked, rebuttoning his shirt and tightening his tie.

"Not that I know of. And I would have known."

"Colomba said that she had seen her with the mechanic who killed himself." He pretended to think hard. "What was his name again?"

Lupo snapped again. "Loris Mantoni? That junkie? Not on your life."

"Maybe she didn't know he was a junkie," Colomba put in.

"Everyone knew it." The waiter brought the glass of bourbon and Lupo turned it slowly in his hands. "Especially the Carabinieri. He'd been raising hell since he was a minor."

"Narcotics every time?"

"And aggravated fraud and stalking, even though when he did it, it was basically just busting people's balls. There were also a couple of involuntary mental health commitments." He shrugged. "Lately, he'd been clean, but that didn't last. Still, it wasn't all his fault. His father is a real piece of shit. He beat the brains out of Loris, and by the time he was done, the boy was an idiot."

"Who is his father?"

"A guy who's always drunk and hangs around in the bar in Conigliano. He beat his wife, he beat his son, and he still beats anyone he takes a dislike to. He's done some time behind bars, too, always for crimes on the general level of stealing chickens. Now he's a truck driver. Gaspare is his name."

Colomba jotted that down.

"Is there anything else you need? I have work to do," said Lupo.

"Just tell us why Martina wanted to get out of Portico."

Lupo stiffened. "Who fed you that nonsense?"

Dante narrowed his eyes and Lupo felt as if he were being X-rayed. "Maybe you didn't know about it. Because maybe the young woman bypassed you and spoke directly to the high command."

"Impossible."

"Then why had she given up her rental?"

"Did you talk to her landlady?" Lupo asked uneasily.

"And we searched her apartment, too," Dante said, still staring at him. "Don't worry, there wasn't anything interesting."

"Why should there have been?" Lupo asked, in a tone of voice that sounded less relaxed than he'd meant it to.

"Do you know that you just relaxed your shoulders? What were you worried about?"

Colomba squeezed his arm. "Can I talk to you for a second, Dante? It seems to me we're wandering a little far afield."

"Not so. It was Martina who put the hammer in your house, CC. And Lupo knew it."

9

Colomba had seen Dante play this game many times before, but she'd never gotten used to it. He used words like electric shocks to trigger certain emotions, and then he read them. But how had he managed to link the hammer found in her backyard with Martina? She'd never suspected the young woman for a second.

Still, there could be no doubt that Dante had hit a bull's-eye. Lupo had turned red and was struggling to conceal his dismay behind a mask of anger. "I don't give a fuck who you think you are, don't you dare insinuate anything of the sort."

"I have no intention of telling anyone else about it," Dante replied, unruffled.

"You can count on my discretion, too, Lupo," Colomba said, supporting Dante's play. "And I can assure you that whatever you tell us will help track down Bonaccorso. Was Martina working with you?"

"No, and I didn't know anything about it," Lupo grumbled after a few seconds. "I only figured it out later, on my own."

"How?"

Lupo pulled his wallet out of his pocket and reached into it. He took out a piece of brightly colored cloth, which he then laid in front of Dante. "I found this among her things. If you try to lay a finger on it, I swear to God I'll shoot you."

"CC . . . do you know what this is?"

Colomba recognized the Disney-style patterns. "It looks like a piece of Tommy's pillowcase. Which is what the hammer was wrapped up in."

Lupo nodded and put the scrap of cloth back in his pocket. "Martina was the first to arrive at the Melas home. Maybe she found the hammer and hid it, but I swear to God I have no idea why she would have done anything that fucked up. The only thing that occurred to me is that she might have been trying to protect the boy, but why she would have decided to hide it from you . . ."

Dante gestured to Colomba: Lupo was speaking the truth. "I don't believe that this was Martina's idea. I think that Bonaccorso must have talked her into it," he said.

"In order to frame the Deputy Captain?" asked Lupo, who was starting to see the light.

Dante nodded. "Bonaccorso is afraid of Colomba. He knows that sooner or later she's going to get her hands on him."

Colomba was certain that Dante was lying, but she didn't let on.

Lupo stood up. "How long is this story of Bonaccorso going to remain a military secret?"

"Until he's caught, and maybe even after that," said Colomba. "I'm sorry."

"I talk to Martina's parents nearly every day. They're sure their daughter was killed in the line of duty. I won't allow anyone to tell them that she slipped on a banana peel."

"That won't happen," said Dante. "I promise you. And we'll keep you briefed on all the developments in the investigation, if you'll keep your lips zipped with the intelligence agencies."

Lupo pointed his finger right at her face. "Make sure you do, or I'll come looking for you."

He turned to go, and Dante smiled at Colomba. "We have an ally."

She seized him by the lapels of his jacket. "The next time you try something like that, I'll upend you into a ditch. Why didn't you tell me about Martina? I'm not very fond of playing the fool."

"Because I just figured it out here and now."

"Don't make me laugh."

10

When they got back to Mezzanotte, Alberti and Esposito were finishing dinner; they'd moved the kitchen table outside and placed it on the patio. "Thanks for waiting for us!" said Colomba. "You could have locked us out while you were at it."

"We waited for you, but it's ten o'clock . . ." Esposito justified himself.

"We kept some pasta warm for you, Deputy Captain," said Alberti. "*Sugo del poliziotto*, cop sauce, with everything we found in the fridge. And without meat for Signor Torre."

"Thanks, but I'm not hungry," he said, heading around the house to his bedroom, while Colomba scarfed down the leftover pasta directly from the pan before heading off to take a shower.

In the meantime, Dante got the two men to help him haul the kitchen sofa out into the backyard, and he stretched out on it, staring up at the night sky and ruminating while chain-smoking.

After the surge of excitement of the first day's investigation, he'd plunged back into the deep well of sadness that always followed any time spent thinking about the Father. He hated the man, but the Father was also a part of him, the person who had been there as Dante grew from a child to a man, his captor but also his mentor. Dante thought back to the silo, where he'd been confined for thirteen years, only snippets of which he could even remember, snippets that were hard to place. In his memory, everything unfolded the same way, over and over: the Father's visits, studying, the intelligence tests, and the grueling puzzle sessions . . . to say nothing of the pain from the clubbings he was forced to inflict on his own hand every time he behaved like a "beast that had to be punished." He couldn't remember the day of his kidnapping. He could only remember the day of his escape, when he'd caught the German off guard; everything that surfaced in his mind from his life prior to that moment was a lie, Dante knew it: false memories shaped by his jailer, day after day, year after year. Could Leo really be the solution to the mystery of his identity? Or were the memories of the Box nothing more than a nightmare?

"Still got the blues?" Colomba asked him, sticking her head out of the glass door. She'd changed into her usual threadbare track suit.

Dante sat upright. "I'm just thinking about the past, a past that never dies. And I wonder what my brother had in mind, when he decided to bring the war here."

"What war?"

Dante gave her his usual wicked grin. "The war between Good and Evil, no? Why didn't he leave you be? Why did he abandon me like a bag of garbage?"

"I was hoping you could tell *me* that."

Dante tapped his fingers on his forehead. "There's nothing but empty space in here. And you're the cop, after all."

"Ex-cop . . ." Colomba muttered.

"That's right, you're a civilian consultant." He smiled. "Do you think the intelligence agencies might have anything useful on the mechanic?"

"Maybe so, but I don't intend to ask them about him. They haven't linked his suicide to Leo, and I don't want to be the reason they connect the dots. The same thing applies to Tommy and the Father. Every piece of information we ask for is another piece of information we give them."

"Won't Di Marco notice that he's being cut out of the loop?"

Colomba made room for herself on the sofa and tugged a piece of blanket over her. "I spent ten years managing superior officers who wanted *immediate results*. I know how much rope I can take."

"So how do you plan to operate?"

"In classic tradition: wearing out shoe leather."

11

During the week that followed, while Dante recovered his strength, a little more each day, Colomba and her team tracked down friends and family of Loris and Martina, doing their best to figure out whether the two of them had met anyone who could have been Leo or an accomplice of his. They came up empty-handed for the most part, however: Martina had confided in a couple of girlfriends that she expected a future promotion, but she hadn't said anything more than that, while Loris's friends—few in number and by and large junkies or alkies—told them that in the past month Loris had cut all ties and just stayed home getting fucked up; and what's worse, without offering any of his old friends so much as a taste.

Colomba also went to meet Tommy's elderly grandparents, the father and mother of Teresa's first husband. They lived in the city of Biella, in a gray apartment house; their skin was the same color as the building. If she'd ever seen anyone who was doing nothing but waiting to die, that would have been the elderly Carabbas. From her meeting with them, Colomba learned only two things: that they hated their daughter-in-law, and that they considered her to have been responsible for their son's death, if only morally speaking. Teresa liked to live life large, constantly busting her husband's chops for not making enough money, and doing everything she could to get rid of her son by placing him in an institute somewhere, in spite of the fact that her husband had been opposed to that course of action, because he loved Tommy.

"Tommy's therapist claims that they had a good relationship, Teresa and the boy," said Colomba, who had introduced herself as a social worker.

"Maybe now," said the old man. "Back in the day, I think that she was just sorry that Tommy hadn't been killed along with his father."

"What about after his death? What happened?"

"What happened is that Teresa left, no more than six months later, taking Tommy with her. She wanted to make money in Greece as a tour operator. And she said that the saltwater would be good for the boy."

"When was the last time you saw Tommy?" Colomba asked.

"I went to see him the day before they left. He was sobbing like crazy. He had understood that he was going to have to leave his country for good."

"Now he's back."

The Carabbas exchanged a glance. "Maybe they should have stayed in Greece," the grandmother said.

Esposito and Alberti, again working as a team, were assigned to take on the mechanic's father, Gaspare Mantoni. Just as Lupo had said, the man spent his time in a bar in Conigliano that was a hangout for truck drivers, when he wasn't out driving big rigs, that is. Mantoni was sixty years old and was short and skinny, with a flattened nose, hard muscles under his checkered shirt, and veins that popped on the backs of his hands.

Esposito decided that the man was a troublemaker the instant he saw him, with both elbows propped on the bar and a glass of red wine in front of him. Esposito flashed his badge. "Signor Mantoni?"

"Here they are again, come back to bust my balls," the man said to the bartender, who prudently pretended to be absorbed in the task of washing glasses.

"We won't take much of your time. What do you say, can we talk outside?"

"I'm fine right here."

Alberti took up a stance behind Loris's father's back, while Esposito dragged a stool over to the counter. He turned to look at the man and said: "You think you're scaring me by acting like an asshole? I eat jerks like you for breakfast."

Mantoni knocked his glass over with a jerk of the elbow, pouring the wine onto Esposito's wool trousers. "Oops."

Esposito let loose with a back-of-the-hand smack in the face. But Mantoni dodged the blow with a feline lunge, then grabbed a bottle off the bar and smashed it on the edge. Alberti grabbed him from behind, forcing him to drop the broken bottle, but the other man launched a kick at Esposito, knocking him to the floor, and pinned Alberti behind him against a column. Voices were raised from the other tables, demanding the two policemen let their friend go, and glasses and bags of potato chips came flying from all directions at the officers.

"We didn't start it!" Alberti shouted, giving Mantoni a hard punch to the kidneys. He whipped around, windmilling his callused fists, but Esposito tackled him around the legs, sending him sprawling onto the floor. The two cops rolled him out onto the sidewalk in front of the bar, while Alberti shouted at the other bargoers to remain seated.

Esposito reached into his pocket for his expandable steel baton and snapped it open with a flick of the wrist. "You want me to stick this up your ass?"

Mantoni laughed and pointed at the red stain on the front of Esposito's trousers. "You forgot to put in your tampon, you little pussy."

Esposito smashed the baton into his teeth, crushing his lips. "I'll put your tampon in for *you*, you piece of shit."

Mantoni whipped around on all fours, spitting blood and chuckling. "All right. What the fuck do you want?"

Esposito slammed the baton down again, this time on his back. "I want to talk about your son. You understand, you dumbass mule?"

The man leaned back against the wall and rolled himself a cigarette, soaking it in blood. "What the fuck do you want with him? He's dead."

"We'll ask the questions," Esposito replied, letting the steel baton swing back and forth right in front of the man's nose. Mantoni didn't seem especially daunted. "When was the last time you saw him?"

"At the morgue. They brought me in to identify him."

"Before that!"

"Two months ago. I went to his shop to get a new set of tires."

"And you never saw him alive again?"

"No."

"Did you know that he was doing drugs?"

"I thought he'd given that up, but people like him never quit." Mantoni lit his crumpled, red-stained cigarette. "They just take a break, so that they enjoy it more when they start up again."

"Maybe he needed some help," said Alberti.

Mantoni shrugged. "Maybe so. But who the fuck am I to try to teach other people how to live?"

"So the whole month before he killed himself, you never once talked to him?" Esposito asked.

"On the phone, a couple of times."

"About what?"

"What the fuck do you care?"

Esposito slammed the baton down onto the man's thigh.

Mantoni rubbed it. "Fuck off. One of the tires was worn out, and I wanted to return it, but he never opened the repair shop up. Both times, he hung up on me, with some excuse."

"What excuse?"

"He said that he was talking on the other line. But don't ask me who with or what about, because he didn't tell me." He spat the cigarette butt down a sewer grate and stood up. "Can I go now, or do you want to count the hairs on my dick?"

"Do you know that we could arrest you for assaulting a law enforcement officer?" said Alberti.

"Then arrest me, what am I supposed to tell you?"

"Fuck off. Go on, get out of here." Esposito gave him a shove.

Without turning around, Mantoni gave them the finger. "If you change your minds, I'm right here."

While the two policemen were recovering from the brawl with Loris's father, Colomba came back from Biella and managed to drag Dante off the sofa in order to go meet Demetra Melas. The woman had moved to Caglio, a small town not far from Portico, but a bit farther down in the lowlands. She was in a farmhouse that had been adapted for use as a group living facility, for the most part inhabited by old people who kept chickens and rabbits in their patches of the garden. Demetra used her patch of land to sit at a small plastic table, smoking, yelling at her neighbors if they made noise, and throwing rocks at the chickens. She kept a pair of Doberman pinschers she'd had sent to Italy directly from Athens. When the dogs saw Colomba and Dante arriving, they leaped to their feet snarling.

"The lady ex-cop has come to pay a visit." Demetra laughed. "And she even brought her handicapped friend along for the ride."

"How could I miss such a gracious social occasion?" Dante stepped away from his walker and extended his good hand toward the dogs' snouts.

Colomba clutched the pistol in her jacket pocket with the torn lining. "Don't do anything stupid."

Dante scratched the Dobermans behind the ears, and the two dogs immediately stopped barking and greeted him delightedly. "Don't do anything stupid like what?"

"Don't touch my dogs!" Demetra yelled.

"And don't you keep them on chains," said Dante, unhooking them.

Colomba put her hand on the grip of her sidearm again, but the two Dobermans ignored her and trotted around the courtyard, peeing repeatedly. Demetra went to get them by the scruff of their necks, and angrily locked them up in her mini-apartment.

"Do you mind telling me what else you want from me?" she asked.

Dante leaned on the walker. "To tell you that you'll never see your brother's money," he said laconically.

Demetra's eyes narrowed. "It's Tommy's money."

"The money is going to be placed under judicial seal because it's the proceeds of illegal activities. When the investigations are complete, you'll be lucky if you aren't under judicial restraint yourself."

Demetra laughed wholeheartedly. "How idiotic. Your brain is as lame as your legs."

Dante took off his glove. "My name is Dante Torre. Your brother changed my IV bags for a year and a half while I was being held prisoner by a terrorist named Leo Bonaccorso."

Colomba hauled him away. "Are you planning to tell everyone every single detail? I mean, okay if it's Lupo, but even this slut—"

"If you'd rather torture her, be my guest. Otherwise, this is the only thing we have to offer in exchange. In any case, if she's had anything to do with this, she already knows all about it, and she knows that we know, too."

Colomba huffed in annoyance. "So be it, but if you keep this up, they're going to shut down this investigation before we can even get started." She grabbed two chairs and turned to look at Demetra. "Now let's have a chat."

Demetra surprised them both by pulling out a cheap, outlet-brand bottle of brandy from under the table. "Then let's drink to your health, Torre." She poured the liquor into two plastic cups: Colomba didn't even touch hers, Dante grimaced after sniffing at his. "You're famous, even in Greece. Someone kidnapped you in Venice, right?"

"Right."

"It's obvious that my brother had nothing to do with it, but I'm not interested in running any risks. How much money do you want?"

"I'm not trying to blackmail you, Demetra. There's nothing I can do to help you to inherit that money by proxy. Tommy's money is going to remain frozen for years, unless it turns out that your brother was innocent. But . . . that's impossible. Your brother really did act as my jailer on Bonaccorso's behalf. When the story becomes public, you'll know all the sordid details." Colomba realized that Dante was playacting once again.

Though she didn't like it, she could guess at his objective.

"It wasn't him," said Demetra.

"How can you be so sure?" Dante asked.

"Because he wasn't a bad person. He was a coward, like all men, but he wouldn't have hurt a fly. Plus, it would have disgusted him to care for you. He couldn't even bring himself to get a tick off a dog."

"I never said that it had been his idea."

Demetra crushed her cigarette out on her heel. "If he did it under duress, then he was innocent."

"That depends on how badly they threatened him and how much he got out of it. There was certainly a lot of money in his account . . ."

"If you say so in court, they'll believe you," said Demetra. "Or are you trying to avenge a death?"

"We need evidence," said Colomba. "Revenge has nothing to do with it."

"Then let's get back to the reason we came here in the first place," said Dante. "To see Tommy. To ask him some questions. His money is none of my concern, but if I do find something out, that'll be to his benefit as well."

Demetra looked at him, mulling it over. At last, she said: "As you can imagine, he's not in my custody yet. Otherwise I'd have left for Greece, taking him with me. The judge says that he has to wait until the completion of the investigation into my brother."

"But can you visit him freely?" Colomba asked.

"Yes."

"The next time you go, tell the director that you want to have him examined by a psychiatric expert."

"There's already that clown Pala."

Dante glared at her. "Do you want to get your money or not?"

"Okay."

"Trust me, you need to speak in person to anyone you reach out to," Colomba weighed in. "Don't forget that you're still a person of interest and that they're probably monitoring your phone calls." She wrote down her cell phone number on a used train ticket and handed it to her. "Call me from a pay phone. And don't use names."

Demetra took the rumpled ticket with the tips of her fingers, the nails spangled with tiny enamel stars, and slipped it under her bottom. "There's one at the intersection. I'll use it. In any case, if there's anyone who was blackmailing him, it was Tommy's mother."

"You already told me that she didn't like you."

"That's not the only reason . . . Aristides and I had been quarreling for years, mainly on account of his 'girlfriends,' if we can dignify the term. But he never held a grudge with me for more than a week. He'd send me a gift from some corner of the world, or he'd call me to send his best wishes. This time, he didn't do it." A drip of mascara ran down her cheek, under her left eye. "I ought to have reached out to him. It's the only thing I blame myself for in this whole fucked-up story."

13

That evening they had dinner with Bart at the Mago Merlino farmstay, while the policemen stayed home to count their bruises. This was the first time that Bart was seeing Dante wide-awake, and for half an hour the two of them talked uninterruptedly, partly about the last year and a half, partly about Dante's state of health, which he claimed had never been better, though he was always exhausted by the time evening rolled around. The two women had *passatelli al ragù di carne*, while Dante picked at a dish of black truffle bruschetta—black truffles were easy to find in the forests around there. Bart updated them on her investigations at Villa Quiete, which so far hadn't produced results any different than the findings of the military scientists.

"It was a public building and there are thousands of genetic imprints, but the only one we were able to identify was yours," she said, looking at Dante.

"Not even the Melases'?" asked Colomba.

"No. The same thing for the fingerprints and other strange particulate matter. Whoever it was, they were very careful."

"Did you do the exam on my brother's samples?" Dante asked.

"Yes, but he isn't your brother," said Bart.

"Leave that alone," said Colomba. "He's fixated about this thing."

"I'm not fixated . . . So you collected them personally in the NOA dormitory?"

"I did, with my team, why?"

"Dante is convinced that Leo intentionally left the samples to be found," said Colomba.

Bart thought it over as she ate her tiramisu; she was the only one who had ordered dessert. "If you don't take the samples directly from the person, there's always a margin of risk, I suppose."

"Don't give him any leeway, Bart . . ." said Colomba.

"Then my brother's DNA really could be in that clinic."

"I'd have noticed. We used yours as a baseline. Certainly, if Leo wasn't your blood brother, then we'd have no way of knowing."

The waiter arrived. "Would anyone care for an espresso?"

Dante smiled. "We all would, but not here. My survival kit has arrived, at last."

14

Back in his room at the farmstay, Dante's survival kit consisted of twenty or so cardboard boxes packed with clothing, bags of whole-bean coffee, assorted pharmaceuticals purchased on the Deep Web, two laptops and a desktop, an iPad, a countless array of chargers, three Kindles, a sixty-inch OLED television set, a Pure radio, a ring-shaped Dyson air purifier, and, most important of all, a professional-grade espresso machine on a base, which Dante lovingly preheated with all the focused care of an astronaut performing maintenance on his spaceship. He'd stealthily rummaged through the survival kit, found a couple of tablets, crushed them into powder, and snorted them, and now his pupils were enormous again. Bart and Colomba pretended not to notice and waited while he ground a handful of blackish and irregularly shaped coffee beans in a wooden hand grinder. As he turned the handle, it made as much noise as a jackhammer, then he filled the espresso machine's filter baskets with the fine powdered coffee.

"At last, I can put an end to my abstinence. Let's celebrate with a little something from Misha's Mundi Coffee. Peruvian. Probably the rarest brew on earth. I already wanted to let you try it before Venice, but it was vacuum-packed and it's kept perfectly. Notes of tropical fruit, hay, and brandy, among other things."

"And does it come out of the butt of some wild animal?" Colomba asked suspiciously.

"Mmm . . . yes."

"Oh, come on now . . ."

"It's not my fault that digestive enzymes have exceptional effects on the coffee beans. This was *processed* by South American ring-tailed coatimundi. They're members of the raccoon family, and I assure you, they weren't mistreated."

"All they have to do is poop out coffee so we can drink it," said Bart, sprawled on Dante's bed. She'd been working till all hours at the clinic and she was exhausted.

"The coffee beans are rinsed of the excrement and then roasted at four hundred and fifty degrees Fahrenheit. And there is excrement in everything we eat, like the peanuts on the counter of a bar. Half of them contain traces of fecal matter left by the waitstaff."

"That's true," Bart confirmed.

"I'm going to throw up now," said Colomba.

Dante sniffed at the filter basket before twisting it into place. "How long has it been since you had any, CC? I've never seen you drink an espresso since you thawed me out."

"More or less since when we lost you," said Colomba, gazing into his eyes.

Dante remained motionless for a few seconds, then turned around and faced the espresso maker to keep from showing how deeply moved he was.

Dante put five porcelain demitasse cups under the spouts and started the machine up. The room instantly filled with the sweet aroma of espresso. Colomba took her cup, her hands trembling, and not just because she was afraid of dropping it; Bart's eyes were glistening. Alberti took a cup for himself and another for his partner, concealing the bottle of grappa he planned to use to spike it. Dante tossed back his cup in little more than a sip, then made two more for himself in rapid succession without another word. Colomba had no sooner finished hers—it seemed a little bland, she thought, but she kept her impression to herself—before she asked for another, even if the caffeine had immediately set her heart racing. "You're actually back. I still can't quite believe it."

"Maybe this is all a dream, and you're bleeding out right now, dying on the floor of the Palasport back in Venice," said Dante.

"Don't even joke about it."

Bart asked for a refill. "That's the problem with the brain. It processes all the incoming information from the sensory organs, but sometimes it just creates new information out of nowhere, and there's no real way of telling the difference."

"Will the two of you just cut it out?" Colomba grumbled. "I have nightmares as it is."

"She hates science," Dante said to Bart with a complicit smile.

"She's a genuine old-school knucklehead cop."

"If the two of you want to be left alone, I'm happy to comply," Colomba said in an acidic tone.

Bart dragged her down onto the bed and gave her a hug. "Cut it out, dummy."

Dante made himself another espresso. "Speaking of science, I wanted to know what Bart thinks of my theory about Martina. I have to make a confession, ladies: I talked to Lupo today."

"Who's Lupo?" Bart asked.

"A carabiniere," Colomba snapped. "Why did you do that?"

"Because I promised to keep him informed of our progress, and because I wanted to know if he'd give us a hand."

"We don't need him," said Colomba.

"That depends . . . I figured that, seeing as Dr. Bartone was around here, she might be able to help confirm my hypothesis about Martina."

"Dante thinks that she was knocked out with an insulin injection," Colomba explained.

"How could I confirm that without doing an autopsy?" Bart asked, baffled. "Where's the body?"

"Still in the Pesaro morgue, waiting for the completion of the investigation," said Colomba.

Dante smiled apologetically. "Not exactly."

15

At two in the morning a butcher's refrigerator truck parked in the hospital courtyard and two male nurses wearing carabiniere boots eased a gurney out of the back door. Lashed to the gurney was Martina: the male nurses were Lupo and Bruno. They had put a mask over her face and she was swathed in a sheet up to her chin.

Martina was rolled down various hallways to the diagnostic radiology ward, where they placed her on the bed of the CAT scanner, which continued shuttling back and forth for a full hour, bombarding her with enough radiation to fell an elephant. Controlling the movements of the scanner was Bart, whose eyelids were drooping from lack of sleep, but whose movements were still characterized by her customary diligent precision.

With her X-ray scalpels, Bart sliced into Martina's abdomen, digging deeper millimeter by millimeter, creating three-dimensional images thin enough to allow her to search for anomalies. Finally, between one suture and the next in the leg of the Y that had been carved into Martina's torso by the medical examiner, she identified a subcutaneous hematoma no bigger than the head of a pin. It ran down at a ninety-degree angle into the body, to a depth of 5.6 millimeters: the average length of an insulin hypodermic needle.

"You nailed it," she said to Dante. "And I want you to know that I expect a giant pack of coffee to show off to my friends."

"You can count on it," said Dante, leaning forward and elaborately kissing her hand. Lupo pocketed the report, in accordance with the agreement he'd made with Dante to keep his lips zipped until the Bonaccorso investigation had been completed.

The corpse was starting to stink at room temperature. It was wheeled back out to the refrigerator truck and taken back to the morgue in Pesaro, where the night guardian, an old acquaintance of Bruno's, given his arrest record as a flasher, had willingly agreed to turn a blind eye to the unorthodox transport of a corpse entrusted to his keeping.

Colomba, on the other hand, drove Bart back to Rimini. When she got back at daybreak, she rushed into Dante's room, hoping to wake him up, but he was already doing muscle exercises, stretching an elastic band with his feet, dressed in a mime's overalls.

"I'm sleepy as hell, but I'm just too furious with you," said Colomba. "You busted my chops about how I lied to you, and now you're pulling stunts like this behind my back. I'm thinking about sending you back to Rome." Dante put down the elastic band and mopped the sweat off his brow with a terry-cloth towel.

"You're right. Want a cup of coffee?" he asked, going over to the espresso machine.

"My heart is still racing, and I'd like to sleep until noon."

"Then how about a Moscow Mule?"

"Okay, but quit changing the subject! Why did you make a side deal with Lupo without telling me?"

"Because we would have gone back and forth about whether or not it was a good idea, and I didn't want to tell you about it unless I was a thousand percent sure that I was right."

"You're always a thousand percent sure that you're right."

"True, but in this case I was hoping I was wrong." Dante made a couple of cocktails in the copper mugs that had come in the survival kit, after filling them with crushed ice. "I didn't want to hurt your feelings." He turned on the MP3 player and started a compilation of Asha Bhosle songs, turning up the volume until it provided an irritating background soundtrack. "I was hoping to avoid that."

"Now you're just pulling my leg. Spit it out."

"Why did Leo kill Martina the way he did? He could have murdered her in a thousand different ways, in any of a thousand different places, but he killed her right there, near Melas's hideout, which was the riskiest thing he could have done."

"Maybe he just planned to imprison her in the hayloft, and then something else happened we don't know about yet."

Dante shook his head. "I looked on the map, there are crevasses and isolated clearings the whole way between here and where she was killed. Even if he'd drugged her there and not a stone's throw from your house, he could have gotten away and tossed her body practically anywhere. Same thing applies if she'd been following him, which I don't think happened."

"I don't believe it, either. She wouldn't have abandoned her assigned post. She was on a stakeout."

"Exactly. Which means Leo wanted her to die there. Because he wanted someone to find Melas's hideout and rescue me. You were just the first one to get there."

16

Colomba sucked on her cocktail, stalling for time. She was too tired to think fast. "So you're saying Leo killed Martina as a way of making sure someone found you," she said.

"Yes. You weren't moving fast enough, and I was dying, tied to a bed."

"Come on, that doesn't hold together," said Colomba, doing her best to keep her anxiety at bay. "All Leo would have had to do is make an anonymous phone call to the police or to me. Why would he have done it in such a contorted manner?"

"So he could stay in the shadows. He sent Tommy to your house, he got Martina to plant the hammer. What other reason would he have had, except to get you to take the bait? He knew that they'd never prosecute you for it."

"Really?"

"And the phone call in Milan . . . You told me that you never could figure out why he called you, right? Here's the answer. He wanted to get you to guess that he knew where you lived, without telling you directly. I'm running away, but in the meantime I'm warning you . . . Do you believe that?"

"And do you believe that I'm an idiot?" Colomba shouted at him.

Dante started polishing the espresso machine. "I knew you'd lose your temper."

"Leave that thing alone. It's already gleaming," said Colomba, getting to her feet while her anger changed to shame. She forced herself to speak in a calmer tone. "If Leo abandoned you, it's because he had to burn his bridges after they found the *Chourmo*. He knew from Romero that the DCT would trace it back to him unless he did."

"That's something that only those idiots in intelligence could come up with. He had a reason for abandoning me. He had a reason for getting you involved. Just like he had a reason for killing Martina the way he did."

"What reason?"

"I haven't connected all the dots yet. But just think of my brother as a spider tucked away in its hidey-hole, tugging on its web"—and here he waved his hand in a circular gesture to take in the surrounding hills—"in all directions. And if you jostle his web, he won't come out again. Martina, Loris, the Melases, his neighbors in the apartment building in Milan. They all jostled his web, and they all died. It's no accident." Dante took one of Colomba's hands in his. "You saved my life, and who knows how many others. The blood of these victims falls on my brother and on all those people who chose to do nothing to stop him. Not on you."

Colomba's eyes were glistening. "I'm sick of it, Dante. I feel as if I reek of death."

"Let's get out of here. I mean, like right now. Let's just dump those two dumb cops and run away."

Colomba shook her head. "No, no. I can't. There's Tommy. Leo may have just used him to get me out of hiding, but I don't want him to wind up like all the others . . . I don't want to get a phone call one of these mornings so I can go down and view his corpse, too."

"Then get ready for some more surprises, CC. None of them good."

17

Colomba slept until one in the afternoon, and when she finally woke up she found a text on her phone from D'Amore, asking her to join him in Rimini, where he was supervising Bart's work. So Colomba had to go the whole way back a second time, though this time she left the driving to Esposito.

D'Amore was waiting for her in front of Villa Quiete, leaning against one of those delivery vans that the intelligence agencies used for surveillance and stakeouts. Written on the side was the name of a nonexistent construction company, along with phone numbers that connected to an answering machine, to avoid arousing unnecessary suspicions.

"Would you care to say hello to the doctor?" D'Amore asked as he walked toward her.

"I'd just as soon let her work undisturbed," Colomba replied. She wasn't sure she'd be able to keep a straight face if she saw Bart again. They walked down to the water, talking as they went. The seashore was a little over a half mile away, and a pair of plainclothes NOA officers trailed along behind them at a discreet distance. They were the two nonbrothers.

D'Amore put an oversize e-cigarette up to his lips. "We understand how Bonaccorso blew up the apartment building in Milan. He sabotaged the electronic control panel of the heating system. It was connected to the internet, and he just sent a command to turn off the burner and bypass the thermocouple and safety valve. The room filled up with gas and then . . ."

"*Boom*," said Colomba. "No explosives?"

"None at all. That's the reason the bomb-disposal technicians weren't able to do anything to stop him. A couple of them were still inside when it happened," said D'Amore, with a veil of sadness in his eyes.

Colomba understood that there was something personal at play here, but she didn't ask about it.

"I'm really sorry," she said. "Did you find anything useful in the rubble?"

"No. The only good news is that the woman who lived next door is out of danger now, and soon she'll be able to start talking to us. You never know."

They reached the waterfront esplanade known as the Lungomare Fellini and leaned against the parapets that separated the sidewalk from the beach. Beneath them, the sand and the breakwaters were immersed in the greenish glow of the late-winter sun. The smell of brine was overwhelming.

"Do you think that Leo brought Dante here in the sailboat, and then went back and sank it?" Colomba asked.

"It's hard to imagine he wouldn't have been noticed by the coast guard. Still, it's a remarkable coincidence you should have asked me that, because we've finally turned up something on the *Chourmo*. It used to be called the *Solea II*, and it was the property of a Greek shipowner who died later in a shipwreck near the island of Zakynthos."

A lightbulb lit up in Colomba's head. "Isn't he one of the people that Giltine killed before coming to Italy?"

"Yes."

"So the Melases were connected to Belyy . . ." Colomba said in surprise.

"The late Signor Melas's father certainly was," said D'Amore. "He had a lot more money than the inheritance he left his son. At least ten times as much. And nearly all of that money was sent abroad. We've lost track of it, after Hong Kong." He blew out a cloud of vanilla-scented vapor into the chilly air, and then waved it away with his hands.

"What was the shipyard good for?"

"Considering that many of the boats they repaired wound up being sent to African countries and then were frequently sent back for 'special maintenance work,' we can theorize any number of things, ranging from arms trafficking to blood diamonds, but we've only started investigating in that direction."

"But the son sold it all."

"Maybe he just didn't want to be involved. Or else he figured he already had enough money. But there's something even more important. We've always wondered how Bonaccorso knew that Giltine was about to unleash a bloodbath in Italy," said D'Amore. "Now we think that he just followed her yacht. And that means that Bonaccorso knew where to look."

"Because he knew the Greek shipowner," said Colomba, suddenly short of breath. This was the first piece of information about Leo she'd been presented with that had even an inkling of a chance of being true. "So he was a part of the magic circle."

"That would explain a lot of things, wouldn't it?" D'Amore asked. "Except for one: Why did he let his boss be killed? If he knew that Giltine was planning the massacre in Venice, he could have alerted Belyy and saved his skin."

D'Amore spewed out another cloud of vanilla-scented smoke. "Belyy had set up a small empire of his own in the private security business and COW was a useful screen organization. But there has never been an empire in the history of the world that someone hasn't tried to overthrow. Maybe Bonaccorso was working for the revolution."

Colomba suddenly glimpsed the image of Tommy's playing card in her mind's eye, and understood. "Or else he was working for the new king. And still is. Which is why he's still out there sowing pain and death."

18

Dante looked at Loris's little single-family house, leaning on a tree on the other side of the street. He was wearing a studded leather jacket over a *Metal Gear Solid* T-shirt.

"There's no security," he said to Alberti, who was looking at him through the window of the parked car.

"Weren't you already convinced that Loris was Bonaccorso's involuntary accomplice?"

"Yes. But that's not enough for me. Come on, get out of the car." Dante waited for Alberti to turn off the engine and lock the car. "You may have seen Leo twice, but to me he's the man who inserted a fucking valve in my gut."

"I understand that, Signor Torre. But still . . ."

Dante interrupted him. "My brother knows me down to the last pore in my skin. But I don't know a damned thing about him. I don't know why he followed me for two years before kidnapping me, I don't know what he was doing here, and most of all, why *he put me* here. So now I want to know things that, in another situation, I would have just taken for granted. Is that clear?"

"You're afraid that he's smarter than you," Alberti said with a smile.

Dante sighed. "Exactly." He put his weight on the walker and pointed at the front door bedecked with the judicial seals of the criminal court. "Open the door with your universal cop passkey."

"No way."

Dante made his unsteady way over to the front door. "No problem, I brought my kit. Help me stand up, if you wouldn't mind." Dante pushed the walker aside and crouched down in front of the lock, while Alberti steadied him with a hand on each shoulder. It was a pretty ordinary kind of lock, and Dante opened it in a matter of seconds with a set of fine metal hooks, and then put them away in their leather case. When he pushed the front door open, though, the dark lobby closed in around him. "You go in first, while I smoke a cigarette outside."

"I can do it for you, if you want."

"No. Thanks. Just roll up all the shutters and open all the windows." Dante leaned against the outside wall and looked up at the sky, seeing nothing but a giant cage. He mopped the icy sweat off his brow.

Alberti put on a pair of gloves and a pair of shoe covers and entered Loris's home for the second time. The place stank pretty bad, but there was no garbage in sight and all traces of drugs had disappeared, including the cigarette butts. He opened the place up wide as had been requested, and looked out onto Portico from above. It had been a nice bright day and the setting sun was turning the roofs red.

"Are you enjoying the panorama?" Dante asked as he came up from behind. He'd recovered, but his breathing was still labored.

"It's not bad here," said Alberti.

"Sure, if you're a cow. There must be a base for a cordless phone around here somewhere," he said. "Do you remember that he was holding the receiver when he died?"

"Maybe it's down in the repair shop."

"No. The number of Loris's landline matches up with his home address. There is no phone service in the repair shop."

"Isn't it kind of too far for it to work?"

"Exactly," said Dante, still standing at the window. "And there's another strange thing. The mechanic's dad told you that he was always on the other line. The only other line is his home number, but in the last year he's received practically no phone calls at all."

Alberti finally found the cordless phone base under a pillow. It was disconnected from both the phone jack and the plug. "It looks like it wasn't being used, Signor Torre. Maybe it really was just a prop."

"Open it up, if you don't mind."

Alberti did as asked, unscrewing the cover on the base with a scorched pocketknife he'd found in the sink. Inside he found a battery wrapped in duct tape and a SIM card connected to a chip the size of a postage stamp. Alberti composed music, so he knew a little something about electronics, and he could see that the transmitter that sent the signal to the cordless receiver had been disconnected from the phone circuit and rerouted to the chip. "There's something odd about this. I don't think it's a phone tap," he said.

"I think it's the exact opposite," said Dante, and plugged the base in, making a contact with one of his lock-picking tools. Sparks showered in all directions.

"Look out, you're going to get a shock," said Alberti in alarm.

Dante showed him that he'd been using his gloved hand. "It's insulated. And where I'm touching it, I don't think it's any more than twelve volts. Hold on . . ." He let loose some more sparks. "Do you hear anything?"

"No."

Dante looked around and then, on the floor, buried under a pile of old sports magazines, he found a stereo. He turned it on, pulled the audio cable out of the CD player, and stripped the jack with his teeth, laying bare the metal wires inside. He spit the plastic sheath into an ashtray.

"You're contaminating a crime scene, Signor Torre."

"We work with the double-oh-sevens, Alberti, we have a license to kill." He spat out another little chunk of plastic. "If this doesn't work either, I give up." Using the bare wires, he touched the interior of the cordless base. The stereo sputtered, then there was nothing but static.

"Something's making a contact . . ." said Alberti.

Dante turned the volume all the way up. "Tell me if you hear anything that's not just white noise."

Alberti felt his teeth vibrate. "It's like fingernails on a blackboard," he said.

Dante turned it off, put the cordless base into his overcoat pocket, and limped over to the door. "Come on, we're done here. I need something to drink."

Alberti tried to put everything back as it had been and clumsily replaced the judicial seal on the door handle. He caught up with Dante on Portico's main street and together they walked down to the town park, where a little gazebo was serving as a bar. Dante drank a glass of vodka, straight, sitting on a bench. As far as he was concerned, there was no point in ordering a cocktail unless the bar had at least one certificate of excellence.

"What was that stuff?" Alberti asked.

Dante lit a cigarette. "Have you ever heard of Nevada? The company, not the state. According to the intelligence agencies, it was one of COW's subsidiaries. After Belyy's death, there was a complete reshuffle of the board of directors, impossible to trace it back to him."

"Never heard of it."

"It was founded in 2010 in Washington, DC, and at first it had only one customer: the United States government. It worked in the sectors of cryptography and secure communications technology. Then, seeing that business was booming, it started selling systems to private citizens. And do you know what one of their most popular products is? The ultrasound acoustic dissuader."

"For mosquitoes?"

"No, for human beings. If you turn it on, all the young men and women and boys and girls under the age of twenty-five take to their heels, and stop loitering around your shop windows or smoking crack in front of your apartment house entrance. They call it Teen Buzz, and the device that generates it is called the Driller." Dante held up the device they'd removed from the cordless phone. "This is a Driller."

"And grown-ups don't hear anything?"

"No. You're not thirty yet, so you're in the range, while Loris was younger than you and suffered the full effects of it."

"It's connected to a SIM card. So it turned the cordless into a cell phone."

"That means that, even if Loris unplugged it, it would still work. So my brother calls that number and the whistling starts. Loris starts being unable to sleep, having nightmares, snorting coke just to stay awake, and he skids off the rails. At that point, Leo starts talking to him directly through the SIM card. He tells him that his girlfriend is dead and that he needs to take revenge. *Kill Colomba Caselli. Woo-oo-oo.*" Dante imitated the sound of a cartoon ghost.

"And was it Bonaccorso who installed this in his house?"

"Or maybe an accomplice." He turned the Driller over in his gloved hand and pulled out the SIM card. "It's a Dutch Lyca Mobile, anonymous. There's no way to get call records. Do you have any fingerprint powder with you?"

"You've developed a strange idea of the work I do, Signor Torre . . ."

"Yes, that it's pointless. Let's go buy some glue."

Colomba returned from Rimini tired and starving, and found Dante, Esposito, and Alberti playing junior chemist on the back porch. They'd built a sort of mini-greenhouse with some coat hangers and something that looked very similar to . . . "That's the garment bag for my down coat," said Colomba.

"It was lying around . . ." said Dante.

"Sure, in my closet." Colomba looked at the "greenhouse" more carefully. Inside it was a drinking glass full of some slimy transparent substance, another that was smoking, and a broken chunk of plastic. "What is that stuff?" she asked.

"Gorilla Glue with cyanoacrylate. Glass of hot water. And Driller," Dante explained, pointing to each object. "The hot water is there to hydrate old fingerprints. The cyanoacrylate vulcanizes them, making them visible."

"We found the Driller at Loris's house," said Alberti.

Colomba stopped him. "Start over. From the beginning."

Dante told her everything, while the fumes from the glue were bonding with the grease of the fingerprints, turning them three-dimensional. And she told him all about her conversation with D'Amore. "The king is dead, long live the king," Dante commented. "And something tells me that the Nevada company has just jumped onto the winner's bandwagon."

"But is Leo the King of Diamonds or does he just work for him?" asked Esposito. He opened the plastic bag and pulled out the Driller, then he dusted it with powdered pencil graphite. A series of black fingerprints appeared on the battery.

Colomba took a picture of the fingerprints with her cell phone. "It wouldn't take D'Amore two seconds to run them down on the system," she said, "but I'd just as soon keep this part of the investigation to ourselves."

"I'll ask a partner of mine for a favor," said Esposito.

"That might not be necessary, even though I hope it is. Hold on." Dante found the file folder on Martina that he'd left on the kitchen sofa, which now stood under the trees in the back of the house. He still couldn't stand to stay indoors for long, especially in the dark, and the night before he'd slept outside wrapped up in a cocoon of blankets. He brought the file folder back to the patio and compared Martina's fingerprints with the ones on the Driller. "A waste of time," he said with some irritation. The fingerprints matched exactly.

"She didn't even use gloves, what a dope," said Esposito.

"She thought she was working for the good guys. Working for someone who could have her transferred to Rome. Why should she wear gloves?" said Colomba, boiling over with rage. "Leo got her to put this thing in Loris's house to use it when he killed her."

"That guy is sick in the head," said Esposito. "I really am starting to think he might be your brother, Genius."

PART THREE

THE TWO KINGS

BEFORE

The man who used to call himself Leo Bonaccorso revs down the out-board motor and sets the autopilot. Behind him, a life that is already starting to dissolve; before him, Nothingness.

Mu.

When he tries to explain to someone what "Mu" means, he rarely if ever manages to make himself understood. According to Zen it's the symbol of that which cannot be described or defined in any way: Nothingness. And Nothingness is the only god he believes in. The most powerful god, before which the universe itself will eventually succumb. And so, what is the only answer to questions such as right or wrong, Good or Evil?

The man who used to call himself Leo Bonaccorso steps out onto the deck and unwraps an energy bar, seeking within himself the lingering traces of the last identity he'd put on. From time to time a thought occurs to him that stubbornly remains alive, as if the mask refuses to let itself be deleted. A regret, a nostalgic yearning. When he finds a thought like that, he writes it on a scrap of paper and sets fire to it.

What's rebelling against his will this time is the name of a woman with green irises that change with her mood and the weather. He writes that name on the wrapper of the energy bar, lights it, and watches as it falls into the sea, turning into a shower of sparks. He sniffs at the scent of the ashes it's been transformed into, and he feels purified.

The watch on his wrist vibrates. The man who no longer has a name looks out at the sea one last time—a reminder of the infinite array of possibilities that Nothingness endows him with—and then goes below-decks, stepping into a cabin that the prior owner of the boat used as a storeroom. He had tossed everything in that cluttered room into the water, except for an extraordinary assortment of narcotics and poi-

sons, synthesized or blended with a masterful touch that verged on the artistic. He fills an insulin syringe with an opioid solution, then steps toward his prisoner to administer the dose, exactly as he's been doing regularly for days.

Dante is curled up in a fetal position in one of the berths, naked except for an adult diaper; his wrists and ankles are fastened tight with duct tape, and a rubber ball is jammed into his mouth with a bit, part of the standard gear for masochists. He's awake now—he always wakes up between one dose and another—but his eyes are glassy. His jailer pats him on the head, then proceeds to change his diaper and wash him with a soapy bath sponge. Dante starts to come to, kicking his legs like a seal. The other man waits for his eyes to focus, then loosens the mouth bit.

"It's lunchtime," he says.

Dante licks his cracked lips. "No," he murmurs.

"You can either eat like this, or through a tube stuck down your throat. Which do you prefer?"

"Kill me."

"Don't be so melodramatic."

The man with no name takes another energy bar out of his pocket, unwraps it, and places it against Dante's lips. At first he sucks on it hesitantly, then he starts biting it. It's soft and he has no difficulty. His jailer lets him drink a glass of isotonic solution, then he disinfects Dante's lips and rubs a dab of balm onto them.

"Don't put that thing back on me," Dante says. "Please."

"It's for your own good. You'd be capable of severing your veins with your teeth." That's not a wisecrack: he's pretty sure that Dante would try, and he's even more certain that he'd succeed. "You just need to be brave, little brother," he says. "It's almost over. And you'll never even remember waking up again. That's how it always is."

Gripping Dante's left arm tightly, he makes his veins pop, and then he delicately slides the thin hypodermic needle into his flesh.

And it is at that moment that the world turns upside down.

The cabin tilts thirty degrees, and the man who was Bonaccorso falls backward, hitting the door. The bed is screwed to the floor, as is only right and proper in a gas-powered boat, but Dante slides out of it, half-stunned, hitting the planking of the hull. Wrists and ankles are still bound with duct tape, and the drug coursing through his veins keeps him in a dull state between sleep and wakefulness.

There's a smell of chemical fumes, then the engine dies. Without even bothering to try to look out the closed door, the man without a name calculates his chances of survival. The Chourmo is taking on water. From the angle of the deck, he can tell that he has less than two minutes to try to get out, and his odds are growing worse with each passing second.

Water is starting to seep underneath the door. He resists the rational imperative that ought to drive him out of that cabin and grabs one of Dante's feet; he drags him closer, into the puddle that's starting to form, then he frees his hands and feet and starts strapping him into a life jacket.

Dante mutters, "You killed her" and "blood."

The man who was once Bonaccorso hits him in the face. "Your friend is fine," he says. "If I'd wanted to kill her I would have twisted the knife in the opposite direction."

Dante's hand restrains him, feebly. "I'll die of radiation," he mumbles.

"It's not radiation that you need to worry about." The boat tilts even more. A lamp breaks off the wall and rolls toward them. Mu pushes it away with one hand and lifts Dante with the other, holding him single-handed the way one does with sleeping children. He opens the doors and steps into the bilge surging with icy water and kerosene. There's a wooden crate floating with a scorpion clinging to it.

By now, the water has reached his waist, and he's walking toward the ladder, which with the Chourmo keeling over on one side has risen to an angle of almost ninety degrees. He uses Dante as a flotation device, then he pushes him onto the ladder, by now practically horizontal. The bubble of air in the bilge is keeping only the stern of the boat in the air, as far as the quarterdeck and part of the starboard hull.

There's a small explosion toward the bow, when the kerosene that has spilled out of the fuel tanks catches fire on the surface. Now the Chourmo looks like nothing so much as a comet with a long glowing tail on a sea covered with black smoke.

Dante opens only his left eye, rolling it upward into the socket. "Then what do I have . . . to worry about," he finally manages to get out.

"The right question is who, little brother. If you ever run into him, you'll certainly recognize him, and if you do . . . run as fast as you can." He grabs Dante and with a twist of the hips hurls him down, into the flaming sea.

CHAPTER 1

For a forensic scientist, night is an investigation's best friend, because sometimes light covers things up instead of revealing them. If it's a matter of getting blood to react with an application of Luminol, you might only need dim light and a powerful black light, but what Bart and her team were trying to find in the hallway of the Villa Quiete clinic was far more evanescent than mere bloodstains.

The hallway leading to the room where Dante had been held prisoner was sealed now, and a device that looked like nothing so much as a smoke machine from a film set was spewing a vaporized solution of sea salt and distilled water into the air. Two of Bart's assistants dragged the machine from one end of the hallway to the other, careful not to step where they'd already passed.

Bart turned on the ultraviolet lamp and put on her goggles. "Lights!" she shouted.

Outside the door to the stairway, D'Amore was helping one of Bart's assistants to open the cover of the junction box. Unlike the forensic technicians, he wasn't wearing a head-to-foot jumpsuit—only gloves and shoe covers—but he was steering clear of the points that Bart was checking at that time. "Exactly what is she looking for?" he asked the assistant.

The assistant was a woman in her early thirties, wearing heart-shaped eyeglasses, which she pushed up to the bridge of her nose before answering.

"Do you know what aequorin is?"

"I'm afraid not."

"It's a molecule that can be found in certain jellyfish. Very similar to the luciferin found in fireflies."

"The stuff that makes them light up."

"Bioluminescence, exactly," the assistant confirmed. "Luciferin has also been found in certain crustaceans and types of plankton that emit blue light when stimulated. Off Skerki Banks, there are a number of microorganisms that possess these physical characteristics. If we find samples of DNA or particulate matter that has been contaminated by aequorin or luciferin, and that doesn't belong to Torre . . ."

"Then they might belong to Bonaccorso or perhaps an accomplice." D'Amore put the e-cigarette into his mouth with a broad smile. "That strikes me as a fine idea."

"If there were a Nobel Prize for forensic science, Dr. Bartone would have won it long ago," the assistant said with great conviction. "We've sprayed the hallway with a solution of distilled water and sea salt, because an essential component of bioluminescence is calcium ions. Let's hope it prompts a reaction, even if it's been nearly a year and a half."

D'Amore pushed aside a length of black plastic tarp that had been pulled over the doorway into the hall and peeked in through the glass. At first all he could see was darkness but then, suddenly . . .

Inside, Bart, her eyes already accustomed to the dark, was holding her breath. She'd hoped to find tiny scattered sparks of light, but now, before her eyes, there glittered a galaxy of blue stars.

The NOA officers relieved each other, starting a new shift, over at the dog shelter, and a black car moved away, turning back and forth in the switchback curves. Dante followed the headlights until they vanished behind the trees, then he put the boom box on the table, pushing aside the dirty plates and Alberti's regulation-issue PM12 submachine gun. He started up the playlist of *Krrish 3*, a movie he'd watched at least a couple of times in the original Hindi, then he took a seat at the head of the table, carefully easing himself down with his shiny new wooden walking stick. He hadn't eaten with the others. His eyes looked demented, and there were new circles underneath them.

"Where did you get that?" Esposito asked, pointing at his walking stick.

"It came today," Dante replied. "A Ham Brooks classic. My legs are working better, and I don't need the walker. At least I don't seem like an old mummy anymore."

"Big improvement." Esposito stood up. "I'm going to get some sleep. Good night, Deputy Captain."

"You're a big boy now, you can stay up late with the grown-ups," said Dante.

"No, thanks. I can't take any more of this Arab hurly-burly you make me listen to all day long."

"It's Indian, not Iraqi. And even if they were Iraqi, they have other words for it," Dante said. "Is there a special course you have to take to be a Neanderthal policeman, or did you just recruit him special?" he asked Colomba.

She grabbed the cane out of his hands and slammed it down onto the table top.

"That's enough bullshit. Sit down, Esposito. This concerns you, too," she said grimly.

Dante poured himself a glass of vodka to cut the tremors caused by the mix of caffeine and Ritalin. "While I was under anesthesia, I had a dream. My brother was in it. Every so often I remember another snippet of it. While nearly everything else disappears, Leo remains perfectly clear in my mind. I can hear his voice. And I see water submerging me."

"Okay . . ." said Esposito. "And we care about this why?"

"In my dream, my brother wanted to warn me against someone. Maybe the conversation never actually took place, maybe it's just my subconscious, but I'd say that this is the gist of the matter. Leo killed Belyy and let Giltine destroy his magic circle of accomplices. Impossible to think that there wasn't someone behind him, providing him with information and logistical support."

"Someone from COW who wanted the old founder dead," said Esposito.

"Most likely. And now? Does he have a new boss? Who is he killing for?"

"Maybe for himself."

"Or maybe he just hasn't finished the job," said Alberti.

"There you go," said Dante. "So he must have some gray eminence from COW in his sights."

"And you think *he* lives here?" Colomba asked acidly.

"No, *you* live here. But let's take it one step at a time. Esposito, you're a policeman with a great deal of experience. How do you catch a fugitive on the run?"

"You try to find out where he sleeps, who brings him food, or money . . ."

"But what if they're all dead already, or out of the game, like Belyy's magic circle?"

"Then you look at his relatives. Or doesn't he have those, either?"

"No relatives. No name and no face."

Esposito shrugged. "Then I'd give up. I'm not Merlin the Magician."

"Leo can't give up. Because he knows that the person he's looking for, who survived the massacre, knows him and can't wait to take his revenge. CC?"

"Try to make sure that it's this person who sticks his nose out of hiding."

"Exactly. My brother is continuing to kill so as to attract his enemy's attention. And from the way he's operating, he's absolutely terrified of this enemy."

Bart's assistants were photographing like crazy with their special cameras capable of picking up luminous radiation invisible to the naked eye. Their jumpsuits were dripping from the ambient humidity.

"It's too much, Dr. Bartone," one of them, Robin Singh, said. Robin was a young man, barely twenty years old, who already had two university degrees in the hard sciences. "Bonaccorso couldn't have been dripping wet when he got here. Maybe there's something in the paint that's causing a reaction."

"Take samples and check the spectrometry." Bart took off her goggles to give them a wipe. "If they match, lay out a grid and take it all home. Imagine tiles ten centimeters on a side. I want a sample for every tile."

"Aye-aye, Doctor," said Robin.

"And keep a note of where you took it from."

Bart put her goggles back on and followed the bioluminescent wave all the way back to Dante's prison, where the only wall that seemed to have been contaminated by aequorin was the far wall. While the phosphorescence faded as the molecules oxidized, Bart seemed to see a shape through the shadow. She shut her eyes, then opened them again, trying to look with her peripheral vision, off to one side where the rods were more light-sensitive.

Just as it had seemed to her: an entire section of the wall—the central portion—wasn't giving off any light at all. The glowing wave stopped there and started up again immediately on the other side. A section roughly the size of a French door.

Bart hurried to delineate the boundaries with adhesive markers that were phosphorescent in their turn, though in another hue and still visible in daylight.

"Turn on the lights!" she shouted as she shut her eyes. The fluorescent overheads flickered to life, and Bart opened her eyes again and looked at the wall in front of her. All that could be seen were her markers; the rest was perfectly uniform. She tapped with her gloved hand on the section she'd marked off. It made exactly the same sound as the rest of the wall.

D'Amore stuck his head in. "Something good, Doctor?"

"I'd like to think so. That would be the first time that a cockamamie idea led to something good, even if it was my idea. Do you know if the military checked this with sonar?"

"Yes. But they didn't find anything."

Bart rapped again. "But there's definitely something here. They checked for explosives and everything, right?"

D'Amore nodded again.

"Robin!" Bart called out. "Let's do another exam with sniffers and sonar. And if we don't find anything strange, then let's start drilling."

Dante took a pack of cards out of his pocket and spread them on the table. He took off his glove and started to shuffle them. "My brother is looking for someone, and he's made use of a very expensive tactic, in terms of human lives." He turned over a card, apparently at random: it was the king of diamonds. "To Tommy, Leo is the King of Diamonds. A perfect choice of suit, considering the role played by COW's money."

"Ah, speaking of money. The bitch called me while I was in the shower. She wants to meet in the late morning at the group home," said Colomba.

"I'll have nightmares for years . . . Oh well." He spread the cards out in a couple of fans. "So let's say that the King of Diamonds, alias my brother, is looking for . . . the King of Spades, considering that the spades are swords in European decks?" He folded the fans of cards back up into a deck, and the king of spades appeared at the top of the deck. No one clapped. Dante set the deck down on the table, then continued with the jack and queen of diamonds. "These are the Melases." The *sette bello*, or seven of diamonds, a crucial card in the game of Scopa. "This is poor Martina. Suggest a card for Loris, CC."

"That would have to be the two," she said apathetically.

Dante cut the deck using his good hand, and turned over the central card. It was the two of diamonds. "Here are Leo's victims, or maybe we should say, the bread crumbs he scattered for the King of Spades to gather and follow." He distributed the cards over the table in order of death, in a chain that culminated at the king of hearts. Or king of cups, in the Italian suit. "Which would be me."

"Cups, definitely. But only because there's no such thing as a king of pills," Colomba muttered.

"What about us?" said Alberti.

Covering his good hand with his bad one, Dante produced the ace, queen, and jack of clubs. "Sorry, CC, I'm going to elevate you to ace of clubs. Especially since the billy club is the universal symbol of you cops."

"We should club people more often, truth be told," said Esposito.

"We said that my brother is afraid of the King of Spades and that all the spades are dead." He gathered all the cards of that suit into a mini deck and covered them up with his bad hand. "And that he was therefore looking for something to lure him into a trap. What do you think that would be?"

"Dante, please . . ." said Colomba, not at all amused.

"Okay, I'll tell you." He raised his hand. Instead of the mini deck, he now held the king of hearts. No one had noticed when he'd picked it up from the table. "*Me.*"

"Why would the King of Spades be so interested in you, sir?" Alberti asked.

"Maybe he wants to split my head open and see what the Father did to it," Dante replied. "Because, let's not forget, Leo has had dealings with him, too. In fact, he probably was a member of his organization, since he focused on Tommy, who was one of the Father's victims, even if we can't say how or when. That can't be an accident. Maybe, once the Father was out of the running, my brother set about finding a new boss. And he decided to use me as a pawn. That would explain why Leo started pursuing me directly after the Father's death."

"There's something I don't understand, Signor Torre," said Alberti. "Why here, of all places?"

Colomba turned her head, clearly irritated. "According to Dante, because I live here."

"If my brother's enemy is interested in me, then he knows Colomba and he's probably been keeping up to date on the things that have been happening to her. My brother made things happen here in the hopes that the King of Spades might come around here in person and stick his nose into matters."

"And was he successful?"

"All I know is that Colomba, luckily, managed to find me before he could. Otherwise, who knows what would have happened to me."

Colomba felt her breathing become labored, and the sounds around her turned liquid and distant, as if they were coming from the far end of the valley that stretched out before them.

"CC, are you okay? You're looking very pale."

Colomba clutched at the table. The world had started to spin: no, even worse, to break up into dark patches, shadows that echoed in her ears, that slid past on either side of her field of vision.

Shadows that were screaming.

Colomba threw herself to the floor on all fours, knocking her chair over behind her, and took a punch at the portico, skinning her knuckles against the wood.

Dante dropped down beside her and put his arm around her shoulders. "Breathe, CC . . . just breathe."

She shoved him away and threw another punch. And then . . . her lungs were suddenly uncorked. Slumped on the floor, Colomba started breathing again, feverishly, wiping away tears of pain.

"CC . . . what happened? What did you see?" Dante asked her.

"If Leo had something in mind at the clinic . . . Are you sure there's no danger right now?"

Dante understood and cursed himself for an idiot. "Bart," he gasped in a whisper.

5

Bart's staff had redone the environmental analysis twice in Dante's room at Villa Quiete, without once turning up traces of explosives or toxic substances. Just to make doubly sure, they also took samples from the wall and the ceiling, but all they found was paint, cement, and dead bugs.

At that point, Bart ordered the battery-powered drill with vacuum attachment brought to her. There was a clear plastic bell around the drill bit which allowed the dust and residue from the drilling to be sucked away and then conveyed through a corrugated hose into an airtight container at the worker's feet. Two advantages at once: no environmental contamination and the possibility of preserving samples from the drilling.

With Robin's help, Bart took just a couple of minutes to penetrate the cement barrier, punching through into what seemed like a gap between the brick walls. The tiny electric motor of the vacuum cleaner started straining, and for fear of burning it out, Bart hastened to turn it off: those gadgets were as delicate as porcelain and every bit as expensive.

Robin pointed to the clear plastic shroud. The cement dust had clustered along the length of the drill bit instead of being sucked away toward the mouth of the vacuum hose. "There seems to be a pressure differential," he said.

"That's odd . . ." Cautiously, Bart tipped the handle of the drill ever so slightly. The plastic bell was clamped to the wall, like a suction cup . . . as if there were a vacuum on the other side of the wall. The pull wasn't that powerful, and if Bart had released it, the drill would have fallen to the floor, but something told her that wouldn't be a very good idea.

The assistant with the heart-shaped glasses called her from the far end of the hallway, waving her cell phone. "Doctor," she said.

Like everyone who was working in the "hot" zone, Bart had left her cell phone outside in order to avoid interference with the delicate equipment and machinery. If they had decided to bother her, it must certainly be something urgent. "Who is it?" she asked.

"He says that he's a friend of yours who just got back recently. He seems to be very upset."

"Bring it here, please," she said to Robin. "I'd rather not move the drill."

"If you want, I can take over . . ."

"No."

Robin hurried to get her phone and held it up against her ear.

From the earpiece came Dante's voice, sounding upset: "You need to get out of there immediately."

"Why?" she asked.

"I'm afraid there's something dangerous in there that just hasn't been found yet. The bomb-disposal technicians are on their way, but until they get there, make sure you don't touch anything."

Bart felt the drill suddenly become very heavy in her hands.

"I'm afraid it's just a little too late. Have you ever heard of bombs that work on a vacuum?"

Dante took a minute to answer. "No, but . . . there are certainly altimetric detonators . . ."

". . . that trigger an explosion when they detect a shift in atmospheric pressure," Bart finished his sentence for him, while a trickle of sweat ran down her back.

The silence from the other end of the line was more explicit than a thousand words.

"All right," said Bart, doing her best to seem less terrified than she actually felt, "then I'd better keep my finger in the dike, here, like the little Dutch boy from the story. Do your best not to waste any time."

Robin put the cell phone away and looked at her, worry stamped on his face. "So, Doctor . . . What do we do now?"

Bart massaged her right forearm, which was already starting to ache from being held motionless. "Get everyone out of here. But first bring me some silicone and a chair."

6

When Dante and Colomba, accompanied by Alberti, arrived in Rimini a little after midnight, the Italian army's NBCR (Nuclear, Bacteriological, Chemical, and Radiological) teams had already surrounded the clinic. Colomba had had dealings with them before, two years ago, when she'd been packed into a train contaminated by cyanide: she hadn't enjoyed that encounter, but she knew how very efficient they were.

Bart's assistants were waiting outside the perimeter, closely watched by soldiers in camo uniforms, but Colomba had only to say her name and she was ushered through the cordon. With the assistance of a female suit wrangler, she undressed in a van and put on a uniform very much like the ones worn by the NBCR team, which included an absorbent full-body undergarment and another airtight suit in yellow Tyvek; she also dangled a gas mask around her neck, but didn't put it on.

Alberti waited in the car; Dante, as expected, refused to ruin his look and only agreed to wear some heavy boots and a glove for his good hand. He was on edge and Colomba would have preferred not to have him come along, but he had threatened to throw himself under the tires if she'd tried to leave him behind in Mezzanotte. What's more, he had an unbeatable argument.

"I don't know what value my brother places on me, or for that matter what his adversary thinks about me," he had said, putting on a show of confidence, "but they definitely won't pull any funny stuff if I'm in there."

And so, for the first time, Dante saw the place where he'd been held prisoner. Brightly lit by halogen floodlights, the clinic appeared to him in a diabolical guise, with the cooling towers on the roof looking like twin horns and the main gate identical to an ironic, gap-toothed smile. Panic froze him to the spot before he could even enter.

Colomba noticed. "Would you rather stay outside?"

"No. I'm tired, that's why I'm walking slowly," he lied, with a quaver in his voice. "You go ahead, I'll catch up."

Guided by a soldier, Colomba went to Bart's side, where she continued to hold the drill. Now Bart was sitting on a folding chair, surrounded by members of emergency teams who were monitoring her condition in real time. They had unscrewed the vacuum hose and sealed the hole, and then they had slipped two upright boards beneath her arms, fastening them with duct tape to help her to support the weight of the drill. But there was no way to pull it out of the wall without letting air into the hole, and the plastic dome prevented them from being able to loosen the chuck holding the drill bit. Around the rim of the little plastic dome a thick bead of silicone had been applied; Bart could hear it creak every time she relaxed her muscles even slightly. The pain in her arms filled her eyes with tears.

Colomba stroked her hair. "Maybe it's just a random air bubble," she said.

"Air bubbles push the air outward," Bart replied, panting slightly. "This one's sucking the air in. If it's a booby trap, whoever laid it thought it through very carefully. The inverse pressure also prevents the escape of particulate matter and chemical traces from whatever explosives might be in there."

"I can't take over for you, can I?"

"The soldiers asked me the same thing, but I'm afraid even to take a breath. Nothing sticks to this fucking wall," Bart said, clenching her teeth. "And after all, I'm the one who pulled the boneheaded move, I don't want to drag anyone else into it. So I'd just prefer you get somewhere safe, outside of the blast zone."

"You always say we don't spend enough time together, and now you're trying to send me away?" Colomba retorted, sitting against the wall. "I'm used to keeping desperate cases like you company."

In the meantime, Dante had managed to make his way as far as the lobby. He had just taken a seat on a radiator right beneath the unsettling mosaic depicting the Virgin Mary and the sleeping patient when a man walked up to him. The new arrival took off his gas mask and stuck an e-cigarette in his mouth.

"Do you want a real one?" Dante asked, lighting up a cigarette of his own.

"I've given up smoking, but the nicotine helps me to stay awake." He stuck out his hand. "My name's D'Amore, I work with Colomba."

Dante didn't shake the extended hand. "Di Marco's bagman," he said.

D'Amore laughed. "You don't even know me, and already you dislike me?"

Dante huffed in annoyance. "How much money do you have in your pocket?"

D'Amore looked at him, stumped. Dante waved his hand impatiently, as if telling D'Amore to speed it up.

After pulling out his wallet, D'Amore replied: "Sixty euros."

Dante pulled out the same sum in cash and laid it on the floor.

"Do you want to bet I know more things about you than you think I do?"

D'Amore smiled. "I forgot that you're a mentalist."

"I don't even know what that means . . . Do we have a bet?"

"Well, since all we can do is wait here anyway . . . You're on." D'Amore laid his money on top of Dante's.

Dante theatrically cracked his knuckles—the ones that worked, anyway. "Okay. You've spent a lot of time out of the country," he said at random. This was his opening shot.

"And you say that because . . ."

"Your boots are too heavy for the season and they're scuffed up by the sand from some desert. I know a little something about sedimentology. Those scuff marks were made by a hard silica sand. Like the kind you find in Egypt."

D'Amore struggled not to look at his shoes, but it was too much for him. "I was there on vacation."

Dante smiled. "If that were true, you never would have told me. Let's see . . . Your left arm hurts you, but not too badly."

D'Amore said nothing.

Dante smiled again. "You're trying to control yourself. That means it's something important . . . People act differently with recent or chronic pain. They tend to handle it better if it's old, let's just put it that way."

"I can imagine."

"Your pain is chronic, or at the very least you've had it for a while. And seeing that you've admitted working outside of the country . . ."

"I never admitted a damn thing."

Dante snickered. "And you just reiterated the point, quite clearly . . . I'd say that your return to Italy from some sandy place and whatever happened to your shoulder are connected. War injury?"

"Now you're just guessing. I'll take your money."

Dante pinned down the money with the tip of his cane. "Don't you try it, gambling debts are debts of honor. Let me see your hands."

"Why?"

"I'm no mentalist, but I am a palm reader. Hurry up, your money is making my mouth water."

D'Amore took off his gloves.

"No recent calluses, you've been doing office work," Dante said after examining his hands closely by the fluorescent lights. "You don't spend much time at the shooting range, either, to judge from your index finger. If you look at Colomba's forefinger, there's a much more evident thickening of the skin."

"You said it yourself, I'm a paper pusher."

"But your fingers are covered with faint scars, from burns and razor cuts. Old stuff, and if I didn't know who you work with, I'd have guessed a cook or an electrician. But you weren't a cook, were you?"

"No," said D'Amore, and for the first time there wasn't a trace of bonhomie on his face.

"Bomb-disposal expert? If you'd made a wrong move with an IED, you wouldn't be here, but the fact that you *are* here makes me think that you know something about clearing explosives. But then, maybe you weren't the one who made the wrong move," Dante said with a barb of malice. "You caught a piece of shrapnel, maybe because someone snipped the wrong wire, but it wasn't you. You put your life at risk, and now maybe the reason you wear that Buddha bracelet is to remind yourself that you're living your second life. A sort of reincarnation."

"That doesn't—" D'Amore started to say.

"Hush. There's no need," said Dante. And it was true: the micro-expressions that D'Amore had kept under control until that moment were now dancing across his face. Dante could read them and guide them, using his words like a conductor leading a symphony orchestra. "Forgive me, I've awakened some ugly memories. I really didn't mean to," he said, provoking the other man. "Now that I look more closely, I can see that the bracelet was clearly intended for a more slender wrist than yours. You had to cut it and then lengthen it. Whoever made that mistake with the bomb was a very skinny man. Or a woman? Your woman?"

"Keep your money. I've had enough," said D'Amore.

Dante gave it back to him. "I don't want your money, I just wanted to make it clear to you that you can't pull the wool over my eyes. And that I'm going to know if you try any funny stuff with Colomba."

D'Amore tried to come up with a witty retort, but he was interrupted by a beeping sound from the radio.

"We've found something," said the soldier on the other end of the line.

"I'm on my way," D'Amore replied. "It was a pleasure to chat with you, Signor Torre."

Dante smiled complacently. "Of course it was."

Down in the boiler room, D'Amore found Colomba standing in front of the sewer outlet. The grate had been removed and just then a bomb-disposal technician, covered with mud, was emerging from the main.

"C-4," he said, after removing his helmet. "There's enough to bring down half the neighborhood. They've mined the whole perimeter of the hospital and then poured two feet of cement over top of it. We can't get rid of the explosives until we find the detonators."

"It must be connected to the wall of the room where Bart is," said Colomba.

The bomb-disposal technician shook his head. "We haven't found anything that runs that far. The sewer runs in the opposite direction."

D'Amore grimaced. "Let me take a look," he said, putting his mask back on.

He took a lot more than a look, because he was down there for half an hour, taking over as supervisor, moving cautiously through tunnels that were so narrow he could only crawl through them. At last, between two sewer drainpipes, he found a narrow rubber tube that disappeared into the cement. He pushed a fiber-optic cable through next to the tube, and found that it was connected to a sort of sealed glass case, about the size of a television set.

"Here you are, you piece of shit," D'Amore said.

CHAPTER II

The glass case was connected via the slender rubber tube to a space in the hollow area behind the wall of the room where Dante had been held prisoner. With great care and a few prayers, D'Amore sealed it, blocking the suction of the air; Bart let go of the drill, sobbing from the pain in her arm. One by one, the soldiers isolated the wires leading to the glass case, and then they took it away in an armored truck. They opened it with a robot, and inside they found a child's balloon. In a vacuum, it had remained inflated because what little air it contained had expanded, but if the glass case had filled with air, the pressure would have flattened it and set off a passive switch.

"I've seen plenty of booby traps, but this one is unusually twisted," D'Amore said to Colomba. By now it was seven in the morning, and the sky was brightening. "To say nothing of the amount of time it must have taken someone to set it all up."

"He had time on his hands . . ." Colomba murmured. How many other innocent lives were in potentially mortal danger at that exact moment?

"I can't quite see what his line of thought is," said D'Amore. "If he'd planted a bomb under Torre's bed, that would have made sense. He would have killed the hostage and the rescuers. But planting a bomb in a wall that might be demolished by sheer chance, and maybe in twenty years . . . what kind of sense does that make?"

"None," Colomba lied.

"But you suspected it anyway."

"Dante is the anxious type."

They looked each other in the eyes, glimpsing nothing there but a wall of exhaustion. "We can talk about it at the briefing."

"Not today. I have things to do."

"Major Tom to Paloma Blanca," her radio crackled, as if in confirmation of the words she'd just said.

"Cut it out," Colomba replied, "this is the emergency channel."

"We're falling asleep out he—" Colomba stepped out into the garden and the communication turned into a burst of static: the scramblers had been activated and they blocked the signals the minute you set foot outside the building.

Dante and Bart were on a bench in the park, wrapped in a thermal blanket.

"You look so cute, the two of you," said Colomba as she reached them.

Bart laid her head on Dante's shoulder, while he wrapped an arm around her. "You can be our maid of honor."

Colomba felt an unreasonable pang of annoyance. "Come on, let's get out of here. Alberti is warming up the car."

Dante put his dark glasses back on to protect his eyes from the rays of the sun. "Why don't you come with us?" he asked Bart. "We can celebrate the narrowly averted danger. I have some infusion coffee slow-brewing, a fine Sulawesi aged in whiskey barrels, perfect for iced coffee, even though the temperature outside isn't exactly ideal yet."

Bart smiled. "I love that brew and I'd be happy to drink some. But I think I'll just go take a nap and get back to work—that is, if there's anything left to find after the bomb-disposal technicians are done sweeping the place."

But Dante had focused on her first sentence. "When have you ever tried Sulawesi?"

"A couple of months ago, at Starbucks."

"You went all the way to Seattle? I know that they have a reserve of Sulawesi there . . ."

"No, they've opened a boutique roastery in Milan."

Dante looked at Colomba with the eyes of a child who's just been told he slept through the New Year's fireworks. "You didn't tell me . . ."

"You just narrowly escaped being blown sky-high, and you're worrying about Starbucks?" Colomba snapped.

"I'm a time traveler, the world changed while I was sleeping. Did we get Pizza Hut, too?"

"No pizza. And we're not going home. We have an appointment with Tommy, remember? So up you get, on your feet." She gave him a hand and pulled him to his feet.

"What about 7-Eleven?"

Colomba settled the fedora low on his head, pushed down to the bridge of his nose. "Enough's enough."

As soon as she was in the car, Colomba fell fast asleep, like a rock, and woke up half an hour later, more tired than before, and with the mark of the seat belt pressed into her cheek. Behind her, Dante was ending a phone call.

"Who were you talking to?" she asked him.

"Lupo. I told him about the bomb in Rimini."

"Jesus, you really don't know how to keep your mouth shut, do you?" she asked, shutting her eyes again.

"Around here, Lupo is Big Brother, and if I want to get information I have to give something in exchange."

"This time, whose turn was it?"

"Loris's turn. We found proof that Leo was manipulating him with the Driller, but why him? How did he choose him? When I was delving into his past, I chanced upon an interesting coincidence." Dante lit a cigarette, and Colomba rolled down her window. "When he enrolled in therapy following the abuse, they sent him to the same treatment community where Tommy has just been transferred. Pala has been working with that community for years. So probably he and Loris met there."

Colomba shook her head. "Di Marco's men went over it with a fine-tooth comb. And after all, Pala's been living in San Lorenzo for twenty years, he wasn't catapulted here by Leo like the Melases."

"But don't forget that he's Tommy's therapist. Maybe my brother didn't pick him at random. He didn't know the territory and he needed information about the victims."

"Listen, I may not be as good as you at reading people, but after being fooled by both the Father and Leo, I'm a lot less trusting than I used to be. But Pala is clean."

"Maybe he just talks too much at the corner bar. Maybe my brother put a microbug under his chair. But you'll admit that it's possible?"

Colomba nodded. She looked at the clock on the dashboard. "We have time to swing by his place before we go see Tommy," she said. "Hit the siren."

Alberti turned on the roof flashers and accelerated well over the speed limit.

Dante gripped his seat belt tight and shut his eyes.

S andro Pala could see himself in the mirror of the half-open door of his clothes closet, lying stretched out on one side in bed, and he didn't like what he saw one little bit, in spite of the gentleness of the faint early-morning light.

"I'm too fat," he said. "It's not just a matter of looks, it's a matter of health. I'm at risk of heart attack, diabetes, and all kinds of cancer."

"So why don't you go on a diet?" asked Caterina, sitting up and leaning back against the headboard. She, too, was naked, but without an ounce of excess fat, fit enough that it was clear she worked out with weights on a daily basis. She stroked his hair.

"Because it puts me on edge. And that doesn't go well with the work that I do." He looked at the reflection of Caterina's face, next to his now. "Now that we're on the subject, I have an ethical misgiving."

"About what?"

"About you."

Caterina laughed and wrapped herself around his back. Feeling her legs clamped around his hips, Pala stirred. "About me," she whispered in his ear.

"I'm twice your age and you work for me," Pala replied. The condom he was still wearing creaked with his new erection. "Did I take unethical advantage of my position? Did I seduce you by playing on my role as an authority figure, a father figure?" He gripped her thigh. "Did I coerce you into this in any way?"

"Don't be silly. If I'd waited for you to make a move, I'd be an old lady by now," she said.

Surprised, Pala glanced at the reflection of Caterina's face in the mirror, next to his own: she had a harsh expression he'd never seen before. Pala felt a sudden sharp stab of pain in his ear.

"Shusssh," she said as she pressed down the plunger of the hypodermic needle that she had slid into the shell of his ear. Pala pushed it away and tried to get out of bed, but the rapid-acting insulin was already taking effect. A diabetic normally injects between twenty and fifty subcutaneous units: Pala was dealing with more than a thousand suddenly coursing through his bloodstream, destroying the sugar in his blood and transforming it into reserves to be deposited in his liver and bones. It was the equivalent of sucking all the gasoline out of a car's engine and filling a spare tank for potential future needs, but leaving nothing for the pistons to burn. Suddenly deprived of fuel, Pala's body was starting to shut down. First he lost his vision, then his sense of balance.

"Help, help me," he mumbled, but his words turned into a scream when a terrible stabbing pain burst into his head. His brain was hungry, but there was nothing for it to eat. It was desperately filtering his blood in search of crumbs of nutrition and pushing water out of his pores. His heart rate shot up to 200: Pala vomited his breakfast into his lap and fell to the floor, drenched with sweat and cramping violently.

With his last conscious thought, he tried to grab hold of the dresser, pulling down over him a stack of shirts neatly ironed by the housekeeper; they covered him like a funeral shroud. But he wasn't aware of it: he'd slid into a hypoglycemic coma and the tremor had turned into convulsions. Pala slammed the back of his head and both his heels against the bedside carpet, and his eyeballs rolled up into their sockets.

Caterina, who had been standing watching him the whole time from the foot of the bed, bent over to check his physical state. His heartbeat was very faint, his skin was cold and clammy. He was still alive, and he remained alive while she was gathering the sheets off the bed and the condom from the puddle of piss that was collecting between Pala's legs. Then she put on a pair of latex gloves and her shoes and made the rounds of the bedroom, wiping the places she had touched with her bare flesh—the nightstand, the door, the head of the bed she'd grabbed with both hands while pretending to come while Pala was on top of her, and of course, his body, in places that an employee normally wouldn't touch.

She put her checkered skirt suit back on and checked the psychiatrist one last time: Pala's breathing was shallow and fast, he wouldn't be around much longer. Caterina wiped the acid sweat from his hands, then went to pick up the bag she'd left in the lobby that morning.

It was very heavy.

When they reached Pala's office, Lupo and Bruno were already standing outside the front door.

"I'm not going in," said Dante.

"Sure, don't worry about it." Colomba helped him out of the car, a little roughly. "Just remember that Lupo knows who you are, but the rest of the world doesn't, so do your best not to be noticed." After a second, she added: "Sorry, I take that back, it's pointless."

She went over to join the Carabinieri, who turned around to look at her for a second, briefly interrupting their thunderous pounding on the door.

"Good morning, gentlemen," Colomba said. "What seems to be going on?"

"Nothing, for now. And if you get back in your car and drive away, nothing will happen a minute from now, either," said Lupo.

"Let's skip the threatening preamble, shall we, for just this once?" said Colomba.

Lupo pointed at Dante, who was unsuccessfully trying to hoist himself up to the windows by hooking his cane onto the sill. "Your friend . . . *Whatshisface* . . . got me thinking. I checked with Martina's parents: Pala had been her therapist after a nasty skating accident that was giving her nightmares."

"That's a nice coincidence . . ."

"I just want to have a short talk with him, and see how he reacts. I come in peace, at least for the moment."

"Too bad he isn't home."

"And that he isn't answering his cell phone, either," Bruno weighed in.

"Can you trace his phone, CC?" Dante asked from behind, brushing the plaster dust off his jacket.

"Only if we want D'Amore to take him off our hands," said Colomba. She tried shaking the door, which didn't budge a quarter of an inch. "It's armor-plated, you're not going to be able to kick it down." She turned to speak to Dante: "*Whatshisface*, take a look."

Dante bent down and scrutinized the lock. "It'll take me ten minutes or so. I won't break anything. There are no signs of alarms, there's not a lot of traffic on this street, and people tend to steer clear when they see the Carabinieri." He looked up. "Which tells us a lot about what people think of you."

"I can't do anything of the sort. It's an abuse of power," said Lupo.

"Then get back in your green squad car and get out of here," said Colomba. "Because I frankly don't give a damn."

The two Carabinieri exchanged a glance. Bruno shrugged his shoulders. "You decide. After all, I'm retiring soon."

Lupo sighed. "All right, but if we find any incriminating evidence against Pala, it's up to me to decide what to do with it."

"When, and if, that happens, we can talk about it. *Whatshisface*, chop chop."

Dante extracted his lock-picking kit and with a SouthOrd "jimmy" checked the inside of the tumbler with both eyes shut, trying to make a mental map of it. He discovered that the security lock had eight pistons arranged along different axes. If you tried to use the classic "bumping" technique used by most burglars—inserting a pick and hitting it to make the pistons open—they'd go out of alignment and the lock would be frozen in place. He would have to move the pistons carefully, one at a time, determining the correct elevation to unblock them.

"What a pain in the ass," he muttered, spilling a chunk of the ash extending from the tip of the cigarette he clamped between his lips.

"Wait, but who are you, exactly?" Bruno asked.

"Inspector Whatshisface from the French Sureté, *mon ami*," Dante said, putting on a Peter Sellers accent and continuing to insert increasingly slender metal picks.

"Go get a box of gloves from the car, would you please," Lupo said to his partner, sick and tired of that buffoonery.

When Bruno returned, Dante was using ten or so metal picks all at once, orchestrating them in an intricate array with his fingers, even using the fingers of his bad hand. One decisive twist, and the door swung open.

"Voilà," he said, pushing it all the way open. "Knock yourselves out." He sat down on the step and put his leather glove back on.

"Aren't you going in?" Bruno asked as he distributed latex gloves.

"I'll stay out here on the lookout, in case the cops pull up."

"Ha ha, you're so funny," said Bruno as he walked past him into the front hallway. Dante heard him mutter something that sounded like "slimy spy," which led him to deduce that Bruno thought he worked for the intelligence services.

The deserted office, illuminated by the big windows, seemed to Colomba subtly different from the other times. Grim, alienating, cold. While Bruno and Lupo were splitting up the rest of the rooms between them, Colomba rummaged through the psychiatrist's office, where she had certainly shown Pala the worst side of herself. There was nothing that she shouldn't have expected to find, but when she pushed aside the De Chirico painting that hung over the little couch, Colomba found a safe with a numerical keypad, roughly the size of a television set with a fifty-inch screen. Might Pala have jotted down the combination somewhere in that office?

An instant later, she heard Lupo curse from upstairs, and she raced up the spiral staircase. In terms of style and furnishings, the residential section of the building was similar to the office where Pala received his patients, but three times the size and with all the inevitable signs of private life, duly hidden from the patients: laundry hampers, sandals and slippers, a book lying open on the bedside dresser, a pair of reading glasses. Lupo was squatting down next to Pala's corpse, which lay sprawled on its back, half-covered by the clean laundry that had spilled down over it.

"Fucking goddamned hell," said Colomba.

"Don't go in, I've already made enough of a mess as it is," said Lupo.

"How did he die?"

"I can't say. There aren't any evident marks."

"Wait." Colomba remembered seeing some trash bags in the ground-floor bathroom. She ran down to get them and put two on her feet. Then she went over to the corpse and cautiously raised one arm.

"He's already starting to stiffen," she said. "He's been dead for at least two hours. Help me out here, I need to turn him on his side."

"We shouldn't be messing around with him."

"I know that. When I count three."

And so they discovered that there were no marks on his back or shoulders, or on the backs of his legs.

"It looks like a heart attack," said Colomba. "But I don't think that's what it was."

"Neither do I," Lupo snapped. "Let's see what Dr. Tira has to say. Or your friend. By the way, is she all right? I have to say I find her very appealing."

"Yes, she just got a bad scare."

Lupo reached the hallway with a single leap. "I'll report this to dispatching. You and Whatshisface get the hell out of here, because I don't want to have to explain your presence along with everything else."

"Are you looking to have the investigation taken out of your hands again? Because that's exactly what'll happen the minute this becomes official. The military will arrive and they'll put everything under judicial seal."

"That's what they'll do eventually, anyway."

"But we can still make sure that it happens only after we've checked that there's nothing that might prove useful." Colomba smirked awkwardly in embarrassment. "Dante trusts you, otherwise he would have steered clear of you, and I trust him. But if you want to miss out on the opportunity to understand what's going on here, go ahead, pick up the phone."

Lupo nodded. "Okay." He checked the time on his cell phone. "It's eight twenty. What time do the patients start arriving, usually?"

"I think at nine, or nine thirty."

"Bruno!" Lupo shouted.

The veteran carabiniere climbed the stairs, jokingly complaining all the way about the effort, but when he saw the corpse he immediately turned serious. "Sweet Jesus," he exclaimed. "Is that Pala?"

Lupo nodded. "Move the car and shut the blinds downstairs. Let's pretend no one's in here. Then stay here and keep an eye on who comes and who leaves."

Bruno turned around and started down the stairs, but Colomba managed to ask him: "Would you send me Alberti and Whatshisface, please?"

"Whatshisface . . ." Bruno muttered. "All right."

Dante arrived a couple of minutes later, walking with his eyes shut, and in fact he had to let Alberti lead him. He stopped at the door and pulled up his T-shirt to filter the air: Colomba had thrown open the windows, but his sensitive nostrils still didn't like the smell.

"There's a dead body and it stinks," he said, keeping his eyes shut tight.

"It's Pala," said Colomba.

"My condolences to one and all. *Au revoir.*"

Colomba stopped him. "Make an effort."

Dante took three deep breaths, leaned on his cane, and took a quick circular look around the room, then shut his eyes again. "I looked. Can I go now?"

"No. Did you notice anything?" asked Colomba.

"A fat corpse and the sunlight glistening off a puddle of piss."

"Aside from that!"

Dante breathed deeply again. "There's a part of the floor that's cleaner. And it wasn't the housekeeper, because it's too irregular and there are broad patches that haven't been polished. Downstairs, in contrast, the floor has been beautifully buffed. Maybe the killer cleaned up. How did this torturer of defenseless brains meet his end?"

"There are no signs of violence, but it was painful. It could have been a stroke, or it could have been insulin again," said Colomba.

"Plausible. I saw that the sheets were all tangled, but are they dirty, too?"

Lupo looked at them carefully. "Not very. A few splashes of vomit."

"Can you sniff them around the middle?"

Lupo obeyed, at first hesitantly, but then with growing conviction.

"It just smells of detergent or fabric softener. The one with the teddy bear."

"Try again. Tell me if it smells of sweat or of a human being in general."

Lupo, patiently, did as he was told. "No."

"As far as you know, was Pala gay or straight?"

"Do you want me to sniff his butt while I'm at it?" Lupo asked.

"All right, I asked for that." Blindly, Dante grabbed Alberti's arm. "Go see if you can find any dirty sheets in the laundry room or in the bathroom," he said. "If there aren't any, then the man or woman he was in bed with killed him, and they got rid of the sheets to avoid traces of things like DNA. Hi-ho, trusty steed!" Alberti led him out of the building.

"They're not going to accept my nose as evidence in court," said Lupo.

Colomba didn't answer. She'd suddenly been illuminated by an image: Caterina catching her bullet on the fly.

So do you hunt, too? Colomba had asked her. *Not with a rifle*, Caterina had replied.

"We need to find the secretary," said Colomba.

The Educational and Therapeutic Community of the Guardian Angel of Portico, familiarly known as the ETC, was a trio of square buildings in the industrial zone, surrounded by a couple of acres of grounds. The males lived in one building, the females in another; the smallest of the three buildings served as a daytime activities center. It housed eighty or so residents, all between the ages of fifteen and twenty. Some had been sent there by the juvenile court, others by social services. Most of them had themselves been the victims of abuse and mistreatment.

In the immediate aftermath of his parents' murders, Tommy had been sent to the boys' building, and he'd practically never emerged since, in spite of the invitations the social assistants had extended to Demetra to take better care of him. Since he'd been at the center, Tommy had turned completely inward, and by now he interacted with no one, except to some very bland and minimal extent with the staff and the volunteers, and even in those rare cases without ever speaking; if they tried to force him to speak, he'd shout and pound himself in the head with his fists. Most of the time he was calm and well behaved, though. He tied his own shoes all by himself, and ate with a spoon, put away his coloring books when he was done with them, and stayed inside. They'd given him a roommate to make sure he didn't hurt himself: a sixteen-year-old boy who'd been drawn into the social service system when he was twelve because he'd been abused by his mother's boyfriend.

Laura Patti, the supervisor, was sixty years old and gray-haired. She had accompanied Tommy to his parents' funeral, and in that context she had shown considerable skill, because she'd managed to keep him calm the whole time. Laura loved the work she did and the kids she took care of. And that spelled her fate when the woman who had been Pala's secretary turned up at her office door, on the second floor, above the daytime activities center.

"I wasn't expecting you today," Patti said, shaking hands with her. "Tommy's in his room, but pretty soon he has a meeting with a consultant sent by his aunt."

"I know, that's why I'm here. We'd rather have Tommy meet the consultant in the office, with Sandro. I'll take him and bring him back this evening."

The supervisor leaned against the edge of the desk. "Tommy doesn't like being out in the open air."

"I'm trying to get him used to it . . ."

"According to my experts, it's not doing him a lot of good. The other day, you took him for an outing, and he was upset all night long. We had to sedate him. Tell Sandro that we prefer for him to have his meetings in our institute."

"Certainly, starting next time—"

"No. You have only the best intentions, and I understand that, but now the boy is my responsibility. And you're not a psychologist, unless I'm mistaken?"

The woman who had been Caterina looked up at her. Her eyes were enormous and very dark, veined with a melancholy you often see in certain veterans when they come home from war. "No, I'm not a psychologist." Laura Patti raised her hands to defend herself, but she wasn't fast enough.

5

Pala's corpse was turning increasingly gray and ashen, but Caterina couldn't be reached on her cell phone; Bruno had gone to find her, even checking her home address, but in vain.

"What do we know about her?" Lupo asked as he finished unscrewing the shade on a lamp in the office.

"Alberti!" shouted Colomba. "Tell us about Caterina."

He leaned down from the spiral staircase. "Italian, of Eritrean birth. A degree in philosophy," he said. "She'd been working for Pala for three months. No prior offenses, a magnificent résumé featuring previous employment as a dental hygienist and a private nurse. Nothing suspicious."

"But she should have been here already," said Lupo.

"I know," said Colomba. "And there's not a fucking thing here."

Lupo pointed to the safe. "There's *this* bitch. Do you think Whatshisface would know how?"

"I'm an escape artist, not a thief," Dante shouted from outside.

"So what happens if they lock you up in a safe?" asked Colomba.

"I'd die immediately."

Alberti's head appeared again over the railing. "I found Pala's cell phone," he said. "At least, I think it's his. It's locked."

"Where do you keep your ATM passcode?" Lupo asked Colomba. "And don't tell me you remember it by heart."

"On my cell phone, with a fake area code. You think it works for safes, too?"

"Well, I'd give it a try, at the very least."

"Alberti, unlock it," said Colomba.

"How am I supposed to do that?"

"With a thumbprint," said Colomba.

"You aren't thinking of . . ." said Alberti. He stopped talking.

"Put a couple of bags on your feet," said Lupo with a hearty laugh. Alberti vanished.

The corpse's thumb did the trick, and in the phone directory they found a name that they all agreed was suspicious: *Le Chiffre*. The first attempt to use the combination was unsuccessful, but when they entered the supposed phone number backward, the safe door swung open, leaving them all slack-jawed.

The safe was packed with cash. All of them two-hundred-euro notes. Colomba checked a couple of wads of bills: they were real.

"You can certainly make money as a psychiatrist," Lupo commented.

6

The woman who had once chosen the name of Caterina left the ETC office, dangling the supervisor's bunch of keys in one hand, with a small red stain on her light gray boot. She noticed it while she was walking through the garden, and she discreetly wiped it off on a bush. Then she cut through the vegetable patch where some of the boys were putting young seedlings into pots, and headed decisively toward the dormitory. She moved with confidence, smiling at everyone she met, and no one was surprised to see her in the area that was off-limits to visitors: she'd already been there dozens of times, and they all knew her.

Tommy was in his room, kneeling on the bed; he was coloring a drawing of a palm tree and he had chosen to use black for the fronds. When he saw her, he emitted a loud and inarticulate bellow, leaped to his feet, and started rocking on his heels.

It was the first time that she'd seen him do anything of the sort, and she was afraid that it was the onset of a fit: he was twice her size, and she didn't know how to calm him down on her own. She smiled at him.

"Ciao, Tommy. I've never been able to tell if anything I say gets into your head when I talk to you, but I hope so. We need to go for another drive. Come on, I'll buy you some ice cream."

Tommy continued rocking on his heels. The woman regretted having used up all the insulin.

"Don't make me mad, Tommy," she said sternly. "Be a good boy and put your shoes on. Get moving!"

Tommy accelerated his oscillations back and forth, accompanying them with a sort of ululating howl that seemed like a fire alarm. The woman gave him a smack in the face. Tommy fell silent, rubbing his reddened cheek, his eyes darting around in search of an escape route.

"You don't want another one, do you?" the woman asked.

Tommy shook his head, shuddering.

"All right, put those fucking shoes on and come with me. And you'll be sorry if you open your mouth again."

Trembling, Tommy put on his fur-lined clogs and, jerked along by the woman, descended the building's stairs. A few people greeted him, others said hello to the woman, but she kept walking, eyes straight ahead. Thanks to the supervisor's bunch of keys, she was able to open the building's service door, emerging onto the courtyard where the employees parked their cars. Tommy dug in his heels at the doorway, shielding his eyes against the sun with the back of his hand. After ordering him to stay there, the woman opened the gate, ran to get Pala's car, and pulled into the courtyard in reverse.

"Get in," she said, leaving the engine running.

Tommy shook his head, twisting his wrists.

She opened the trunk of the car and pulled out the lug wrench. The morning sun gleamed off the chrome plating. "Get in or I'll crack your skull and stuff you in the trunk. You decide." Tommy reluctantly climbed into the car.

As she drove out of the courtyard she crossed paths with a volunteer on a moped, who took advantage of the open gate with a friendly wave of thanks. He had an appointment with Laura Patti, so he was the one who found her body.

7

Fifteen minutes after the call from the ETC had been put through to the Portico Carabinieri station, Master Sergeant Nerone phoned Lupo.

"Apparently the Melases' son has disappeared, too," he said, still incredulous that another murder had taken place in his jurisdiction. "They're searching the building, but . . ."

Lupo wiped the sweat off his brow. "Send all the men over there," he said. "And alert the magistrate who's on duty. I'll be right over." He hung up and went back to the others, who in the meantime had finished straightening up the rooms that they'd searched.

It was a hard blow for Dante.

"That makes no sense," he said from outside. "They could have kidnapped him and killed him whenever they wanted. Why today?"

"We'll worry about that when we find him," said Colomba. "What are we going to do with Pala?" she asked Lupo. "Do you want to make it official?"

He shook his head. "No. If Tommy really has disappeared, I'll have a good excuse for going to look for him."

"And the money?" asked Dante, sticking his head in the door. "Split it up into equal parts?"

"I'd like to be able to say the thought hadn't occurred to me," said Bruno, who had just come back inside.

Colomba shut the safe door and punched a bunch of random numbers. "End of the temptation. Let's go."

Once they arrived at the ETC, Lupo went in to speak with his colleagues, and came back out an hour later.

"Tommy is no longer in the building," he confirmed. "And the supervisor was hit hard in the face and then strangled with the phone cord.

Vigevani will be here soon; if you want to take a look at the corpse, you'd better hurry up."

Colomba shook her head. "I've had enough for today."

"Me too," said Dante, sprawled on the car hood smoking a cigarette. Inside, Alberti was snoring, keeled forward onto the steering wheel.

"There's one more thing," Lupo went on. "Pala's secretary came in through the front entrance about two hours ago. She didn't return her pass at the exit, but she's missing, too."

"So she took Tommy," said Colomba, with a pang in her heart. "Why didn't anyone try to stop her?"

"She seems to have gone out the back way, and anyway she could come and go as she pleased here. Pala often came here to meet with the kids, including Tommy. But the other day she came here by herself and took him for an outing. When the boy came back, he was in a state of shock."

"Let's go take a look at Tommy's room before the SIS get here. Dante, are you with us?"

"I'll sit this one out."

As soon as Colomba and Lupo vanished into the building, Dante tapped his cane against the car window, right next to Alberti's ear.

"Wake up!" he shouted.

Alberti lurched. "What's going on?"

"I'm bored."

"Please, I haven't slept since yesterday."

"You want some Nuvigil?" asked Dante, proffering a small white pill in his begloved fingers. "They give these to fighter-bomber pilots when they have to fly all night long."

"Oh, God no." Alberti yawned and opened the car door, extending his legs. "What do they say about the boy?"

"That Pala's secretary kidnapped him." Dante tossed the pill into the air and swallowed it dry, gesturing for the water bottle.

Alberti passed it to him. "And she works for Bonaccorso."

"Or else for the person that my brother is looking for, or else she might even *be* the person that my brother is looking for. And she'd been there, under his nose, the whole time. The King of Spades might be a queen, why not?"

"That makes sense. Working for Pala, she would have known every-thing that was happening, without being discovered."

"You think it makes sense? She left five million euros in cash behind and murdered another person, in full view of anyone who cared to watch. It doesn't make that much sense to me."

Alberti yawned again. "Maybe Tommy is worth more to her than five million euros," he said.

The woman who had once called herself Caterina now had a different car, a different name, and a black wig with smooth hair. Tommy was slumbering in the back seat, knocked out by the benzodiazepine that she had forced him to drink, mixed with a bottle of fruit juice.

By now, the woman told herself, they must have found the supervisor's dead body. And, if she'd been unlucky, there was already a manhunt under way for her. The police would already be scanning car traffic, and airports and train stations would have been alerted. There wasn't a chance of a black woman traveling with a white boy standing six feet tall passing unnoticed. Luckily, though, she wasn't trying to leave the region. If anything, she was heading inland, sticking to the narrow, rocky roads that she'd been forced to learn by heart. In daylight or darkness.

The landscape turned dry and withered, the cars thinned out and became infrequent, and the coloring of everything went from ochre to a dark yellow. Slowing down to keep from cracking an axle in the numerous potholes, the woman drove into an abandoned town, rolling past half-crumbling houses with their windows walled up. She finally came to a large refinery, reduced by neglect to little more than a steel skeleton, surrounded by rusted-out fences and piles of garbage. Alongside the pitted, rutted road ran the rails of a railway line, no longer in use. They terminated in a large industrial shed, in ruins like everything else.

The woman who had been Caterina opened the gate to an area that looked like an open-air gravel dump. She parked behind a gigantic rusty earth mover and texted someone on her cell phone, then hastily destroyed the phone.

From that point forward, everything needed to work without a hitch.

Gaspare Mantoni heard the *ping* of his cell phone in his pocket and immediately understood what it was about, but he didn't look at it, not right away. He did things on his own time frame, and anyone who said differently would get a kick in the teeth. He ordered another glass of red.

"This time, give me a good one. Open a bottle."

"Really?" asked the barkeeper. "Are you celebrating something?"

"A funeral."

"Whose?"

"Mine."

The barkeeper laughed, but stopped instantly when Gaspare glared at him, eyes narrowed in a way that scared him.

"Hold on, are you not well?" the barkeeper asked.

"Never felt better in my life," the other man replied. "Open the bottle, for fuck's sake, or I'll come back there and get it myself."

The bartender uncorked a bottle of pinot noir for him and filled a clean glass. "Don't do anything stupid, now, you're one of my favorite customers." Gaspare tossed the glass back in a single gulp. "Put it on my tab, I'll be back later," he said, laughing silently at his own wisecrack.

Out in the street, he read the text—it was exactly what he expected it to be—and stuck his cell phone under the spray of a public drinking fountain. He'd been hoping for an arc of electric sparks, but to his disappointment the screen simply flickered and faded, and then turned off entirely. Gaspare then hurled the phone at the outside wall of a church, laughed in the face of an old woman who'd turned to stare at him, and climbed into the cab of the tanker truck that awaited him on the parking plaza, the symbol of the Eni oil company on its side.

When he went to insert the key into the ignition, however, he realized that his hand was trembling. He got mad at himself, and at the empty feeling he had in his belly. It occurred to him that he was still in time to pull out, go home, and pretend nothing had happened . . .

Yeah, nothing, at least until he started shitting blood. And from then on it would only get worse, until he became a completely useless waste of oxygen. A farting old man dying like so many other farting old men. His fellow truck drivers wouldn't give a damn about him, just like he didn't give a damn about them, and they'd forget he'd ever existed the day after his funeral.

Gaspare Mantoni turned on the engine, and he felt the rumbling vibration fill his whole body. Was it the engine that was wreaking havoc in his belly, or had it just been the food in prison? Not that it much mattered, by this point. He turned around and headed off down the provincial road.

They'd remember him. Oh, how they'd remember him.

10

W ait, why did you bring this nut job here?" asked Nerone, standing
  guard at Tommy's room, when he saw Colomba arrive.

Lupo was exhausted and on edge. "Speak to me in that tone of voice
one more time and you'll be in a world of shit," he told him. "Go on,
take a hike. Get out of here!"

Nerone turned beet red. "Sir, yessir," he said, and then did as he'd
been told. Colomba and Lupo shut the door behind them. The room
stank of dirty socks, but it was clean and big enough to accommodate two
single beds with patchwork covers, a pair of small desks, and a clothes
closet. Colomba immediately identified Tommy's side of the room: his
bed was definitely the one that had been neatly made, and the same
applied to the desk with books and crayons perfectly lined up and tidy.

"What are we looking for?" asked Lupo.

"Anything," Colomba replied.

They lifted mattresses and rummaged through clothing, without
finding anything interesting, however. Colomba opened the twin doors
of the clothes closet and had no difficulty identifying Tommy's clothing:
it was twice the size of his roommate's. Here, too, however, not so much
as a crumb, in the pockets or in the cuffs. But his size 13 work boots, on
the other hand, had left a sprinkling of dust on the bottom of the closet.

While Lupo went to make peace with Nerone, Colomba took the shoes
in a bag to be tested, along with a handful of coloring books, and brought
them to Dante. He was still sprawled on the trunk smoking a cigarette,
while Alberti had gone to wash his face in the restroom of the dayroom.

"Now it's your turn to take a sniff," she said, extending the exhibits
in his direction.

Without changing position, Dante took the coloring books and waved them in the air. "If I finish coloring them, will you give me a piece of candy?"

"I'm starting to get sick and tired of you. Why are you so twisted?"

"Because I don't understand a fucking thing in all this. I was convinced I was the chosen prey, instead I discover that it's Tommy. And if that's the case, then I was left in the hospital to slowly die as nothing more than a piece of decoy bait. I'm just a discard."

"Put aside your wounded pride and see if you can do something useful. If the coloring books aren't good for anything, then at least look at the rest."

Dante put the bag down on the hood and studied the boots. He even took out the insoles.

"What can I tell you that you don't already know? They were purchased in Italy, and used very little."

"What about the particulate matter?"

"I don't have bionic eyes. All I know is that it's full of sulfur."

"What do you mean, sulfur?"

"You know that stuff they have on matchsticks? CC . . . All right, I get it that you're not a chemist, but the color is unmistakable, and so is the smell. They use it in agriculture as a fertilizer, and all around here is nothing but fields." He picked up a pebble the size of a pinhead and held it against the light. "Even though this doesn't seem to have been refined . . ."

Colomba didn't wait for him to finish talking but called loudly for Alberti, who came running back from the dayroom.

Dante slid to the floor, using the cane to brace himself.

"Why are you so upset?" he asked, baffled.

"Do you know what my paternal grandfather did for a living?"

"No, what?"

"He was a miner."

CHAPTER III

The little town was called Sant'Anna Solfara, and it had started to die at the end of the fifties, when the sulfur mines had been shut down. Digging the mineral out of the ground had become less and less profitable, in spite of the fact that the miners were paid a pittance and worked under inhumane conditions, always at risk of breathing firedamp, as they called methane.

The woman who had been Caterina got out of the car, shoving Tommy into the dust.

"Get walking," she told him. "Pretty soon, I'll leave you in peace, and if God is willing, I'll get a little peace of my own." She said it to him in German, a language she hadn't spoken in years, afraid it might ruin her Italian accent. After all, it didn't make any difference to Tommy: all he understood was rough treatment. She pointed him to the entrance of the nearest mine, with a rail car parked in front of it, piled high with yellowish rocks.

"There. Come on. Get moving," she ordered, giving him a swift kick in the ass. Tommy started crying, but he did as he was told. They reached the bars that prevented access to the mine, but the woman simply opened the padlock, shoved Tommy inside, and shut the gate behind her.

The mouth of the mine had been transformed into a little museum, with vintage photographs on the walls and shelves loaded down with sulfur soap bars and other souvenirs. Behind the museum was a gallery that led to the shaft that went down to a depth of a thousand feet. There were lights marking the route, but they were turned on only for paying visitors; at that moment, the entrance looked like an arch done in black paint, like the tunnels created for Road Runner by Wile E. Coyote.

"Get moving," said the woman who had been a great many different things, none of them true, poking Tommy in the shoulders with her keys.

Cautiously, Tommy stepped into the darkness. They descended, following the rails of the mining carts, and when the outside light had vanished entirely, she reached into her pocket and pulled out a little flashlight. The gallery resonated with the muffled echoes of their footsteps and the distant sloshing of running water.

Once they had descended fifty yards, the woman identified the wooden bench she had been told to look for. She told Tommy to take a seat and, rummaging around behind the bench, she found a waterproof backpack, damp and covered with dust. Inside was a badge holder and lanyard to hang around her neck, an ID with a photograph of Tommy, and a ticket for *The Wonders of History*. The backpack also contained several short hypodermic syringes with plastic caps protecting the short, sharp needles.

By the light of the flashlight, she read the final instructions printed on a sheet of paper.

The syringe contains Seconal.
The rest of the equipment is behind the freight elevator cage.
Arrival is scheduled for noon.

On the back of the sheet of paper was a photograph of an old man with black skin.

The woman looked at the picture and wiped her eyes: she was crying.

Colomba got in behind the wheel, where Alberti usually sat, but before driving away, she rested her hand on the gearshift, undecided.

"What are you worried about?" Dante asked, stretched out as usual in the back seat.

"I'm not worried, I'm just remembering," she replied. "The last time I decided to operate on my own, forty-nine people were killed."

Dante sat up behind her and leaned closer. "Put it like that, and you seem like a mass murderer, but you know it wasn't your fault."

"Ninety-nine percent of me knows it, Dante. Otherwise I never could have survived. But that one percent will torment me forever. Caterina can work alone or with an army, she might be the Queen of Spades or a simple henchman, but she has Tommy in her hands."

"And you think you're going to help him by informing the Carabinieri? Have you ever heard of friendly fire?"

"I wasn't thinking of the Carabinieri."

"CC . . . the military is only going to fuck things up."

"So far, I've done all the fucking up that needed doing," said Colomba, picking up her cell phone.

D'Amore read the text from Colomba in the hotel in Rimini where he was staying. He'd just finished showering, and a network of fine scar tissue glittered on his chest and back. As requested in the text, he downloaded Signal and used the app to call her back.

"It's the office phone," he said. "Let's be careful we're not being monitored. What's going on?"

"I'm going to give you a piece of news you'll be receiving soon anyway. Tommy has been kidnapped by Pala's secretary."

"The psychiatrist? How is he involved?"

"He's dead. Don't ask me how I know."

"I long ago stopped asking that kind of question." D'Amore picked up the hotel's pad of letterhead notepaper and used his teeth to take the cap off a pen. "Where's the corpse?"

"At his house. But right now, what I'm interested in is Tommy. Maybe I know where Caterina is taking him, but I don't know if she'll be waiting there alone, or with an army."

"Tell me what I can do to help you."

"First I want assurances from you: you won't do anything that would endanger the boy."

"Absolutely, I would never."

"D'Amore . . . if you were your boss, I wouldn't even try this, but I'm telling you this in the hope that you aren't rotten to the core, the way he is. I want you to swear it to me, I want you to swear it on whatever it is you hold dearest."

D'Amore heaved a deep sigh. "Things can get complicated in the field, and you know that better than I do. I can't promise you that everything will turn out fine, just that I'll do my very best. Is that good enough for you?"

Colomba thought it over for a moment, covering the microphone even though there was no one talking in the car.

"Okay," she said at last. "I hope that I haven't made the stupid mistake of the century. There's a small town twenty miles outside of Portico. It's called Sant'Anna Solfara. Probably Tommy and his kidnapper are there, somewhere close to the mines."

D'Amore checked the route on his online map. "I can get there in an hour, using the men I have here in Rimini. Maybe a few minutes faster if I can get a helicopter to take off from Pisa, but I'm not certain."

"No helicopters. No camo uniforms. I trust you." Colomba ended the call.

"So are the troops arriving on camelback?" Dante asked.

"Yes, but they're going to get there after us. Until they do, we're going to have to make do on our own," she replied, and finally put the car in gear and pulled out.

The last details that would link Caterina to the woman who was almost done getting ready in the mine shaft were the color of her skin and the wry twist at the corner of her mouth. Everything else had changed, completely. Her contact lenses had shifted her eyes to green; the uniform of a volunteer nurse of the Sovereign Military Order of Malta, with a dark blue overcoat with leather frogging, had replaced the checkered skirt suit; and a black veil now covered her braids. She even had an ID badge hanging around her neck on a lanyard, with a recent photograph of her and yet another fake name.

Behind the cage of the freight elevator, the woman had also found a red blanket, a pair of sunglasses, and a little white cap with the Maltese cross. And a wheelchair, neatly folded up. She opened it out and pushed it toward Tommy, who had remained sitting on the bench the whole time, banging a rock rhythmically against the wall of the shaft. He'd been doing it so long that the palm of his right hand was red and scraped. When he saw her, he clumsily threw the rock in her direction, but he didn't even graze her.

The woman took his face in her hands. His skin was cold and clammy with sweat.

"I told you once not to act like a fool. Have you forgotten?" Grabbing him by the hair, she dragged him to the wheelchair and forced him to sit in it. "Stay there," she told him.

She went back to get the backpack where she'd found her instructions. Resisting the temptation to take another look at the photograph glued to the document, she found the syringes, took the cap off one, and hid it in her hand.

"This is only going to hurt for a second," she told Tommy. She planted the needle in his thigh through the denim of his jeans and depressed the plunger until the syringe was empty. Tommy twisted, losing one of his sandals, but the Seconal deprived him of strength before he could get to his feet. His head lolled back and he breathed laboriously, eyes wide open and a streamer of drool hanging from his mouth.

The woman checked his heartbeat, then covered him with the blanket—once she'd unfolded it, she saw that at the center of it was a large white cross—and put the glasses and cap on him.

From outside the mine, in the meantime, came the distant echo of voices and laughter.

Within a charming natural setting, the archaeological mining park offers a unique experience, allowing visitors to stroll through the environment and structures that once formed part of the industry of Sant'Anna's yellow gold: sulfur," Dante read on his cell phone. "Who wants to climb down into the bowels of the earth to see how they used to mine sulfur? Raise your hand."

"I sure didn't know they'd built a park to commemorate it," said Colomba, accelerating into a curve to pass a car ahead of them.

"Maybe if we turn on the roof flashers . . ." said Alberti, suddenly remembering why he preferred doing the driving, when he could.

"No."

Dante stopped reading and leaned forward, clutching his knees in the position they tell you to take during an emergency landing. He'd read the instructions plenty of times, even if he'd never boarded a plane in his life. The mere idea of being sealed into a flying metal tube made his stomach hurt.

A truck driver honked his horn as Colomba swerved in front of him, cutting him off just in time to avoid hitting an oncoming three-wheeled Piaggio pickup truck loaded with wood in the opposite lane.

"Are we still alive?" Dante asked with his eyes closed.

"For now," Alberti replied.

"Tell me some more about the park," said Colomba. "We're almost in Sant'Anna."

"It opens at noon, and only on weekends," said Dante, picking up the lit cigarette that he'd dropped on the carpet.

"So the park is closed today," said Colomba.

"So much the better, at least we'll have fewer innocent visitors to protect."

"The whole town must be full of sulfur dust," Alberti commented. "They might even be outside the perimeter."

Colomba bit her lip. "It's a risk. There isn't much in the town except for the mine, unless things have changed since I was a little girl," she said. Her grandfather had taken her there a couple of times and had told her about life as a sulfur miner. She had imagined them as the gladiators of her school history textbook: muscular, half-naked, and with pickaxes instead of swords. "It's also true that Sant'Anna Solfara isn't exactly an ideal spot for a fugitive. There's just one street that connects to the provincial road."

They emerged from a tunnel, and just as he was shutting his eyes, Dante thought he glimpsed on an advertising poster the words SULFUR MINE.

"Stop," he said without looking. "Please, CC, stop and go back until we reach the sign."

"Dante, we're in a hurry. What sign?"

"The colored one."

Colomba slammed the brakes on so hard that he practically spat his guts out, then put the car into reverse, forcing the driver of a semitrailer behind them to veer onto the shoulder. Dante heard the driver shout, even though he had both hands over his ears. On a series of panels outside the tunnel were a number of advertising posters, stuck up one atop the other, all for concerts and food fairs dating back to the previous summer, but Colomba easily spotted the one that Dante was referring to. Against a background picture of the mines of Sant'Anna were the words SUFFRAGE MASS FOR THE VICTIMS OF THE EARTHQUAKE and—in smaller print—PRAYER AND REFRESHMENT STOP OF THE "CYCLIST-PILGRIMS" OF VIA LAURETANA.

"That's today's date," said Alberti.

"And the time?" asked Dante, who had cautiously uncovered only one ear.

"Ten minutes ago."

5

The echo of the chatter and laughter in the mining park was covered by the metallic creaking of a metal roller gate being opened. The woman in a nurse's uniform had patiently waited for that moment, but her heart started racing all the same. She waited a couple of minutes to regain her calm, then stood up and adjusted Tommy in the wheelchair so that it seemed as if he were sleeping; as a finishing touch, she tugged his cap down over his forehead, snug against the top of his glasses.

From above came voices and the sounds of footsteps, drawers being opened and shut. With an electric buzz, the lights went on along the ceiling of the gallery.

The woman pushed the wheelchair toward the exit. At the last curve, she crossed paths with a young man and young woman, both in their early twenties, wearing matching T-shirts that read ITINERARIES OF THE SPIRIT.

"Good morning, Mother," the young woman said with a smile.

Mother. Right, she thought, and after greeting them with a sober nod, she walked into the souvenir shop. It was jammed to the rafters, half of the customers nuns or priests in tunics, the other half old people with walkers or in wheelchairs. Her uniform was perfect for blending in with the crowd, and she decided that everything was going according to plan.

Before being Caterina, the woman dressed as a nurse had lived a life that constituted a succession of bad choices and worse luck, with only an occasional flash of light when she managed to pull off a job that didn't end in a black eye or a pair of handcuffs. She drove very well, and once she had been the driver for an automotive smash-and-grab robbery of a jewelry shop in Cologne—she'd driven through the plate-glass window—

organized by a pair of Polish cousins. They had studied the routines of the jeweler and his employees, they knew when the private security guard got off work for his lunch break, and they'd calculated exactly how long it would take the German *Polizei* to get there, as well as how long it would take them to get away. The two cousins' precision, however, had been nothing compared to the way her life over the previous year had been scheduled and predisposed. But then, the reward she'd been promised would allow her to live very comfortably for quite some time. She wasn't even interested in the cash she'd left behind in Pala's safe: that money, she had been told, would serve to mislead the investigation, and to point accusing fingers at the psychiatrist.

She emerged into the open air with Tommy. The mining park had become a town fair, with food trucks selling sandwiches and grilled corn on the cob, a little cotton candy stand and a balloon stand next to it. The large dirt plaza where the mouths of the mine shafts opened out now contained at least two hundred people. There were families with children, bicyclists with their narrow black shoes, and lots and lots of volunteers and religious, with their entourage of the sick and the aged. They were gathering around the white tent where mass would be held. A pair of loudspeakers were spewing organ music and the chants of the Laudamus.

The woman looked around her with all the clarity of surging adrenaline. A little boy fell down and started crying; a group of cyclist-pilgrims with their bikes slung over their shoulders were walking toward one of the bars, singing a mountaineering song; the metal sausage griddle sizzled with grease when the cook tossed twenty pounds or so of fresh meat onto it; a man with a hermit's beard and a white tunic was vigorously clanging a bell while waving a sign with photographs of undernourished African children. Tommy shifted his position. She looked closely to make sure that he was still out like a light, then she went over to a stand selling religious books and glow-in-the-dark plastic statues of Our Lady of Loreto, filled with holy water. It was ten minutes past twelve noon, and for the first time, she wondered whether the rigid program that she had followed until that moment had failed just at the crucial instant.

Then a two-tone horn echoed from the street and a white tour bus with the Maltese cross on the side came through the front gate and parked next to the mountain of gravel, on the far side of the open plaza. The woman pushed the wheelchair in that direction.

Her ride had arrived.

6

Colomba parked on the sidewalk and looked out in concern at the crowd gathering around the white tent.

"At least they can't run away without us seeing them, since there's only one way out," said Alberti.

Dante pointed to a group of priests in tunics. "Maybe Leo disguised himself as a priest, like Nicolas Cage in *Face/Off*."

"Do you think that Caterina is about to hand Tommy over to him?" Colomba asked, intentionally ignoring the wisecrack.

"It's possible. Unless he wants to join the pilgrims to make his escape unnoticed. Or do both things at once. But for us, the point is another: Do we go in or do we remain hidden?"

Colomba chewed on her lip, undecided. "If Leo, or Caterina, recognizes us, they could start shooting into the crowd. Or use Tommy as a hostage."

"I don't think he expects to see us here," said Alberti.

"But he might have taken it into account," said Dante. "For all we know, he might have hired half the people here in tunics that we can see around us."

"For all we know, he might have planted a bomb just like he did in Milan," said Alberti. "Or he might have already strangled Tommy."

Colomba felt a stab of tension that shut her lungs down, and she planted her fingernails into her palms. "Fuck," she murmured.

"CC," Dante broke in, "what would normal procedure be in this case?"

"Cordon off the area, identify the hostage, move him to safety, then neutralize the target," Colomba reeled off the steps mechanically. "But in order to do that, we'd have to wait for D'Amore . . . And in the meantime, Leo or Caterina could kill the hostage or hop over the fence someplace we can't see."

Dante shrugged his shoulders. "We don't have any way of knowing what my brother has in mind. So just do what your former colleagues would do in your situation: dump the hot potato into someone else's lap."

"Tommy isn't a hot potato." Colomba shut her eyes for a second, trying to regain her calm and peace of mind. "Just tell me whether you think Leo is willing to blow himself up just to keep from getting caught."

Dante had a brief flash from his dream in the Box, when the water was submerging everything. This time, Leo wasn't waving goodbye with a smile: he was peering at him closely, with a look of concern, and telling him to run.

"He's not a suicide bomber," he replied. "But one thing is for sure, if he's in here, he's figured out an escape route."

Colomba nodded. "Then we need to find a way to get in without being noticed."

Alberti pointed to a food truck that was setting up on the main road. "What do you think of that?"

7

The woman who had murdered the psychiatrist whose secretary and lover she had once been stopped about thirty feet short of the white tour bus, pretending she was tucking the blanket in around the boy in the wheelchair she was pushing. Actually, though, she was looking at the group of volunteers and nurses of the Order of Malta who were getting out of the bus in small groups, accompanying octogenarians and invalids wrapped in blankets very much like the one she had found in the mine shaft. Half of the volunteers were of South American or North African or Central African origin, while the other half seemed to be made up of Asian women; they were all pushing wheelchairs that two powerfully built male nurses were extracting from the tour bus's luggage compartment, unfolding, and then helping the nurses to get their patients into.

The woman spotted a skinny little volunteer waiting for her ration of skinny old bones; the other woman had an age and a complexion roughly compatible with her own. When she saw that the young woman had been assigned a mountain of human flesh, she realized that she'd found her match.

Like in some elaborate choreography, nurses, caregivers, and patients spread out in an intricate array over the sandy ground, in an alternating pattern of white uniforms, dark-blue overcoats, and red blankets. The skinny woman stopped near the locked entrance to a mine, and after letting herself be overtaken by the colorful tidal wave, she headed toward the tent where the Te Deum was now being broadcast.

The woman pushed Tommy's wheelchair toward the wheelchair pushed by her "colleague," who shot her a worried glance and, on the verge of tears, said something to her in French.

"Italian or German," the woman retorted.

"Is that you?" the other woman asked nervously in Italian. "Are you Caterina?"

"I used to be."

The nurse raised the cap covering the face of the mountain of flesh, revealing a swollen face and a warty schnozzola.

A mixture of horror and pleasure seethed in her belly. "What's happened to him?"

"Cirrhosis of the liver. He's in the final stages. I gave him a sedative."

"Did you talk to anyone on the bus?"

The young woman shook her head. "I never once took off my gloves, I never once took off my veil, I was never here. Before I leave I'll go into one of the bathrooms and I'll change my clothes, then I'll take the train and go home," she said as if repeating a lesson from memory. Then she added, without changing her tone of voice: "I just needed money. I want to go back to my country."

"You don't have to justify yourself to me. Where did you find him?"

"In Rome. He lives alone. But I didn't find him. I was told where he lived."

"Did you see who gave you your instructions?"

"No. Did you?"

The woman who had been Caterina shook her head, then pinched the old man's cheek. He didn't react. "How am I supposed to wake him up?"

The young woman looked around, then handed her a hypodermic needle wrapped in a piece of toilet paper. "Whatever it is you need to do to him . . . do me a favor, and do it in a hurry. I want to get out of here."

"I'll be back here before the end of the mass. In the meantime, you take this one aboard the bus and wait for me. If the driver asks you anything, just tell him that your patient is tired and needs to sleep."

"They'll notice it's not the same person."

"And they aren't going to give a damn. Just put him in the last row. And if he starts to get worked up, there's a syringe for him, too, in the pocket on the back of the wheelchair."

The woman took the old man with her and pushed him toward the control cabin of the ropeway conveyor that years ago had brought the raw minerals to the refinery, and which now consisted of nothing more than a bucket hanging thirty feet off the ground. The cabin, which still held some portion of the original controls, had once been locked, but the last time she'd been here, the woman had replaced the old padlock with a new one. And so she had no difficulty opening the lock, pushing the wheelchair inside, and shutting the door behind her. No one saw her. If it had been a different kind of party, there would probably have been kids everywhere rolling joints or making out, but this was a party for good Christians, and good Christians never go where they aren't supposed to. The woman took out the hypodermic needle wrapped in toilet paper, and only at that moment did it occur to her that she didn't know what was in it, and whether this should be an intramuscular injection or a venous one. She chose his deltoid. For a good thirty seconds, nothing at all happened, then the old man started trembling and coughing. Another two minutes went by before he regained consciousness; the whole time, she stood right in front of him, savoring every second.

Finally the old man opened his bleary eyes and focused on her, but he didn't recognize her. And how could he, if the last time he'd laid eyes on her she'd been six and covered with blood?

The woman felt a pleasurable sensation of warmth rise from her belly.

"Ciao, Papà," she said.

8

While Alberti remained at the entrance to the park, awaiting the arrival of the counterterrorism squad, Colomba and Dante slipped windbreakers with a picture of the pope on the back over their clothing, and donned the cyclist-pilgrim caps that they'd purchased at a souvenir stand. Then they approached the proprietors of the café food truck, promising them a cash payment if they helped them, and threatening them with arrest if they didn't. One of the two accepted; the other stalked off in annoyance.

And so Colomba and Dante managed to enter the mining park, peering out at the strolling visitors from the interior of the food truck, and after circling the plaza once, remaining as close as possible to the crowd, they parked behind the tent where the faithful were gathering.

There were no walls, just the canvas awning warding off the sunlight overhead, and so Colomba and Dante saw the crowd assembling while the priest, with the aid of a couple of altar boys, put on his ceremonial vestments. In front of the altar—a simple wooden table with an ostensorium, a cross, and a candle—was a large space without benches, reserved for gurneys and wheelchairs, already packed with old people and invalids.

"You know that believing in an invisible, infinite, and omnipotent being can be considered a sign of mental illness?" Dante said, peering out at the faces.

"From my point of view, thinking that the universe created itself is even more of one."

"So your God lets people like Leo and Caterina go around murdering people and kidnapping kids."

"It's called free will. But you *don't want* to get bogged down in a theological discussion at this exact moment, right?"

"Right."

Colomba asked the driver to park close to the souvenir shop.

"We aren't authorized to park there, they'll tell us we have to move," the man replied. "They don't even have sockets for us to plug in, no electric power."

"Just tell them that you have a problem with your engine, and that you won't try to open for business," Colomba said. Then, to Dante: "I'll take a walk around and get right back, you stay here."

"Okay," he said, having already spotted the liquor bottles. Colomba tilted the visor of her cap low over the bridge of her nose and stuck her earpiece into her right ear. It was flesh-colored and virtually invisible, and it connected by Bluetooth to the radio she wore at her waist, next to her handgun. She checked to make sure none of that could be seen under the windbreaker and got out.

"Can you hear me?" she murmured.

"Yes," said Dante, who had the radio propped up on the counter, with the volume turned down low.

"Yes, Deputy Captain," said Alberti. "Esposito has just arrived."

"Tell him the channel," said Colomba, and stepped into the little shop crowded with children and nuns, where she pretended to be interested in the sulfur cream for greasy skin. Next to the shop, there was an arrow pointing the way to tours of the mine the way it was a hundred years ago.

"Are you open?" she asked the clerk behind the counter.

"Certainly! Come right in."

"I can't hear you very well, Deputy Captain," Esposito said in her ear.

She moved toward the shop window, between the display cases of antiqued postcards. "I'll bet you can't, there's a lot of rock around here. Where are the others?"

"They're dribbling in a few at a time."

"Confirm that," said D'Amore, piping in on the frequency. "What's the situation? Have you identified the target?"

"No. None of the three. But the area is enormous."

"Describe it to me."

"There must be at least twenty-five acres of land, with lots of blind spots, crumbling old buildings, and factory sheds. There are about three hundred people, all concentrated in the central space. Many black and Asian women, many priests and nuns. Two Carabinieri are in charge of maintaining public order, fire trucks and ambulances are parked at the entrance. The whole area is enclosed by a barbed-wire fence, which gives onto the fields and the township road."

"We've cordoned off the perimeter. They're not getting out that way, unless they've already left."

"Snipers?"

"Two, on the roof of the abandoned factory, at nine o'clock. We'll call the front gate six o'clock, the big tent the center of the area, and the enclosure at the far end twelve o'clock."

Colomba looked for it, peering carefully, but from there she couldn't see it. "Oscar Kilo Yankee," she said. "But remember what you promised me."

"Me and Espo are ready to come in," Alberti broke in.

"Start checking the tour buses." Colomba thought it over for a second and added: "At eleven o'clock, more or less."

"I'll send in four of my men and have them start from the other end," said D'Amore. "There are very few of us, given the number of people."

"I didn't expect this crowd," said Colomba.

"I'm Falcon One, my men run from Two to Eight. The snipers are Eagle One and Two. You're Rome One, and your men are numbered progressively. Open channels."

"Oscar Kilo Yankee."

"This is Rome Two and Three, and we're going in," said Esposito's voice. Without a hint of sarcasm, for once.

"Rome Four is going to have himself a nice cold vodka and tonic," said Dante's voice.

"Stop playing with the radio," said Colomba.

"Yessir, Signor Rome One."

Colomba descended into the tunnel and soon the official communications channel in her earpiece turned into hisses and bursts of static. The gallery into the mine was deserted and bare, save for the emergency lights lining the rock walls. Colomba would have sworn that it was identical to when her grandfather had taken her down there.

She continued until she reached the locked freight elevator cage, but that was the end of the walk: after that, the gallery was blocked off by a heavy gate with a lock plugged up with dust. It probably hadn't been opened in centuries, and that was a good thing, because who knew how many miles the galleries went on, between forking branches and communication tunnels.

And then she noticed that behind the gate, tossed by a steady draft, something was rolling along. She stuck her arm between the bars and grabbed it on the fly: it was a bunched-up pair of fishnet panty hose.

Colomba went running back to the souvenir shop to get decent radio reception, just as the loudspeakers were blaring out the priest's echoing voice.

In the name of the Father, the Son, and the Holy Ghost.

"Rome One here," she said. "I found an item of clothing that may belong to the target. She used the gallery open to the public to change clothes, right behind the souvenir shop, at three o'clock," she continued as she walked back toward the food truck.

D'Amore asked her if there was any more evidence, and she answered no. "But find someone who has the keys, I don't know if there's anything else."

Amen.

"Roger, Rome One," said D'Amore. "Falcon Four and Five, head over to three o'clock."

Colomba waved at the food truck driver, who was smoking angrily as he mulled over the money he'd lost, then she rapped at the closed metal roller blind. "Dante, I brought you a pair of stockings to sniff," she said.

When he failed to reply, she leaned in to look through the narrow gap. The kitchen of the food truck was empty.

9

*A*nd with your spirit.

The echoing loudspeakers penetrated into the control booth of the ropeway conveyor. The woman who had been Caterina understood that her time was almost up. She leaned over the man sprawled on the ground, who was staring up at her through his tears, his shirt unbuttoned and wide open, revealing the belly swollen with the abnormal buildup of fluid and covered with the bruises from paracentesis. In the effort to escape, he'd fallen out of the wheelchair and now he was flat on the dirty floor, incapable of rising. His stretchy-waisted trousers had fallen down his rickets-ridden legs, revealing the adult diaper he wore because he had lost all bladder control. He'd shit his pants and reeked of it.

The man's daughter gazed at him without compassion.

"You remember my mother?" she asked him. "She survived for a whole month after you left, did you know that? Even if she didn't understand a thing anymore." She pointed to her temple. "You broke something in her head. With your fists. And I helped the nurse to wash her. I was six years old, and I was cleaning my mother because you'd beaten her into a coma." She hunkered down to look at him more closely. "What was it she did wrong?"

"Nothing . . . nothing." The old man's voice scraped and hissed. "I was drinking. I didn't mean to—"

"I'll tell you what she did wrong. She found out what you were doing to me. And she tried to stop you."

The old man flailed and struggled in his effort to speak, but he just coughed, red with the effort of breathing.

"They took out my ovaries. At age six. From the infection that you gave me. Right after my mother died." The woman took off her veil and overcoat and hung them on the door handle. "Do you know what the nurses said?" she continued. "That it was just as well. At least that way I wouldn't bring another miserable bastard just like me into the world, another *Neger*." The woman got a waterproof white jumpsuit out of her bag and put it on, crushing her braids under the hood.

"Forgive me," the old man wheezed, and he made a last desperate attempt to get to his feet, but his daughter shoved him back into the wheelchair with her foot.

"I would have forgiven you if you'd come back to get me. I would have let you do anything to me if you hadn't abandoned me. And probably I'd be dead now, as a result. But instead, here I am. You never came back, and I grew up."

She pulled the box cutter out of her purse and started by cutting off the man's nose.

D'Amore caught up with Colomba at the food truck. He was wearing a cap with a photograph of the pope and in one hand he was carrying a pamphlet listing the initiatives of the Order of Malta.

"Did you find him?" he asked.

She shook her head. "I looked under the tent and all around the various stands."

"If he'd been dragged away against his will, one of my men would have seen it. Could he have left voluntarily?"

"I hope so." The phantom pain in her belly was so strong that Colomba was forced to crouch. "Still, I can't help but think that Leo organized all this to get him back. I know that's crazy, but everything that's happened is crazy. God . . ."

"Falcon Four," said the radio.

"Go on," D'Amore replied.

"There's a woman who matches the target's description. She's dressed as a nurse and she's pushing a wheelchair with a man whose features we haven't been able to get a sighting on, but he could be the hostage. In the area around the tour bus parking lot. Eleven o'clock."

"Everyone converge but maintain safe distance. Eagle, do you see anything?"

"Negative, we're blocked by the ropeway conveyor."

D'Amore put a hand over the microphone. "Are you going to come or do you want to stay here and wait for Dante?" he asked.

Colomba planted her fingernails into her palms until drops of blood appeared.

"Let's go," she said.

Dante waited until two of D'Amore's Falcons moved away from the book stand. The two men wore hats and sweatshirts identical to those worn by the pilgrims, but it was obvious from the way they held themselves and moved and covered each other's blind spots that they had military training. And then there were the slight bulges around belly and thigh, the hard eyes, the fake smiles, the slight tilt toward the side of the head with the earpiece.

Dante moved around behind a little bar on wheels, shaped like a lemon, and from there he saw the Falcons cross paths with Esposito and Alberti; after a rapid exchange of observations, they all moved off at a brisk pace toward the tour bus parking lot.

Something's happening, he thought.

As soon as the policemen and the soldiers vanished behind the old processing plant, Dante slipped into a crowd of schoolchildren, and after edging his way through them continued toward the small mountain of mining slag, next to which stood the sulfur kilns, a series of inclined stone basins the size of swimming pools, arranged in a stepped array. In the nineteenth century, they were used to filter and distill the unprocessed sulfur: now they were just enormous trash cans, receptacles for the garbage that people threw from the road.

Had Colomba already noticed he'd disappeared? he wondered. He could imagine her losing her mind and cursing his name.

But what else could he do? Tell her that while she had been walking deeper into the mine, the boring wisecracks of the cops playing hide-and-seek had vanished from the radio, replaced by just one voice that had frozen him to the spot? A voice that had persuaded him to slip stealthily into the crowd that trudged along fetidly like a thousand-headed monster, and to put up with the sticky hands of the children, the myriad bodily odors, the foul breath of strangers mixing with the air that he breathed, the particles crawling with the bacteria from their sweat?

To the kilns, the voice had said. *Alone. You'll have all the answers you've been looking for.*

An instant later, communications had started up again between the Falcons and the Eagles, but Dante hadn't heard them: he'd already stepped out of the van, worried that Colomba might arrive and stop him. He hadn't thought it through, he hadn't weighed the pros and cons.

His legs wobbly beneath him, Dante walked up the wooden catwalk that climbed to the kilns, his heart racing, drenched with sweat. Sitting on the central sulfur kiln was a man. The minute he saw Dante, he grabbed a couple of crutches and rose from his seat.

"Hi, little brother," he said. "We have three minutes. Don't waste them."

12

Tommy shouted.

The young woman who'd taken delivery of him leaped to her feet in surprise, banging her head on the tour bus's luggage racks: she'd hoped he'd sleep longer than this, but instead he must have just awakened. And now he was looking around in terror.

"Be good, Tommy," she said to him. "Soon you'll be home." Tommy started struggling and twisting and he emitted another shout. She rummaged through her purse and found the syringe, but he was moving too vigorously, and without meaning to, he swatted her with a flailing hand. The syringe rolled away down the central aisle of the bus.

"Everything all right back there?" asked the driver.

"Yes, yes, it's fine. Don't worry about him," the young woman replied, doing her best to hold Tommy still. But it was an impossible challenge. He was fast, and he was big. And very strong. He tore off her veil, and when she tried to put it back on, he crushed her against the armrest, swatting at her with his open hands. She was forced to stand up again, and once again she hit her head against the overhead luggage rack. Tommy climbed over her and started pounding on the rear door.

"Hey, look out, he'll break it!" said the driver.

"I don't know how to calm him down!" she replied, slipping into a state of panic. "He's having a crisis."

"If you don't know how to control him, what do you think I can do about it?" asked the driver, opening the doors.

Tommy teetered, but managed to hold himself upright by grabbing at the doorframe. He shouted again, and this time a couple of passersby turned to look; it must have been a fairly common sight, that day, because soon the two strollers looked away and continued along the way.

The young woman grabbed the syringe and hit Tommy in the back with it, but she had forgotten to remove the cap and the needle snapped off.

"Please, calm down," she said.

Tommy paid her no attention, leaped to the ground, and started running, waving his arms as he emitted shouts and incoherent yawps. Blinded by panic, the young woman got out in her turn, but instead of chasing after the boy, she headed for the porta-potties.

13

Dante's brain had exploded, unable to withstand the force of the satori: everything he had ever imagined, everything he had ever believed, had been wrong.

"What the fuck happened to you?" he stammered.

Leo smiled under the network of scars that rendered his face unrecognizable. "I fought the war, little brother. And I lost." He no longer had any fingers on his right hand, and his legs terminated above the knees. His left eye was half-closed by scar tissue. "You were there when it happened, but you've forgotten all about it."

A fragment of the dream scratched at Dante's memories. *The water. The odor of kerosene.* "The shipwreck," he said.

Leo nodded and sat down again. "When the second fuel tank exploded, I was too close to the *Chourmo*. The explosion stunned me and the current dragged me under. You had the life jacket, and they got you out of the water right away."

"Who took me away?"

"If I knew, they'd be dead by now. You may not remember, but we had a long conversation on the boat. I explained that you had to help me catch him. You were . . . stubborn, but I knew that you'd understand in the end."

Dante's head spun, and he, too, sat down on the wall, remaining a few yards away from Leo. "You can't have killed Martina. Not in the state you're in."

"And I wouldn't have done it like that. I really liked her. She always brought me coffee." Leo gave him a crooked smile.

"Jesus . . . you worked for Lupo."

Leo nodded. "I put his phone calls through."

"So it wasn't you who locked me up in Rimini."

"No."

"And you didn't kill the Melases."

Leo shook his head.

"And . . ." Dante stopped: it was the only question he really cared about, but he couldn't ask it. The mere thought of turning it into actual words drained him of all energy.

Leo understood all the same. "And I don't know who you are, little brother."

The crashing wave of disappointment and rage brought Dante out of it. "Then why the fuck do you keep calling me that?"

Leo reached into his pocket and pulled out a black-and-white photograph, which he set down on the top of the low wall. "That was taken in Berlin in 1980." It was two men sitting on a bench, against the background of a nondescript brick wall. One of the two men was lighting both their cigarettes. Dante recognized him and looked away.

Don't look outside. Be obedient. Be clean.

"The Father . . ." he said, trembling with fear.

"Our Father. When you were ten, we shared a cell. I was fourteen, and I was taking care of you."

"I was in the silo . . ." Dante stammered.

"No. That came later. First you were with me, at the Factory." Leo looked at the watch he'd fastened to one of his crutches. "We still have two minutes."

"I'm not letting you go . . ." Dante tried to say.

"You can't even stop me. Don't waste your time."

"Who are you?"

"*Mu*. I'm a void."

"Why Venice?"

"Look at the other man in the photograph. You've seen him, only much older and much better tanned."

Dante looked back at the picture, his eyes half-closed as if it were gleaming with dazzling light. "Belyy. The founder of COW. Fuck. So he and the Father worked together?"

"They knew how to plan for the future. The Cold War was over, the Soviet Union was destined to collapse. Belyy started to transfer the most promising boys, and the Father was kind enough to keep them in safe custody. I don't know where you come from, but I spent the first fourteen years of my life inside the Box. Giltine was my sister, but unfortunately she was completely off her rocker."

Tommy fell at the bottom of the small mountain of slag, got to his feet, and with blood streaming from his nose went on running. He tripped over one of the uprights supporting the walkway that led up to the kilns and fell again, slamming his face against the first step. This time he didn't get up again: he curled up in a fetal position and started crying.

Dante, thirty feet up, saw him. "The boy . . ." he said.

"One of the officers who are infesting this party will take care of him." Leo held him tight. "We still have a minute."

60 SECONDS

Colomba had seen Tommy emerge from behind the trees and fall on the catwalk. At the exact instant that she swiveled in his direction, gripping her pistol, D'Amore's voice exploded in her ear.

"Rome One. We don't know if the hostage is alone. Abort."

"If they shoot me, you'll find out," she said, reaching the base of the sulfur kiln.

Tommy was rubbing his face, and blood was gushing from his nose. Colomba bent over him.

"It's all right, Tommy," she said to him. "I'm here. I'm here."

The boy grabbed her in a bear hug. Colomba returned the hug, gripping the pistol in her right hand. "Hostage safe. We need medical support," she said into the radio.

"All right. Acquire target," said D'Amore.

40 SECONDS

Alberti and Esposito were the two officers closest to the sighting. They drew their handguns and ran toward the young woman who was opening one of the porta-potty doors. A little boy stepped out of the next toilet over and, at the sight of the drawn pistols, started shouting, but the young woman was unable to react fast enough. Alberti threw her to the ground and aimed his gun at the back of her head.

"Police. Don't move."

Esposito twisted her arm behind her back and, after searching her, handcuffed her. "Rome Two. We have the *fucking whore*."

Alberti took the veil off the young woman's face. "It isn't her," he said, his heart lurching.

"What do you mean it isn't her?" said Esposito. "She was with Tommy!"

Alberti turned the girl over roughly. "Where's Caterina?"

20 SECONDS

Caterina put the jumpsuit into her purse and put the veil back over her face. At her feet was a slowly spreading puddle of blood diluted with a liquid that looked like urine, but which had issued directly from the sliced-open belly of the man sprawled on the ground. Quarts and quarts of excess abdominal fluid.

She saw herself reflected in that disgusting gruel. She smiled.

She was free.

10 SECONDS

Leo led Dante along the platform, staggering.

"I was convinced that you were behind it all, that you were the King of Diamonds. But instead, you didn't even play this match."

Leo smiled for the first time. "That's why I'm throwing the whole deck into the air," he said, and smashed his head into Dante's face.

Dante couldn't see a thing, and he lost his balance, staggering backward toward the mouth of the sulfur kiln. He tried unsuccessfully to grab the edge.

"No!" he shouted as he slid toward the bottom of the kiln.

"Don't believe anything, little brother," Leo said from above. "Don't believe anything."

ZERO

The tanker truck being driven by Loris's father punched through the gate around the mining park as if it were made of plywood, right at the point that the soldiers would have described as "three o'clock." The truck was a hulking beast from the early nineties, forty metric tons on six axles, and there were very few things that could even begin to halt its forward progress, even at just five miles per hour.

Gaspare Mantoni bumped over an earth berm and then rumbled down the long, deserted ramp of dirt, spraying mud and gravel as he went. He uprooted a hedge, then rammed aside a café food truck parked outside a souvenir shop; the food truck tipped over, landing on the proprietor, who had gotten out to smoke a cigarette, cursing all the while against his partner, who'd left him to deal with those fucking cops. The handle of the metal roller blind caught him at the base of his spinal cord, then the side of the truck crushed his head like a walnut, and it did the same thing to two young people from a local Catholic association a few feet away.

Gaspare swerved, and after ripping out one of the corners of the tent, he headed straight for the altar. The first one to go under the wheels was the priest himself, followed seconds later by the crowd of the sick and the faithful clustered around him as they made pointless attempts to turn and run, stampeding each other underfoot in a screaming tangle.

Gaspare, his senses dulled by alcohol, barely even noticed. He'd driven drunk for most of his life, successfully filling the tanks of half the countryside around Portico with fuel for heating and cooking, navigating paths barely wide enough for goats, so he certainly wasn't having any difficulties here, on what was basically flat land. If he kept running over things and people, well, *fuck*, it was because he liked doing it.

He slammed into a group of priests who were running for their lives, feeling like a bowling ball smashing into a triangle of pins, and then emerged into the tour bus parking lot. He swerved again and smashed into the white bus with the red cross.

Gaspare left this world at that exact moment, when his frontal bone smashed through the windshield. The driver of the tour bus that Gaspare's truck had smashed into was tossed backward by the airbag and, out of the corner of his eye, saw the tanker truck sail into the air like a scorpion's tail, amid the screeching sound of twisted sheet steel. The rear of the tanker truck came plummeting down onto the nose of the tour bus, and the safety valve, jammed shut by years of neglect, suddenly popped open, freeing into the surrounding air the thirty thousand liters of liquid propane gas under forty-five bars of pressure, which immediately turned into an expanding plume of gas, shooting out at a velocity of nearly two hundred meters a second.

The shock wave and hurtling wall of air kicked up a swirling cloud of dirt and grit that riddled the walls of the porta-potties and the bodies of two young women who were hastily getting dressed; the cloud then moved on to machine-gun the girl between Alberti and Esposito. But the two of them didn't even notice it happening, because they'd been swept away an instant before, with their eardrums shattered.

They were still in midair when the liquid propane gas entered into contact with the flame.

Alberti saw his partner's body sail away like a cannonball.

The wall of air and the cloud of flaming gas and vapors overturned the vans and trucks that had been spared by Gaspare's tanker truck, blowing them up in a chain reaction, burning the guy ropes holding up the tent, charring the benches, and slicing like an incandescent scythe through the crowd of running people, the NOA agents and the Carabinieri who had pursued the tanker truck. They hit the mountain of mining slag, which flew into the air like so many champagne corks and rained down on Colomba, her arms still wrapped around Tommy, then they tore loose the cables of the ropeway conveyor, crumbling the control booth into bits, transforming Caterina into a glowing, seething cloud, and then climbed and climbed, until they lapped hotly at the summit of the sulfur kilns.

Dante was still sliding toward the bottom when everything became intolerably bright. His brother's silhouette at the top of the kiln became a patch of color in the white.

And an instant later, he was lost in all that whiteness.

PART FOUR

THE CHILDHOOD OF EVIL

*W*hen the door opens and a tentacle of light makes its way into the small, exposed-brick room, the boy without a name snarls and crouches, ready to lunge. He spends much of his time on all fours, because in the world of darkness where he grew up, that's the safest stance. Where he grew up, you recognized others by their smell. Where he grew up, if you weren't a predator you soon became food.

The man in the doorway is tall and skinny; he wears a loose factory-worker jumpsuit, and dark glasses over a silk ski mask. As soon as he sees him, the boy without a name lowers his eyes and stops snarling, because he is now in the presence of the man who will decide his fate. He calls himself the Father, he speaks Russian with a strong foreign accent, and he expects absolute obedience.

"Come," he says to the boy, turning his back on him without waiting so much as a second. The boy could attack him. In the dark world, no one ever turned their back on anyone. But the dark world is far away now, and he doesn't even know how far away because one day he woke up and he was already here, between these walls, and he must have slept for days, maybe months, because the faint daylight that filtered down through the high ground-level windows had been enough to make him scream from the stabbing pain in his eyes.

The Father heads off down a long dusty hallway, lit by bare lightbulbs, and the boy follows him, hunched over, knees bent, hands ready to clutch, feet ready to kick. He sniffs at the new smells, listens to the old sounds that filter from behind the endless succession of closed doors: shouts, sobs, screams, and the sound of flesh tearing beneath repeated blows.

"You grew up in a hostile environment," says the Father, still in Russian. "And that made you what you are . . . it made you a good Son. But now you need to learn to be something else. Because the secret of survival is the ability to adapt to your environment, do you understand?"

"Yes," the boy whispers, even if it's not entirely true: many of the words that the Father utters are completely unfamiliar to him.

"Your reflexes must become a choice, they have to stop being an imposition of the worst part of you . . . the beast part. Do you understand?"

"Yes. Beasts die."

"Very good. Whereas you are going to survive. And you're going to have a roommate."

The Father stops in front of a door. He pulls the bolt and opens it. The crude glare of a fluorescent light illuminates a skeletal young boy bound to a cot with leather straps, foam dripping from his mouth, an IV inserted into his vein. He's wearing an open hospital gown, and there's a hole in the cot to let his excrement drop into a bucket beneath.

The stench makes the boy's eyes water.

"A difficult patient," says the Father. "He has a stubborn, oppositional, whiny personality." He raises the ski mask to uncover his lips, and pops a licorice stick into his mouth. "I'm having quite a hard time overcoming his resistance. In spite of the terapia."

He's uttered the last word in Italian, and the boy looks at him, uncomprehending.

"Terapia means treatment." The Father points to the IV tube. "Insulina," he says, in Italian again. "In the proper dosage, it provokes a shock that starts the brain up again, and that I hope will eliminate certain forms of rigidity. He receives the treatment twice a week, alternating with perineal electromassage and baths. There have been some improvements, but he's not cured yet. Do you understand?"

"Yes."

"I'm counting on you to make sure he learns obedience. In return, he will help you to learn to reason. He has a very elevated intelligence quotient and a superior ability to process ideas, even if it's often hindered by his morbid sexual proclivities." The Father takes a rag off a hook on the wall and uses it to mop the prisoner's sweat-drenched face. "I hope I won't have to use techniques that are more invasive than these. I'd just as soon leave him intact. But il medico pietoso fa la piaga puzzolente," *he adds in Italian. Roughly speaking, it means a doctor must be cruel to be kind. He pulls the IV out of the prisoner's vein and puts a bandage on his arm. Then he lifts the bound boy's head and helps him to drink a glass of water and sugar. The boy spits most of it out, his eyes rolled up into his head.* "I'm going to leave you here with him. Once he recovers, take him to your room. From this moment forward, you're bound together, do you understand?"

"Yes," *says the boy without a name, looking at the prisoner and wondering whether it might not be better to kill him immediately, suffocate him the minute the Father turns his back.* "Does he have a name or is he like me?" *he asks.*

The Father lowers the ski mask again.

"You can call him Dante."

CHAPTER I

The operations required to recover and identify the victims at the mining park lasted two weeks, because the miles of tunnels required the intervention of teams of spelunkers.

But the most challenging area to inspect actually proved to be the parking lot, where the sheet metal and steel beams of the tour buses had fused with the structures of the ropeway conveyor, producing a razor-edged tangle of twisted metal. In the end, there were thirty-nine corpses recovered, but everyone agreed that there would have been a far higher number of victims if Gaspare Mantoni had plowed directly into the parked buses instead of playing a demented game of *Grand Theft Auto* in the middle of the crowd: even with all the ensuing panic, the ones who didn't wind up crushed beneath the wheels of the tanker truck had managed to escape, making it to a safe distance from the epicenter of the explosion.

Among the thirty-nine confirmed victims, there were nuns and monks, a number of park personnel, the clerks at the souvenir stand that burned to the ground, the cotton candy vendor and his colleague who sold balloons, the priest who was saying mass, the woman called Caterina and her father, the young woman who had helped Caterina, three NOA officers, two Carabinieri, and a policeman from Rome who had been slammed against a brick wall.

His name was Claudio Esposito.

Esposito's funeral was held with high solemnity at the Basilica of Saint Paul Outside the Walls, along with services for the other police officers and soldiers killed in the massacre.

Among those attending were Esposito's widow and two children, who were living through their worst nightmare come true. Among those attending were the highest authorities of the Italian state, including the prime minister, who delivered a speech decrying the dangers of Islamic extremism. Among those attending were Di Marco and the highest ranks of Europe's armed forces and intelligence services, who all applauded respectfully. Among those attending was D'Amore, breathing with some difficulty as a result of his cracked ribs, with a distant look in his eyes as he thought of other deaths in other lands. Among those attending were Martina's parents, as she was commemorated among the other innocent souls, fallen to the violence of terrorism. Among those attending were Lupo and Bruno, still in a state of shock at the discovery that Bonaccorso had lived among them for months without anyone noticing. Among those attending was Alberti, his arm in a sling and his head covered with burns, supported by his girlfriend as he sobbed helplessly: in what seemed like the blink of an eye, he'd lost two partners with whom he had been sure he'd grow old.

Also among those attending was Colomba, riddled with bruises from the collapse of the hillock that had protected her and Tommy from the explosion. She didn't approach her former colleagues or the family members of the deceased, but remained among the ordinary people who were attending out of a sense of fellow feeling or in order to be able to see themselves on television. With her hair in a buzz cut and her eyes blackened, no one recognized her. No one except Santini.

"This is all your fault, you miserable bitch!" he shouted at her, after pushing his way through the length of the procession. He was stinking drunk and could barely stay on his legs.

Colomba tried to change direction to avoid him, but Santini followed her. "Esposito was in the personnel office!" he railed. "Why the fuck didn't you just leave him in peace? Why did you drag him into your insanity?"

The procession continued to stream past, and the mourners pretended not to see them. Colomba tried once again to move away, and once again Santini planted himself in her path.

"What the fuck do you want from me?" Colomba said listlessly.

"I want you to get out of here!" Santini shouted, his back increasingly bowed as he leaned toward her. "Get out! This is no place for you. You have no right to be here."

Two plainclothes policemen pushed their way through the crowd. They were Santini's security detail, and they must have been worried when he'd rushed off without warning. One of them locked arms with their superior officer.

"Sir," he said. "Please, let's go. It's not worth it."

A glint of lucidity appeared in Santini's eyes, and he took a couple of steps back. "Just make sure she gets far away from here."

There was no need: Colomba let the procession stream past, and soon she stood all alone on the deserted cobblestones. In the end she headed off through the streets of Rome, navigating toward a home that no longer felt like it was hers.

She walked past the Hotel Impero on Via del Corso, but she didn't stop: she didn't feel up to it, not yet.

In the week that he'd spent on the rooftop veranda of the penthouse suite of the Hotel Impero, drinking straight vodka and espresso, smoking cigarettes and tossing back pills, Dante had been forced to manage another lost piece of his life, starting with the ten hours spent in the belly of the sulfur kiln before the Protezione Civile search teams managed to dig him out.

The bottom of the ramp had been smeared with motor oil and Dante wouldn't have been able to climb up and get out under his own power, even if he'd been sound of mind. But he most certainly wasn't. After the explosion he'd lost any sense of self. His rescuers had found him half-naked, covered with soot, bellowing inarticulate phrases and animal sounds. He'd even tried to attack them. Fortunately, among the rescuers was the emergency room doctor from Portico who had admitted him to the hospital under the name of Signor Caselli after Villa Quiete, and he had put in a call to Colomba, who was still combing through the rubble in search of Dante.

By now it was impossible to continue to keep news of his rescue a secret, and so the chief of police had issued an official announcement, stating that the leader of the ISIS cell that had kidnapped him had been killed during the massacre at the sulfur mines.

Dante had no alternative but to lock himself away in his suite at the hotel, avoiding everyone, without distinction: journalists, rubberneckers, but also old friends. Even Roberto Minutillo, his lawyer and friend for many years, was unable to get in to see him.

Only his adoptive father, Annibale Valle, had refused to stop trying.

He was a bearded Falstaffian man in his early seventies, who managed to hold his nearly 450 pounds of weight upright with the aid of a couple of canes. Now, though, he was sitting on a pair of chairs that had been pushed together and staring at Dante, who was in turn doing everything he could to ignore him.

"You can't just stay in here, avoiding everyone, for the rest of your life," Annibale said as kindly as he could.

Dante put out the butt of his cigarette in the melted ice at the bottom of his glass.

"Forget about it, Dante," Annibale went on in a gentle voice. "I've been watching you fight and suffer your whole life, and maybe the time has come to stop. For your own sake, as a way to protect yourself. Those things that you think you know—"

"Things that I think I know," Dante interrupted him, parroting his words. He got out a clean glass and poured ice and Beluga vodka into it. "That's what you used to say even when I was trying to explain to you that the Father was still alive." He flashed a nasty smile. "Before I found out that I wasn't the real Dante. Before I found out that you had lied to get out of jail, since you were accused of having killed me. Sorry, of having killed *your son*."

Annibale looked down. "Dante . . . what do I have to do to get you to forgive me? I love you, Dante."

"I don't have to forgive you for anything," Dante said as he lit another cigarette. "The first thing I learned the minute I got out of the silo is that people lie, and you're no different." Then, after a long silence, he asked: "Do you ever think about him? Your real son?"

Annibale sighed. "You're my real son, too—"

Dante threw the glass hard onto the floor. It didn't break, but the vodka started dripping over the edge of the balcony down into the garden below. "Do you ever think about him?" he asked again, without raising his voice.

Annibale nodded. "All the time."

"And what do you think about?"

"Come on, Dante. It's not fair . . ."

"Please."

Annibale blew his nose on a paper napkin. "About . . . about what he would have been like when he grew up. Whether he would have been like you," he said in a broken voice.

Dante grinned. "I'm not like anyone else. Except for a psychopath who helped to murder a bunch of people."

"I'm a void," Leo had told him.

"It's all over now. You have to move on."

For the first time, Dante turned to look Annibale in the face. He looked old to him now, with those cheeks that sagged like a turkey's wattles, and the veins standing out in sharp relief on his hands. He thought to himself that children should never see their parents get old, that everyone should be born and grow up alone, to avoid the pain of saying farewell. "Without a past, there is no future," he said. "Just a really shitty present."

"You've almost been murdered three times. Isn't that enough for you?"

Dante reached down to pick up the glass and filled it up again. "I'm a gambler, Papà. I keep betting until I break the bank. Or somebody breaks me."

Colomba didn't have many friends left among the ranks of law enforcement, but she hadn't alienated them *all*. The guard at the front desk of the morgue at the Umberto I Hospital wrote her a pass and put in a good word for her with one of the attendants.

"No more than twenty minutes, Signora," the attendant told her, after pulling out the correct body tray in the mortuary refrigerator, and then he left her alone.

Colomba sat down on the stool, and after heaving a sigh, loosened the straps and pulled down the sheet. Leo's half-frozen face—greenish, with the chin askew and the eyelids lowered—didn't frighten her in the slightest. Whoever he had been while alive, mercenary or psychopath, was no longer there. But the autopsy had revealed old wounds that might date back to his adolescence, and his DNA, which didn't match the samples previously on file, had been useful in reconstructing a piece of his family: Giltine really was his sister, as he had told Dante; or actually, half sister, because they'd had a different mother. All they had in common was their father.

Belyy.

"I believe that hell exists," she told him. "And that you're there right now, burning and suffering for everything you've done. But if the devil is actually an impartial judge, he ought to acknowledge that you had a few mitigating factors."

She lowered the sheet a little further, uncovering his chest, ravaged by the autopsy and burns almost certainly dating back to the wreck of the *Chourmo*, since the burns from the liquid propane gas explosion were concentrated primarily on the back of his body.

"Because what Belyy did to your mother, the things you experienced as a child, it all helped to make you what you were." Now she pulled the sheet all the way down and looked at his amputated legs. The irregular flaps of the scars. "Though I also believe in free will, in personal choices. And you made your choices . . . and you chose that strange sort of life you lived."

Leo was killed by the shock wave and the heat from the blast, an impact that was too much for an already debilitated body: that's what she had been told at the last meeting of the CASA select committee that she was invited to. If he'd been just fifty yards farther away, he would have survived.

"But you didn't want to survive, you wanted to die before I could find you and kill you myself. You even denied me that last fucking satisfaction. I didn't even get a chance to tell you to your face how you disgusted me. How much you . . ."

She burst out sobbing so hard that she couldn't even catch her breath. She got down off the stool and curled up in a corner of the chilly, tile-lined room.

And that's how Bart found her.

5

Bart helped Colomba to her feet and forced her to go out with her to get a bite to eat, in spite of the fact that Bart herself was dropping with exhaustion: she'd come down to Rome to take part in the meeting of the National Committee for Order and Public Security, and she'd come by the morgue only to make arrangements to transport Bonaccorso's corpse to LABANOF, where she planned to do further testing.

It was still cool out, but they nevertheless took seats at an outdoor table in the San Lorenzo quarter, not far from Dante's old apartment. People did come around to take pictures of the place, but nobody seemed interested in buying it, because of the radical renovation that he'd had done on it. Bart ordered a full meal, from antipasto to dessert. Colomba ordered just a salad. The thought of food turned her stomach.

"Gaspare Mantoni had a colorectal carcinoma," said Bart. "And even though he was penniless, he left his wife a million euros. In an offshore account."

Colomba toyed with her fork and said nothing.

"Whereas the other guy that they found, torn to bits in the control cabin, was Pala's secretary's natural father. He didn't have long to live, either."

Colomba nodded. "They told me about that, too." Caterina's real name was Andrea Muruts, and Muruts was her mother's surname. She was a second-generation German citizen, a prostitute and an armed robber who had spent most of her life behind bars, first in institutions, and later in prison. "They found out that Teresa met her as soon as Muruts was released from prison. Probably, Teresa was the one who recruited her and sent her to work for Pala."

"At the behest of the King of Diamonds . . ."

"He was really good at recruiting well-chosen individuals. But the counterterrorism magistrates have established beyond the shadow of a doubt that he's dead, and good riddance to him."

As soon as she said it, Bart realized that she might have picked the wrong subject. "How is Tommy?"

"I haven't seen him once since he was admitted to the hospital." Demetra had shown up with a battalion of lawyers, claiming the court had given the boy poor treatment and exposed him to an array of risks. "All I know is that he'll be leaving soon for Greece."

"Maybe his aunt isn't as much of a bitch as she seems."

"No, she'll milk him for what he's worth and then abandon him in some shitty institution."

Bart sighed. "Sweetheart, you can't fix all the world's problems . . ."

"Usually I just create new ones," Colomba replied bitterly. "But don't worry, I really am retired now. It's all over, as the intelligence agencies state in their official version of events: Leo organized it all and now he's dead. The Melases were his accomplices, Loris and his father helped him to kill Martina. Caterina, or actually, *Andrea*, helped him to kill the Melases and to steal their money in exchange for his help in taking revenge on her father. The young woman who helped Andrea is dead, and she was doing it for money. Certainly, Leo simply made an honest mistake with the tanker truck, he should have made his escape earlier, but so much the better, right?"

Bart sighed. "You have to admit that from a certain point of view, it's all eminently plausible."

"Leo was at the mines to save Dante, not to kill him. Pala was clean but in his safe he had 4.8 million euros with the fingerprints of the Melases all over them, and he didn't run away when he could have. But why look for anything else, at the risk of having something else come out that it might be better to keep quiet?"

"Are you planning to pull any more of your bullshit moves?" Bart asked, with a hint of worry in her voice.

Colomba spread both arms wide, in her jacket. "When they put an end to my consulting deal with CASA, they revoked my permit to carry a firearm and all my security clearances. And after all . . ." She shrugged. "Who the hell cares? If I hadn't persisted, Esposito would still be alive."

"And Dante would be dead." Bart looked at Colomba. "Why are you making that face?"

Without looking up, Colomba answered: "When he recovered consciousness in the hospital, he told me that he loved me."

Bart almost dropped her fork. "And what did you say?"

Colomba didn't answer. Exactly as she had done with Dante, before taking off at a dead run out of his tent at the hospital.

6

Dante managed to convince his adoptive father to get out from underfoot without plunging into another crying jag, then he made himself an espresso with a blend of Arabica and Indian coffee beans, and then he went back to the rooftop veranda, staring up at the transparent ceiling. He turned on his iPad and connected to the virtual hard drive that he had on a secure encrypted site, and on which he'd placed all the documents he'd received from the intelligence agencies concerning COW, along with everything he'd found online about private security agencies. Ever since Bush Jr. had authorized them in the Second Gulf War, private security agencies had become economic powerhouses, publicly quoted on the stock exchange.

The death star at the center of COW's mercenary galaxy was F3, originally founded in South Africa by Belyy immediately after his escape from the Soviet Union. Half a million employees, two-thirds of them in the Middle East or Africa. In the last two years it had been supplying governments and multinational corporations not only with soldiers but also with risk evaluations and strategic analyses. It had revenues of thirty billion euros a year, and it had also recently acquired Atlanta, one of the world's largest companies specializing in security technology.

Then there was Fegiz Protection Services, with headquarters in London and offices in Afghanistan and Bahrain. Until Venice, it had taken in more than three hundred million euros a year for support services to the American army in Iraq, finally ending up in serious trouble because of a video that showed several of its men shooting civilians. After Venice, it had subcontracted its Pentagon assignments to a company specializing in mercenaries from Latin America, acquiring a leading company in the automation field. SonDy Corp, on the other hand, had been founded in the nineties as a private airline, and it was in the business of transporting personnel and heavy machinery to and around high-risk areas. Along with F3, the year before it had acquired White Elephant, one of the world's largest cybersecurity corporations, with headquarters in Berlin. White Elephant had, in turn, acquired a majority stake in the American company Atomic Ray, which produced military drones purchased by, among others, the Italian Army. And Atomic Ray in turn owned a Silicon Valley incubator for facial recognition systems.

Dante crumbled a Provigil tablet and mixed it into a glass of straight vodka as he continued leafing through documents and internet sites. In spite of what Leo had told him, he couldn't find any link between the Father and Belyy . . . until a name leaped out at him: BlackMountain. It was a financial holding company with headquarters in Portland, Oregon, that had millions of shareholders around the world. It distributed to several of the Father's accomplices a sort of pension, and it was also the chief investor in a chain of group homes for disabled children called Silver Compass, and it was there that the Father had hooked and reeled in a number of his victims. Dante discovered that, after Belyy's death, BlackMountain had invested heavily in all the new operations of the former COW companies.

It wasn't much, but it was enough to reassure Dante that his brother hadn't lied to him till the bitter end. For the umpteenth time in the past week, he asked himself what he felt about him, and in particular about his death. Relief? Sadness?

It would have been nice to talk it over with Colomba, but there was still that whole story of what had happened in his tent at the hospital . . . He picked up the room phone and called the hotel's director of security.

7

C ould you really not have noticed a thing?" Bart asked.

Colomba huffed in annoyance. She'd quickly regretted her decision to accompany her friend to her hotel, because Bart simply wouldn't stop talking about Dante. "I've spent half my life working in close contact with men," she replied. "Stakeouts, late nights in the office . . . If they don't try anything, then I just keep to myself."

"But Dante didn't try anything."

"Which is actually a pity. I would have just told him to go take a cold shower, and that would have been the end of it."

"I would have hopped right into his bed."

Colomba turned to look at her. "How much have you had to drink?"

"Two beers. But Dante is definitely hot, plus he's intelligent and easy to get along with . . . And I'm single."

Colomba shook her head, unsure whether Bart was yanking her chain.

"Did the two of you ever talk about it again?" Colomba's friend asked her, for the second time.

"No. But I'm afraid that sooner or later the topic is going to resurface. For now, I'm just avoiding him."

They'd reached the Hotel Romano, and suddenly the brightly lit city, with its streets and thousands of years of history, struck Colomba as very beautiful, in spite of everything.

"Isn't it strange that when Dante disappears, you search for him, and when he's around, you're the one who disappears?" Bart asked as she was waiting for her key at the reception desk.

"Those are two different things."

Bart gave her a hug. "Sure, but the mechanisms are universal, sweetheart. Don't be a stranger, come see me soon, all right?"

Colomba called for an Uber to take her home, and flopped down into an armchair in her living room. Once that chair had been her favorite: now it seemed as lumpy and alien as the rest of the apartment. It reeked of dust and dampness, and the three cactuses that she had once tended on the balcony were now brown and dry. And then there was the life of the city, something she was no longer used to, the sound of the traffic coming in through her window, the smell of the Tiber.

She saw herself sitting on that armchair for all the years to come, slowly getting covered with dust just like the stack of used books on the floor next to the armchair. She'd bought them all at the used book stand across from the Teatro Adriano. On top of the stack was *Gravity's Rainbow*, which Colomba had given up on after the first few pages, and which she now had no desire to pick back up, with all its stories about cocks and missiles. Dante might like it, with his maniacally obsessed interests.

That's enough thinking about Dante, she told herself, and mechanically started rummaging through the books in search of a title that appealed to her.

Then D'Amore knocked on her door.

8

D'Amore was wearing a charcoal-gray suit and a white shirt, and he had a trench coat folded over his arm. He didn't seem lighthearted right now: he was just a soldier in civilian attire.

Who's just had to go bury his men, Colomba thought.

"Am I intruding?" he asked her. "They told me you'd gone home and I just wanted to check in on you."

Colomba gestured for him to come in. "Are you still keeping me under surveillance?"

"I left a squad car parked downstairs. Just for the first little while."

Colomba shrugged her shoulders and went back to sit in her armchair, kicking off her combat boots. "I don't have a fucking thing to offer you, except for the nocino walnut liqueur that my partners gave me after I got out of the hospital."

"I used to drink it when I was a kid."

"Then pour yourself a glass and feel young again. It's under the sink, next to the Comet scrubbing powder."

D'Amore took off his jacket and went into the kitchen. His formal attire looked good on him, Colomba decided as she watched him go. She wondered if that was a mask, just like his lighthearted demeanor, or whether that was actually the real D'Amore . . . assuming that there was one, of course.

He came back with the walnut-shaped bottle and poured a couple of fingers of the brown liqueur into two colorful plastic cups. He handed one to Colomba and took a sip of his own.

"Exactly the same as I remember it: too sweet and too bitter, at the same time," he said, and sat down in the armchair facing Colomba. "I heard that Santini started a quarrel with you at the funeral."

"He was drunk and he had a good point. I should have left Esposito alone, let him live his life." A knot surfaced in her throat and she focused on her glass.

"You had perfectly good reasons to get him involved."

Colomba nodded imperceptibly. "I trusted him. But I treated him badly. He must have died cursing my name."

"We're all heading in the same direction, Colomba. And once you come to the end of the road, it makes no difference."

"Is that your philosophy of life?"

He looked up for a second; his eyes were bloodshot. "Do you have a better one?"

"Not right now. Were you friends with any of them?"

D'Amore poured himself some more nocino. "No. Still, I sent them to their deaths." He toyed with the pendant that dangled from his wrist. "I shouldn't have had a field command, I'm no longer an operative."

"But you were once."

"That's something we have in common. Have you thought about what you want to do, now that Bonaccorso is dead?"

Colomba shook her head.

"Are you going to go after the King of Diamonds?"

She looked at him over the top of her glass. "No courtesy calls in your line of work, are there?"

D'Amore gave her a weary smile. "No one sent me here, I swear to you. Can't I just worry about the well-being of a colleague?"

"If you're not worried about men who died needlessly . . ."

D'Amore gripped his glass. "Now you're being unfair."

"In spite of your official versions, you know perfectly well what happened at the mines: someone wanted to kill Leo and they did it by unleashing a massacre. Unfortunately, you lot have no interest in finding out who that was. Or else you already know, and you want to keep him as a friend."

"I can't be friends with someone who killed my men," said D'Amore. "And we aren't going to interfere with the civilian magistrates as they conduct their investigations."

"They aren't going to find out anything without help from the intelligence agencies, and you know it."

"I may not like that, but there's nothing I can do about it."

Colomba raised her glass. "Give me some more." Her eyes had taken on an olive-green sparkle. D'Amore leaned toward her and Colomba let herself lean against his shoulder. She felt his breath on her ear, with pleasure. For a second. Then she straightened up.

"No," she said.

D'Amore retreated. "Sorry, I didn't mean to make you uncomfortable—"

"Oh, I'm not. But you're going to have to look elsewhere for a quick fuck to chase away grief."

D'Amore picked up his jacket and trench coat and got to his feet. "I'd better go. Will you stay in touch, every so often?"

This time, there was no need even to reply.

D'Amore smiled and left. After getting into her pajamas, Colomba noticed that he'd left a flash drive on the armchair.

9

Colomba scrolled through the files on the flash drive, and since she didn't understand a thing she was looking at, she put her combat boots back on and went out the door.

It was 1:30 a.m., and outside her front door there weren't many parked cars. And only one car had two people inside. It wasn't hard to guess that they were D'Amore's men, but Colomba had absolute confirmation of the fact when they followed her taxi all the way to the Hotel Impero.

The night desk man was a new face, and since she wasn't wearing the fancy clothing of the hotel's usual guests, she was forced to announce her visit.

A couple of minutes later, she saw a bald, muscular man wearing a jacket and tie walk toward her.

"Let me show you the way, Deputy Captain," he said.

"Excuse me, but who are you?" Colomba asked in surprise.

"I work for Signor Torre. Please, come with me."

The man accompanied her to the door of the suite, knocked once, and then opened it with a key of his own.

Colomba had expected to find Dante awake, but more importantly, alone. Instead, two men dressed just as nicely as the bald guy were scanning the room for bugs; they'd even dismantled the ceiling lamps.

Dante was out on the terrace, and his eyes looked like he'd been getting high. The material that had cluttered his bedroom in Portico was now scattered all over the suite around him, including his espresso machine, now paired with an automatic coffee brewer. In spite of the fact that the sliding windows were all wide open, the air was impregnated with tobacco smoke and coffee.

He waved hello. "Insomnia?" he asked wearily.

"Of a sort. Who are these people?"

"Contractors," he replied as he lit a cigarette.

Colomba straddled a chair. "Have you lost it?"

"I made a well-considered decision to choose an Italian company that has never worked with our government. You see? I don't need you. You can stop worrying and go home."

Colomba heaved a sigh. "Dante, I care about you. You're my best friend."

"Well, welcome to Friendzone.com then . . . What do you want? Were you sick and tired of drinking the stale old liquor you have at home, so you decided to come on over to Dante's open bar?"

Colomba tossed him the flash drive. "D'Amore left me this. But it's all numbers, not my field."

"Three," Dante called out, "could you come here for a second, please?"

One of the two well-dressed technicians came out on the veranda. He checked the flash drive, probably with an eye for explosives, viruses, and microbugs, and finally gave it back to Dante. "Clean," he said. "We're done in there."

"How many bugs did you find?"

"Just two, Signor Torre. Standard-issue ministry equipment."

"They underestimate me. Thanks, we'll see you tomorrow."

Three and his partner left the suite.

"What the fuck kind of name is Three?" Colomba asked.

"I got it from watching *House*. Like him, I don't want to establish terms of familiarity with someone who might die on my account."

"Why do you think you're in danger?"

"I don't," Dante replied. "But when I track down the King or the Queen of Spades, I'm going to need protection and logistical support in order to kill him or her. They're also going to testify in my defense, if I wind up having to act in legitimate self-defense."

Colomba wondered if she was dreaming. "Jesus, Dante. What on earth have you got into your head?"

Dante took a sip of coffee. "You wanted to find my brother. I want to find the person who killed him, along with a bunch of other people."

"You want to risk your neck to avenge a murderer?"

"*One of us*, CC." He held up the flash drive. "Do you or don't you want me to read it?"

Colomba nodded. "Please."

Dante stuck it into the port on his laptop and scrolled through the contents. They were all Excel files.

"These are monetary transactions," he said after chain-smoking a couple of cigarettes. "From four years ago, credits and debits from a business industry in Belize. BI's are shell companies used to put money through offshore banks, for purposes of tax evasion."

"What about those?" Colomba asked, pointing to several highlighted account entries, both outgoing and incoming.

Dante studied them. "They're not on the original document, so I'd have to guess that these are notations made by your friend or someone working for him. By the way, did you take a tumble in the hay with him? You've got his aftershave all over you."

"If you think you're embarrassing me, you can forget about that."

"Too bad, it's lots of fun to embarrass cops," he said. "Ah, here's the legend of the accounts. Does Markopoulo Mesogaias mean anything to you?"

"That's where the Melases had their boat repair yard."

"One of the most active accounts comes from there. Hundreds of millions of euros."

Colomba yawned. She was having a hard time keeping her eyes open. "And the account belongs to?"

"That's not shown. But on the same account we see incoming transactions, money from . . ." He stopped, truly interested for the first time since he'd opened the file. "BlackMountain. And White Elephant!"

Colomba remembered that name, too: it was on the counterterrorism list.

"All the transactions start and end on the same date," said Colomba.

Dante hesitated for an instant, then said: "Let me check a couple of details," and then he did some quick Google searches. At last, he shut the laptop, satisfied.

"Well? After all, I know you can't wait to tell me," Colomba said to him.

Dante clasped both hands behind his head. "The war between Leo and the King of Diamonds? It was the Father who triggered it."

10

The suite had a guest bedroom with its own bathroom. Colomba had slept there frequently before Dante was kidnapped, and she found the mattress exactly as she'd remembered it, collapsing on it fully dressed, taking her clothes off only at the first light of dawn, just so she could get up and lower the blinds and then go back to sleep.

When she finally got up, Dante was in the living room, looking like Adam Ant, talking to Three and the bald guy who had come down into the lobby the night before to usher her up to the suite.

"Sorry," she said. "I'll make a quick cup of coffee and then leave you to your work."

"Deputy Captain, good morning," the two men said, practically in chorus.

"I slept in the guest bedroom."

"Good to know," said Three.

Colomba cursed herself for an idiot. What godly reason had there been to specify that detail? Dante handed her a mug as big as a washbasin, filled with coffee he'd made with the brewer.

"Do you really have to sweep for so many bugs?" she asked him.

"No, Deputy Captain, we just need to make one phone call highly secure," Three replied in his stead, and from his valise he extracted a laptop, which he connected to an external audio chip and to a cell phone. "Unfortunately, it's not possible to completely encrypt the call, because both sides would have to be using the same software. We can only cover up Signor Torre's voice by using low frequencies. Every time that Signor Torre speaks, anyone tapping the line will hear a very staticky communication."

"You should have just told him to download Signal, that certainly would have cost less," said Colomba, trying to be funny.

Three shook his head, still the complete professional. "The individual is in solitary confinement in the special high-security wing of Rebibbia Prison."

Colomba was left breathless for a second. "Are you trying to talk to the German?"

Dante nodded. "He has the right to call his lawyer, in view of an upcoming appeals hearing." He pointed to the cell phone connected to the computer. "Borrowing his phone cost me an extra twenty thousand euros."

11

The phone calls that convicts make from prison are always monitored and recorded, except for the ones to their lawyers. But the German was an exception to that rule.

He seemed to be in his mid-sixties, but he was still muscular, with a powerful neck, long white hair, and a boxer's broken nose. He had scars from knife wounds and gunshots all over his body, as well as three consecutive life sentences without parole for his acts as the Father's accomplice.

That was all that the investigators knew about him, more than three years after his arrest.

What his real name was, and whether or not he was even German, remained a mystery. For that matter, the German had never opened his mouth, and when a prison trustee in charge of sweeping floors had asked him one too many questions, the German had shoved the broom handle down the man's throat.

At exactly half past noon, he was taken out of his cell by two officers of the correctional police, carefully searched, handcuffed, and led to the booth of the officer who was in charge of security at one of the wing gates, a tiny broom-closet-sized room. Around the booth was a cordon of MOG officers, the Mobile Operating Group, the SWAT teams of the correctional police. Normally, the phone calls were done in the visiting room, but the German was an exception when it came to that as well.

The switchboard dialed the lawyer's number.

Dante answered with an exaggerated rendition of the lawyer's Neapolitan accent, and was put through to the German. Colomba had rarely seen him so vibrant with tension.

"Good morning, Mr. German," said Dante, almost in a falsetto.

On the other end of the line, there was a moment's hesitation. The German knew that when his phone appointment rolled around, he wouldn't actually be talking to his lawyer, as the correctional police believed; he didn't know, however, who he *would* be talking to. "Good morning, Counselor."

"Did you receive the postcard?"

"Yes."

Dante nodded to Three, who started up the low frequency. "From this moment on, only you can hear *me*, but the eavesdroppers will be able to hear *your* voice loud and clear. Do you understand?"

"Yes."

"Complain about the poor quality of the line."

"I'm afraid I can't hear you, Counselor," said the German.

"I imagine that in a couple of minutes someone will interrupt this call, so let's waste no time." Little by little his tone had become more confident.

"I don't have anything to tell you, Counselor."

"In fact, I'm the one who's talking to you. And you'll be listening."

"As you think best, Counselor."

"I've seen the accounts, and I had a little chat with Leo before he died. I know that the Father and Belyy worked together before the fall of the Wall."

Without so much as an instant of hesitation, the German replied: "I told you the last time we met: look out what you poke your nose into."

Dante remembered that phrase very clearly, as well as the circumstances in which he'd heard it. Shortly before being kidnapped in Venice, he'd gone to see the German in Rebibbia Prison, in search of information about Giltine. It hadn't been a friendly encounter and, just at the thought of it, Dante felt a rivulet of sweat slide unpleasantly down his collar.

"The Father used a financial shell company to pay people like you. It was called BlackMountain. And from a close study of your savings account, I'd say that you had profitable dealings with a few companies that have recently taken over COW. Here's the way I see it: Belyy was an old beat-up relic of the Cold War, and he believed in his soldiers, whereas the Father liked to compare himself to Mengele, and he believed first and foremost in the development of scientific research. In the end, the

Father was ready to challenge Belyy for the throne, but he died before he got the chance. If there was ever a King of Diamonds, it was him."

"I don't know what you're referring to, Counselor. I don't know much about that kind of thing."

"In fact, you were strictly a discard. Leo was the real face card. Judging from the things he did, it's obvious that he had plenty of military experience and highly placed connections. He was a contractor, one of the children that Belyy probably had by raping female prisoners. The Father took him and turned him into his own remotely guided missile against Belyy. I just want to know from you why, once Belyy was dead, he decided not to stop."

"And you're asking me?"

"Yes. Whatever role you might have played, you've been benched by now. The Father, Leo, Giltine, and Belyy are all dead; the new generation of technocrats who are bringing COW into the third millennium don't give a damn about you. Do you want a minimum of satisfaction? Then use me. Who was Leo working for?"

There was another extended silence. And Dante wasn't the only one sweating in the room.

"For no one," the German finally said. His voice had lost all expression and sounded like a late-model GPS.

"Then why did he go on fighting?"

"For love," said the German.

In the penthouse suite of the Hotel Impero, the temperature seemed to plummet.

"Are you quite done, Counselor?" the German asked aggressively.

"No," Dante replied, emerging from his momentary study. "Leo was killed, too, and by someone who put in a lot of effort to do it. Someone who loved Belyy or someone who hated the Father and all his ilk?"

"The second thing that you said. If he could, he'd set fire to the whole world just because *he* set foot on it."

"Who?"

The German laughed. "Look at yourself in the mirror, kid," he said. And then he hung up.

12

While Dante sent Three to return the cell phone to the German's lawyer, to ward off a situation in which someone decided to go see him first, to ask some awkward questions, Colomba tried to recover from the shock of having heard the German's voice. She remembered as if it were yesterday the night the man had attacked her, as brutal and unstoppable as the Terminator, and every bit as icy.

"What postcard were you talking about?" she asked.

"It was the photograph that Leo gave me before dying. I had his lawyer mail it to him."

Colomba shut her eyes as she counted to ten. "Why?"

"I wanted confirmation that it was authentic. If it hadn't been, he'd have hung up the phone the minute he heard my voice."

"If he was telling the truth, the Father and Belyy went on waging war against each other even after they were both dead. A feud."

"Through their . . . creatures." Dante sniffed at himself. "I'm going to take another shower. I smell like fear."

"What did he mean when he told you to look in the mirror? That the guy looked like you, or that it was all your fault?"

"I think the first of the two," Dante replied, slipping into his bedroom. "The King of Diamonds passed through the Father's claws, and like me, he didn't wind up dissolved in a drum of acid. And from the way he moves, I'd say that what happened to him is more or less the same as what happened to me."

"How much does all of this organization cost you?" asked Colomba, raising her voice so she could be heard through the wall. In the meantime, she prepared a cappuccino with the espresso machine.

"Thirty thousand euros a day," Dante shouted from the bathroom. "Plus a series of extra expenses."

"But do they know that you don't have a penny to your name?"

"They insisted on being paid in advance. Two hundred thousand euros. And another two hundred thousand as a deposit."

Colomba realized that she'd used almond milk: she threw it all away and opened a sugar-free Red Bull. "How did you talk Annibale into underwriting it?"

"I didn't," he replied from the shower, talking through the stream of water. "It was my money, the payment for my own hard work. It's my base fee for opening the locks of the dead."

Colomba ran straight into the bathroom and hurled the can of Red Bull at the silhouette behind the pebbled glass of the shower stall. The glass panel cracked.

"Hey!" shouted Dante.

"I'm going to kill you," said Colomba.

Dante turned off the water and hastily emerged from the shower stall with a towel wrapped around his waist. "For what, for having taken money that should have gone to the slush funds of the intelligence services? Money that could have gone to your friend Aftershave D'Amore?"

"I told you not to do it."

"And I listened to you, at least as long as my brother was alive. Then I called up Santiago and I gave him the address and combination. The Carabinieri still hadn't come by." Santiago was a former member of the Cuchillos, a Latino criminal gang, a drug dealer who had broken free of his former brothers and who now made a living by doing jobs on the Deep Web. Dante trusted him to the exact same degree that Colomba *didn't*.

"How much did you get paid?"

"Six hundred apiece. He was the one who got the money out of Italy. Now I have my own BI. It's in the Cayman Islands. Do you want to report me to the police?"

"Don't talk nonsense. But you can't do this thing without me."

"I thought you'd pulled out."

"I'm not letting you go it alone."

Dante turned his skinny back on her and switched on his electric shaver.

"As you like."

"But I handle the troops. Tell your security contractors that from here on in, I'm the sergeant major."

"Be my guest. Just for your information, when it's all said and done, if there's anything left over, I'm going to use it to get far away from here." A tuft of red hair fell into the sink. "And I'm not going to reappear magically in an abandoned clinic around the corner from your house."

"Good, because you're a real pain in the ass," said Colomba, concealing her dismay.

"Go get dressed: we're going to have visitors soon."

CHAPTER II

The King of Diamonds had started playing chess at age ten. He didn't have chess pieces, back then, or even sheets of paper to draw them on; and anyway, he'd been in such extreme pain that he often couldn't so much as lift a finger. But his mind actually seemed to feed off that pain, growing stronger as the pain grew worse. While his body seethed and twisted, his thoughts became crystal clear and finally lifted him out of the world of flesh. In the mental chess matches that he played without interruption, he became the pieces that he moved, and he could clearly see the future of each and every one of them, as if their lives were unreeling before his eyes. He knew when a bishop was about to be taken and when a queen was going to check a king; and he knew when an apparently insignificant move at the opening of play would irremediably compromise the endgame.

As he grew up, the King of Diamonds had come to understand that the world was all one giant chessboard, and that men and women had their fates decreed, they just couldn't see it yet. They were dominated by the simplest of stimuli—hunger, desire, fear, and pain—and their reactions could be charted on a grid with only a few minor variants: a coward was always bound to run away in the face of danger; a lover would always plunge into the river to save his beloved.

If he knew an individual even only superficially, the King of Diamonds was capable of guessing with a high likelihood of accuracy what they would eat for breakfast, or what magazine they would choose to leaf through in a hospital waiting room. He also knew how to force them to make specific choices, very different from what they might have chosen only moments before, obviously without their being able to guess that their future was being decided elsewhere. He would construct intricate game plans, where men fell and died in their dozens without so much as a clue to why. He planted seeds that sprouted only years later. Most important of all, he was careful to pick up on signals marking the moment in which his pawns first caught the scent of the invisible presence that was deciding their final destiny, so that he was ready to distract them, just as the hip-swiveling and comely assistant of a stage magician is busy distracting the audience's gaze far from where the dove is hidden.

And now, standing looking up at Dante's hotel, the King of Diamonds realized that it was time for a diversion.

F or days, One's men had crisscrossed Italy, tracking down and inter- viewing the Father's survivors, trying to convince them to meet with the man who had saved them. Not all of them had accepted, and not all of them were capable of putting up with the stress that the trip would have entailed, but six of them had said yes. Luca Maugeri, of course, arrived in Rome with his father: Luca excited, his father ill at ease in his too-long trousers. On the other hand, it was both of Rug- gero's parents who accompanied him; he was thirteen years old but he looked much younger, his face marked by fetal alcohol syndrome; the Father had sold video footage of his imprisonment to a pedophile, one of the many methods he used to finance himself. Then there was Luigi, age fifteen, epileptic: the Father had convinced everyone that he had been drowned in the river and that the current had swept his body away, never to be found. Cesare, close to sixteen, was the eldest of the group: autistic and with a slight case of arrested mental devel- opment; he was the one that Luca called OG; accompanying him was the doctor from the clinic in Florence where he'd been living since his rescue. Fabio's mother and father hadn't come, either, but then, they had a very good excuse: the Father had killed them with a contrived gas explosion. Fabio was twelve, just like Benedetto, who showed up dressed in denim from head to foot. He was the only member of the crew who had been found by his doctor to be entirely free of pathol- ogies or developmental impediments; his parents looked around as if wondering what they were doing there.

The contractors led them through the hotel kitchens to avoid surveil- lance cameras, and then sent them up a few at a time to the top floor. Waiting for them at the door to the suite was Colomba, called upon to welcome them as honored guests while Dante tried to summon the energy required to greet that group of strangers.

She thanked them all for having accepted the invitation, and showed the adults to the living room, leaving the kids to wander freely throughout the suite. Luca started explaining to Cesare how the plasma display television set worked; the two boys seemed to have made friends quickly. Ruggero and Luigi, on the other hand, went straight out onto the terrace because, like Dante, they suffered when confined to close quarters, though not with the same intensity as him. One and Four kept an eye out to make sure they didn't hurt themselves, and from the way that One smiled at the kids, it was clear that he had children of his own.

"Dante would like to meet with the boys for an hour or so. He'll do it out on the terrace, where we've also laid out some light refreshments. But I'm going to have to ask you to remain here, inside, for the whole time they're having their chat; you can see the terrace from this living room, there's railings and there are . . . bodyguards. You'll be able to go and pick them up when you like, but Dante would like some privacy for the chat."

The doctor objected, Benedetto's parents objected, but Colomba had no difficulty bringing them around, because they all knew that without her and Dante the boys would still be locked up in the shipping containers. What's more, she was the "heroine of Venice," and in the end that put an end to the protests of even the most insistent holdouts.

Dante emerged from his bedroom only after all the boys and their guardians had been ushered out onto the terrace. He had the look in his eyes of someone who feared an outbreak of Ebola, but he put a brave face on, and when Luca and Benedetto ran to hug him, he managed not to hurl himself over the terrace railing as his instincts told him to.

Parents and guardians went back inside, and Colomba helped the boys to get seated, distributing orangeade and pastries. The most frightened one of the group was Benedetto, but without looking at him, Luigi took his hand, and he calmed down immediately.

"Well," said Dante, looking at the palms of his hands. "My dear boys, as you know . . . um, I too experienced . . . eh . . . the same adventure as the rest of you. The same *misadventure* as you. I should have said misadventure."

"Yes, we know that, Signor Torre," said Benedetto. "The Man from the Silo."

"Silo!" Luigi shouted. Cesare laughed.

"You can call me Dante, and I hope we can be on a first-name basis," he said. "We are colleagues because we've lived . . . well, I already told you, I think. In any case . . ." Dante picked up a small set of bongo drums that sat on the table. "I haven't turned into a beatnik, even if you probably don't even know what that means, but with this you can hear me more clearly." With stunning speed, he tapped and scratched on the drums for thirty seconds or so, but it only took a few seconds before the boys all fell silent, in astonishment. When he stopped, they all laughed, except for Ruggero, who imitated the others only at the end. Benedetto even clapped his hands, and Dante bowed with a smile, triggering new and even more fervent rounds of applause.

"Do you mind if I ask what you told them?" Colomba whispered.

"*The German has stinky feet*," he replied.

The German was taken back to the cell where he lived twenty-three hours a day, after the sixty minutes of fresh air in the deserted prison yard. That was the one time a day when he ventured out, aside from the shower, which he also always took alone. He had no books and no newspapers, and he watched no TV, except for the news first thing in the morning. The rest of the time, according to those whose job it was to keep an eye on him, he did nothing but stare at the wall or exercise. He seemed not to suffer in the slightest from his isolation.

The one activity he indulged in was reading the dozens of letters he received every week, after they had been subjected to the study of the prison censors, of course. His case had prompted a great deal of curiosity . . . and much more than that. Directors wrote to him, offering to make a movie about his life; writers who wanted to help pen his memoirs; women and men who wanted to marry him; women and men who wanted to string him up by the testicles for what he had done to dozens of children in the service of the Big Bad Ogre.

The German read everything and responded to none of them, but the photograph of the Father and Belyy in Berlin hadn't gone into his wastebasket with everything else. Dante had arranged to have a few phrases printed on the back to make it look like an old postcard and had mailed it from someplace outside of Rome, with anodyne greetings from his lawyer.

The German got up to go to the bathroom, and without letting himself be filmed by the surveillance video camera, he pulled out the photograph.

The bathroom of his cell was a toilet with a sink, concealed behind a low wall that stood about five feet tall, so that the guards could always monitor what he was doing while still offering him a bare minimum of privacy. The German sat down on the toilet and laid the postcard in the small sink. He put the stopper in the drain and turned on the faucet.

He came back half an hour later for another "session." In the sink, the water had turned faintly greasy; the photograph, drenched, had stuck to the bottom of the sink.

Pretending to wash his face, the German leaned over the sink.

"Good boy," he murmured. Then he drank all that disgusting water.

An hour later, Dante's hand ached and he was drenched with sweat, but with all the furious pounding and scratching of the Code that he'd done on the bongo drums, he'd managed to involve all the boys in the conversation. Luckily, he'd also discovered that there are abbreviations capable of making it all go much faster, like the ones used in texting.

Aside from Luca, every one of them had spent between two and four years imprisoned in the shipping containers, and the Code was an old, nasty habit buried deep under their skin, impossible to root out. At the same time, though, Dante understood that it had saved them, at least in part. In the darkness of those months and years, they'd been stuffed with psychopharmaceuticals, subjected to electroshock, left to freeze or to boil away in torrid heat, exactly like what had happened to him.

They'd been abandoned without food for days, they'd been forced to sleep with the stench of their own feces, and then to do crossword puzzles and tests like the ones from school, in exchange for a little drinking water for every correct answer. But thanks to the Code, at the end of each "exam" or "treatment," they'd had friends to comfort them, someone to complain to, someone to share their thoughts with.

And now, through that same Code—and then, a little at a time, through actual words—Dante managed to learn from the survivors things that had never been revealed to their parents and therapists. Such as, for instance, that Ruggero hadn't been able to prove he was capable of behaving like a "son," and so he had been left to his own devices for sixteen months; no tests, no challenges of any kind: the Father had simply abandoned him, even though the German and the other henchmen continued to bring him food and water. Benedetto, on the other hand, had rebelled, whereupon he'd been strapped to his bed for months on end, forced to defecate through the hole in the cot that the Father called the "cuckoo." And then Cesare, who had been subjected to sleep deprivation until everything around him had turned first white, then black; the next thing he'd seen was the face of the policeman who had opened the door of his shipping container. At the time, he still didn't know he'd lost a year of his life.

Dante listened and concealed behind a forced smile all the anguish, sadness, and horror that swept over him with every new discovery that actually didn't really qualify as a discovery, because it felt to him that he'd been listening all the while to the story of his own life. He drank vodka and liquid benzodiazepine without letting the boys see him do it, and he knew that now he'd start having recurring dreams of the silo, but still, he remained focused, even when Cesare told how the sleep torture took the form of a combination of deafening noises and blinding lights, which were turned on and off again at a series of irregular intervals.

"And none of you even noticed the noise?" he asked the others.

Luca and Benedetto shook their heads.

"OG was in shipping container two, right?" Dante asked.

"Two," Benedetto said, and Luigi confirmed by tapping out the same number.

"When Cesare didn't write . . . Benedetto, you were three, right? . . . then your communications were interrupted. It's like the telephone game: if someone's missing, the message comes to a halt."

They all nodded.

"But it didn't happen with OG," said Dante.

Colomba, who had been forced to go back inside to handle the adults like a hostess, noticed that something outside had changed, and she took advantage of that opportunity to go and tell Dante it was time to stop, because the parents were starting to get nervous.

Dante nodded. "Send everyone home, except OG. Tell them to find him a room here, with the doctor, and if he makes any trouble, tell One to write him a check out of the expense account."

"You like having plenty of money, but that's not going to last if you keep it up like this," Colomba warned him.

"It's not a problem," he said grimly. "Today, for the first time, I had definitive proof that the Father had another prison. And OG—Cesare—was confined in it."

5

The doctor objected, of course, threatening to bring the juvenile court into the matter. Dante raised the offer to twenty thousand euros, which the doctor arranged to have deposited in the clinic's bank account, thus winning points in everybody's estimation. He and Cesare were given a double room on the same floor as the suite to make security simpler.

This was Colomba's opportunity to chat with Three, and that's how she found out he was a former colleague.

"I worked for the Ministry of Justice's postal and communication police with Lieutenant Anzelmo," he told her. "Now he's an inspector at Segrate. I know that he helped you to catch the Father."

Colomba nodded.

"None of my business, but do you think that there's someone else around as bad as that bastard?"

"Maybe someone worse."

By the time all the guests finally left the room, Dante was exhausted. He was mixing himself a cocktail in a gigantic glass when Colomba received a phone call from the last person on earth she would have expected: Demetra.

"What do you want?" she said, too tired to be polite with anyone.

"I don't want anything. But Tommy wants to say goodbye to you before leaving. He didn't actually say so, but he made it very clear to me."

"You threatened me if I ever got near him again . . ."

"If you don't want to come, that's not my loss. I'm sick and tired of all you cops."

Demetra ended the call and Colomba immediately alerted the head of operations to ready a transportation group for her. It took just five minutes before an armor-plated Mercedes staffed by a female body builder and a bearded contractor wearing a bow tie came to pick her up in the hotel's rear courtyard, while an escort vehicle followed a short distance behind, communicating with the other contractors via discreet earpieces. They seemed like soldiers, and they probably once had been, before discovering that it was possible to earn better and risk less.

Colomba wasn't used to sitting in the back, so she asked the guy with a beard to get in back instead.

"Are you armed?" she asked the female body builder behind the wheel, whom Dante had called Nine.

"Yes, Deputy Captain," she replied.

"How are you going to sort things if my former colleagues stop us?" Colomba knew perfectly well that by Italian law, armed personal protection was delegated solely to law enforcement or the armed forces. Security guards were allowed to protect banks and buildings, or else the transport of valuables, but not people, unless it was with a special authorization that she felt certain no one had requested.

"We're armed guards transporting valuables," Nine explained. "We've been assigned to transport a valuable asset belonging to Signor Torre."

Colomba rubbed her forehead. "Which would be what?"

Without taking her eyes off the road, the body builder pointed to the glove compartment. Colomba opened it and found a Barbie dressed in lamé, still in its original packaging.

"What's this?" she asked.

"It's a Pink Jubilee Barbie from 1989," said Bow Tie from the back. "A collector's piece. It's worth about a thousand euros."

"In practical terms, the price of this drive to the airport," Colomba retorted.

"It meets the definition of a valuable asset," Nine said seriously. "But if anybody starts shooting at us, don't worry, we'll cover you, too."

6

Demetra had given her an appointment at Terminal 1, in the Alitalia lounge.

Nine pulled over, then put the doll in a metal briefcase with a stylized little man casting a shadow on a wall. "You're going to have to keep it with you if you want us to accompany you inside," she said.

Colomba was on the verge of refusing that condition when she remembered that she wasn't armed: the King of Diamonds would be unlikely to attack her in an airport, but he might have convinced a flight attendant to do the stupidest thing in his or her life. She took the briefcase, letting Bow Tie lead the way through the maze of corridors in the airport. It was Friday evening and there was a long line at the metal detectors, probably because of the number of weekly commuters leaving the Italian capital. Overhead, the television screens were showing news reports on the funeral services held the day before.

The lounge was next to the Area B check-in, and they went in with Bow Tie's card. He clearly wasn't new to this sort of thing.

The lounge was something midway between the waiting room of an exclusive physician and an English pub, and it was very crowded. Demetra and Tommy were sitting in the farthest row of leather chairs, next to a vintage map of airline routes. Demetra was reading a magazine and didn't even bother to look up. The only one to react at the sight of Colomba was Tommy: he leaped to his feet, ripping the wire of the headphones he was wearing, and ran straight at her, squeaking like a bat and pushing his way through the passengers standing in the aisle.

"It's all good," Colomba said to her escort. "He's a friend," she just had time to add before Tommy lifted her bodily into the air, making her drop the briefcase. She returned the hug, to the extent that she was able, but then made it clear to him that he needed to put her down, because he was holding her so tight that she couldn't really breathe. Tommy's hair was shorter, and he still had bruises on his face from the rain of stones that had hailed down on him at the mines, in spite of the fact that Colomba had jumped in front of him to protect him.

"You're going to a nice place," she said to him. "The sea is beautiful in Greece. Do you know how to swim?"

Tommy shook his head, holding his arm around her neck. It must have weighed a couple hundred pounds.

"Maybe someday I'll come see you, what do you say? That way I can tell you what I find out about your parents. Because I'm not going to forget about you, okay?" Colomba said, in a voice that was cracking. "I'll go get the address right now from your aunt. Meanwhile, you stay here with my friend, okay? That's this guy right here, with the dumb tie."

Tommy looked at the bow tie as if he'd never seen one before and tried to grab it. The bodyguard lunged backward, and soon the two of them were chasing each other around the room, darting and dodging.

Demetra remained obstinately focused on her magazine until Colomba was practically on top of her.

"Ciao, ex-cop lady," she said reluctantly.

"How did you arrange things with the court?"

"Everything's taken care of, my lawyers fixed everything. Tell your friend that, considering what the police did, I don't feel obliged to give him a cent."

"Dante doesn't want anything from you," Colomba retorted.

Demetra smiled. "Everybody wants something," she said, and went back to her magazine. It was called *Hello!*, but it was in Greek.

Colomba pushed it down rudely. "If you mistreat him, I swear I'll come and get you."

"And why would I do such a thing?" She smiled. "He's my nephew after all, isn't he?"

"And are you letting him fly in first class with you, or are you having him put in with the luggage?"

"They don't want noisy children in business class. He'll be fine in economy."

"Even though he's paying for the ticket," Colomba said, furious now.

"No, it's my brother who's paying. So long, ex-cop lady."

Colomba clenched her fists as she tried to keep from steaming over and went back to Tommy, who was victoriously brandishing the bow tie. Its former owner, on the other hand, was massaging his neck. "Ready to go, Deputy Captain?" he asked.

"Not yet," she replied.

She took the bow tie out of Tommy's hands, extended it as far as was possible, and put it around his neck, just under the curly hair at the back of his neck, soft as the plumage of a baby chick. "That way you'll remember me."

Tommy hugged her again. "I love you," he whispered in her ear.

7

While Colomba climbed back into the car with a hole in her heart the size of Greece, Lupo was sitting on the bed of the two-star hotel that the Ministry of the Interior had reserved for him in the EUR district, just a short walk from the Palazzo della Civiltà Italiana, the Fascist-era building that everyone in Rome simply called the Colosseo Quadrato—the Square Colosseum.

The room, with its green wall-to-wall carpets and patches of humidity on the walls, overlooked the hotel kitchens and reeked permanently of cooking grease. But Lupo's stomach had been bothering him even before unpacking his bags in that hotel room: it seemed to go along with the dull echo still in his ears of the voices at the procession the day before.

He was just placing the ornamental saber of his dress uniform into its travel case when the clerk called up from the reception desk, announcing a visitor. Lupo went downstairs in shirtsleeves, convinced it must be some colleague passing through.

Actually, though, it was Di Marco. He was sipping an espresso at the counter of the little bar at the front entrance, his raincoat draped over his shoulders. His arms were no longer in casts, but he was wearing an elastic wrapping on each wrist. Lupo turned to look out onto the street. Just outside the front plate-glass window was a dark blue official car, with two men inside and the roof dome flashing.

"Colonel . . ." he said, snapping almost to attention.

"Sergeant Major," Di Marco replied. "We met briefly at the ceremony yesterday, but we haven't had a chance to talk. Can I get you something?"

"An espresso, but you're my guest here, I'm staying till tomorrow."

"Please, have a seat," said Di Marco, gesturing for him to sit at one of the tables in the dining room, with its uninviting, somewhat sticky

Formica top. "I wanted to get to know you better, because I know about your role in the Bonaccorso investigation."

"Inevitable, seeing that he started his killing spree in my jurisdiction."

"Inevitable, seeing that Colomba Caselli lived in your jurisdiction," Di Marco shot back.

Lupo read the cartoon on the packet of sugar: it was the one about the patient who's afraid he's boring, while the psychologist, unknown to him, is fast asleep in his chair. "True enough, sir."

"Luckily, she didn't get you involved in the massacre at the mine," Di Marco continued with a fake smile.

"I don't consider that lucky," said Lupo. "I ought to have been there, and I wish I'd been there."

"And have you ever wondered why Caselli made sure you weren't?"

"Because she wanted the special forces."

"Or maybe she just didn't want you."

Lupo shrugged. "We're not exactly best friends."

"What do you think she's doing right now?"

"I don't know and I don't care, Colonel."

Di Marco pulled a handheld computer out of the inside pocket of his raincoat, turned it on, and held it out to him. "Go ahead and scroll through the photographs."

Baffled, Lupo did as he was told. The pictures had been taken at the entrance to the Hotel Impero, and they showed men in suits and ties entering and leaving the building. A couple of them were wearing earpieces. "I'm guessing they aren't members of the hotel's security team."

Di Marco nodded. "They're private security. The agency is called Shadow, and the ones in the pictures are all ex-cops. They were hired by Signor Torre, but . . . if you look at the next few pictures, you'll see that they're working with Caselli, too."

Lupo placed both hands flat on the table; he had a broken fingernail, and it was only with a certain effort that he was able to keep from chewing on it. "How do I fit in with all this?"

"I'm starting to wonder whether Caselli told the whole truth about what happened at Sant'Anna Solfara."

Lupo sat in silence. Di Marco stood up, setting a business card down on the table. "In case you find out anything else. I think that Corporal Martina Concio, as well as my men who gave their lives at the mines, deserve to have any shadows cleared away from this horrible story. We need to make sure that anyone responsible is severely punished. Good day, Sergeant Major . . ."

Lupo stood up in his turn, nodding goodbye to the colonel, who left the café without a backward glance and climbed into the car that stood waiting for him.

"Son of a bitch," he muttered under his breath.

But the photographs had wormed their way into his head.

8

D ante was sprawled on the sofa on the terrace smoking a cigarette when Colomba returned to the hotel.

"Everything okay with Tommy?" he asked without looking up from the tablet.

Colomba shoved him over and then got comfortable, her legs draped over his. He didn't push her away. "He told me that he loved me. He has a nice voice when he isn't shouting, midway between a child's voice and a grown-up's. Musical. I was about to cry."

"A bunch of people are declaring their love for you these days," Dante said, getting comfortable and continuing to read. "And it freaks me out a little bit to have you so close to me."

"Get used to it. I can't hold you at arm's length as long as we're working together. And anyway, Demetra was having just a little too much fun with it all. God, I hate that woman! Her brother left twenty-five million euros to his son, and she's going to spend every last cent of it on facelifts."

"You should have told her that her brother's money probably came from the Father's money laundering. Probably it was him, or his father, who handled the account that we saw."

"And counterterrorism knows that. When he left that flash drive, D'Amore wanted to make that clear to me."

"To help you or to get you to drop the case?"

Colomba shrugged. She couldn't say. "How did you leave things with Cesare?"

"I'm checking everything we have about him. We don't know anything about how he was kidnapped. His parents said that he just walked away by himself one night, opening the door and running out into the street.

But his medical file is interesting. Here, read it," he said, handing her the iPad.

"Blah, blah, blah . . . Pathetic state of health, undernourished, et cetera, et cetera . . . *Keloid scars on the soles of his feet from cuts sustained by having walked on sharp or abrasive surfaces.*"

"He's the only one with that type of scarring out of all ten," said Dante.

"One of the Father's experiments?"

"Either that, or else in the other prison he had to walk on a floor that wasn't as smooth as the bottom of the shipping containers. And if he wasn't given proper medical care, as I'd have to imagine, there's a chance that small foreign objects were encapsulated in the scars. Like the dot of ink on your hand."

Colomba had accidentally stabbed herself with an ink pen years ago, and it had become a permanent tattoo between the thumb and forefinger of her right hand. "Absolutely not," she said. "I'm not going to let you start carving away at that poor boy's feet."

"Do you seriously think I would do such a thing? But—"

"No buts out of you," said Colomba as she got to her feet. "Cesare has already been through enough. Maybe there's some evidence in your bad hand, for that matter. Why don't you have them open it up?"

Dante took off his glove and used his right hand to spread the twisted pinkie and ring fingers apart. In the webbing between the two fingers, there was one scar that was lighter than the others, circular and roughly the size of a coin. "Exploratory surgery," he explained. "I had them run a fiber-optic cable inside to check and see if there were any extraneous bodies that couldn't be detected by X-rays. It was painful, but there's nothing I wouldn't have done to catch the Father. And now I'd do anything for even a scrap of new information about the King of Diamonds."

9

When they explained Dante's idea, the physician who was Cesare's legal guardian seemed much less reluctant than Colomba.

"Keloids are painful and annoying, especially on the soles of the feet," he said to her. "And they get inflamed whenever Cesare plays soccer. I've asked his parents to pay for laser treatments in a clinic, but they said it wouldn't be necessary and that he'd just grow out of them."

"Can you authorize it?" she asked.

"Yes," the doctor replied. "As long as I'm allowed to decide what kind of treatment he'll receive, and how and where."

"It would be done here. If you're in agreement, Dante has just rented the whole spa, which is closed at this time of night. We could have the surgery done on one of the massage beds. It will all be sterilized and, of course, you'll be able to watch and you can put a halt to the operation at any point if you're not satisfied with the hygienic situation."

The doctor stopped to think for a few seconds. "When can we do it?"

"Right now, if you're in agreement," Colomba replied.

"Gosh." The doctor leaned toward her. "Excuse me, but by any chance is Signor Torre actually Tony Stark in disguise?"

Colomba limited herself to a polite smile—she didn't have any idea who Tony Stark was—and after saying goodbye she confirmed with the head of the Shadow agency to go ahead.

When she got back to the suite, sitting on the terrace with Dante were Cesare and Luca, who were counting the illuminated windows in the buildings facing them. Maugeri Sr. was sitting uneasily on the sofa, with an espresso demitasse in his hand.

"I told Signor Maugeri that it would be better if Luca stayed to help his friend," Dante said. "And left tomorrow."

"I think that would definitely make him feel better," Colomba confirmed.

"All right, fine, but I honestly don't understand what's happening," Maugeri said nervously. "First you show up at my house, then you tell us to come here, as if it were a matter of life or death. Maybe I really ought to talk to my lawyer." He flashed an apologetic smile. "I don't have anything against you, and I know I owe you everything, but I don't want my son to get caught up in something that frankly seems a little dubious."

"Do you seriously think that your son helping a friend seems a little dubious?" Dante asked in the tone of voice he used when he was studying someone.

"No," Maugeri hastened to reply, "but I'd much rather he left everything that happened to him behind him, rather than continuing to wallow in it."

Dante narrowed his eyes. "It's not an experience you can easily forget about, and you seem much more upset about it than he does. What's worrying you?"

"Nothing!" Maugeri was on pins and needles by this point. "I'm just thinking about my son."

"Is there anything *we* ought to know about, Signor Maugeri?" Colomba asked, going along with Dante's tactics.

"For fuck's sake, you already know everything there is to know," and he stood up. "And tomorrow morning I want to be driven home, with Luca."

"No problem," said Colomba. She really didn't want him underfoot a minute more than was necessary.

10

The surgical team at the clinic that Dante had rented at great expense installed its own equipment and sterilized the room, discussing the upcoming surgery with the physician guardian, who approved every step. Dante didn't feel up to being present, and so it was Colomba's responsibility to oversee it. And so she was able to get a look at the soles of the boy's feet, which were covered with bubbles of scar tissue of various sizes.

For the entire time of the surgery—an hour—Luca held Cesare's hand. When it was done, the boy's feet were slightly reddened, and a few crumbs of dried skin had collected on the operating bed. Colomba asked Three to take the skin to an analysis lab.

"There's something rough here," the nurse said all of a sudden, as she was massaging Cesare's feet with a soothing cream.

The dermatologist put on his magnifying glasses and carefully examined the spot the nurse was pointing to. "It's a small encysted splinter," he confirmed. "We're going to take that out, all right, Cesare?" The boy wriggled uneasily under the medical floodlight, but Luca smiled at him reassuringly. Or actually, he smiled into the empty air: the two boys almost never actually looked each other in the face. The surgical extraction proved to be painless, because it was a splinter just a few millimeters in length, as slender as the spine of a small cactus.

It, too, was added to the small bag of evidence to be taken to the laboratory.

The results came back at dawn, to the utter astonishment of Colomba, who was used to the biblical time spans of forensic laboratories. She trudged out into the suite's living room in her pajamas, where she found Dante wide-awake and serving coffee to all the contractors on duty. She took advantage of the chance to toss back a double espresso shot while reading the report, which had arrived in a watermarked envelope closed with a wax seal. It looked costly.

In the document, illustrated with enlarged photographs of microscopic views, the laboratory explained that what had mainly been found in Cesare's skin fragments was dust, but that the splinter contained formaldehyde, phenol, and wood fibers.

"Bakelite," said Dante.

"Didn't they used to make telephones with Bakelite?" Colomba asked, yawning so hard she almost dislocated her jaw. It seemed impossible that only a short time ago she had decided to give up the hunt for the King. Now she was working hours that were longer than when she'd been on full duty at the Mobile Squad.

"Yes, and View-Masters, molds, toys, costume jewelry, buttons, and about a billion other things," said Dante, trying to assume the full lotus position on the sofa, unsuccessfully. "Fucking arthritic joints I have . . ." he muttered. "Is there a colorant?"

"Traces of dark pigment, either black or dark brown," Colomba read on. "Now that I think about it, the rifle I used at the police academy had dark brown Bakelite parts. It was a relic, a genuine antique."

"OG! Fuck!" shouted Dante, rolling as if in a delirium to grab his laptop. "What an asshole. What an idiot I am. I should have realized it immediately!" He turned the screen so she could see it: he'd gone to a page on warisboring.com, where there was a photograph of a submachine gun with a folding stock that looked distinctly vintage. The submachine gun was called an OG-43.

"I even knew about this gun. I studied these things, for fuck's sake!" He pointed at the grip on the perforated barrel. "It looks like wood, but it's Bakelite. Bakelite!" he shouted again, and collapsed on the bed. "God . . . why does the world have to be so small, why do I always wind up right back where I started from?"

"Start explaining or I'll lock you in the closet," Colomba threatened him.

He jumped off the bed and his legs almost gave way beneath him. They hadn't fully regained their strength. "The OG-43 submachine gun was developed for the Fascists of the Republic of Salò, after the armistice in the Second World War," he said. "You know, the ones who preferred the Nazis to the Americans."

"Go on . . ." said Colomba, who was starting to get irritated.

"There was only one factory that produced it. Only one, you understand? The Manifattura Armaguerra. After Italy's Liberation, it was converted into a repair shop, and then it ran out of repair work as well, and ever since the sixties, the sheds just stood there, gathering dust. The place is falling apart by now, but four or five years ago they started clearing it of asbestos."

"How do you know that?" Colomba asked, unable to grasp the reason for his excitement. "Do you know the history of every Italian manufacturing plant?"

Dante, who was wheeling around the room like a dervish, suddenly slammed to a halt, red-faced, his frogged jacket wide open, vents flying. "The reason I know it is I used to ride my bike past there! That fucking place is in Cremona, CC. The Father's Factory has always been there, right under my nose."

CHAPTER III

The officers of the correctional police banged the cell bars every night to make sure they were still perfectly intact, but when it came to the German, they did it first thing in the morning, too, as well as at the start of each shift, because they didn't trust that muscular, taciturn son of a bitch any farther than they could throw him. For the same reason, they never went into his cell if there were fewer than four guards in the group. They were accustomed to seeing him work out when they entered the cell, so they were astonished to find him sprawled on his cot, with his face turned to the wall.

"On your feet, Kraut," said one of the guards. "Come on, show yourself." The German didn't react, and with a caution he'd never shown even with Cane Pazzo, whose name meant Mad Dog and who was a Camorra torpedo, the chief inspector reached out and gripped the German's shoulder and turned him over. The German was stiff as a board: his eyes were open wide and he was trembling with fever, his skin yellowish and cold; the blanket was soaked in vomit.

The officer tried to bring him to with a couple of sharp slaps to the face. "This guy is going to die on us," he said.

"Let him die," his partner retorted. "He killed children, this piece of shit."

"Don't talk bullshit, we'd be the ones to get in trouble for it." They handcuffed him and dragged him off down the hallways, because he was a heavy man and could barely stay on his feet. When they finally got to the infirmary, the German retched again loudly and spewed bile onto the cot they were trying to lay him down on. The doctor on duty took one look at his eyes and hurriedly checked his heart rate. "Looks like poisoning. Did you find anything odd in his cell?"

"We didn't check," the inspector replied.

"Could you send someone to do that, please, and right away?" the doctor asked. "And we need to alert the warden's office: we need to take him to the hospital."

The inspector nodded, but with a smirk. Who the fuck cared.

Stopped at the front gate of Rebibbia Prison for the standard search, the veteran ambulance driver explained to his young colleague the way things worked.

"If it's a chicken thief, they'll just put a guard in the ambulance with us and an escort team in a squad car to follow us. If he's dangerous, they might put two guards in the ambulance, and two escort cars. If he's *very* dangerous, then four guards will ride in the ambulance and there will be more follow-up cars than a presidential procession."

When they finally brought out the German, four guards got into the ambulance—all of them full MOG officers in riot gear—while there were six escort cars, including an armor-plated vehicle. The patient was handcuffed to the gurney, hand and foot, a security precaution that the older paramedic had never seen in his career, especially not with a convict who was in his sixties.

"Who is this, anyway?" he asked the MOG officer next to him. "Dracula?"

"Basically," said the other man, with his jaw clenched, as the ambulance took off, heading for the Sandro Pertini Hospital, where there was a penitentiary medicine ward with twenty or so beds. Bars everywhere, but private rooms: for someone coming from Rebibbia, it was like going from a cheap bed and breakfast to a five-star hotel . . . but the level of security was just as high. The drive from the prison took only twenty minutes. More or less halfway there, they drove over a viaduct across the Aniene River, one of the twisty-turny tributaries of the Tiber, and it was as they were crossing that bridge that, without warning, the ambulance swerved into the opposite lane, crashed through the cement parapet, and plunged into the water running between tree-lined banks thirty feet below. The vehicle slammed nose-first into the rocky riverbed and then slumped over onto its side.

The escort vehicles following behind it screeched to a halt and the MOG officers leaped out of their cars, guns leveled. In the wreckage below them, nothing was moving. The head of the escort left some of his men to halt traffic and keep their weapons trained on the partly submerged ambulance, and climbed down with the rest of the unit to the bed of the river, making their way down the steep bank, littered with broken bottles and plastic bags. Forming a human chain to keep the current from sweeping them away, and holding their weapons over their heads, they finally reached the ambulance. The front of the vehicle was completely submerged, and given the murky condition of the water, they couldn't even see the person at the wheel. The head of the escort pulled open the ambulance's rear door, and the air from the cab gurgled beneath the surface of the water, producing a red bubble that burst upward, splashing violently and momentarily blinding him.

When his vision cleared, the first thing that the chief officer of the armed escort saw was the head of one of his colleagues. He had a pair of handcuffs stabbed into his eyes.

Dante was looking out the rear window of the armor-plated car, tormenting his *Star Wars* tie clip. He'd dressed formally—except for the tie clip—the way he always did when he set foot back in Cremona, in a subconscious attempt to seem a little more normal. Or maybe just as a form of self-protection.

When he was far from Cremona, he was able to avoid thinking about his fucked-up past, but whenever he came back to the city, it all bobbed to the surface again, making him feel like more of a phantom among men than ever. After battling with himself, he finally called Annibale and let him know that he'd be coming to Cremona. "I don't know what time it'll be, but I'll try to swing by to say hello."

"So this visit is business, not pleasure," said Annibale, resuming his worried tone.

"No, I'm still trying to break the bank. And there might be something in Cremona that can help me. Chill a good bottle for me."

Colomba, who had nodded off, her head against the car window, woke up with a start.

"Where are we?"

"We're almost in Cremona. It won't be long now."

All around them, the landscape had turned into the flat expanse of the Po Valley, an unbroken procession of wheat fields, tiny towns, and huge farmhouses in varying states of disrepair. For Dante, the setting for a nightmare. When he dreamed of the Father, he'd often see him chasing him down the rows of plants, while he, little more than a child, ran barefoot, unable to outrun him.

"Maybe there's some truth in everything that Belyy and the Father imagined," Colomba said suddenly. "Maybe the treatment really can create people capable of thinking and acting differently."

Dante snorted. "Electroshock and isolation only damage the mind."

"And yet Leo managed to outsmart the counterterrorism agencies of the whole world, and the King maneuvers other people like so many puppets, and you're one of the most brilliant people I've ever met . . ."

"Maybe we were all born geniuses. We were destined to do great things, like inventing engines that can run on tap water and teleportation devices. The Father kept us from doing that, the same way he kept everyone he dissolved in acid from ever doing anything again."

One, at the wheel, turned to look at them. "We're here."

The contractors parked their three cars next to a roundabout along the road that ran past the former weapons factory. The structure consisted of a series of industrial sheds with pitched roofs and large windows, standing on bare ground amid patches of trees. Some of them were still in good condition; others, deeper into the vast property, couldn't conceal the effects of decades of exposure to weather and vandalism. In contrast with what Dante remembered, on one of the outside walls, thousands of square feet of solar panels had been installed. A sign stated in large letters that construction would begin soon on a large outlet store.

"If there was ever anything here, it's gone by now," Colomba said, pressing her face between the bars of the gate.

"I don't expect to find anything remarkable," said Dante. "But until more or less five years ago, Cesare was a prisoner in here. And someone had work done on the solar panels after the Father was killed and the German wound up in prison." He turned to Three and Four. "How is it going with the drone?"

"Two more minutes and we should be ready, Signor Torre."

"The drone?" asked Colomba.

"That's included in the price," Dante said with a grin, but a very strained one. He lit a cigarette. "If that's the Factory Leo was talking about, then a piece of my life took place in here."

"Are you hoping that you'll be reminded of something when you see it?"

"Quite the opposite," he said. "I already have plenty of fucked-up memories."

While cars raced past all around them, Three and Four readied the Snipe. It was a tactical military drone, no bigger than any toy drone, utterly silent and equipped with both a normal video camera and an infrared camera; it weighed a mere 140 grams—about five ounces. They flew it over the area, piloting it with the greatest of ease by means of a tablet, and then Dante asked them to concentrate on the section where the buildings were in the greatest disrepair. The Snipe didn't have a great deal of autonomy—the batteries had to be switched out every fifteen minutes—but in no more than an hour's time they had an eminently acceptable mapping of the area, which Dante, lying in the back seat with his laptop propped up on his thighs and the radio earpiece in his ear, compared with the official plans he'd found online.

"Maybe we ought to go in on foot," said Colomba. She was outside the car, leaning against the side and looking at the surrounding area. The contractors, dressed casually so that they didn't look like a group of Mormons, were pretending to be passersby or rubberneckers, except for the IT experts, who were hunched over in the car behind them. "After all, sooner or later we're going to have to do it anyway."

"It's 220,000 square feet," Dante retorted. "If we don't know where to look, it would take us a lifetime."

"Are you sure you don't just want to have fun playing with the drone?"

"Would that be so bad?" Dante activated the radio's microphone. "Let's make another circuit, maybe next to the storage shed, the light-colored one with the round roof, but this time let's use the thermal sensor."

Three and Four obeyed and in the streaming video on Dante's computer there appeared, poking out from amid the shrubbery, a half dozen pink circles, invisible to the naked eye; one in particular was next to a pile of bricks. "What do you think those are?" he asked Colomba, who had stuck her head into the car.

"All I know is that they're slightly warmer than the ground around them. Maybe they're air vents from some sewer line or other. You can get that effect if there's rainwater running through them, which has absorbed the heat of sunlight and is starting to evaporate."

"From the vintage photographs, there don't seem to be any air vents," Dante replied. "Let's go in."

Colomba shook her head. "I don't want to offer an easy target to a sniper. Let's wait for dark."

Dante suggested spending the hours remaining before dark at the bar, so they went with a group of contractors in search of one. They were within sight of the bar they'd chosen when Colomba heard her phone buzz.

Alberti's voice was so shrill, sobbing, and shocked that at first she had a hard time recognizing it.

When he told her what had happened, Colomba was forced to sit down on a low wall and catch her breath.

D'Amore reached the site of the incident while it was still light out.

"I've never seen anything like it," the deputy chief of the correctional police who was in charge of the investigation and the manhunt told him.

"Isn't it great that the world still manages to surprise us, every so often?" D'Amore replied, his thoughts elsewhere.

"Not like this, sir. This way, please," the other man said, inviting him to follow him down to the banks of the Aniene. The ambulance was still in the water, but next to it was a Zodiac belonging to the correctional police, and aboard the inflatable craft were a couple of officers from the forensic team in white overalls, snapping pictures. "The corpses are all still inside, if you'd care to see them."

"I don't care to, but I have to," D'Amore replied.

With a wave of his hand, the deputy chief asked the pilot to steer the motorized dinghy over to the bank, and in a short while they were both transported to where they could look in through the open rear door of the ambulance. D'Amore realized that the correctional officer hadn't been exaggerating: the gurney was still where it belonged, but the handcuffs that had held the German in confinement were dangling empty, except for the pair that he'd stabbed into the eyes of the dead MOG officer, who was now bobbing in the fetid water. A second officer had his head twisted at a ninety-degree angle, and the third had been beheaded completely. The last MOG officer was wrapped around the paramedic, maybe because when the ambulance plummeted over the side of the bridge, they'd been thrown together. They both showed signs of gunshot wounds.

"The German did all this on his own?" asked D'Amore.

The deputy chief nodded. "He opened his handcuffs with a piece of twisted metal, probably taken from a food tin."

"And your colleagues didn't notice?"

"I think he only opened one handcuff, at first, the one that was covered by the oxygen tanks. The boys were tense, they were locked and loaded, even if that's against regulations."

"And once he got free he grabbed the gun," D'Amore said, acting out the scene. "Then he fired at your colleague and at the driver. And while the ambulance was falling into the river, he did the rest."

"He must be strong as a bull, even if he seemed like he was on his deathbed," the deputy chief murmured.

The Zodiac took them back to shore. D'Amore almost slipped in the mud while getting out of the boat, but he turned around and helped the deputy chief to get out. "What is it that he ate?"

"Something toxic that altered his heartbeat and caused diarrhea and hemorrhaging. Probably arsenic." He showed him a picture on his cell phone of a few shreds of wet paper. "It was a postcard. He tore it up and flushed it down the toilet, but we found it in the sewer lines. We think that's where the arsenic was. We're trying to figure out who sent it to him."

In one of the fragments an entire face could be seen. D'Amore recognized it even though it was badly faded. "Very good," he said wearily to the deputy chief. Then he shook his hand. "Keep me informed."

"Naturally, sir."

D'Amore had parked just outside the area marked off by police barriers, and as he got into the car, he pulled his cell phone out of his pocket to call Di Marco. He'd just sat down when he felt a sudden terrible pain in his left leg. He looked down: there was a pair of scissors sticking out of his thigh. A hand that reeked of swamp water clamped over his mouth. "We need to talk, cop," said the German.

5

O h Jesus," Dante murmured when Colomba told him about the German. "We're protected, Dante," she said, trying to reassure him.

"Protected?" Dante had turned the color of the outside of the bar. "He killed six people while strapped to a gurney! How the fuck do you think it's possible to protect us from him?" Until Dante discovered the Father's true identity, he'd always believed that his jailer had been the German. He'd seen the German through a crack in the wall of the silo as he led another prisoner through the fields. Dante had never found out who that boy was, but it was 1989 and the only survivor of the prisoners of that period had been Dante, even though he now believed that the King and Leo formed part of that group.

"We've already caught him once," said Colomba.

Dante pressed his hands over his ears, walking in a circle. A couple of the customers from the bar who had stepped outside to smoke looked at him curiously. "What if he let us catch him on purpose?"

"Dante . . . calm down."

"What if he's the King?"

"He was under surveillance twenty-four/seven," Colomba replied. "He couldn't exactly go around tossing corpses into the woods."

"Maybe he had accomplices. Other puppets who had no idea they were puppets." Dante took off his jacket: his shirt was drenched with sweat. "And do you think it's an accident that he escaped today, of all days?"

"How am I supposed to know?" asked Colomba, who once again was beginning to feel an unpleasant pang of pain in her lungs.

"It's because I called him," Dante persisted. "He understood that I was getting close to the truth."

"Why would he have cared? They're all dead."

"Except for the King. Let's get out of here, CC. Let's drop everything."

Colomba hugged him; Dante was trembling. "And then? Are you willing to look over your shoulder for the rest of your life? They'll catch him, they'll catch the German, he won't be able to get out of Rome. But anything we aren't able to figure out today is going to torment us forever." She looked him right in the eyes. "I won't let them hurt you, I swear it."

Dante leaned his weight on her shoulder and brought his face close to hers. It was a slow, endless moment, and Colomba thought he was about to kiss her, but Dante stopped just a fraction of an inch short of her lips and turned aside. "Okay, okay. You're right."

Colomba started, slightly embarrassed now. "Do you want something to drink?" she asked awkwardly.

Dante nodded. "Yes, please. Could you bring it to me out here, though? I just can't manage to come inside." He hunkered down on the ground, using his cane for support. "I'll sit right here, Three and Four can keep an eye on me. I'll tell the others that we can get moving as soon as the sun sets."

6

A t seven, the area of the former weapons plant was shrouded in darkness, except for the side of the building with the solar panels, where a line of lamps had been installed. Dante checked the padlock on the gate, and then opened it so quickly that Colomba couldn't figure out how he'd even done it.

"One," she called out at that point. "Please leave someone to keep an eye on the road, and then everyone else, inside with us."

"We can't violate private property, Deputy Captain, even if it's abandoned," replied the chief of the Shadow agency, smiling apologetically. "If someone reported us to the police, we'd lose our license."

"What if something happens in there?" Colomba objected.

"We'd call the police and then head in to get you. The law is very restrictive on these matters."

"At last, I've found someone who follows the law," said Dante. "Even if this wasn't exactly the right time for it."

"What kind of weapon do you carry?" Colomba asked him.

One showed her the Glock 17 he wore on his belt. "I can't give this to you, Deputy Captain."

"No, but I can steal it from you. That's what I'll tell them if they catch me, and you can report me to the police and tell any story you like. I probably won't need it—according to the drone this whole place is deserted—but I can't let Dante go in there without protection."

One looked at her for a good ten seconds, his face impassive. "Okay," he finally said. And, scanning his surroundings for anyone who might be watching, he handed her the gun. "I'm going to trust you."

Colomba smiled back, checked the handgun, and slipped it into her pocket. "We need flashlights."

"We have something better," said One.

o   o   o

Apparently, also included in the price of the package, along with the drone, were the latest generation of night-vision goggles. Three showed them how the goggles worked and then helped them to get them fitted comfortably to their foreheads. Dante, who loved electronic gadgets, forgot his fear for a few seconds and started experimenting with the zoom function. "Bionic eyes. Cool."

They went in, switching on their goggles once the light from the road was blocked by the surrounding trees. The ground around them suddenly switched into shades of green, with yellowish shadows. The noise of the passing traffic on the Via Paullese had vanished, and now the only sounds to break the silence were their footsteps and their breathing. Dante held his cane out in front of him, and he used it to smack bushes or move garbage out of their path.

"Everything okay?" One asked over the radio.

"It's all good."

"Haven't you invented any cool battle handles?" Colomba whispered.

"There's no need, it's just us. And the communications are encrypted. They have better products than what the police use."

A gust of cool wind made the treetops toss. Dante started; Colomba felt a stab of tightness in her stomach. They stopped to wait for silence to return.

"How many times have you done this sort of thing?" Dante asked.

"Actually, never. I'm not a marine."

They skirted the skeleton of a half-ruined office building, which loomed up gigantic in their night-vision goggles, as if ready to crush them, and they found themselves face-to-face with the warehouse with the round roof.

"That's where they stockpiled the weapons," said Dante. "The Allies never bombed the place, and production went on uninterrupted till the very end. One of the workers who was employed at the plant was killed after the war had ended, on April 25, Liberation Day. The Nazis didn't yet know the war was over, and when he tried to tell them, they shot him." He checked the location of the circles on the tablet the contractors had loaned him. "They ought to be around here somewhere, but I can't see them."

Dante went on: "The night goggles work differently from the thermal sensors. And the temperature of the area has shifted, it's become more uniform." Dante looked around, amping up the intensity of the infrared projector he wore on his forehead. "But that's the pile of bricks right there."

It was the very same pile they'd seen with the drone. Colomba looked at the ground and bent down and felt it without finding anything, then she took off her tactical backpack and pulled out a folding shovel. "If the circles aren't going to do any good, then what?"

"Let's just look everywhere," Dante said, "starting with the parts that haven't been rebuilt. How's it going?"

"The ground is hard. You might consider giving me a hand."

"I don't want to get dirty."

"I think I'll just bury you here . . ."

About a foot and a half down, the shovel hit something hard. Colomba leaned down to dig with her hands, and Dante knelt down beside her. By the greenish light of the night-vision goggles, they could glimpse something that seemed like the top of a cement chimney, with the vent sealed and loopholes along the sides, roughly the circumference of a serving platter.

"I continue to think that this is just a way into the sewer," Colomba said, brushing dirt off the narrow vertical apertures.

"No, it's an air intake," said Dante.

"For what?"

"A bomb shelter. The construction style looks German, but I'm no expert. It's not marked in the official plans, because it was a military secret."

"And no one ever found it?"

"The Father certainly did. We just need to find the entrance." Dante let himself flop down on the pile of rubble. "Unfortunately, I don't think I'll be able to go in with you."

7

D'Amore had never felt pain like this. It was like burning and freezing at the same time. But there was no flame and no ice: only the German's hands, and his scissors.

Flat on his back on the floor of the hut—one of the many that lined the banks of the Aniene—where the German had dragged him after making his way through the various roadblocks in D'Amore's car, D'Amore couldn't move. And he kept his eyes closed. He didn't want to see what that white-haired man had done to him. Only once, an infinity ago, had he dared to look at the arm the German was ravaging. It had been sliced open lengthwise, like in an old anatomy textbook, with the artery intact and the hemorrhage blocked by a tourniquet made out of the laces from his shoes. The German had waited until he was done with his work on the other arm before he started asking questions, and D'Amore had answered every one, promptly, eagerly, better than he had done at school, without reservations, without hesitation. Because every time he hesitated, it just meant another cut, another nerve ending exposed.

Torture isn't an exact tool. If the pain is too powerful, you'll say anything to make it stop, mixing truth and imagination. Your memory is destroyed, you lose any sense of self-awareness. But if the torturer is good at his job, he knows how to keep you right on the edge. And the German was very, very good at his job. What's more—D'Amore had learned this at the expense of one knee, the bone of which now protruded from the bleeding flesh—the German could sniff out any and all lies.

Now the German was putting on the clothing that he'd taken off D'Amore before starting to torture him, even though it fit tight over the man's gorilla chest. D'Amore realized that the torture was over now, but also that that hut was going to be his tomb. And so, why not . . .

"Do you know who the guy that Colomba is looking for really is?" he asked.

The German barely looked at him. "I know who he used to be, but I don't know who he's become."

D'Amore blacked out for a minute, and another fragment of his life was gone. When he came to, the German was putting his shoes on.

"Why?" he asked again. "Why . . ." He stopped: he couldn't even begin to ask the question.

But the German seemed to understand anyway. "Do you know how many breeds of dogs there are?"

D'Amore shook his head.

"Neither do I. But there are a lot. And once, long ago, there was only one breed. Someone took those dogs and bred them until he managed to produce dogs the size of mice and dogs the size of horses. But before producing a new breed, there were thousands of dogs that came out all twisted and wrong, or else mother dogs died giving birth because the fetus was too big." He leaned over him. "You tell me, were the dogs happy about this? Did they understand the reasons behind what was happening to them?"

D'amore shook his head again.

The German picked up the scissors from the floor. "You see? Even you don't understand."

"But why are you doing it?"

"Out of love," said the German. And he cut D'Amore's throat.

8

Colomba had the men send the drone up in flight in the hopes that a view from above might help her, but it was no good: they couldn't find the entrance to the old bomb shelter. She was about to give up hope when an idea occurred to her.

"Do you have anything that can generate heat and light?" she asked One, after walking back to the gate.

"Like some kind of fireworks?"

"Exactly, something like that."

One pondered for a moment. "We have some flashbangs. Not military grade, naturally. They're airsoft flashbangs, but they're pretty loud."

"I'll take a couple, and I want you to get ready to send up the drone when I alert you."

Colomba went running back to Dante with the flashbangs: to look at them, you'd say they were identical to the real ones, even if they were much less powerful than those used by the army. "Do you like playing with firecrackers?" she asked him.

Dante gave her a look that required no words.

"Then grab your shovel and get to digging."

Colomba and Dante opened two more chimneys before they found one that wasn't plugged up with dirt. They broke the cover, then peered inside: there was just an empty tube that ended in nothing.

"Perfect," said Colomba.

"I get what you want to do," Dante broke in. "It's a good idea, it seems like something I might have come up with."

"It would have occurred to you, too, if you weren't spending all your time looking over your shoulder for fear that the German's going to jump you." She activated the microphone. "Send up the bird," she said.

The drone arrived a few seconds later, and Colomba told them to make it climb until she had a panoramic view of the area. She tossed the first flashbang down the chimney, covering the tube with a brick. The bang sounded incredibly loud to her, but from out on the road One said it had sounded like a tiny firecracker. Colomba tossed in the second flashbang, too, and then Dante checked the pictures on the tablet from the moment of the explosion. The drone had managed to intercept a tongue of flame that pointed toward the shed with the round roof, stopping just a couple of yards short, where it spread out into a luminous sphere.

They moved over to the point that they'd identified, Dante struggling along behind her, resting his weight on the cane. "I think we're going to have to start digging again."

He clicked the microphone. "Ten thousand euros to anyone willing to come give us a hand."

"Sorry, boss," One replied. "We can't. But thanks for the offer."

When they were done digging—Colomba took care of most of the work—they'd unearthed a cement manhole, covered by a number of wooden boards. Colomba shoved it aside with her feet. Underneath was a hole big enough to fit into, and through the cobwebs and roots it was possible to glimpse a metal ladder that ran down about fifteen feet, terminating just above a pool of stagnant water.

"Sure you don't want to come along?" she asked Dante.

"Not awake, and if I was unconscious I wouldn't be a lot of help. But have them send the drone, so I can follow you from overhead, live. That way I can tell you what you need to do."

"You can tell your grandmother what she needs to do."

Dante threw both arms wide. "I'm so sorry, but I don't even know who she is."

Holding the drone like a video camera, Colomba descended a couple of steps, checking to make sure the ladder was solid. It didn't even creak. "I'm going. If I don't come back, send scuba divers," she said.

Dante leaned over, pressing his face close to hers. "I wouldn't want to have any regrets, just in case you never come back," he said. And he gave her a kiss on the lips.

Colomba was caught off guard, but she grabbed his head to keep him from pulling away. "I'm not a little girl." She pulled him closer and stuck her tongue in his mouth. "This doesn't mean a thing, do you get that? I'm not in love with you and, physically, you're not even my type. But I love you, and I don't want to lose you, okay?"

And she slipped down into darkness.

9

Colomba went down the steps, the drone clamped under her arm, her mouth smacking of the taste of tobacco and alcohol. The taste of Dante. Had she done something stupid? Probably, but this wasn't the time to think about it, all the more so because her foot was meeting nothing beneath it now: she had reached the bottom of the ladder. She slipped the drone underneath her jacket and grabbed the bottom rung.

"I can't see a thing," Dante told her.

"Don't bust my chops," she replied, and after extending her leg until it touched the surface of the water, she let herself go, finally landing on the floor below. The water reached up to her ankles and it instantly started leaking into her combat boots through the eyelets for the laces. It was cold, but tolerable. Something moved and darted away: Colomba just hoped that it wasn't a hungry rat.

On one side of that sort of well was a metal door that didn't seem old enough to date back to World War II, locked with a heavy chain and a padlock the size of a fist.

"Do you want to come down and open it?" she asked, framing it with the drone.

"If you want, I can teach you . . ." said Dante.

"Forget it." Colomba set the waterproof tactical backpack down in the water and pulled out a small sledgehammer. It took about fifty or so blows from the hammer, but in the end the hasp of the padlock broke away.

"It takes a gentle touch . . ." said Dante.

Colomba opened the door, braced against the gust of smoke from the flashbang, and stepped in.

It was a hallway of unfinished cement, with a row of doors very much like the one she'd just opened, but all without padlocks; as she went by, the water swirled and agitated, churning up whirlpools of rotten leaves and dirt. It felt like walking through a sunken ship, but that was a thought that brought back bad memories, so she forced herself to focus on the present. "Dante, can you hear me? Can you see?"

"Yes," he replied in a faint voice. "Those are cells. The Father held people prisoner down here."

Colomba kept walking. "Wait before you say that, maybe it's just storage."

"No. No. Oh God . . . I'm about to vomit."

"It's all okay, Dante. Please, just calm down."

"I was down there, CC. They kept me down there . . ."

"And now I'm down here. And I need you. So get a grip on yourself," she said in an intentionally harsh tone.

Dante remained silent for a few seconds. "Okay," he finally said in a firmer voice. "You're right. Let's see what's in there."

Colomba opened the doors. They were rooms measuring roughly seven by ten feet, with a ceiling tall enough not to have to stoop, all of them windowless. The first room was empty, while in the second she found a rusted cot with a hole in the center. In the third room, an old, worn, barely legible sign read OG-43—STORAGE.

"Cesare," said Dante. "He was in there."

Because of the goggles, Colomba couldn't make out the details very clearly, so she lifted them off her face, but that only plunged her into utter darkness. She turned on the flashlight and shone the beam of light onto the walls. They were covered with scratches, and she didn't doubt for a second that those scratches had been made by human fingernails. She imagined a child locked up in there, desperately trying to get out. She imagined a young Dante. He was making strange sounds in the microphone, and Colomba realized that he was crying. "Stay tough, Dante."

"Yes, yes . . . But we need to get Bart here, we need to figure out who was here."

"As soon as we get out," she said.

The last door was painted green, but the paint had all flaked away. Behind it, Colomba found a gynecological examination bed with stirrups for the legs. "Dante . . . the Father never took girls, did he?"

"No."

"Strange." She checked the rest of the room with the flashlight. There was an old file cabinet, green like the door but in better condition; the drawers were empty, though, except for a few sheets of paper that seemed to be handwritten medical reports, unfortunately now completely illegible on account of the damp. Colomba stuck them into her backpack and illuminated an old blackboard standing nearby: there was a single word written on it, the chalk seeming to have carved and scratched the black surface.

SKOPTSY.

"Do you know what that means? Dante?"

His voice reached her as if he were being suffocated: he was still trying not to cry. "Yes, yes. I know. That goddamned bastard. That monster."

Colomba turned off the flashlight and, after putting the night-vision goggles back on, she retraced her steps. "Is it the name of some Russian?"

"No, it was a Christian sect in eighteenth-century Russia. They practiced mortification of the flesh and suffering. They believed that their God wanted offerings . . . The same offerings that psychiatrists once implemented with the patients who were too agitated, whether adults or children. *Cleansing*, they called it."

"So, what you're saying is . . . ?" Colomba asked.

"They castrated them, CC. And now I understand why the King is so full of hatred."

10

Climbing out of the well proved more strenuous for Colomba than entering it had been. When she emerged onto the surface, Dante was kneeling on the ground, tears streaming down his face.

Colomba felt herself being assailed by a wave of rage, but also a strange sense of melancholy. She was just sorry that she hadn't been there when Dante, still a child, was kidnapped by a maniac who decided on a whim what tortures to inflict on him. She wished she could have taken him by the hand when he emerged from the silo, and when he'd been bounced from one clinic to another, entrusted to doctors who, perhaps, in their own past careers, had done the same things that the Father had inflicted on generations of patients: electroshock, ice baths, physical restraints . . . and castration, as she had just discovered. She wished she could have been there when Dante had seized his own independence, concealing his fragility behind a tough and coarse attitude toward the world. *But I'm here now*, she thought. *Even if it's not exactly the way he'd like*.

"I'm sorry," she said to him.

Dante raised his head. "It's the history of the world, CC. It's not just the Father. People like me have undergone the worst tortures for centuries. And they continue to undergo them today." He wiped his face, smearing dirt on it as he did. "There was a doctor—his name was Moniz—who had invented a method for calming his patients, a method more efficient than castration and electroshock: he trepanned their skulls and injected alcohol to burn the cerebral matter."

"In concentration camps?" Colomba asked in a faint voice.

"In hospitals. He was awarded the Nobel Prize for medicine, CC. The Nobel Prize." Dante sighed and, leaning on his cane, got to his feet. "Castration provokes long-term effects, and one of those effects is osteoporosis. We'll have to ask Bart to—"

One's voice interrupted them. "There's a problem."

"Go ahead," said Colomba.

"The traffic isn't flowing the way it ought to. I'm afraid they're cordoning us in."

"Okay, we're heading out now."

She didn't have time to finish that short sentence before her cell phone vibrated in the backpack. She was only able to find it on the tenth ring: it was Lupo. "Caselli, you have two minutes to get away from there."

"From where?"

"You know perfectly well."

Evidently, the head of the Shadow agency had been right about the traffic. "How the fuck were you able to find us?"

"There's a bug in your car. We put it on you when you were at a service station, getting gas. Di Marco isn't happy with what you've been up to."

"I understand, but we haven't broken any laws."

"He's going to prove the opposite. D'Amore is missing and the German has escaped, he's beside himself with rage."

"And what do you have to do with all this?"

"It's very difficult to do my job without getting dragged into the messes that the intelligence agencies keep creating. A friend of mine tried to warn me about it, and now I see that he was right. So I had a moment of doubt, and I made the wrong phone call. Get going. Before much longer, you won't be able to get out of the area."

"Hold on . . ." Colomba took a breath. "Under the Factory there's an old bomb shelter. The Father held children prisoner down there. Don't let Di Marco get rid of what's in there. Many families might finally have answers about children who vanished without a trace."

At the other end of the line, there was a pause. "I promise you that I'll do my very best," said Lupo.

"Thanks." Colomba broke the cell phone against a rock, then threw away her earbuds. "Leave everything behind, Dante."

"What about the team?"

"There's nothing we can do for them, and they certainly have good lawyers. Do you think you can climb over the fence on the side where the solar panels are?"

"No . . ." he replied.

"Okay, then, let's just wait here until they come and arrest us."

Dante heaved a sigh of frustration.

11

B efore he was kidnapped, Dante had been far more agile than Colomba; but now, instead, she had to help him by pushing from below. When he landed on the other side, he dropped his cane and wasted time trying to retrieve it.

"Can't you just get another one?" Colomba asked, urging him to get moving toward the first fork in the road leading to town.

"It's a Ham Brooks classic, I told you that before."

"And I still don't know what the hell that means. Is it valuable?"

"Have you ever heard of the Man of Bronze?"

"No, but I know lots of people who definitely deserve no better than a bronze medal. Is that good enough for you?"

They heard the turbocharged engines even before they saw the cars, and they threw themselves behind the hedges that lined the road, letting the troop trucks filled with NOA agents rumble past them. From a distance they could hear sirens wailing and excited, shouting voices: the team had been captured.

Dante snapped a sharp military salute. "Farewell, it has been an honor to serve the fatherland at your side."

"A burden, if anything. At least now you'll save a fair bit of change."

"No, I'm afraid not. Shadow is going to be able to keep the deposit. By now, I think that all I have left is enough to get far away from this country." Dante was starting to pant, and he slowed his pace. "I'm sick of living here, surrounded by spies and state secrets."

Colomba shoved his shoulder to restore his sense of brio. "Like where?"

"I've heard good things about Sweden."

"It's fucking freezing and they speak an incomprehensible language."

"Well, I never leave the house anyway."

They'd walked a mile or two away from the area around the Factory, and Colomba decided they could afford a brief halt. The fog had descended, and they could see very little around them.

"Okay," she said, "we're covered with mud, we don't have a cell phone, I have a handgun I have no right to carry, and we're in the middle of nowhere, without a car. Any suggestions?"

"Let's steal one," Dante replied promptly. "I know how to start one without the key."

"Next suggestion?"

"Cremona is in that direction, about four miles away," Dante said, pointing randomly. "And at Annibale's house I have some changes of clothing."

"They'll come looking for us there, too."

"But not right away, I hope. All we need to do is get changed and get him to lend us his car. Even if it isn't obvious just where we could drive it."

"One step at a time," said Colomba.

It was a long walk, and one that was burdened by the weight of fear, because somewhere around them was the King of Diamonds, busy searching for them, as well as the German, out on the loose. But at least the fog helped to conceal them.

Annibale lived in an eighteenth-century palazzo in the historic center of Cremona. By the time they reached the building, it was eleven at night. Dante hit the buzzer three times in rapid succession.

"That's the family buzz," he said. The street door clicked open and he and Colomba walked into the main living room, the size of a parade ground, with all the windows wide open. Dante looked at them with utter relief. He knew this house, and like any familiar place, he had a hard time being shut up in it. Still, even there, it was better to have the windows wide open.

"The housekeeper must be in her room, asleep," he said. "Papà, are you awake?" he called.

"Upstairs."

Like the first and last time that Colomba had been in that building, Annibale Valle was awaiting them in his bathrobe, sitting in an armchair. Unlike the last time, however, he wasn't alone.

Standing behind him, with a hand on his shoulder, was Tommy.

"I thought you'd never get here," he said.

12

Colomba fell to her knees as her lungs tightened so violently that she expelled all the air in her body in a single gasp. The room had filled with darting shadows, and Dante's screaming voice seemed to be played on a disk spinning far too fast. Everything was wrong, she thought, certain that she must be dying. But above all, *Tommy* was wrong. It had been his face that felled her, dropped her to her knees—not her surprise. It no longer had the kind gaze and the vacuous expression: his eyes were hard as stone and they glittered with intelligence and hatred.

Dante shouted again, Valle twisted uncomfortably in his armchair, and Colomba tumbled over onto her side as the shadows devoured her, shrieking with electric hisses. Tommy laughed, and it was the most horrible sound she had ever heard in her life, bad enough to outstrip even the sound of the shadows that were looming closer now, flickering out one after the other. In the black void that was consuming her, she heard the sound of a slap, and then a hot burn on her cheek. The shadows backed away, slithering out of her field of vision. Dante had slapped her in the face.

Colomba bit the floor, chipping a tooth on a crack in the hardwood parquet. This time, she was the one who screamed as the pain in her mouth surged down her nerves and inflamed her brain.

"God," she said, sitting up.

"Not exactly," said Tommy. "But everyone creates their own god, in their own image and semblance. I chose myself."

Colomba looked at him, unable to accept that the person standing in front of her really was the same boy she had protected. "This isn't you," she said, somewhat foolishly.

"Skoptsy," said Dante.

Tommy shrugged. "Good boy, you took a tour of the Factory."

"So the Father really did kidnap you . . ." he said.

"In 1979."

Once again, Colomba came close to being unable to breathe. "That's not possible, you'd be Dante's age."

"Eunuchs who are castrated as children develop differently," said Dante, without taking his eyes off Annibale, who trembled as he wept. "They don't get white hair, their whiskers don't grow."

"Exactly," said Tommy, sitting down on the armrest of his father's armchair. Only then did Colomba notice that he was holding a kitchen knife pressed against the back of Annibale's neck. "Testosterone has a number of contraindications. Castrati like yours truly have a good ten years' extra life expectancy compared to the uncut. But there's another thing that's even better." He touched his temple. "No distractions. Ah, yes, while we're on the subject, Colombina, toss me your handgun. You couldn't shoot me before I cut the old man's throat."

"Please . . ." Dante whispered. "Papà, don't worry," he said.

Tommy laughed. "Poor little thing."

Colomba tossed him her handgun and Tommy stuck it in his belt.

"Tommy never existed, then?"

"Of course he did, and he was a burden for his mother. She'd already tried to get rid of him, but it hadn't turned out well. I took care of him, one less mental retard."

"That's not possible, the DNA—"

"Caterina gave us a hand and took care of me while they did the exam. A minor exploit in sleight of hand. I set aside samples before disposing of the corpse."

"How did you know?" Dante asked, staring at him. "How did you know about her, how did you know she wanted to get rid of her son?"

Tommy slapped Annibale on the back. "Go on, tell him."

"No . . ." he whimpered.

Tommy pointed the knife at his left eye. "Come on."

"I'm sorry . . . I'm sorry . . . But I warned you to leave it alone . . ."

"Come on, old man," Tommy said again. His thin voice clashed with the threatening tone and his grown-up posture. Colomba wondered how she could have been so wrong about him. How she could have missed it. But Tommy had had a whole lifetime to learn how to pretend, how to dissimulate, a lifetime frozen in the physical appearance of an eternal overweight adolescent.

"I didn't know . . . I didn't know what to do with the boy. With Dante. But there was a rumor going around . . ." He broke off and looked at Tommy. "Please."

"Beg all you like but keep talking. I have an airplane to catch."

"There was a rumor that . . . someone could take care of them."

Dante gripped the cane so tight that it creaked. "You gave your son to the Father?"

Annibale, trembling, nodded.

"But do you realize what you've done? Do you even realize?"

"Now I do. Now . . ."

"Now it's too late!"

Colomba tried to keep her cool. "And he wasn't the only one."

"No. The Father offered this service when they cut his funding. There were plenty of people eager to get rid of their pain-in-the-ass children, kids who hadn't learned to talk when they reached the age for it. Tommy's mother had just been unlucky, because the German fucked things up. He was supposed to murder the husband and take the boy, but Tommy took off running and the German had to let him go. When I showed up, the mother was so happy. She thought we were going to conquer the world together."

"Jesus," said Colomba. "And Maugeri, too, right?"

"No, his wife. And he'd figured it out, oddly enough. He was always such an idiot. But then most people are idiots. Ninety-nine percent of the population. Then there are people like me and your friend. People who know how to think."

Colomba didn't understand how on earth Dante had managed to lunge forward so quickly. One moment he seemed prostrate with grief at the revelation, and the next he had leaped to his feet and shot toward Tommy brandishing not one but two canes. Then she understood that one of the canes was nothing but the sheath for the other, which was actually a blade.

Tommy was taken by surprise when Dante hit him on the arm holding the knife, but he quickly threw Dante to the ground like a broken reed, and then grabbed the blade out of his hand. It was a sort of sword, which had the knob of the walking stick as its grip.

"This is nice, where did you find it?"

"Fuck yourself," said Dante as he tried to get to his feet. Tommy aimed Colomba's pistol at him. "If you move, little Colomba, I'll shoot him instantly." Then he stepped on Dante's left arm, putting his full weight on that foot, and ran the gloved bad hand through with the cane-sword, nailing it to the floor. Dante let out a piercing shout, and Tommy seemed to observe him with extreme interest. Colomba tried to react, but he wiggled his finger at her disapprovingly.

"I can see you, Colombina. Don't interrupt, I'm still talking to . . . let's call him my brother." He leaned over Dante, who was desperately clutching the wrist of his bad hand, trying to stem the hemorrhaging. "You know why I'm here, right?"

"*Look at yourself in the mirror*," Dante murmured, remembering the German's words.

Colomba understood, and it was another sudden whiplash. "You're Valle's son. You're the real Dante."

Annibale wiped his nose on his sleeve. "Yes."

"You even took my name, kid." He hauled off and kicked Dante in the face. Dante spat blood. "That's something I can never retrieve, at this point. I've become Tommy Melas, and it's as good an identity as another, until I'm done getting back what belongs to me. Then we'll see."

Colomba realized that Tommy was about to fire, and that she only had that brief, slender possibility. She was still hunched down, and she lunged at Tommy. Maybe she'd succeed in knocking him off balance, but Annibale lifted his leg, caught her in midair, and tripped her so she fell to the floor. "I'm sorry. He's my son, you understand that?"

"I think we'll get along famously, you and I," said Tommy.

Then he pulled the trigger.

Colomba felt her shoulder explode and saw the shadows return. She started crawling toward Dante, *her* Dante, leaving a trail of blood behind her like the slime of a snail. He seemed incredibly far away, and the distance only continued to grow. Tommy shot her again, and this time she tasted blood in her mouth. But it didn't hurt, not anymore. She brushed her fingers over Dante's side, and he turned his head to look at her, his eyes glazed over.

"I'm sorry," she said to him. Or maybe she only thought it. Tommy was getting ready to pull the trigger a third time when a cyclone with white hair turned the room upside down.

For Colomba, on the verge of unconsciousness, it was like witnessing a series of static images in a vacuum world. Tommy raising the handgun. Tommy pulling the trigger. The German lunging at him, wrapping both arms around him, yanking the weapon away from him. Tommy in turn wrapping the German in a bear hug and wrestling back. The German biting into his face and ripping away one entire cheek. Tommy opening his mouth to scream. The German pounding him with fists as massive and heavy as rocks. Tommy on his knees. The German with Colomba's pistol in his hand, and a burst of flame emerging from the barrel. The back of Tommy's head literally exploding. The German firing again. Valle, now without a face. The armchair tipping over backward, the German firing once again. Valle's throat turning into a bloody crater.

Darkness.

The German bent over Tommy and spat in his face. "You should have finished the treatment, kid."

He checked the magazine: he still had two bullets. More than sufficient. The German turned to fire the kill shot into Colomba's head, but then he noticed that Dante was no longer lying on the floor. Dante was standing right in front of him, drenched in blood, his left arm dangling inert, his good hand firmly gripping the cane with the blade. Dante darted his arm forward as if brandishing a banderilla, and hit the German dead-center in the eye.

"I *did* finish the treatment, asshole," he said. Then he passed out.

The German didn't die until a couple of seconds later; he toppled forward and as he hit the floor, the Ham Brooks Classic sword punched out through the back of his head.

When Lupo entered the apartment he found himself looking down on a horrendous spectacle, with blood everywhere, even dripping from the overhead lamp, and five ravaged corpses. Then he realized that two of the five corpses were still breathing.

EPILOGUE

The real Tommy had never been either fat or tall, and he was certainly not especially well liked. His corpse, discovered in Greece not far from the hotel where Teresa had worked, was malnourished and his body bore many marks of mistreatment. His mother had kept him locked in the house all that time, treating him as a burden she couldn't seem to rid herself of. Annibale Valle's son had solved that problem for her, by cutting the boy's throat and burying him.

Colomba would go on wondering for the many long months and years that followed whether she had never glimpsed Tommy's real face simply because the ostensible boy was so skillful, or rather because she hadn't *wanted* to see it, caught up as she was in her role of a paladin riding to battle against the dull, obtuse world. Probably, it had been a combination of the two.

Multiple investigations were still under way, but what it had been possible to determine up to that point (or at least what she had been able to learn) was that Tommy had escaped from the clutches of the Father immediately following his death, when the monster's organization had collapsed. Thanks to the evidence found in the Factory, which Lupo had successfully managed to save from the shredders of the intelligence services—which earned him a swift kick in the ass and a transfer back to Portico from Di Marco—four more prisons had been discovered, scattered around Italy, and sadly dozens more corpses of teenagers who had been eliminated in a variety of ways. Traces of the Code had been found here and there, but just which of the prisoners had created it remains a mystery. In one of these prisons an open cell had been found, so rare a circumstance that it was one of the first to be gone over by the forensic squad: in it they had found the DNA of the real Dante, and the genetic analysts now all agree that it belonged to Tommy, and that Tommy/Dante had been able to escape from that cell immediately after the death of the Father, when Colomba had slaughtered his various accomplices. The prison had been concealed deep in the foundations of an apartment building, so buried in cement that Tommy, probably, felt certain that it wouldn't be discovered anytime soon. Bart was working on it full-time.

Tommy might very well have been the Father's longest-held prisoner, and he'd learned everything that he needed. His contacts with the world of contractors, which he'd used adroitly to have the *Chourmo* sunk and to take Dante prisoner, in turn; the lists of parents who had entrusted their differently abled sons to the Father in the hopes that he might heal them and in any case get them out from underfoot; the foreign bank accounts . . . Tommy had used all this to destroy what remained of the Father's domain, and to build himself a considerable personal fortune. All that he lacked was a public identity, seeing that he couldn't use the identity of Annibale Valle's son, and the investigators felt certain that his plan had been to feign a miraculous "cure" from the symptoms of autism that he knew how to counterfeit so skillfully, after which he'd be able to live the way he thought he deserved.

Like a king.

During his three years of freedom, Tommy had hopscotched across Europe like a giant bloodsucking tick, draining of their assets many of those whose names appeared on his list, as well as manipulating an array of individuals into doing as he wished, without their ever quite realizing it. Collaborators and collaborationists from the Father's and the German's spheres of influence had been ravaged and murdered, while Melas, who had had the bad luck of being not only the sole heir to the man who laundered the Father's money but also the parent of an unwanted child, had been very, very cooperative, because Tommy had a gift and a skill for terrorizing people and persuading them to follow him. And in the end, as always, Melas had been deleted from history. Colomba was starting to think that maybe Demetra wasn't the black sheep of the family after all. They'd found her in a hotel in a state of profound narcosis, after Tommy had forced her to miss her plane by feigning a hysterical crisis and trashing the Alitalia lounge.

While Colomba was recovering from her wounds at Celio military hospital, graduating from suspect and defendant to free citizen, she read all the volumes of *Doc Savage: The Man of Bronze* that she could get her hands on. Doc Savage was a hero of the American pulps in the thirties, a sort of gigantic genius, undefeated in hand-to-hand combat and in science. He had five assistants, and one of them, a lawyer named Theodore Marley Brooks, also known as Ham, went everywhere with a sword cane.

"Do you know, I'm really enjoying myself?" said Colomba once she was capable of getting up on her feet and out into the garden, and Dante was finally able to come see her, after spending a month in hiding before his name could be cleared. As best she was able to understand, Santiago had rented Dante the roof of the apartment building where he lived. Dante had returned to his fine former fettle, with longish hair and a panama hat, and seemed to be a cosplay version of David Bowie. His bad hand was healed, though it was even more crooked and twisted than before, but as long as it stayed in its glove that wasn't evident. As for his spirit, the various pieces were having a hard time holding together. Valle's death had come as a blow. The man who had raised him had been willing and ready to sell him out to a murderer, only because that murderer was his *true* son. If Tommy had arrived in Cremona ahead of Dante and Colomba and was ready and waiting for them, it was for one reason only: Annibale had given him a heads-up after the phone call from Dante.

"It's as if I've had to review my entire past life, again," he said to her, handing her a thermos full of what he claimed was the world's finest Irish coffee: Irish whiskey, aged sixty years, and medium-roasted Kenya Konyu coffee. "That is, if I even have a past at all."

Colomba took just a small sip and felt her head start spinning instantly. "Well, one thing's for sure. You're not Dante Torre."

"My ass. I earned that name, I deserve it." He took back the thermos and took another drink. "But I killed the only man who knew who I was."

"And who remains a mystery, even now that he's dead."

"All self-respecting Dr. Frankensteins have a faithful Igor, but let's just hope that something turns up . . ." He looked at his hands, one of which was sheathed in a well-made glove. "I never thought I'd be capable of such a thing. But we're all probably capable when the time really comes."

While he had been hiding out from the arrest warrant in his name, Dante had studied the sheets of paper that Colomba had gathered at the Factory. They came from a place called Villa Blu, which in spite of the Disney-sounding name had been a sort of concentration camp for children run by a psychiatrist nicknamed Dr. Electrode, on account of his uninhibited use of electric shocks, especially as applied to the testicles of misbehaving young boys. Villa Blu was shuttered in the wake of the passage of Italy's Basaglia Law in 1978, and the Father had been happy to offer his services to the families who would have preferred a son they could show off in society. Cesare's parents were indicted and faced trial, and they were soon to be joined by a great many other parents.

The woman who lived across the landing from Romero had been indicted, too, once she emerged from her coma. She'd never seen Leo, of course: she'd lied in exchange for money to buy herself a lifelike silicone newborn doll: the one that Colomba had mistaken for a real baby. She'd never had a child at all, she'd only pretended to have one, and she was so deeply attached to that doll that she'd gone back into the flames to rescue it . . . whereupon it had melted onto her flesh.

"It's incredible the way Tommy managed to pull the wool over everybody's eyes," said Colomba. "Even when I was in Milan, and I was convinced I was talking to Leo, it was really him on the phone the whole time."

"I'm really good at imitating voices, too, you know. Have you ever heard my Mickey Mouse imitation?" He smiled bitterly. "He made a fool of me, too, CC. I was looking for the gray-haired grand old man of private war-making, not just a bad copy of myself. But you, in any case, have an excuse. Your maternal instinct. Your biological clock, ticking away."

"Idiot. It was just that he really seemed like a teenager. None of the health care professionals ever noticed a thing."

"He had a first-class prosthetic device and no one ever did any serious, in-depth exams, knowing where to look. And when the supervisor at ETC started to make insistent noises about doing some, he had her killed. In any case, I sent a good bottle of whiskey to Lupo. He more than deserved it. He was the only one who never trusted Tommy."

"And I always treated him like a creep, along with everybody else who wanted to bring charges against Tommy."

"Tommy was good, really, really good at it. Hidden in plain sight just like Leo, but physically much more powerful and capable. And then there was the sulfur on his shoes, the crowning touch, his masterstroke. He was sure you'd figure it out." It was Tommy who'd planned the Melases' move to Portico, precisely so he could get close to Colomba and bring her into it. And when he was confined at the group home, he hadn't had any difficulty getting out at night to take care of his various errands.

Martina had probably recognized him, the night she was murdered.

"Luca writes me often," Colomba said. "He says that he made the right decision, to trust me and to reveal the Code to me. Now Cesare practically lives with him."

"Maybe Maugeri is less of an asshole than we thought," said Dante.

"Compared with the others, he's practically a saint. And Luca is growing up very well, he's using his disease as an instrument, not as a limitation: a feature, not a bug." Colomba gave Dante a play jab: he'd slipped into a reverie, staring into the empty air. "What's up with you?"

He took another sip, a way of stalling for time. "I've got an idea about why they were so interested in kids on the autism spectrum," he said. He handed her a newspaper clipping about how there was a far greater concentration of adults with Asperger's in Silicon Valley tech companies than the national average.

"Are they good at making software?" Colomba asked.

"No doubt about it, but I think the real issue is something else," he said, leaning on his cane. He didn't need it and there was no longer a blade inside, but he was convinced it looked good on him. "Evolution."

"Evolution?"

"Do you know why there are so many people with high blood pressure? Because people with high blood pressure tended to wake up more easily, not like you: you sleep like a diesel engine. And if someone tried to kill them in their sleep, they'd react. Now, though, high blood pressure is no good to anyone, or practically none. Many scientists, however, think that the autistic are the people of the future, better suited to move through a world buried in an avalanche of information, because they're capable of finding the right details without getting distracted."

"What about you?"

"I'm very adaptable, if the coffee is good." He heaved a sigh. "Leo wasn't my brother."

"We knew that."

"No . . . but he believed it. He really believed that he'd been in a cell with me. Instead, it had been with Tommy. The real Dante."

"Are you sure?"

"Bart didn't find so much as a trace of me in the Factory. We're going through the archives of Villa Blu, to see whether by any chance I had ever been admitted there, and then . . . made to disappear like many other kids. For now, though . . . I'm just glad he wasn't my brother, not even my adopted brother, but I'm sorry about his death."

"Seriously?"

"Yes. He was a victim, too, just like Giltine, just like Tommy. Like so many victims, they turned into killers and torturers, but Leo . . ." He shook his head. "Right up to the very end he obeyed his own butchers. The photograph he gave me wasn't just for me."

"He knew that you'd show it to the German."

"He was the only one who could confirm its authenticity. When you know the way a person thinks, you also know what he's going to do." He looked at his pocket watch and stood up. "All right, it's time for me to go. There's someone who wants to buy Annibale's house, and I can't wait to get rid of everything that remains of him. Aside from his watch, which goes perfectly with my cane."

"Are you still thinking about going to Sweden?"

"Or else Antarctica seems rather appealing. There are icebreakers that offer some very nice tour cruises. I don't know how to swim, and I'm afraid of being in water where I can't touch bottom, but I think I could get used to it. I'd like to see something beautiful, for a change."

Colomba shut her eyes, then reopened them. "Go ahead, ask me."

"To marry me?"

"Stop clowning around."

Dante gathered his courage. "Would you come with me?"

Colomba smiled.

AUTHOR'S NOTE

Many of the things that I describe in this novel are true, even if they've been adapted. Villa Blu doesn't exist, but there did exist a Villa Azzurra—a different, lighter shade of blue in Italian, an azure instead of a navy blue—concerning which I would urge you to do a little research for yourself. You will discover that certain forms of medieval treatments inflicted on the neurodiverse have survived right up until the present day.

The Manifattura Armaguerra in Cremona exists, too, and that story is more or less as I told it, with the exception of the bomb shelter, which I made up. It's a piece of Italy's memory as a country, as well as Cremona's, but it's a monument to the darker times of history, too.

The history of the autistic in Silicon Valley is true, as is the story of private wards. I changed the names of the private security companies, but the things they do and their revenues really are just as I described.

If you're interested in doing any further reading, I'm providing a few useful links, in part as a way of saying thank you to my sources of information. But first and foremost, I want to thank you readers, for taking this long, strange trip with me.

Autism and new technologies: https://www.dailymail.co.uk/wires/afp /article-3762402/Autism-Silicon-Valley-asset-social-quirks.html

Manifattura Armaguerra: https://www.cremonaoggi.it/2018/02/21 /larmaguerra-cremona-storia-affonda-le-sue-radici-nel-primo-dopoguerra

Villa Azzurra: https://www.vanityfair.it/news/storie/17/01/20/manicomio -bambini-libro-alberto-gaino-edizioni-abele-storia-angelo-torino

Inspiration for the Father: https://www.infermieristicamente.it/articolo/7777 /dalla-violenza-dell-eletttromassaggio-alla-violenza-dell-abbandono

Castration and longevity: https://www.lesswrong.com/posts
/2w9FEdFiMwnGLbAZf/effects-of-castration-on-the-life-expectancy
-of-contemporary

Contractors: https://www.usnews.com/opinion/blogs/world
-report/2015/10/08/pentagon-needs-to-cut-shadow-contractor-work
-force and https://www.securitydegreehub.com/top-security
-companies-operating-primarily-outside-the-united-states

ACKNOWLEDGMENTS

There are three people without whom you would never have been able to hold this book in your hand: my agent, Laura Grandi; my editor Giordano Aterini, who stayed up into the wee hours with me; and my wife, who supported me, encouraged me, and gave me numerous perceptive in-depth critiques. I should also thank Chiara Caccivia, who gave the first draft of my book a thorough *technical* edit; Alessandra Maffiolini, who is the historic memory of this trilogy; Carlo Carabba; and, of course, the entire Mondadori staff.

Pergola 2017–Milan 2018